Night Departure

and

No Place
(Case Dismissed)

Night Departure

and

No Place
(Case Dismissed)

by Emmanuel Bove

Translated by Carol Volk

Four Walls Eight Windows
New York • London

A Four Walls Eight Windows First Edition

Copyright © 1995 Four Walls Eight Windows
Copyright © 1988 Éditions de La Table Ronde
English translation copyright © 1995 by Carol Volk

First Printing May 1995

All Rights Reserved

No Part of this book may be reproduced, stored in a retrieval system, or transmitted in any form, by any means, including mechanical, electronic, photocopying, recording, or otherwise, without the prior written permission of the publisher.

10 9 8 7 6 5 4 3 2 1

Four Walls Eight Windows
39 West 14th Street, Room 503
New York, New York 10011

Designed by Morgan Brilliant

Printed in the USA

Library of Congress Cataloging-in-Publication Data

Bove, Emmanuel. 1898–
 [Départ dans la nuit suívi de non-lieu. English]
 Night departure and no place (case dismissed) / by Emmanuel Bove : translated by Carol Volk. — 1st ed.
 p. cm.
 ISBN 0-941423-91-3 : $25.00. —
 ISBN 0-941423-98-0 : $14.95
 I. Title.

PQ2603.08703713 1995   92-43032
843'.912—dc20   CIP

Table of Contents

Foreword by Raymond Cousse — vii

Night Departure — 1

No Place (Case Dismissed) — 185

    Part One: Friends and Relatives — 187

    Part Two: Prison — 351

    Part Three: Toward Freedom — 413

Foreword

Night Departure and No Place are Emmanuel Bove's last works. We chose to publish them together because they can be read continuously as well as separately, the intrigue of No Place beginning where Night Departure leaves off.

The two novels were originally published separately. The first in Algiers, in 1945, with Éditions Charlot; the second in 1946 with Robert Laffont. These details are not irrelevant. Night Departure appeared in the latter third of 1945. Emmanuel Bove died in Paris on July 13 of that year. Edmond Charlot, whose archives were destroyed by the OAS during the war in Algeria, was unable to arrange for Bove to hold a copy of his book in his hands, but it is certain that Bove played a role in its publication. A month and a half before his death, feverish and emaciated, unable to leave his room, he wrote as a post-script to his last existing letter: "I am publishing." The comment was significant. Bove had always refused to publish in an occupied France. He had intended to make his way to England, and it is therefore not surprising that *Night Departure* is dedicated to General de Gaulle.

Finally he found himself in Algiers, where he arrived in November 1942, the eve of the Allied landing. He remained there until October 1944, date of his return to Paris. It was in Algiers that he wrote the two novels presented here, which have never since been republished. It was there too that he established ties with many writers and artists, notably André Gide, Saint-Exupéry, Max-Pol Fouchet, Albert Marquet, Henri Jeanson, and Philippe Soupault. The state of his health worsened. "Bove led almost a nocturnal existence. Sometimes he brought his hand to his face, not so much to smother a cough as to conceal a grimace brought on by the pain. He often disappeared for a stay in the hospital but didn't speak of his illness," remembers Enrico Terracini.

In his 1945 datebook, Bove wrote on March 28: "Fell ill." Deathly ill. Up until that point, the datebook is full. From that day forward, for the few hundred days he had left to live, the pages are blank, except for April 20, his birthday. There he noted: "47 years old," underlined three times and with an exclamation point. From then on, silence. These poignant details reveal his extreme discretion.

By the time *No Place* appeared, Bove had been buried

for over a year, and his body of work with him. New gods—of the Sartre-Camus-Aragon persuasion—were ushered in in the name of Liberty regained and the Revolution to come. The Boves, the Calets, the Hyvernauds, and the Guérins were forgotten, those who placed decency over literary vanity, those whose refusal to be deceived began with a refusal to be deceived about themselves. The truth is that the status of "great" accorded certain writers rarely corresponds to a simple honesty on the part of these writers about themselves.

No Place refers not only to Bove's final book. This generic title can be applied to his entire body of work, not to mention his entire existence. No doubt the author, in the situation in which he found himself, thought of this. The titles of his four final books (*Un homme qui savait* [*A Man Who Knew*], *Le piège* [*The Trap*], *Départ dans la nuit* [*Night Departure*], *Non-lieu* [*No Place*]) tell a tale in and of themselves. Written during the war, these novels are also set against a backdrop of war. While they can be read on a primary level, they can also be approached, particularly the latter two, as a vast novel of initiation.

The lead character in *Night Departure* and in *No Place* is no less cowardly than the "hero" in Bove's twenty previous books. In the earlier novels, nonetheless, the character was a coward a priori, refusing to undertake any sort of action, as much out of powerlessness as out of principle. Here, he finds himself on the other side of cowardliness, in a sense, after the consummation of an act, in this case the murder—the accidental murder—of two German guards. We might imagine that this act would liberate the narrator. On the contrary, it only increases his irresolution tenfold, precipitating him into an existential terror—only partly camouflaged by the plot—that leaves him no peace. His infantile doubts and fears are exacerbated until paranoia and horror of life, the potential for which was always present, become concrete and absolute. As if the fact of having acted, as an exception and by chance, had caused irreparable damage. As if all action were a crime, if not THE crime, par excellence. Long held at bay, terror creeps into every pore of the narrator's personality, dissolving his identity. Once the worm is in the fruit, it eats it to the core. The exterior world is but a nightmare—the hallucinated aspect of the story is probably not without some relationship to the state of Bove's health—and the people that populate it irremediably hostile.

I mentioned a novel of initiation, by which I mean an initiation to solitude and death. *Night Departure* recounts the escape of a dozen prisoners from a German camp and ends with the narrator's arrival in France. He returns alone, after having abandoned or lost his companions. The plot can be summed up as follows: from the impossibility of communal life to incurable solitude. Inversely, *No Place* shows the character in a struggle with the hostility or indifference of his countrymen in occupied France. Under the pretext of not wishing to be recaptured—though it is never actually a question of Germans in this book—he tries to break the cursed circle of his solitude. The novel—and with it all Bove's writing—ends with this last setback: Feeling persecuted and terrorized, the narrator decides to look elsewhere for peace and security. The choice of location—Franco's Spain—is ideal.

"I turned around. Two Spanish guards were approaching. I knew they were going to take me to jail, but it didn't matter: I was free."

In short, the only liberty left, for Bove, was in death.

"Mr. Emmanuel Bove died this morning of general debility and heart failure," specified the burial permit.

—Raymond Cousse

Night Departure

For General De Gaulle

Chapter 1

We had just spent two weeks packed together in cattle cars. Entire days had passed with no movement of the train. Then, suddenly, it took off. Now we were freezing from the wind. A grey powder fell from the sides of the train and rose from the floorboards, irritating our throats, drying our nostrils. At one stop, we were given permission to gather a bit of straw, but it was old straw and crumbled to dust in a few hours. My comrades huddled together. I preferred the cold. When the train went full speed and one of us was smoking, we all feared a fire.

It was dark when we reached the Biberbrach camp after a twenty-three kilometer march from the train station. Now we were to be divided into groups. We waited, seated on the frozen ground, for the formal triage to end. Despite their famous knack for organization, the Germans were confused and kept moving us around. Everything was done in an orderly fashion, but in the meantime, we were still outdoors.

Pelet sat down each time. I had clung to him from the start: as we were boarding the train, they had pushed him to one side and me to the other. I followed him anyway. They had tried to kick me back in line, but a scuffle broke out and I was able to slip past.

What would happen now? Pelet wasn't moving. He was hunched over pitifully, his head almost touching his knees. I slapped him on the back. He sat up and looked at me sadly. "Whatever happens, stay near me," I told him.

I didn't know him, but I was afraid of our being separated.

In my five and a half months as a prisoner, all I could think of was escaping. Not once had I worried about the future, so confident was I in my ability to act decisively. I was sure I wouldn't let the right opportunity pass. But after holding out for so long, I began to realize I had an unfortunate tendency not to consider any of the opportunities that arose to be the one with all the right elements for success. If I didn't change my approach, I might still be waiting for the perfect moment in a year or two. I started to feel miserable. I realized I had to act. But nothing is worse than making a decision based not on favorable circumstances, but on having waited too long.

My health had so deteriorated I was sure I'd be

hospitalized. Several years back I'd had a case of pleurisy; I still had a pain in my side, not to mention the digestive tract problems that resulted from the condition. The doctors all thought I required special care. I was surprised when the French military doctors didn't give me a discharge. But after all the deprivation and bad treatment I had endured, I was even more surprised when the camp commander found nothing wrong with me. When I showed him my certificates, he didn't even bother reading them. Stories of Kraut savagery came to mind. I asked for a second opinion, which was equally unsatisfactory; then I sent a written request. While waiting for the response I learned that my father had also sent a letter to the German authorities, with additional supporting documents, requesting my liberation. All this was ridiculous, but you never could tell. For a long while these slim hopes were all that kept me going.

I tried by yet other means to have my case reconsidered, but it was no use. If I wanted to preserve the little strength I had left, it was foolish to beat my head against a wall; better to adjust to the circumstances and continue to care for myself despite the hardships of camp life.

These were difficult days. When you're weak there is nothing more demoralizing than having to perform physical tasks that would exhaust even a healthy man. Added to the worries of imprisonment itself were the problems of eating better, avoiding heavy loads, and so on.

My fellow prisoners were willing to help me some, but eventually they tired of it. I considered abandoning the struggle, letting myself go, even if it meant falling ill. Instinctively, I rejected the idea. Instead of chatting for hours and playing cards at the end of the workday, I made myself herbal tea. I had to do this secretly so as not to be accused of self-indulgence.

In the beginning it was pretty easy, as there was relatively little surveillance. Gradually, however, as camp life became harsher, I realized I would no longer be able to lead this double life. I was afraid. The moment when my frail health would fail me seemed imminent.

I had my darkest thoughts in the evenings. My health, to my surprise, had gotten better not worse. My stomach troubles had disappeared along with my insomnia, and I could eat whatever trash they served without a problem; yet it seemed to me I would surely have a relapse. I saw myself admitted to a hospital too late to arrest the damage, cared for summarily without a serious examination by people who had absolutely no reason to help me, and ending my days in a nondescript hospital room, the victim of negligence and indifference, for the life of one man means little when millions like him are fighting on the battlefield.

But these worries were nothing compared to a feeling of dread that weighed on me, an amplified version of something I'd felt already as a private in the French army: the sense that something could happen to me indirectly, merely because I belonged to a particular human group. For this reason I spent my time giving advice, calming the nervous, getting involved in secret intrigues. I was afraid of a rebellion, of someone attacking one of the guards, of an injustice that might cause a mutiny. The fact that I couldn't leave, that I was partly responsible for anything that might happen, that I had to stay with my fellow prisoners even in the event of an epidemic, a bombing, or a counterattack, made me constantly ill at ease.

Though he rarely spoke to me, I was obviously the one whom Pelet liked the most. He often looked at me adoringly, as if we shared a bond that was absolutely incomprehensible to our companions. He had a rather homely appearance: leaden skin, circles under his eyes, sweaty palms, a soft-looking bone structure, and yellow spots on his teeth where the enamel had worn off.

Sometimes he took me by the arm and dragged me away from the others to read me letters and show me photographs of his wife and son. He couldn't understand why, from the Germans' point of view, families that didn't love each other had the same advantages as those that did. Sometimes I found him sitting in a corner, like a neglected child. If I approached him, he pretended to hate me as much as he did the others, just to annoy me. To snap him out of it, I would tell him we'd soon be free, that I was in the process of preparing an escape. But his reaction was the opposite of what I anticipated. You would have thought I was trying to drag him into a dangerous adventure without taking into account that he was less able to defend himself than the rest of us, that where sad human specimens such as himself were concerned, it didn't matter whether we escaped or not. My concern for him might be sincere but it was also shallow. Yet if I left him alone, he eyed me suspiciously, as if I were avoiding him. As time passed, he became more and more unpleasant. He seemed to blame us for his misfortunes. And on the pretext that he and I were connected in some special way, he made it clear that he expected me to right the situation.

Chapter 2

We had been at the Biberbrach camp six weeks when a small incident brought me great pain. A kind of cabal had formed against poor Pelet. His suffering combined with his haughty airs got on everyone's nerves. They all banded together to talk about him in a superior, pitying tone that disgusted me. They made fun of the way he insisted on calling himself a family man when he had only one child, and they found other things to mock as well. He deserved sympathy, they said, but everyone had troubles; there was no reason why his should count more.

Bisson was assigned to warn Pelet to change his behavior, that if he didn't become a better companion no one would talk to him any more. At this I suggested that we had to be understanding of the poor fellow and indulge him since he was suffering.

"What about us, aren't we suffering too?" they observed.

I answered, yes we were suffering, but we were also better able to handle it. In the end I got them to leave him alone.

My intervention had a rather strange result. Several days later, Pelet suddenly took me to task, accusing me of having conspired against him. I was responsible for the animosity he was sensing. I told him that if he wanted to be that way about it, I would no longer have anything to do with him, that he was petty, that I had too many worries for him to create new ones out of thin air.

Suddenly he softened, asked my forgiveness, told me that he knew full well that it wasn't me, but that I had to understand how much he suffered from being without his wife and child. I pointed out that his situation was no worse than everyone else's. He said he was aware of that, but nevertheless his situation was worse since he was suffering more than we were.

From that day on, he got in the habit of coming to speak to me whenever he saw me alone. It might have seemed we were sharing secrets. Yet he never had anything to say. I found this flaunting of a non-existent intimacy distasteful. No matter how cold I was to him, he never got discouraged. When others could see us, he rolled his eyes and looked sad. One day he told me he had received a map of southern Germany. He was willing to show it to me, but only if I promised not to tell anyone. He also told me that during the night he had heard the sound of a train carried by the wind. I pitied him more and more. I found myself in the painfully awkward position of being liked by a man everyone hated. Sometimes I snubbed him, but most of the time I consoled him. He would return to find everything he'd lost—his wife, his child, and also, I added to make him happy, his apartment. Despite this, he often said that I, who had no family, couldn't understand.

Baillencourt, who was the only one to wear an identity tag around his neck, was becoming increasingly despotic. It suited him. He had real influence over some of our comrades: Jean and Marcel Bisson, Baumé, Billau, even Pelet. One day he called me into a corner and announced that the date of our escape was set. We were going to attempt the great adventure (to use his expression) the following Saturday, at three in the morning.

I asked him why that day, why that time? He gave me all sorts of reasons. "And who decided this?" I added. He looked at me with astonishment. He seemed uncomfortable saying: "I did." Instead he simply said, "It's been decided . . . it's been decided . . ."

As soon as I was alone, I reflected on his plan. It was an ordinary plan. Anyone could have come up with an equally clever one. The truth was that with or without a plan, we had to get out of the camp without getting killed and then travel more than four hundred kilometers through Germany without getting caught. I kept my reservations to myself, for fear of being excluded. I wanted to be counted in. I wanted to be able to decide for myself up to the very last minute.

The next day, Baillencourt said he had something extremely important to tell me. He still had that air of being the sole master of the situation. I made an effort not to let my bad humor show.

"I'm listening," I said. "No, no, not now," he answered. "Come see me at around eight o'clock." I asked him why he couldn't tell me right away what it was about. He claimed it wasn't safe.

At eight o'clock, I made my way to our meeting place, which was not without danger. With great to-do, he drew the map of Germany that Pelet had shown me from his pack. "I just received this," he said stupidly.

By the glow of his cigarette lighter, he showed me the route we were going to follow, then explained to me at great length the cunning means by which he had managed to procure all the information necessary to elaborate his scheme. I kept quiet so as not to be rude, but I thought it had been absurd to bother me for so little. Nothing is more dangerous than these people who want to be important. As I gazed at the barbed wire, the rampart walks, the guards at their lookouts, the searchlights beaming across the camp, Baillencourt was busy with his pencil, marking out the route we should follow on the map of a country that was utterly foreign to him.

Once in bed, I told myself that if I really wanted to escape, I had to do it alone. Of course, that wouldn't be a very nice thing to do to my comrades. While appearing to share their hopes and disappointments, I was secretly planning to abandon them. But they were so stupid, so unaware of the true difficulties, that in reality I had no choice.

Ideally I would escape alone, minimizing the risk by means of some chance occurrence, a mistake, a substitution, or by landing a job, a position for which I would be qualified by my knowledge of German, or even through the friendship of an officer, a bureaucrat, or someone else strategically placed. I would disappear from the camp without attracting attention, the way a man is removed in the army upon orders from higher-up; I would avoid jealousy and gossip, without giving the others a chance to say: "Why not us?" without giving anyone the idea of imitating me. What one person can do alone becomes impossible with a group. The others might notice, but what would it matter; life goes on and eventually they'd forget. No doubt about it, I'd be better off waiting.

Each night before falling asleep, I dreamt of all these possibilities. My first task was to separate myself from my comrades. I saw myself hospitalized at my father's request. When in need, we give great weight to anything that is done for us from the outside. A thousand times I pictured the German director of some nameless health service reading my father's request. A thousand times I saw him hesitate, lay the paper down, think it over. A thousand times I put myself in his place. Did he have many cases like this one? Did he give the same attention to each of them? Or was he moved by some of them, by mine in particular? Did he feel generous for no apparent reason? Anything is possible, and that thought gave me strength. I saw myself transported to a city. Life changed immediately. I spoke to people with broader intellects, to whom the fact that I was a prisoner of war was of no importance. I managed to win the sympathy of some. Finally, with the help of people who should have been enemies, I managed to return to France. And on that happy note, I fell asleep.

The next morning, when I awoke in the candlelight and saw most of my comrades already getting dressed, I realized I wasn't alone, that they were stuck here too, and that since these fortunate events of which I dreamt couldn't happen to them, there was no reason why they should happen to me. I told myself I had to act immediately, that I couldn't wait any longer. But the situation had never been worse. I had passed up so many good chances to escape, and so many others would probably arise that my sudden decision seemed outrageous.

My comrades were getting more and more nervous. Roger, who was ordinarily so self-possessed, flew into fits of rage at the slightest annoyance. Each time I wanted to trade something I came up against unbelievable resistance, even when what I had to trade was a thousand times better than what I sought in return.

Baillencourt was always trying to make me contradict myself.

Marcel Bisson had suddenly become nasty toward me following a silly incident. I had returned a small sum of money he had lent me. Shortly afterward, stupidly, I admit, I asked him if I had in fact given him back the money. Annoyed, he answered, "No."

Each time he saw me, Baumé said, "Sprecht Deutsch." He was convinced I was half Kraut because I spoke German.

They were starting to make fun of me. When I pretended not to notice, they became increasingly bold. They thought I managed too well for myself. And most of all, I needed things too often; I asked for too many favors and made the mistake of pouting when I didn't get what I wanted. I even got mad one day at one of my comrades who didn't want to sell me a strap he wasn't using. Roger calmed me down. He pointed out that I couldn't insist on his selling the strap. "But it isn't doing him any good!" I'd cried. "It's his," responded Roger. I realized then that I was always on the verge of either getting angry or being too nice. Was I going to stay mad at my comrade or would I instead recognize I was wrong? Clearly, these decisions would produce opposite effects. The fact that at every minute of the day I was at the mercy of my temper like this was beginning to worry me.

Chapter 3

Our preparations were complete. Bisson had even acquired a compass, a slightly demagnetized one it was true, as sometimes the needle didn't move. There was nothing more to do. In the emptiness before our departure, we all sensed the most difficult part lay ahead.

Luckily, a problem of fellowship distracted us. Should we or shouldn't we wait while a certain Durutte, who in any case had played only a small part in organizing the escape, recovered from a foot injury? Should we delay our departure? Should we leave him behind?

My comrades all agreed we should wait. They were superstitious. To launch such an expedition with an unkind act would bring bad luck.

Baillencourt, on the other hand, wanted to keep to his schedule and leave on the night he had chosen, the longest night of the year. But he didn't like the idea of abandoning Durutte either. He decided that we would leave on the appointed day no matter what, and if our friend was still having trouble walking we would all take turns helping him.

I found what was happening increasingly strange. I was worried. I was afraid that at the last moment there would be defections. I even wondered if Durutte wasn't faking it. I shared my thoughts with my comrades. They seemed to think I had a sick mind.

A few days before the escape, Baillencourt took me aside. Although he never listened to anyone, he pretended to act only by consensus. He informed me that he had changed the time of departure. Instead of leaving at three, we would leave at midnight.

"Why?" I asked, as I did each time he made one of his announcements. He told me he didn't want Pelet along, that he found him too cowardly. He might start shouting at a moment of danger; he might faint. This would cause confusion, and so on. Since no one had the nerve to tell Pelet, Baillencourt had decided to move up the time of departure. This way, when Pelet arrived at the designated meeting place, we would already be long gone.

This plan was deeply troubling to me. I pointed out that this was no way to act. We were taking Durutte along after all. Pelet might not be too likeable, he might even be cowardly, but in the end we were all in the same boat. If we really didn't want him to come, we should just tell him so.

Baillencourt blew up. He was the one who had organized everything, who was responsible, not us. He wasn't about to compromise all his work at the last minute. Pelet was capable of taking revenge. If we talked to him, he might denounce us out of spite. If he were only thinking of himself, Baillencourt said, he would run the risk, but there were other people involved, and so on.

Suddenly he calmed down and went to get Billau, Jean Bisson, Breton, Baumé. Our movements since the declaration of war had not completely scrambled the list of men; like a poorly shuffled deck of cards in which the aces remain together, five or six of us had names beginning with B. Aside from Roger, they all responded like generals refusing to sacrifice an army for the life of an individual soldier, men convinced that great acts require a certain cruelty.

All this Pelet business seemed exaggerated to me. The childish simplicity of the escape plan made these grandiose pretensions seem out of place. These conversations, these incontrovertible decisions, this air of sacrifice, had an artificiality about them. This was what scared me. What would really happen in a moment of true danger? Wasn't it possible that the person left behind would turn out to be the most courageous?

We avoided speaking to one another on Saturday, each

pretending to be taken up with personal matters. After the evening soup we made the agreed-upon sign, which indicated that everything was to proceed as planned. I also made the sign, but not without thinking how imprudent it was. If we were being watched, as our behavior seemed to suggest was likely, what better way to reveal our intentions? I had tried my best to convince my companions of this. But it was no use. They couldn't imagine an escape without mysterious or romantic overtones.

I went to bed that night fully dressed, still unsure whether I would go to the meeting point. While the rest of my companions feared betrayal, denunciation, or lack of preparation, I alone was worried about the guards. I saw the danger and they didn't. I could talk about it, scream about it, no one listened to me.

Suddenly at midnight, although up until the last minute I thought I wouldn't, I got up. After a long wait, it is a relief to finally confront danger. In an instant I would be free. I stopped thinking about anything. On the one side was liberty, on the other, physical and spiritual misery. Under such circumstances, how could one doubt the success of the escape?

I reported to the meeting point behind the latrines. It was dark. We proceeded with our hands touching the person in front of us, pretending we were doing so because of the darkness, but in reality because it gave us courage. When we reached the last barrack, we stopped in front of the barbed wire, suddenly struck by the seriousness of our endeavor. However far we had gotten in executing our plan, we could still turn back. The unforeseen event that would motivate us with a sense of the danger, that would make us act like men whose lives were at stake, had not yet occurred.

The camp was cloaked in silence. In the shadows we could make out the barracks, which seemed more crowded together than usual. Thousands of prisoners were sleeping, more submissive than we were, more resigned, perhaps more attuned to reality. We were stunned at the contrast between their general acceptance of a tragic fate and our audacious attempt to escape it. My companions suddenly seemed like children to me. Now in the dead of night, all the preparations, the calculations, the details decided over countless days seemed as if they could have just as easily been arranged by this crowd of sleeping men. And yet these men had made no such preparations. Who was right, us or them?

Now, at the moment of truth, we realized that what mattered, what had real value, were things beyond the common pale: cold determination and the will to risk one's life rather than be defeated. After a few moments we realized that we lacked that will. Baillencourt said some vague words. Then we returned to our quarters.

Chapter 4

The next day, I was ordered to report to camp headquarters to see the commanding officer. On the way, I met Bisson and Pelet. While awkwardly pretending not to see me, they motioned to me with their hands. I approached and told them not to gesticulate when they saw me.

I don't know if Germans act the same with everyone but I've always had the impression that they treated me with special consideration. I had already noticed this at the Muhr camp. Several times I saw one of the officers staring at me when I thought I was part of a crowd and there was nothing to distinguish me from the others. Attracting the attention of those more powerful than you is troubling in a communal situation; it is hard to know if it is prompted by sympathy or antipathy, the outward signs of each being so similar.

This officer had a thin face, so thin that in certain places the bone seemed to jut through the skin. It was hard to fathom the soul tucked behind that fleshless face. When I caught him looking at me, he didn't turn away, but gave no indication that he saw me either. And if some occurrence made me less anonymous, he no longer looked at me at all.

I thought I might be imagining things; I watched him secretly to see whether his behavior toward me was simply his usual behavior. But he never smiled at me, nor said, nor did, anything that might have reassured me.

The situation made me very uncomfortable. It offered no advantages yet took away that of being a nobody, of having the freedom to let myself go if I felt like it, the safe feeling of being unknown. Because of this officer's interest in me, which I might have been imagining, I had to watch myself, to pay attention to the way I looked, to avoid speaking to fellow prisoners who were considered troublemakers when someone could see me. I was in an awkward position, and I wouldn't be surprised if that wasn't all that dirty Kraut wanted.

I headed toward the camp headquarters. I was certain the escape attempt had something to do with this summoning. That I was the one being called in didn't surprise me. What happened at Muhr, happened here on a larger scale. Although I might be a mere private, certain signs, pardon my saying so, indicated that I'd had a bourgeois upbringing and that, socially, I occupied a slightly higher rung than most of my comrades. These signs don't escape the Germans. With their taste for distinctions, they made an effort, through all kinds of little ploys, hints, and delicate mannerisms, to show me they had noticed this difference.

In the beginning, I paid no attention. I joined in the fate of my companions, carefully avoiding being pardoned from a task, for example, as if it had never crossed my mind to be excused. But over time it became difficult; I ran the risk of angering the soldiers whose friendly overtures I ignored.

Thus, against my will, the Germans had coerced from me that minimum of politeness one sees between neighbors who nod to one another without speaking. And this wasn't enough for them. Pretending to believe that a man of breeding suffered more than others at his country's destruction, and that he thus deserved special consideration, they sought to kindle a kind of gratitude in me, to forge a bond between us, as unites people after they've performed simple favors for one another.

This became exceedingly embarrassing, especially since my comrades were not as primitive as the Germans imagined and took notice of the latters' esteem for me. In this way, little by little, the German officers gradually became convinced that I could serve as an intermediary when they wanted to get something from the French soldiers by persuasion, and this, no doubt, was why they had called me in.

I opened the door to the office, saluted with a click of my heels, removed my cap—which looked more like a skullcap—took a few rapid steps and stood at attention near the table where the camp commander was sitting. This discipline disgusted me. I knew that many of my comrades entered this room dragging their feet and had to be bullied into saluting, taking off their hats, and standing at attention. But being under close scrutiny forced me to act against my nature, to behave in a way I knew was appreciated, like a proud man does in civilian life when among people far wealthier than he.

The officer, one of those Germans who are said to be Austrian, offered me a seat. He was a debonair man of about fifty, partly bald, poorly shaved, who in no way lived up to one's idea of a German officer. He prompted you to feel well disposed toward him, as men often do who seem to attach no importance to their assigned responsibilities. The small, hastily furnished office was overheated. An orderly kept shoving big logs into the stove. One had the impression that though makeshift, the office had everything, that while we, the French, had never been so miserable, the Germans were enjoying the best period of the war.

The officer offered me a cigarette and I accepted. But when he offered to light it, I told him I was saving it for a friend.

I then realized I had been called in for an entirely different purpose from what I'd expected. They wanted to put me in charge of a detachment of my choosing; we would be sent thirty kilometers away to reinforce a group already at work on the construction of a railway line.

As soon as I returned to my barrack, I announced the good news. Luck was with us. We were all struck by how close we had come to missing this opportunity. The day before, we had almost embarked on a doomed adventure, and a few hours later, just as we were feeling overcome by sorrow and regret, the Germans themselves were opening the camp door!

Chapter 5

Four days later, we arrived at the large, heavily barricaded villa that housed all the prisoners working on the new line.

The next morning we gathered behind the house in a large field surrounded by barbed wire and covered with pebbles. The sun had barely risen and rain was falling. We made up about a half-company's worth of manpower. In addition to my own detachment, there were prisoners already in place who had come either from Biberbrach or from the two other camps nearby.

Nothing is worse than finding oneself among Frenchmen in this situation, so far from home and yet strangers to one another. We formed a square. From the side facing us someone yelled at Roger: "Hey! Hi, over there, where are you from?"

"From Paris, and you?"

"From Argenteuil."

The German sergeant hadn't arrived yet. Questions and jokes kept coming from all sides. "Any news from your sister?" someone yelled. "Fuck you," someone replied. From time to time, Baumé yelled "Sprecht Deutsch" at me. He didn't let up. Even though it was possible that some of these strangers knew people I also knew, I didn't dare raise my voice stupidly. But I was deeply moved. These men were just like the ones in our camp, but seeing them for the first time gave me the illusion of being in France.

I considered our situation. I had the impression there was no escaping it and that our captivity would become more and more arduous. I thought about my illusions of the last months. Each move was supposed to present an opportunity for escape. Well, this dream had just been shattered. I realized this as I prepared to spend a day in the rain leveling earth with nothing to eat but beet soup. Wherever we went, we encountered the same problems but with a different twist.

We were ordered to stand at attention, but the joking and shouting continued. The German sergeant got angry. Once again, he gave us the command. This time, everyone grew silent. We lined up grudgingly. The order "to the right in fours" rang out. Before giving the order to march, the sergeant waited a few moments, watching us without moving. His message was that discipline was not going to slacken just because we had left the camp.

The rain continued to fall all day, making the work (carrying rails in groups of twenty-four), for which we had no enthusiasm to begin with, even harder. The fact that we pretended to work more than we actually worked made the day seem interminable. By evening, it was ridiculous how little we'd accomplished.

Our group worked in the middle of a field, watched over by four guards who never mingled with us but remained twenty or thirty meters away. The only thing I thought might prove useful was the occasional arrival of a supply truck, but each time one showed up a guard came and stood by.

With great difficulty, using my clout as head of the detachment, I obtained the most sheltered corner of our common room. In the evening, I isolated myself from my comrades and let my feelings of discouragement overtake me. I realized I had been terribly mistaken to think I was a prisoner only because I wanted to be one. For the first time I understood that I was a prisoner for real.

Nearby, Pelet and my friend Baumé sang together in low voices. Labussière, the accountant, joined in. They asked him not to. I closed my eyes, tasting this false air of peace, and fell asleep. Suddenly a noise like a dam breaking loose, like an avalanche, woke me with a start. Someone thought a bomb had fallen on the house. "What's going on?" everyone yelled, sitting up, even jumping out of bed. But as quickly as it had come, the horrible noise faded. It was the Chemnitz express train storming by a few meters away.

I remained awake in the ensuing silence. It seemed to me there was something less strict about this place than the camp. This was because the methods used to confine us had been improvised.

They had turned a large, dilapidated house into a prison. At first glance, the transformation had been complete. The windows were barricaded, but the main reason we were prisoners was because the guards locked our doors at night—the doors weren't prison doors and the windows had planks of wood nailed to them instead of bars. It did not appear to be a prison from which it was impossible to escape, but a house fixed up so the time it took to break out would be long enough for the guards to intervene.

Barbed wire was installed around the house, but less carefully than at Muhr or Biberbrach. I noticed it was rather slack in certain spots. Also, they hadn't thought it necessary to set up exterior surveillance posts, which would have required a guard unit. This would have taken too many men. There weren't enough guards to watch us both day and night; instead, the guards were housed in a room near the front door.

Every night, after inspecting the entire house and testing the planks barricading the windows, they shut us in rooms in small groups, padlocking the doors where the locks didn't work. If someone needed to relieve himself after this, he called until one of the guards opened the door and took him to the latrines. This system was hardly conventional, but it enabled four or five sentries to guard more than a hundred prisoners, night and day.

In the morning, they assembled us in the courtyard. All the guards were there, but only two or three of them accompanied us to work. The others inspected the rooms in our absence, made sure we had nothing hidden, checked the windows.

These windows were clearly their greatest worry. They were well aware that with a simple instrument, or even a brick, the planks could be broken in a matter of seconds. They were constantly reinforcing them. But no matter how they patched them, they couldn't make up for it being a bad system to start with.

Our guards knew these planks were not major obstacles, but they were useful anyway because they would force us to make noise if we were trying to escape. You would have to bang on them repeatedly to break them. By the time you were ready to make a getaway, the guards would have heard the noise.

Eventually I had an idea the Germans probably hadn't thought of. It was true you had to make a racket to break out, but the noise wouldn't be noticed if a louder noise were to cover it up—the sound of the Chemnitz express, for example.

From that day on, this discovery was constantly on my

mind. Finally, I had regained my freedom. I felt joyful. The hope of finding a better way had caused me to ignore many opportunities to escape. The sadness of these last weeks had caused me to reproach myself for this hesitation, to the point of considering myself a despicable, soft, and spineless creature. Suddenly, it seemed I had been right to wait.

Chapter 6

Shortly thereafter, a fear tainted my joy. I wondered if the guards had also thought of this detail and taken precautions we were unaware of, perhaps arranging one of their rounds to coincide with the passing of the train. I tried getting up in the night and listening for footsteps once the train's din had faded, my ear glued to the door of our room. I heard nothing. But I repeated my exercise night after night, for I still wasn't reassured.

My fears subsided. Surveillance in a camp or prison is never executed with the same conscientiousness or attention to detail you would use to watch over someone you care about. I grew more hopeful by the day. I saw myself free already. Just as the train was passing, in a matter of seconds, I would break through the window planks with a stool. I would pick a night when the weather was bad, so the guards, all cozy and warm around their fire, wouldn't dream of going out. I would head toward the corner of the yard where I had noticed the barbed wire was the most slack.

I knew every detail by heart. I had dissected each action in my mind. With a stick I had placed nearby, which no one had any reason to notice, I drew back the first wire. Yet this stick, which ended in a fork, kept getting moved around. Sometimes I found it at the other end of the courtyard. Nothing could be more upsetting than these mysterious individuals who, out of sheer boredom, unwittingly destroy someone else's preparations. Each time I put the stick back in place. Finally I started to worry that the same person might be moving it each time, and that he would find it strange that it kept returning to the same spot.

Again, in my mind I drew back the first wire and ducked underneath. With my right hand, I lifted the next one. With my left foot, I held the third wire to the ground. Then, releasing the first, and still using my stick, I lifted the fourth. Then I did a half turn, sliding into a space overlooked by whoever had installed this tangle of barbed wire and which allowed me to slide through easily. I threw away my stick and drew my knapsacks close to me so they wouldn't get caught. I'd taken the precaution of tying them around my waist with string.

All these moves were executed calmly and methodically. At no point was I obliged to rush. I kept to the side of the road and walked all night. At dawn, I hid in a hole of some sort and stayed there until darkness returned. I've always believed that the best way to avoid discovery is to disappear completely. I calculated that to avoid getting caught during the initial search, with all the anger and upheaval caused by my escape, I would have to fend for myself for about fifteen days.

I therefore needed fifteen days worth of provisions. In fifteen days, if I only walked at night, I could almost reach the French border. Then I would be saved. It would be better, of course, if I had provisions for one month, but where would I get them? And even if I had them, weight would be a problem. I figured I needed five to six hundred grams a day. That meant carrying around fifteen kilos in the beginning. This might not sound like much, but when you have to lug it around, it's a lot.

As soon as I devised this plan, I got mad at myself for not starting earlier. I could have left right away. Eight days ago, in fact, I had received a package from my father and I'd eaten it. At the time I didn't know what my plans were. Now I had to wait for the next one. And the knapsack. Why hadn't I tried to get one earlier?

I told myself I had to stop getting demoralized by this kind of thinking: you tell yourself it's too late and you end up doing nothing. The fact that I still had to round up the necessary provisions was constantly on my mind.

After fifteen days, I succeeded in putting aside about

two kilos of bread, two cans of pâté, a can of sardines, a can without a label whose contents were unknown to me, about two hundred and fifty grams of chocolate, about a pound of beans, a smoked fish of some sort, five patties of a fruit roll mixed with chocolate, a piece of skimmed and dried cheese that was hard as a rock and must have weighed about a hundred grams, a few crackers made with chestnut flour, and a pound of nuts. With the five-kilo parcel I was expecting, if I watched my rations closely, eating only when my hunger grew intolerable, I figured I could hold out for about twenty days.

Chapter 7

When I'd finished my preparations and had a map, a knapsack, and provisions, I moved on to the second part of my scheme. I would tell my companions what I was planning to do as if it were an idea that had just popped into my head, as if suddenly I couldn't stand this miserable life anymore, or worse still, as if I were sure I would get caught but didn't care because anything was better than this hell.

I began by saying I'd received word from home. My mother was seriously ill. It was terrible to feel powerless, not to be able to do anything for her. My father wasn't doing well either. He was being persecuted for his views at the high school where he taught.

"I've had it," I said a little later in front of several others, as if succumbing to a wave of anger. "If this keeps up, I'm going to smash their planks and run. Whatever happens, happens . . ."

No one paid attention to what I said. The next day I started in again. This time, Bisson said, "Don't be a jerk," in the tone one uses with a troubled and suicidal person. I laughingly told him not to take me too seriously. I talked a lot but I was still around, even though I was sick of this life. "We're all sick of it," he replied.

I complained aloud more and more frequently, and over minor things. There were no lights. I couldn't find my shoes. I accused the others of playing tricks on me. It rained on my straw mattress. I had a sore throat, a headache, a toothache. The food was revolting. The water smelled of disinfectant. I hadn't heard from Juliette. The Krauts kept our packages. They treated us like dogs. I had a pain in my groin. I was going to get a hernia. I had no soap, no toothpaste. I had only one extra shirt and it was never dry. I didn't have a handkerchief. Someone was going through my things.

I was saying all this so my companions would become disgusted with how we were living. They also complained, but less than I did. They always resigned themselves to things whereas I continued to protest and fume. But to my surprise, I soon noticed that instead of agreeing with me, instead of joining me in my complaints since they had to suffer the same indignities, they began to distrust me. Yet everything I complained about was true and they knew it. What was even more incredible was that they seemed convinced I was making things out to be worse than they were!

As we warmed ourselves around a piece of wood someone had found on the road, I whispered the following suggestion, "Why don't we all get out of here together?" "You and your ideas!" Momot, a Parisian from Rambouillet, burst out. "So we can get shot a hundred meters from here, or caught, and spend three months in the slammer, with nothing to eat this time . . . No thanks . . . That would be just your luck."

I didn't answer. A candle lit the room dimly. We had undressed after working all day in the rain, but since we had nothing to wear most of us were wrapped in our blankets. While I seemed to be suggesting we all escape together, at the moment I was only thinking of making my departure palatable to the others, of making sure no one would be jealous.

By the silence following Momot's exit, the lack of enthusiasm for his reply, which nonetheless seemed to express what everyone was thinking, I sensed that an escape was not so out of the question for my fellow prisoners, that they were all thinking of it, and though they might be unable to decide to do it themselves, they wouldn't put up much resistance against whoever took the initiative. The truth is they weren't afraid. What held them back was more the fear of embarking on a venture with uncertain results.

When everyone had fallen asleep, I thought for a long time about what I had just seen. My fellow prisoners were men like me. I realized that if you want to take a risk, the best thing to do is appeal to everyone and then act openly. My first experience had made me unnecessarily wary of my companions. I decided to tell them my plan the very next day, to explain it as clearly and simply as possible. Of course at first, as straightforward as it might be, they would be wary. But gradually I was sure they would see the light and understand that if we followed my plan point by point, they too could regain their freedom with minimal risk and under the best possible conditions given our situation. I had imagined escaping alone these last weeks only because I hadn't considered my position from an enlightened enough perspective. In any undertaking, it is important to see things as they are. I had seen that I was a prisoner, but the fact that I wasn't the only prisoner had completely escaped me. This isolated house contained a hundred of us, all in the same boat. I therefore had certain responsibilities. To think I could make things easier for myself by ignoring these responsibilities was a big mistake. It was precisely by assuming my responsibilities, that is, by helping my fellow prisoners, not by hiding what I was planning but by including them in my plan, that I had the greatest chance for success.

Chapter 8

The next evening, when we were gathered together, I told everyone I had an important announcement to make. I motioned for them to come nearer. Some were hovering around Labussière, a strange fellow, watching him fold a bank note so that the allegorical female figure ended up in a compromising position. I told them to come too. Soon everyone was gathered around me, ready to listen, showing me a deference I wanted to be worthy of. Everyone, that is, except for Baumé, who was sleeping and whom we wouldn't have dreamt of waking. In a low voice, I revealed all my preparations since our arrival.

I was still speaking when Momot exclaimed, "You don't have to talk like a secret agent."

This comment flustered me. Some of the others told Momot to be quiet. I went on as if nothing had happened, forcing myself not to take these taunts seriously. I revealed my plan once again.

Just as the express train was passing, one of us (we would decide later who) would take advantage of the noise to break through the boards barricading the window. One by one we would jump into the courtyard. As for the barbed wire, when the time came I would show each of them how to pass through. Our escape wouldn't be noticed until the next morning. We would have an entire night before the alarm was given. Once clear of the house, we would head toward Grigau. This was not a random choice: Roberjack had a married sister near there who lived on a small farm. But it would take time to get there. We would walk all night to get as far from the villa as possible. We would hide at dawn and head out again the next evening. If we covered thirty or so kilometers a night, we could reach France in two weeks. I showed them the map. I had drawn our itinerary in pencil, the stop-points marked by little circles. I told them I spoke German—even though they already knew this—which had enabled me to casually get information about the area from the guards. If we wanted to succeed, we had to avoid contact with Germans as much as possible and eat only from our own food supply. Ten days worth of food was the absolute minimum. We had to begin rationing right away, not even open our parcels. As for me, I already had some provisions which I was prepared to add to the common pile to save time. "That's what I propose," I said in conclusion.

Baillencourt, Durutte, Billau, and Labussière exclaimed that the plan couldn't succeed. First, it was impossible to break the window planks in thirty seconds, the time it took for the train to pass. Even if we managed to do it, it was crazy to think that so many of us could cross all of Germany without attracting attention. Sure, we would walk at night, but that didn't mean that we would never meet anyone. Also, these safe hiding places I had mentioned, where I was counting on spending our days, was I quite certain of finding one at each stop? And was I certain we would all have the physical stamina necessary for such an expedition?

At this point Momot started showing his ill will again. He was determined to escape, but he wanted to have all the cards in his favor. He didn't want to be caught like a jerk. Enough stupid mistakes had been made in this war by others without our help. We all knew what plans were worth, he asserted, anyone could make one. He started getting worked up. He abandoned the serious tone intended to impress his friends. He'd had enough of always playing the fool. From now on, he would act with full knowledge, and not because somebody had told him what to do. Enough was enough. Who needed these people? What we needed were good, upstanding fellows, who knew what they were talking about, who had experience, who had studied the issues, and not people with no knowledge who decided it was their place to give orders and advice.

Labussière said the problem was simple. We didn't need a plan but an opportunity, an opportunity which those who were quick enough would take advantage of. Anyone could come up with a plan like mine, we knew where that led. Things were bad enough already without making them worse.

The other prisoners lost their tempers one by one. I was daring them to escape. I had never dared anyone to do anything in my life, but it was a word they liked to use. "If we had so much courage," Durutte said, "we had only to show it earlier and we wouldn't be here." Baumé hadn't even woken up. He was sleeping in a complicated position, one arm over his head, joining the other hand with fingers clasped while one leg was stretched out and the other bent. Jemmaton the farmer pretended to take up my defense, trying to seem clever. "But he's right . . . ," he kept saying. "I agree with him. And I'm sure we'll get a bunch of them before they get us."

Then Baillencourt claimed I didn't care about anyone else, I was only thinking of myself, I was only pretending to be concerned about everyone else because I needed them. This really made me mad, it was so unfair. I thought of shouting, "He's only saying this because he's afraid," but I held back.

Finally Roger took my defense, which improved my

position. He said that it didn't matter whether our leaders had messed up or not, we had to get out of the fix they had gotten us into. Like it or not, my plan was all we had. Following it was the only solution possible. But the three strong-headed ones held their ground. As for my other fellow prisoners, they voiced no opinions at all.

The very next day, I launched a fresh assault.

Chapter 9

We were gathered in the corner by my bed. Four of us seated on the straw mattress, four others on Pelet's bed, a few standing, and the rest leaning against the wall. I had divided what I had to say into three parts. I was preparing to speak when Pelet suddenly began yelling. His wallet had disappeared, with his money and his beloved photographs.

When he'd looked further and still couldn't find it we began a massive search, but in vain. In the end, I suggested that we put the search off until later, that it would be better to take advantage of our being in one place to talk about serious business.

The others seemed to agree with me. They began listening, but I soon sensed that the fact that I didn't mention the theft and was dwelling on the importance of making a decision about our escape as quickly as possible—after all, we could be sent back to Biberbrach any day now, and then who knew when we'd have another opportunity to break away—was being interpreted as a way of diverting attention, almost as proof that I had something to do with the wallet's disappearance.

At that moment, Billau cut me off. He had been annoying me for a while now, obsessively repeating that he was a Norman, a good Norman, a true Norman, and an old Norman. He said we shouldn't be suspicious of one another, that we should choose one person to search everyone's pockets and packs. No one came forward, so he added that Baillencourt was the best candidate. Everyone agreed. I was beginning to get tired of these three cronies acting as if they were our leaders, but I didn't want to go so far as to propose someone else.

Baumé, who had remained in the back, drew near. He said he preferred that I do it. I immediately protested, insisting that Baillencourt would do a much better job than I would. I noticed the three friends turn to the others with knowing looks upon hearing my name.

Baillencourt began by undoing his own pack, then, as if overcome by a sudden desire to be even more scrupulous, asked one of us to examine it. When no one moved, he began a careful examination himself. He kept showing us proof that he wasn't guilty. "Okay, we know it's not you," I couldn't stop myself from saying aloud. But no one grasped the irony of my statement.

He then went on to other packs. His searches were curious in that although they appeared to be the same for everyone, they were longer for those who were more likely suspects. When he didn't find anything, a discussion arose in which punishment for the thief reached the level of a death threat, so in the end I dropped out of the conversation.

The next morning, as I was unloading a car, Baumé came to me and told me he was the one who had stolen the wallet. He even admitted where he had hidden it. I told him to give it back, or rather to put it back where he'd found it, and not to do it again.

That evening, Pelet found his wallet. I pretended to be surprised when he announced the news. This restitution, however, did not satisfy everyone's curiosity. They wanted to know who the thief was. They whispered among themselves. Neither Baumé nor I joined in this secret meeting. I sensed they suspected Baumé and since I was always defending him and just today was pretending to take no interest in him, they started giving me funny looks. They hadn't forgotten Baumé's request to put me in charge of the search. They didn't go so far as to think I was his accomplice, but they suspected I'd had something to do with the wallet's return.

Our life was too difficult for us to talk about one thing for any length of time. Each time he saw me, Baumé would remind me that he'd asked my forgiveness. Finally I told him not to bug me about it anymore. This idea of forgiveness, which seemed admirable to him, annoyed me. More and more, I had the impression that Baillencourt and his accomplices were going to give us the slip.

I took Baillencourt aside and asked him to tell me honestly what he was planning. I added that if he was planning to escape it was his duty to warn us, so that those of us who also wanted to escape could follow. Instead of answering me, he got angry. He was sick of my constant concern for the others. They could take care of themselves. They hadn't elected me to speak for them, he said, and then made an extraordinary suggestion. When the moment came for us to escape, I should go to the command post and pretend to be choking on something so the guards wouldn't come out.

Thus, despite everything I had done for them, with no ulterior motive and in a spirit of true camaraderie, my companions were flippant about my fate. They found it natural that I should run an added risk, that I should stay behind, that I should get caught so that they, my companions, could flee.

I was careful not to succumb to the ill humor this selfishness inspired in me. I said they were absolutely right, that I had thought of it myself, and that if this was their only hesitation, I was happy to oblige. And the truth is I was being sincere. Since I was organizing everything, since I was pushing my comrades in a direction

I had chosen, it was natural for me to take every possible precaution.

At the last minute I would go to the guard room, claiming to be in horrible pain. Or I would pretend I had a raging fever, I would shiver, I would ask permission to sit by the fire, I would beg them. In case of danger, that is, in the event one of the guards were going outside, I would pretend I was better and return to alert my companions. If I didn't come back, that meant everything was all right, the coast was clear.

Chapter 10

One rainy day when the food was inedible, when the work left to do was worse than usual, when the field surrounding us seemed unending, I approached two of my comrades who'd found shelter under a train car, between the axles, and who, in the only gesture of rebellion still available to them, had left their mess kits out instead of putting them away immediately. They were smoking one cigarette between them, passing it after each puff.

I sat down next to them. I told them this couldn't go on, that I'd had enough, that if it kept up I would do something drastic. I thought that men in the same distressing situation would have similar thoughts. But they kept silent. I told them the only thing left to do was escape, that anything was better than going on in this way. They still didn't answer me. I sensed they didn't trust me. There is nothing more surprising than inspiring distrust when you're down and out, when there is no justification for it.

In order to reassure them, to counter the suspicion that I was pushing others to do what I would hesitate to do myself, I added that as for me, my decision was made. I would rather risk a bullet in the back than continue wallowing in this misery. They gave me awfully strange looks.

My two comrades, crushed by the weight of their captivity, thought there were hidden, mysterious circumstances in my life that gave me an enviable independence. I tried to clear myself by assuring them we were all in the same boat, but it was no use. From that day on, they were wary of me, as if my courage to escape depended on secret connections, as if I were a rotten guy trying to drag them on an adventure they didn't have an equal chance of surviving.

Our duties were far from satisfying. Although I realized it didn't help much, I worked more than I had to in an effort to compensate for my companions. Above all, I wanted to avoid being sent back to the camp. I tried to motivate the others, pointing out that it would be impossible for us to escape from Biberbrach. All they could say was they didn't want to work for Krauts.

The real reason lay elsewhere. When you're suffering, the lowliest sentiments emerge from your heart. All these men, who like me wanted only their freedom, took their revenge for its absence by thwarting the efforts of those who were struggling toward it. When I told them we were better off here than at the camp, they pretended to be indifferent to the pluses and minuses. I tried to move them with arguments we Frenchmen like to hear, that they shouldn't give in to fatalism, that giving up wasn't worthy of "our guys."

One evening, taking advantage of the fact that my comrades were in a better mood than usual, I again brought up the subject of our escape. That day, I had to combat an argument that arose periodically: a rumor was circulating that we were going to be liberated at any moment, that a peace treaty was about to be signed. A guard had heard this on the radio and had repeated it to one of us.

I had been speaking for several minutes when a discussion grew animated behind me. For some reason Momot and Jemmaton were arguing. "You did it . . . ," Jemmaton was saying. "No I didn't . . ."

We asked them to be quiet. Momot replied that no one had ever told him to shut up. Raising my voice, I remarked that under these circumstances we should forget about escaping. Too bad; we would carry these rails until the end of the war. "And let me tell you, we've got a long way to go," I added.

No one was listening to me. The argument had spread. Everyone was yelling at the same time. I heard someone say that they should all listen to me, and another respond that he couldn't give a shit about me, I talked too much, I was a blabbermouth.

I sat to the side on a straw mattress, waiting for things to calm down. Pelet, acting as if he had never lost control, even though he was one of those who had yelled the loudest, came over to me. He said it was shameful. I asked him to leave me alone. He seemed so hurt to be put in the same category with the others that I added, pointing to my comrades, that it was very difficult to hear anything.

The argument grew twice as heated. Now it was a matter of the work that certain people asked others to do for them. Finally, when this senseless debate calmed down, I again addressed my audience. As I was being interrupted from moment to moment, I automatically kept saying, "Please . . . ," adding that I wasn't forcing them to listen to me, but I wanted to warn them that we wouldn't be here forever, that we would be sent back to the camp and would then regret not having taken advantage of the opportunity now available to us.

My companions began counting my "pleases." Eleven, twelve, thirteen . . . To be funny, Baumé, who was standing off to the side, yelled out, "fourteen" just as I was silent. And some of these idiots started laughing!

"What do you want from us?" interjected one of those who had kidded me the most. It was the first time I was being openly challenged. I shrugged my shoulders. "If you really want to get out of here," Labussière picked up, "do it and stop bothering us! We don't need you to tell us what to do. Enough's enough. Let's not talk about it anymore."

Pelet, Baumé, and a certain Mimiague turned to Labussière and told him that indeed enough was enough. "No one's stopping you from leaving if you want to," yelled Durutte. "All we want is for you to stop hounding us."

I said it was true, no one was stopping us from leaving, but we weren't selfish people, and didn't want others to suffer because of us; we would only leave if we all agreed.

Then Momot began yelling that we were all bastards, but his reason was so unexpected I was stunned. We were bastards for having thought for a second that some of our fellow prisoners were capable of denouncing us. They weren't like that. They didn't betray friends, and so on. The others fell silent. I couldn't even imagine what they were thinking.

Chapter 11

A little later on, when everyone had gone to bed, I thought about this scene. I was surprised that young men, far from their families, from material interests, who seemed to have returned to a primitive way of life, could be so petty. I would never have thought that jealousy, envy, and ambition could continue to be so prevalent.

It seemed to me that the situation was messier than before. I had played my cards wrong; it's a mistake to bring up the same topic too often. After hearing me say the same thing over and over, they no longer took me seriously, so that my hopes of getting anywhere with my comrades had dwindled. I had fallen in their esteem. They had always listened to me because they gave me credit for being more intelligent than I am. Now, because I had spoken too much, they realized I was just like anyone else.

It happened that the next day at work I was placed beside the two natives of Rambouillet, Mimiague and Boittard, who still seemed to think they were much better than the others. Mimiague had a small, pointy black mustache. He was always asking the guards for a light and thanking them with a Parisian salute, bringing a finger to his helmet. Boittard had a large, reddish head with alcoholic-looking eyes and the docile manner of a thug who will protect or kill you depending on his orders.

I told them we would be wise to escape, nothing more. The little one put down his shovel, looked me in the eyes, and said, "How much longer are you going to keep bugging us?"

I turned away and went to sit on a log. I gathered every twig of tobacco I could find in my pocket, picking out what looked like bread crumbs, and rolled a cigarette. I saw the guard coming and going a hundred meters away, on the flat road, surveying the stretch of land, with its signal boxes, train cars, spare parts, and stone heaps, amidst which we were scattered.

I told myself it was ridiculous to stick to a rigid plan. I had thought about it too much. Why not take advantage of a moment when no one was looking, or of the generally weary atmosphere, to run away without my comrades or the sentry noticing? If I really wanted to do it, at one point or another I'm sure I'd be able to. But once you left the small oasis of our work site, the surrounding plain went on forever with no trees and no houses. How could you escape without being seen? Jump inside a truck? The problem was that even though the guards were nice, they didn't inspire confidence: they were sturdy, fun-loving men who liked to joke around, give us cigarettes and occasionally a bite to eat and who even pitied us deep down, but when it came to orders they didn't know anyone. If they saw me jump inside a truck they wouldn't even ask the driver to stop, they'd just shoot.

From that day on, I no longer spoke to the two from Rambouillet. Nothing is worse than quarrels like these when you have to go on living together. I had to continually loop around to avoid meeting them face to face, which made for some ridiculous scenes.

One week later, they were involved in a strange incident. For some time, my fellow prisoners had considered Mimiague and Boittard the black sheep. On various occasions we had been scolded by the Germans because of them.

My comrades didn't like that at all. There was always one person who would reprimand the rest, fault us for our stupidity, comment with an air of resignation that it was the same thing over and over, that we didn't know enough to recognize what was being done for us, and so on. Those who complained like this exchanged glances with the guards, gave them knowing looks to show them they were right, that they agreed these guys from Rambouillet were two unworthy individuals.

I personally avoided getting involved in this business. I have always hated these strange friendships between the worst of enemies which the Germans were adept at creating. The idea of being in agreement with them was disgusting to me, even if only on a single point, and even if this agreement remained secret and provided special advantages. Unfortunately, my comrades did not share my scruples.

One evening Mimiague and Boittard must have executed an order so badly that, encouraged by everyone's tacit approval, the guards grew livid. Then a strange thing happened: these two men, who told everyone to take a walk when it came to escaping and who therefore seemed resigned to their fate, began cursing and even threatening the guards. The next day they were sent to a discipline camp. Later on, rumor had it they went to the firing squad.

Chapter 12

I think we would never have left if an unexpected and appalling event hadn't occurred. The differences in our group weren't as great as one might think. We basically fell into two categories: on the one hand manual laborers and office workers from Paris—or more precisely from the Parisian suburbs, because apart from me the Parisians weren't born in Paris—and farmers recruited from Angers. I was continuing my one-man crusade when one of these farmers, Jemmaton, fell ill.

Here I must embark on a short aside. Our house, the House of Misery as Momot called it, was situated three kilometers from the city. The medical officer visited twice a week. If we got sick in between we waited for him unless it was really serious, in which case a guard drove us to the city hospital. Ordinarily, this trip was a welcome change of pace for the guard.

This day, for some unknown reason, the Germans thought Jemmaton was pulling their leg. It's true that Jemmaton was a strong, handsome, strapping fellow and it would have been unlikely for him to fall deathly ill from one day to the next. The guards refused to take him to the hospital and wouldn't even give him permission to stay in bed, forcing him to remain with us.

When we arrived at the work site, Jemmaton had to sit down. Usually when faced with a situation like this, the Germans affect a very humane air, as if to imply that you could count on them as long as you weren't lying. Jemmaton was an honest fellow. He wanted to work, even though he was shivering with fever. He sincerely seemed to believe there was nothing wrong with him. I must say that I was the same way when I had my case of pleurisy.

Jemmaton insisted on working. He hammered metal stakes into the ground for over an hour; then he fainted. I can't say why, but the guards took it very badly. Perhaps the day before, a prisoner had pretended to faint at another part of the work site, and they thought Jemmaton was playing the same game.

One of them got violently angry. He began insulting Jemmaton, threatening him with his rifle and hitting him on the foot. When Jemmaton didn't move, he had him carried to a broom hut.

We were all horrified, especially since we knew that

Jemmaton really was sick. It was at moments like this, which fortunately were quite rare, that we saw the tragedy of our situation. Usually life was simply miserable and monotonous.

As soon as our comrade was laid out in the hut, a guard snapped at us to return to work. In German, I told them they had to be blind not to see that Jemmaton was really sick. They pretended to take aim at me.

At the twelve o'clock break we weren't allowed near the hut. When we went to fetch Jemmaton that evening he was ice cold and delirious. The guards realized they'd made a mistake but didn't want to admit it. Instead they gave us an even harder time. According to them we tended to forget we were prisoners. They were tired of dealing with us individually, which they had often very kindly done, talking to us and giving us tobacco, taking an interest in one because he worked in a bank, in another because he had his own little farm.

On returning to our quarters I yelled at everyone. "What's stopping you is you think some of us will weaken at the last minute. If you were sure that tomorrow, say, all of us would leave together as one, you wouldn't hesitate. Well! It's decided, we're leaving tomorrow."

"Is that an ultimatum?" asked Roberjack, who had a thing for this word. Baillencourt wanted to object. I begged him to remain quiet and told him I would talk to him privately in a minute. I asked him not to destroy my efforts before listening to me.

As soon as the lights were out, I went to sit at the foot of his bed, but we couldn't talk because some of the others, knowing full well how important our conversation was, complained we were too loud.

Then Pelet approached me. I thought he was going to ask me for news, but in fact, he was only thinking of himself. What had happened to Jemmaton had really gotten to him. He still thought he had symptoms of some serious illness. To get rid of him, I said that all illnesses were preceded by a progressive weakening. I didn't know what I was talking about, but I had found the right argument and he returned tranquilly to his place. The next morning, to my surprise, everyone seemed to have forgotten that we were supposed to leave that night. There was no more conversation than usual. Everyone was dressing slowly, as if it were a morning like any other, past or future.

As is common when dealing with matters close to one's heart, I didn't dare speak about it first. I adopted the same resigned attitude as everyone else. I didn't complain. Yet out of habit I almost cursed when I spilled some of the black sap that served as coffee.

We were all in the courtyard shortly before assembly when I saw Cathelnicau speaking to some prisoners in a room on the first floor. I had the impression he was telling them we were leaving that evening, which worried me. I had always insisted on absolute secrecy.

Suddenly, my concern turned to fear. Perhaps they were each looking to bring other prisoners I didn't even know.

Instead of twelve, we would be twenty, thirty, even forty in number. That changed everything.

I remembered Baillencourt's words. I already felt that twelve was the limit. As soon as Cathelnicau moved away from his friends, I went to question him. "You didn't tell them anything, I hope." He told me he had been careful not to, but that they wanted to join us.

I didn't say anything. I didn't even ask how they could want to join us if no one had told them we were going.

My fear only grew. I saw all my careful preparations becoming useless at the last minute. Instead of acting methodically, following a well-developed plan, we were going to trust our luck. It was really incredible how difficult it was to make men understand their own self-interest.

Suddenly an insane thought crossed my mind. In the end, after having arranged everything, I was the one who would lose my nerve. Just then the assembly whistle blew.

During the day, I had occasion to see other conversations going on with prisoners from different rooms. Instead of bringing us together, as our decision, once agreed upon by everyone, should have done, I noticed, on the contrary, more and more distance between us. All my calculations and preparations seemed ludicrous and pointless.

That evening when we were gathered together I wanted to get the situation under control. I felt that we were heading for disaster, that our plan had taken on such proportions that only deaf guards wouldn't notice.

Chapter 13

The train passed at ten after eight. Twenty minutes before, I announced that I was going to knock on the door, call the guard, and have him escort me to the guard room.

They looked at me in amazement. My comrades had completely forgotten that this precaution was their idea. They told me it was unwise, that if the guards were sleeping I would wake them and put them on the alert.

I replied that if they were sleeping, that would prove they weren't planning to make the rounds, and that my waking them wouldn't make them change their minds. Having them take me to the guard room would increase the security of our enterprise.

"It's not necessary, they never make rounds," they yelled from all sides. I answered that we were already poorly prepared in enough ways without adding new ones. Some of them agreed with me, but the majority, I sensed, thought I was complicating things. Others saw my pretending to be sick not as an additional element of security but as an idiotic means of attracting attention.

All my comrades were pretending to be asleep. I felt uncomfortable standing alone among the beds, as if I were up to no good.

At five minutes to eight, as I was preparing to knock on the door, I told Roger I thought it was best to break the boards by having someone ram into them with his shoulder, and to use a stool only if this method proved inadequate, so that the noise wouldn't get out of hand. Then I repeated that if by chance I saw a guard leaving the building, or if I noticed one already outside, I would come back right away.

Just as I was about to knock on the door to call the guard, thus taking the first step toward our freedom, someone got up in the darkness and came toward me to hug and kiss me. It was Pelet. He told me he would stay in the room until I came back, that he didn't want to leave without me. He knew that I had done everything and he trusted only me.

This show of affection moved me deeply. I kissed him in turn. While at this moment the others were thinking only of themselves, while my comrades took no account of all my past efforts and still found it fitting that I should continue to make sacrifices for them, he alone had thought of me.

There was still a quarter of an hour left before the train would pass. I hesitated before knocking, thinking it was a long time to play sick, but I did have to consider that the sentry might not hear me right away.

"What are you waiting for?" I heard someone murmur in the darkness. It then crossed my mind that to ensure my comrades' escape, I was taking the risk of not being able to flee myself. "It's a little too early," I said in a low voice. I couldn't see anything in the darkness, but everything was outlined with extraordinary precision in my mind.

Suddenly I decided to act. I banged on the door as hard as I could and yelled, "Hello, hello . . ." as we did when we needed to go to the latrines. The guards were very understanding, so long as it wasn't too late and there weren't too many calls.

I heard footsteps, then a key in the lock. The door opened. A German let me out. I mumbled a few words; once he closed the door I began groaning. I made my way to the end of the corridor where the entrance was. Next to this, another door was ajar, the door to the guard room.

I stopped. The room was lit. A fire was burning in the stove. I brought my hand to my throat and forehead, and began shaking. I said I was choking and, pointing to the fire, added that I was freezing. The guard, thinking I wanted to go outside, was about to open the front door.

I realized then that I was being too subtle. In an effort to seem realistic, I hadn't wanted to exaggerate the signs of my illness and the guard hadn't noticed anything. I let out a cry, or rather a kind of rattle, and fell to the floor on my knees. Then I got up and stumbled into the guard room without asking. I noticed right away that another sentry was sleeping but that two beds were empty.

I got up as if I were suddenly well again so that I could return and warn my comrades. But just then I noticed the rifles and helmets of the two missing parties. They must have gone out for a night on the town.

I remember that, still thinking I wanted to go to the latrines, the guard who had come for me was unlocking the front door. That meant the other guards were not in the courtyard, or the door wouldn't have been locked. Without a word, I doubled over and slumped down on the chest that was used as a seat by the stove.

The German who was lying down turned over and propped himself up on his elbow. I explained in broken sentences that I must have been poisoned, that I had terrible pains. It was like I was being stabbed at regular intervals in the pit of my stomach. I seemed especially credible as I had had food poisoning once several years before, and knew the symptoms. Also, as the Germans supplied the food, such honesty would make my sickness seem all the more authentic.

Then I started groaning again. The guard acted like a man who might have had a heart once, but who'd taken refuge in insensitivity faced with the overwhelming misery around him. He seemed indifferent to everything. Even if I had been twisting on the floor at his feet, he would have remained impassive. And yet I sensed this facade didn't run very deep.

The German brought me a glass of water. Had he been bringing this glass to his mother or his sister, he wouldn't have revealed any more emotion. He handed me the glass like someone who doesn't want to force anything on you, who leaves you free to drink or not to drink, but I sensed that it pained him to see me moan and wince.

What bothered me was that at the request of my comrades, I had called the guards too soon. Since I was the one who had to do the acting, I shouldn't have allowed myself to be influenced knowing my lack of talent. I was afraid I wouldn't be able to keep it up long enough. The minutes seemed interminable; I couldn't moan so much that the guard would decide to act and yet I had to moan enough for him to allow me to stay in the room. But what would happen if, out of the goodness of his heart, he suddenly offered to drive me to the hospital?

I raised my head. My eyes were teary. "I think I'll be better in a few minutes. The heat is helping me," I uttered laboriously. Above all, it was important not to seem as if I were complaining about being a prisoner. "I must have made a mistake, I must not have been poisoned."

The guard had taken off his helmet and put down his rifle. He was looking at me not knowing what to do. From time to time he spoke to his colleague, but his eyes were closed and he didn't answer.

As the train still hadn't come, I began groaning again, but I had lost my enthusiasm. I felt a sense of well being, as if the danger had passed. The match was won. If my comrades did exactly what we had agreed on, in a few minutes we'd be free. All I had to do was say that I felt better once the train had passed, but not right away, or the guard might make the connection. He would escort me back. Once the door was closed, I would take my turn jumping out the window and join my comrades.

"Are you feeling better?" he asked. I didn't answer.

As the train was taking a long time coming, I began faking pains again. The guard brought me a glass of liquor. Just as he was handing it to me, I noticed a muffled rumbling in the distance. Had I been tied to the rails, I wouldn't have been more frightened.

"I'm feeling better, I'm feeling better . . ." I cried. I took the glass, but despite my best efforts to pretend I hadn't heard anything, I could neither bring the glass to my lips nor put it down. The house began to shake. Then a sound like an avalanche, a thundering collapsing sound, grew louder and louder.

"Drink," the sentry yelled in my ear. I saw his eyes near mine, eyes that were neither masculine nor feminine, in which I saw neither love nor hate. I was still holding the glass in front of me. I was thinking of my comrades. I was thinking that nothing makes us so brave as finding ourselves at the source of danger. In this guard room, I couldn't be better placed.

Suddenly, when silence returned, I heard muffled blows. The windows had resisted! Didn't those idiots realize the train had passed! I bent over and began crying out, spilling the contents of my glass without dropping it.

The blows were still echoing, faster and faster, as if the job were nearly complete.

The guard was heading for his rifle. He put his helmet on. He had a delicate face, beneath this helmet worn as well by millions of others. He called his colleague. When the latter didn't move, he headed toward the door.

The blows kept coming. It was crazy. The guard changed his mind. He came back to call the one who was still sleeping again. At this point I felt all was lost.

At my feet was an ax used for splitting wood. I reached for it and quickly jumped up. I had never fought before, except for once or twice in high school, and you couldn't really call that fighting. I had fended off blows, but I'd never lost control of myself. I'd always made as if the blow I'd received had been excessive for a high school battle. Never in my life had I been possessed by the kind of fury that prompts a person to kill his adversary, to keep fighting even if he's the weaker one in the struggle.

That evening, however, I threw myself at the guard like a madman. He turned around and instinctively held his rifle across his chest as protection. A shot rang out at the same moment. Almost in the light of the explosion—that's how fast it was—I made out a space between the rifle and his helmet. I struck with an upward motion, like when two people swing an object before throwing it.

The German took two steps back as if I hadn't touched him; then I saw the rifle roll from his hands without my even having to strike a second blow. He stumbled, though there was nothing on the ground, and took two quick steps toward me. I stepped back and his entire body fell forward.

Every bit of strength nature gives us to ensure our preservation was present in me at that instant. My fate would be decided in a matter of seconds. I turned around. The other German had woken up. I saw him looking for his revolver and getting up at the same time. He was shaking so hard he couldn't unbutton his holster. It wasn't fear, but having to rush after waking with a start that put him in this state.

For a second I didn't know what to do. It's incredible that one can not know what to do in such a circumstance, if only for a second. This second almost cost me my life. The German took aim. I thought it was all over. I didn't even try to duck it seemed so hopeless. The reflexes nature gives us are too slow.

I approached the German, expecting to be killed at any moment. But he was shaking so hard he didn't shoot for fear of missing me.

I grabbed the handle and a shot fired. I knew I was hit in the hand, but I didn't feel anything like pain. My eyes could have been torn out, I would have felt nothing. I raised the hatchet. I didn't know where I was, if I was striking into the void, if I was being struck, if I was fighting or not.

I was on my knees. I stood up. Everything was calm around me. What was strange was that my right hand, the one that had held the hatchet, hurt much more than my left hand which was bleeding. My fingers seemed broken. It felt like my palm had been crushed by an enormous weight. A few moments passed before I remembered what I had come here to do. I took the keys and ran to our room. But suddenly I was so panicked I couldn't find the key I needed. I had the feeling I would be caught in front of this door I was unable to open. I was terrified. Then, slowly passing my hand over my face, I forced myself to remain still.

When I was conscious of a long moment having passed, I tried to open the door again. I picked a key at random and decided to proceed methodically. A childish idea came to mind: if I had stayed put, this wouldn't have happened. Even though the key didn't fit in the lock, out of habit I tried for a long time to make it fit. Then I tried a second key, and a third. Finally I managed to open the door.

Chapter 14

When I got back inside the barrack, I was surprised to find that Durutte and Bisson hadn't left. Almost at that instant I noticed Pelet sitting on his bed.

"What are you waiting for?" I yelled. My hand seemed enormous. I dunked it in a bucket of water. Then I noticed my haversacks on the bed. We had agreed that my comrades would take them and give them to me later.

As I was slinging them over my shoulders I saw Pelet again. Only at that moment did I realize he hadn't left. Then I remembered that he was supposed to wait for me. Why wasn't he moving, why wasn't he helping me? He hadn't even put on his overcoat. "What are you doing?" I asked him. I didn't understand why he had ignored the tasks I'd assigned him.

I headed toward the window. It was open and the boards

had been torn off. All I had to do was jump. At that very instant, Durutte and Bisson decided to stand between the two beds that had been placed beneath the window. I tried to move them aside. I thought that by pushing them lightly, I would be able to pass. Indeed, they seemed to separate. Bisson moved to the side, but Durutte, as if not knowing where to go to get out of my way, took his place. "Let me out," I said.

They changed places again, but in such a way that they were still blocking the window. Suddenly I realized that they were trying to prevent me from escaping by pretending they didn't know where to go. "Let me out," I screamed.

I was shaking. I was going to get caught. But perhaps it was all my imagination. I turned to Pelet. This man who had always had such a humble expression, who had always shown me a kind of embarrassing deference in daily life in which we shared equally in our misery, who always seemed to be suffering an injustice, was coming toward me with his hands in the air, his hair tousled. He couldn't have hated me more had I killed his wife and son. He grabbed me by the arm, squeezing me tighter and tighter, so that suddenly I realized I couldn't get away.

"What did you do?" he asked me. I suddenly pictured a horrible scenario. They were afraid. They didn't want to leave and they wanted to prevent me from leaving so they wouldn't be accused in my place, so I would have to answer for the murder of the two guards, so they wouldn't have to take the blame themselves.

I broke away with a jolt. Pelet dropped his arms as if hurt by my brusqueness. He was playing a nasty game. He was trying to make me believe that I had caused him great pain, that I didn't understand his feelings, that he loved me. "What are you waiting for?" I repeated.

They didn't answer. It occurred to me that I had acted stupidly. Why hadn't I gone out the front door, since I had the keys? For Pelet? To be true to my word?

He took my arm like a woman trying to win back the man who has beaten her. "Let's think about this . . . ," he was saying. Now I was convinced that he was trying to hold me back so he could turn me in. Yet I didn't try to get away; I pretended to believe that this arm in mine was a sign of affection. But I was afraid, more and more afraid.

"If we don't leave right away we'll get caught," I cried. Pelet let me go. Then he lifted his arms and waved them around like a crazy old man; suddenly he began insulting me, accusing me of doing everything myself, of not listening to anyone, of having fooled them, of wanting to be the cleverest one. Durutte and Bisson agreed. They wouldn't let me get away; they would tell the truth and we'd all be shot together.

I looked for an object to defend myself. No one moved. I sensed that despite appearances, they were thinking more of themselves than of me, and that if I ignored them and went about my business, in the end they wouldn't have the nerve to do anything. "Watch out," I said to Durutte and Bisson menacingly as I headed toward the window. They moved aside. "He's leaving," I heard Pelet say, "we all have to go."

I jumped into the courtyard and took the road next to the rails, where the earth had been packed down. I hadn't walked fifty meters when I heard my comrades jump from the window and run up behind me. I had no fear that instead of coming with me they would try to bring me back to the barracks. I'd already forgotten what had happened. They had their backpacks and blankets. Pelet had put on his overcoat. He told me we had to get off the road we were on and pass under the little bridge and not over it. Our comrades would be waiting for us a little further along, on the left, behind a crumbling wall.

You'd have thought that nothing had happened between us. "You almost blew everything," I told him, without responding to his excuses. And I slapped him as hard as I could. He slapped me back. This made us feel better.

Durutte and Bisson were silent with a defeated air. To encourage them, I told them we were all in this together; that we all had to help each other now.

Our comrades were waiting for us a little farther along, still and silent, some hidden behind the old wall, their feet in the nettles, the others behind a thicket. I found such silence and docility in young men shocking. They gathered around us. Pelet, who I thought had returned to normal, began recounting how there had been gunshots, how I had fired them, how the guards had been killed. I told him to shut up, that this wasn't the time to be talking about all that. Besides, the bastards who had taken no precautions and had made a racket while I was still in the guard room had some explaining to do.

"What are you doing there? Let's go. There's a light on in the house," said Baillencourt, who as usual had gone off to explore by himself and was coming back with orders and information to which his absence lent a certain credibility.

"That's right, we have to go," I said. But Pelet was beginning to repeat the same behavior as in the barracks. He wanted us to all go back to the house. You had to be nuts to think we'd make it to France after what I'd done. The population would help the troops search for us. Once we were caught, we'd all be in the same boat. But if we returned to the barracks now and told them what had happened, I would be the only one in trouble.

I wanted to speak, to say that I had acted in the common interest, and especially to say that what had happened wasn't my fault; I hadn't lost my nerve, whoever had continued to bang on the boards after the train had passed was to blame. They must have been crazy. Just because we were a group, because there were fifteen or twenty of us, didn't mean we didn't have to be careful! If they had listened to me, nothing would have happened.

At that moment, Pelet, who'd become enraged, jumped on me, screaming hysterically. I did it on purpose, I didn't have a family, I was pretentious, I wanted to stand out, I had taken advantage of the kindness and naïveté of my comrades, and so forth.

For a second I thought of running away, of leaving everyone behind. I turned to my comrades; seeing that they were on the look-out, glancing left and right, totally indifferent to what Pelet had just said, totally devoid of any feelings of hatred, I grew confident again.

Pelet was pulling me by the strap of my knapsack. He was so angry that I punched him. He began to scream. I heard the others saying he was going overboard. They grabbed him by the arms and pulled him away. I was delighted to see that no one blamed me, that only Pelet was mad at me, that without him no one would have blamed me for what had happened, that they all understood it was an unforeseeable accident, a risk they had accepted to take.

I felt myself fainting. After everything I had just been through, the joy of feeling in harmony with my comrades, of seeing them interpret events so simply and naturally, was so powerful that for no apparent reason I separated from them and began walking. In my head I heard sounds like bells of many tones. My comrades were calling me, but as if I had been terribly wronged, and as if everyone, knowing this, had to make it up to me, I felt a bittersweet joy in walking away, in waiting for them to run after me.

But I heard cries, and then a detonation. Had the Germans caught us? I began to run, catching my feet at every step, jumping without seeing where I was going to land, scraping myself on the bushes, bumping my head into thick branches. A river blocked my way. I began to wade through it, and in my effort to keep the same pace despite the water, I fell. I got up and fell again. I didn't even know how to hold my breath anymore. I swallowed water and began coughing. Suddenly I saw the blood on my hand and couldn't remember where it was coming from. I had forgotten that the bullet had hit me between the middle and index fingers. When I got to the other bank, I grabbed a branch to pull myself out. It broke. I fell in the water again. I yelled. I thought for a minute that I was going to drown like a child in a few inches of water. Finally I managed to get out of the stream. I zigzagged to hide my tracks. Soon I found myself before a huge pile of brambles. I backtracked. I kept hearing voices. Was it my comrades or the Germans? I laid down flat on the ground. To muffle my breathing, I hid my mouth in the crux of my elbow. I wanted to get up but I couldn't. A horrible fear came over me at the thought of being stuck, paralyzed, unable to run, to use my legs. I still heard noises. Crawling, I managed to slide halfway under a bush.

Then I recognized Roger's voice. He pulled me by my feet, wiped my face with my wet tie, grabbed me under the arms, and stood me up. But as soon as he let me go I fell down. There was nothing to be afraid of but instinctively I began crawling toward the bush from which Roger had pulled me. He stood me up again and put my arm around his neck. After a few short steps, I was surprised to find we were back on the road. I fell down again. It wasn't exhaustion. Physically I could have walked, but emotionally I was at the end of my rope and felt a strange pleasure in being lifted from the ground.

Roger grabbed my arms, but instead of helping I made myself into dead weight. He let me go and I heard him cursing me. Suddenly I felt a blast of pain on my face, then another. Roger was slapping me. I was coming back to life. Encouraged, he continued hitting me harder and harder.

I sat up and tried to defend myself. "Enough," I yelled. "Are you better?" Roger asked, giving me a friendly whack. I got up and we walked side by side. Suddenly I took him by the neck, hugged him against me with all my might and kissed him. "Come on, come on," he said. "Where are the others?" I asked. "They're waiting for us a little further on."

Chapter 15

We found them soon afterward. Pelet and Vathomme had left us, preferring to return to the Krauts.

We hit the road. As I walked I thought about what a destructive role Pelet had played. I had comforted him, guided him, protected him as much as I could. What a lesson! Who would have thought that such a timid man, a man who never opened his mouth except to talk about his son, would one day turn into a fanatical obstructor? I felt uncomfortable even thinking about how much he hated me. My comrades, for their part, had been more clearsighted than I had. They'd never liked him. I should have listened to them, instead of always turning to people whom others don't like. Finally we were rid of him. I felt secure among all these men who owed their present freedom in large part to me. I loved them. They were being themselves. They weren't hiding anything.

From time to time, I couldn't help talking about Pelet. Whereas I continued to suffer from his betrayal, I sensed they were indifferent. Only Roger, sometimes, remembering what had happened, would say to me, "What a bastard, that guy!"

Durutte, who along with Bisson had tried to prevent me from leaving the barracks, approached me. It was clear he regretted his behavior. He explained that he hadn't been all that angry with me, but that, worried about the turn of events and convinced the Germans would ultimately win (there were many who, like Durutte, always thought the Germans would win), he'd obeyed Pelet without realizing what he was doing. He asked for my forgiveness. I saw he was sincere, that he was one of those people who act against their wishes in life, and who, realizing their weakness is leading them astray, naïvely say that they did it despite themselves; since they have no ambition they're not worried this honesty might harm them later on. A simple, honest fellow, in short.

We had already covered five or six kilometers. We had no idea, before leaving, that dogs would give us so much trouble. Whenever a dog barked, another responded in the distance, and so on. It was as if we were walking through a huge pound. It seemed as if the entire countryside was awake. But as we never saw anyone, despite this ruckus, we got used to it and realized it wasn't because of us. The dogs weren't barking to signal our presence, but by a kind of mimicry. This probably happened every night, and the peasants thought nothing of it.

Excitement gave way to fatigue. We walked in silence. The best of friends weren't talking and no longer seemed to know one another. In two hours we had changed so much! We were already thinking of what lay in store and had already forgotten our ten months of captivity. I was perhaps the only one to look back. Pelet's hatred, which I'd never suspected and which had manifested itself so brutally, plagued me; it seemed like an added danger, on top of those I was already confronting. It made me feel I wasn't worthy of my comrades, like I was a kind of black sheep, as if one couldn't be hated without deserving it, without there being something to justify it. Yet they all knew the truth.

I went from one to the next, engaging them in conversation under one pretext or another. But they were tired and didn't answer. To me, this sleepy silence seemed a sign of disapproval. At my wit's end, I lapsed into moments of despondency.

When dawn began to break, we decided to hide until evening. By the slowness with which we were seeking shelter, I sensed that the light didn't frighten anyone. But Suddenly I began to tremble. I looked for Roger. I hardly left his side now; once he even had to motion me to get away. I grabbed his arm. I was thinking of the two guards. He saw how traumatized I was. "Don't think about that guy anymore!" he said. I didn't dare tell him I wasn't thinking of Pelet.

It was almost daybreak. According to those comrades who kept an eye on things, we had covered thirty-two kilometers. Indeed, the countryside here was entirely different from that surrounding the house.

When we had all entered the excavation site where we'd decided to spend the day and I saw my comrades settle down as comfortably as possible, the previous day's drama seemed more atrocious still. To avoid thinking about it, to avoid being alone and to make sure that I would at least have friends, I felt a great need to devote myself to the others. I went about helping everyone, showering each of them with affection. I hadn't hesitated to kill two Germans so they could escape, so all of us could escape. Such an important act must not be committed in vain. I couldn't allow my comrades to fall asleep without first assuring me that they were well, that they weren't in danger.

I told them I was going to see what was happening outside. At this, Baillencourt made a remark that I would have found rather clever in other circumstances: "This time, please don't take any initiatives." I smiled, though I hardly felt amused.

I explored the area surrounding the site. The sky was overcast, but the clouds were uneven in weight, so that immense strips of almost golden sky shone through. In the distance, I saw the hills grow smaller and smaller. It was magnificent. Not a house, not a road, not a telegraph pole. I returned to the site, but not without looking behind me at every instant.

They were all asleep already. I realized I should have told my comrades to organize a patrol, but on second thought this precaution seemed pointless. Then I tried to sleep. I had never felt so alone. My comrades were all sleeping like logs. Deep down, I alone was at war with the Germans, I alone would defend myself to the death if we were surprised, I alone would be shot if we were recaptured.

I woke Roger. I wanted to tell him everything on my mind and was hoping he would comfort me. But he answered in monosyllables. I lay down again. Suddenly, the idea of being in this hole without knowing what was happening around us scared me. I went outside again. The fresh air and open space did me good, but it occurred to me that I was being unfair to my comrades. We had decided to hide during the day. They were hiding; they were doing what we had decided. But I was not hiding. I could be seen. A hunter or a peasant might pass by. Once again, I would have done everyone a disservice.

I returned to my comrades. I had just sat back down when a new terror came over me. Wouldn't the Germans guess our hiding place? Wouldn't they calculate that by walking until dawn we would be here? Wouldn't they be rummaging through all the shanties, all the caves, all the hollows and quarries in the vicinity by now?

This seemed so clear to me that I woke my comrades to tell them. Some seemed to share my fear, but they didn't even get up. Others made a gesture to say that we couldn't look that far into things. We had to be somewhere. The danger would be the same wherever we were. They went back to sleep.

I realized, following this incident, that I was no longer acting rationally and that if I wanted to stay on everyone's good side, I had to get a grip on myself. This time my comrades hadn't noticed anything, but if I kept trying to worry them about possible dangers, they would end up thinking I wasn't in my right mind and would start to distrust me and keep me at more and more of a distance.

I began thinking of other dangers, of the dogs, of possible police round-ups, and of Pelet. I was still afraid of him. He couldn't touch me now, but because of my weakened state, no doubt, I imagined him as having superhuman power. He knew me well. He had told me so many of his secrets that I'd been obliged to share some of my own. If he were to guide my enemies, he would increase their strength. He would alert them to my weaknesses, tell them how I would respond to their maneuvers.

I thought of waking Roger again. Fortunately I realized that I shouldn't cross from an imaginary danger to a real one, and that if I didn't get a hold of myself I would lose the respect of my comrades. They considered me one of their own, a normal man. We were running the same risks together. In my place, they might not have acted as I had, but they fully understood what I'd done. Deep down, they must have thought I was brave, braver than they were. They may have admired me. But they mustn't detect any sort of derangement in me, any strangeness in character. I had killed two Germans. It would have been better not to have killed anyone, but I'd had no choice. My comrades knew this. They had never agreed with Pelet; they thought he was crazy. That question was settled. I mustn't continually rehash the story. And then, after all, this was war!

Chapter 16

My comrades awoke at about four o'clock. They went out one by one to stretch and look for water. Each time one of them left my heart sank. They were oblivious to the danger. They were going too far away. They were acting like soldiers at the front. I held my tongue because I couldn't stop myself from doing the same thing.

Before leaving, I wanted to prepare an inventory of the food we had brought with us, as some, I had noticed, were eating far more than others. We emptied our backpacks. I took a sheet of paper and a pencil and rewrote the list of what each of us had brought. According to the calculations I made before our departure, we should have had enough for fourteen days. Now, less than one day after our escape, I was dumbfounded to find that we had enough, at most, for *two and a half days*. It was incomprehensible.

I tried to find out what had happened. No one could tell me. And the strangest part was that while I was racking my brain trying to find an explanation, my comrades, imagining they were already in France, seemed to think it irrelevant that our plan, in which our rations had been calculated to the ounce, was shattered. And since at this first stage we were already nine kilometers behind—because of me, it's true—the future looked grim.

I had just finished my calculations when Baumé came running in. He had seen a man in the distance approaching our hiding place. Labussière wanted to go see for himself. I held him back. I signaled all my comrades to be quiet. My heart was pounding. From time to time one of them made a remark. Another answered. I yelled, "Shhhh." They imitated me. Everyone yelled, "Shhhh." They thought I was being a little too careful, that even if the silhouette Baumé had perceived in the distance continued to approach, it couldn't be here yet.

I decided they were right. Nevertheless I was thinking how stupid I had been not taking the revolver that had fallen to the floor. Instead of immediately running away from the guard room and wasting time in front of a door I couldn't open, I should have calmly searched for anything that might have been useful later on. We were all unarmed because I hadn't kept my cool. Given the turn of events, I had to be ready to defend myself to the bitter end by any means possible.

I was careful not to say anything. I sensed my comrades didn't share my determination. Were a German to take aim at us, they would all raise their hands. No one would lunge at him, as I had done, at the risk of being killed.

This time it was Durutte who wanted to go outside. I stopped him as well, arguing that it was better to wait too long than not long enough. Finally when darkness had fallen completely, we left.

I was still thinking about that revolver. How was it that my comrades had never thought of arming themselves? For a moment, I wanted to bring the conversation around to this topic. But I held back. After what had happened, I didn't want to seem obsessed with killing people.

A little later on, I couldn't help mentioning to Roger that if we had weapons we wouldn't be at the mercy of a chance encounter, that he should talk to Roberjack about it. There might be some at his sister's in-laws' house in Grigau.

Roger heard me out; then, as if he weren't an escaped prisoner like me, as if he were merely accompanying me on my journey, he whispered, "No, no, better not to talk about that. Now is not the time." I said that if we were to run into a couple of troopers we would let ourselves be recaptured, we wouldn't even defend ourselves. "What can I tell you," he answered, "that's how it is."

After crossing a small wooded area, we found ourselves in an immense, newly-plowed field. I was very concerned about my hand. Instead of healing, it was getting worse.

Night Departure

The bullet had passed between the index and middle fingers, just where they meet, and must have touched the metacarpals since I couldn't move either finger. I had washed the wound in a stream the night before, without even being able to check whether the water was clean.

Now my arm was swelling up and I felt a heaviness under my armpit. I was afraid of infection. I had shooting pains that were getting worse and worse. I also had a fever. At first I'd thought the walking was making me sweat, but I wasn't just sweating. I was also shaking. So it wasn't because of the walk.

And this field that we had just started out on continued for eighteen kilometers. My comrades, who loved shortcuts, didn't even want to follow the grooved paths left by the peasants' carts. We advanced among furrows as yet unpacked by the winter months, forced with each step to climb over huge mounds of hardened earth.

If I lost my strength, if I collapsed in the middle of this field, what would happen to me? What would the peasants who found me the next morning do? There is nothing more cowardly than turning in a wounded man. They might keep me for the day, but after that?

A crescent-shaped moon had risen to our left, a few meters from the horizon. Despite my condition, every time I noticed one of our comrades having difficulty I offered to carry his pack. I had six of them on my back. I wanted so much for everyone to like me I paid no attention to my own strength.

I told Roger I was in pain and asked him to carry one of the knapsacks for me. He looked at me amazed. "You're completely out of your mind," he said. "Why don't you give them back to their owners?" Shortly afterward I did.

Three kilometers further I sensed I couldn't go on. At first I thought I was being too easy on myself. Indeed, although I kept saying I couldn't go on, my legs were still carrying me quite well. I told myself it was a question of will, when suddenly, although I hadn't even slowed down, although I hadn't yet passed through all the phases that in my mind should precede complete immobilization (stopping to catch one's breath, stumbling, leaning on one's neighbors, falling down, and so on), I couldn't put one foot in front of the other! I thought it was because of the weight of the earth sticking to my boots. But without even moving forward, standing in place, I was unable to raise either my left or right foot. I was glued to the earth.

I called out. My comrades didn't stop. I called even louder. They turned around. "I can't go on," I cried.

My face was covered in sweat and since I didn't wipe it off, I felt large drops forming all over. It was torture. Though I so wanted to help, I found myself being a hindrance. What would my comrades do? I thought they would complain, "Oh! him, he's still carrying on . . .Let him fend for himself." I asked Roger to give me his arm. Despite his support, I couldn't take a step. I was exhausted. I hadn't slept in two days. My nerves were raw. From this moment until four in the morning, when I fainted—for five long hours—I lived through a true nightmare. My comrades concocted a sort of seat in which they carried me two at a time, and were constantly relieving each other. I kept thanking them. I didn't know how to show my gratitude. In my delirium I imagined the next night would be the same thing, that they would never abandon me, that my debt would be enormous. I was overwhelmed with confusion.

From time to time I told them, "That's enough, just leave me here, it doesn't matter, think of yourselves, don't worry about me." My distress at being a burden was so visible that their eagerness to help me only grew.

On the way, one of my porters had to stop from exhaustion himself. I then had an attack of hysterics. My inert body began shaking with an intensity I wouldn't have imagined possible given my weakened state.

Further along, something more unpleasant occurred. A light was burning in the distance, in the window of an isolated house. Everyone stopped. I noticed a murmur, snatches of conversation. I gathered my comrades were thinking of silently carrying me to the door of this house and leaving me there like an abandoned child.

They put me down. I tried to get up. "No, no," I cried, "better to leave me here. I don't want to go, I don't want to go . . ." No one could understand my terror. Finally I lost consciousness.

When I came to, I found myself laid out in a meadow.

The sun, surrounded by a cloudy halo, was shining in the middle of the sky. When my comrades saw that my eyes were open, they smiled at me, spoke to me, brought me something to drink. I felt much better. I sat up. "No, lie down," yelled Baillencourt, who always wanted to be the best at everything and in a situation like this was the most attentive. Soon afterward, I was surprised to find that no one seemed to think what had happened last night so important.

After lunch, some in our group lay down to sleep. I used my time to prepare for the long walk that awaited us that evening. I did a few stretching exercises, shaved and washed my feet. I rebandaged my injured hand. The wound was beginning to heal. Roger, who was wrapping it, advised me not to let a scab form too soon.

In the mid-afternoon, after eating only a sardine and a piece of bread, I started to shake for a few seconds. "I must still have a fever," I thought. It was strange indeed that this little meal would cause such a reaction in my system. I couldn't ask my comrades to repeat what they had done the night before. An idea came to mind: modify the schedule and walk only a short distance tonight. My comrades were opposed, which surprised me, as I was the one who had worked out the schedule in the first place.

They had become more confident. I saw them all around me, forming little groups to take care of practical tasks. They no longer bothered to keep their voices down. Of course we were far from any town and were also hidden by thickets. The ease with which they had adapted to our nomadic life worried me; just because we had traveled seventy kilometers didn't mean we were saved.

I thought it would be a good idea for someone to climb a tree and survey the area. My comrades didn't welcome the suggestion. It was overkill. I said it couldn't be overkill when it was a matter of defending our life and our freedom. They shrugged. It is true that even when our lives are at stake, we're happy to be only relatively careful. I remembered a seriously wounded soldier on a street in Amiens. If we had hurried he might have been saved. But we weren't able to hurry. People were running right and left, but minor details kept slowing us down. It was the same thing here in this meadow. We all wanted to take precautions, to stack all the cards in our favor, but there was always something preventing us.

I thought of climbing the tree myself. But what good would it do for only an hour? We had to be on the lookout all the time or not at all. I realized that it was for reasons like these that we often let the most natural precautions slide. Our greatest enemy was the feeling that things were not worth doing if they couldn't be done well. We were vulnerable in so many ways that assuring a single point gave us about as much peace of mind as a helmet gives a soldier.

I therefore gave up on the idea of climbing the tree. I lay down. So much for the hour of surveillance. When I awoke, the hour had passed and nothing had happened.

Chapter 17

The sun was setting. It was starting to get much colder. Someone wanted to light a fire. I objected, asking my comrades to back me up. He said no one could see us because of the trees. I didn't insist. Since my comrades made no distinction between their fate and mine, it would have been out of line for me to worry more about my own security than about theirs. Each time I complained about their lack of caution, I seemed to be saying that my situation was more dangerous. In the end they might find me burdensome.

I sat by the fire, and contented myself with helping disperse the smoke. Dark thoughts passed through my mind. My comrades seemed unbelievably carefree. Instead of concealing the seriousness of my situation, I should have laid it out in the open. I understood why Roger had told me not to talk about arming ourselves. The idea came to mind to have a talk with the more serious ones among us. I took Roger, Durutte, Baillencourt and Momot aside. They felt we should divide up into two or three groups as soon as we arrived in more populated areas. The four of us, for example, could form a group. I said that it wouldn't be very sporting; if the most intelligent among us got together, the others, left to their own devices, would get caught instantly. Roger began to laugh. He said intelligence had nothing to do with it, that Baumé might be the only one who would manage to get home. When darkness had fallen we set off again. Aside from a silhouette in the distance, we hadn't seen a soul since our escape. As the moon hadn't yet risen and there were no stars, we pulled out the compass for the first time. No one but Baillencourt knew how to use it.

We first crossed a pine forest without a single bush. The flat earth was covered by a thin, evenly spread blanket of moss; the trees were spaced like columns, with no low branches. For seven kilometers we had an ideal walk.

Then we came to a road. Some wanted to take it. It was out in the open and followed wide curves. They claimed it wasn't risky. Automobile headlights could be seen so far in advance that we'd have time to hide in ditches off to the side.

I explained why this road seemed dangerous to me. We might encounter bicyclists without headlights, or even people on foot. We might not have time to hide. And the automobiles might very well pass us in a spot where there were neither trees nor ditches nor embankments. If we had to throw ourselves to the ground, someone would always lag behind. But walking through the forest had made my comrades difficult. This wide, flat road was more appealing than the plowed-up fields.

So we took the road. For a reason I hadn't thought of we had to abandon it. Each time a car passed, which happened several times in a row, some of us were slow in getting up, and we wound up losing a lot of time before setting off again.

We decided to cut through fields, as we had been doing until now. We crossed a series of enclosures where sheep and horned animals were sleeping. It was difficult, as each time we had to grope in the semi-darkness for an opening. At first we tried to slide through the hedges, but the earth around them was muddy, even swampy. We would sink to our ankles, even to our knees, and if we tried to go over them our feet would get caught on long branches slipped inside the bushes, probably for reinforcement.

Sometimes, in a corner of these pastures we would see a small log cabin. In such cases I insisted that no one approach it, as shepherds must have lived inside. My comrades paid no attention to my recommendations. They figured as numerous as we were we had nothing to fear from a couple of shepherds alone in the middle of the countryside. I explained that what we had to fear was not the shepherd or shepherds we might encounter, but that through them news of our presence in the region would spread.

After spending several hours clearing a path through all these enclosures, the countryside began to look different. It was becoming rougher and dryer. On the side of a hill we noticed a pile of rocks of all sizes, which made us think there had been a landslide for some reason. In the distance we noticed a bluish chain of rocky mountains lit by the newly-risen moon. A river ran in the depths of the small valley in a direction we couldn't make out.

We stopped to check the map. This was the Blache river. All we had to do was follow it for about a dozen kilometers westward, without worrying about our compass.

Here a disagreement arose among us. Roberjack and Labussière wanted to follow the towpath whereas I wanted to keep some distance from it, again to avoid encounters. They said that if it were up to me we would never get where we were going. I pointed out that the important thing was not how long it took, but that we reached our destination, period.

Finally I gave in and we started along the path. My initial objections began to seem more and more theoretical when we didn't encounter anyone, and I sensed that after another exchange like this, no one would listen to me at all. I resolved to say nothing more, unless a truly serious danger arose.

According to my map, eight kilometers down the road

we would pass a hamlet. It wasn't right on the river, but about a hundred meters away. I had always repeated that one of the main conditions for success was to carefully avoid all inhabited areas. If this rule forced us to lengthen our route by fifty kilometers, it was worth enduring the additional fatigue to ensure our safety.

All my comrades had agreed with me. Yet an hour later when I announced that it was time to bear left to circumvent the hamlet, they protested, insisting it was ridiculous to make a five or six kilometer detour for a small town that wasn't even on our path and which we'd be passing in the middle of the night. We should just keep an eye out. We couldn't make such detours for every little shanty. The war would be over by the time we got to France, and so on.

I let them have their say. I simply pointed out that while this time it might not be very important, one day it might work against us. Roger took me aside, "Don't listen to them," he said kindly.

Soon we arrived at the intersection I had wanted to avoid. Here a very unpleasant incident occurred. I had noticed that the farmers from Angers—Cathelnicau, Vieilh, and Bisson—lagged behind occasionally to cut branches for walking sticks. Now, pointing to the five or six houses in the hamlet with their sticks, the three friends stopped and asked us to wait for them. They wanted to go see if they couldn't pinch a few chickens.

I thought this was going too far. This was out of hand. In the situation we were in, how could they leave themselves open like that? After all, not all the Germans were off fighting. Some of them must have remained in the hamlet. They would run after us with rifles. They would use their telephones to alert the surrounding areas. I told everyone this.

"But what are we going to eat?" Vieilh asked me. I responded that we would indeed be forced to do something of this sort, but we shouldn't do it lightly, without taking every possible precaution, without having examined the site at length.

"It won't make a difference," observed Momot, who always seemed to me to exaggerate his Parisian accent. "Yes, it will make a difference," I cried.

They looked at me as if I were from another planet. I sensed, and couldn't help relishing the idea, that to most of my comrades I was the one who didn't have a clear idea of what we should or shouldn't do.

Then, without listening to me any further, Vieilh, Cathelnicau and Bisson started on the road to the hamlet. I joined them in a flash. Since I couldn't stop them from going, my only option was to stay with them and watch them, to prevent them at least from acting stupidly.

At this point something extraordinary happened. Turning back, they begged my comrades to explain to me that they didn't want me to go with them. I would ruin everything.

In our situation, we couldn't run unnecessary risks. They didn't want me along. They didn't trust me.

It was incredible. I told them they were crazy, that it didn't matter if they didn't understand why; I would go with them anyway. My fate was as much in the balance as theirs. I wanted at least to be present. I didn't want them to think I was opposing this expedition out of fear. I wasn't afraid. My wanting to accompany them was the best proof possible. Then I repeated that if we didn't want to get caught, we should stay together, not do anything alone. I finished in a strong voice with these words: "That said, go if you must."

After half an hour of going back and forth about it, I won my case. We started off again.

We had covered a few hundred meters when Roger, who had been silent during this discussion, approached me. He told me in a kindly tone that I was right to prevent them from pinching the chickens, but I had still exaggerated the risks somewhat. "You don't understand, they're peasants," he told me, like a colonial officer explaining the customs of the indigenous population. "You make them laugh when you talk about telephones. As if people made such a fuss every time a chicken was stolen in the country!"

Chapter 18

In nine nights, we covered two hundred kilometers. One of the greatest dangers we ran was choosing hiding places to pass the days. As we didn't know the areas, sometimes we thought we were in an isolated spot only to find ourselves, come daylight, near houses, or near a logging site or an active quarry.

As a result I insisted one of us stand guard while the rest of us slept. It hadn't been easy to get the others to agree. The strange thing was that this precaution, which I had been so keen on, kept me from getting any rest. Every time I was about to fall asleep under a watchman's protection, I felt an uneasiness wearing away my fatigue. I had the confused feeling that if I did fall asleep, I would awaken to find myself a prisoner. I would open my eyes. I would see the man on duty. I would tell him I wasn't tired, that he could get some rest, that I would replace him.

And at that point I would fall asleep, and my sleep was peaceful because my safety no longer depended on anyone else.

The deprivation and fatigue were beginning to have an effect. We were more and more divided. Some regretted having escaped. Certain comrades spoke of approaching the first farm we came to without worrying what would happen. Some wanted to try to brave it alone! Others wanted us to stay together and share a common fate. Durutte and Momot wanted to go for broke: stop a car, expel the driver, and speed straight ahead. Roberjack begged us to be patient. "We'll soon be in Grigau," he kept repeating.

What worried me was the silence of three of our crew. They looked at me from time to time with shifty expressions. As for me, I tried to keep up everyone's morale. I said we should just continue as we'd been doing, that in reality nothing had happened that we hadn't predicted, and up until now things had worked out pretty well!

The lack of food was especially draining. Some of my comrades thought of digging up vegetables; despite my hunger, this idea didn't sit well with me. I was struck by how quickly we resigned ourselves to extreme solutions. I said this to Roger, who agreed with me. We both found that as difficult as our situation might be, it didn't call for such expedients. We could still wait. This panic didn't bode well. It was a sign of nervousness.

The hostility toward me, which I had noticed already,

only grew. And yet I was bending over backward to help my comrades. Maybe I was annoying them with how cautious I was, but I really only had their interests in mind. I considered myself, perhaps wrongly, responsible for the success of our escape. Yet the hostility kept increasing, to such a degree that I instinctively watched them and was constantly counting to see if all were present: I was afraid one of them would denounce me as the organizer of this escape and the murderer of two Krauts.

Some of them didn't speak to me anymore, but I was careful not to change my behavior. It seemed my very devotion exasperated them. What can one do in such a situation, when kindness and goodness fail to arouse the sympathy of one's peers?

Occasionally I could tell I had a distraught look on my face. When I sensed the hostility I inspired, my facial expression darkened against my will, confirming the suspicions of my enemies. "You can see he's not honest," they seemed to be saying.

I understood this just in time. They were trying to prevent me from being myself. I didn't fall into the trap. I resolved not to change my attitude one bit, to seem as if I didn't notice a thing. But when the signs of antipathy became more widespread and more defined, I began to have trouble maintaining this attitude. It was becoming so sordid; by constantly responding to cruelty with kindness, I seemed afraid. I felt that at any minute I would have to confront the situation.

The next day I did just that. We had taken refuge in an abandoned shack. In the middle was a sort of bench attached to the floor. As everyone was complaining of hunger, I got up suddenly and said, "Wait for me, I'll try to find something." But before leaving I asked if someone would lend me a needle and thread. I wanted to change the shape of my trousers so they wouldn't look like a soldier's. I also cut the collar of my coat, pinning down the front so it would look like a civilian jacket. Everyone watched me without saying a word.

Finally I ventured out with all the available knapsacks. I walked about a dozen kilometers through the countryside in broad daylight, approaching small isolated farms, but everywhere I went I saw men.

When I returned two hours later, I knew they were talking about me. Roger began to cough. Just as I was passing through the door, Baillencourt was pretending to punctuate his words with hand gestures. Others were breathing loudly. I put down my empty knapsacks and in a good-natured voice, one you might use to avoid disappointing someone, said, "Nothing, nothing, nothing . . ."

I looked at Roger. With his eyes he motioned toward the door. I followed him, a little bothered that this discreet invitation was made in front of everyone and trying to counter my discomfort by acting as if I found it natural.

With arms extended as if he were pointing toward the horizon, he said, "I have to talk to you. Watch out." Then, in a loud voice he said, "You see, you should have gone in this direction."

I was in such a state of shock I couldn't hear what Roger was saying. I entered the cabin, determined to know exactly what they had against me. Before I said a word, as if they had guessed my intention, they welcomed me with sneers. I had betrayed them all. I was responsible for everything. I had drawn them into an impossible adventure. It wasn't going to work. They didn't want to pay for my mistakes, and so forth.

I was about to respond when Roger took my arm and led me outside. "Don't start discussing things with them. Wait for them to calm down. They're angry with you right now. It's better to stay calm. You'll talk things out later."

I said that if I was really bothering them, I was prepared to go off on my own. "You're crazy!" cried Roger. "I guarantee that deep down they like you. They're nervous, what do you expect! It's a bad time for us all. In a few days, they'll be the first to regret having been unkind."

I repeated that I didn't want to impose. I had done all I could for them. If they didn't realize that, well, too bad! At least I had a clear conscience. I'd been thinking about continuing on alone for some time now. I only stayed because I thought I could be useful. I was aware of my responsibility in this escape. Because of me, things had taken a far more serious turn than we had expected, and I'd felt an obligation to stay with my comrades. But since they didn't want me, I'd just as soon leave.

As I was speaking I had a secret fear. I was terrified of discovering (for when one has been wounded in a certain spot one is always afraid for that spot) that my comrades would not like this solution. I was afraid, for example, that Roger would tell me, "Sure, but they're not going to let you leave just like that!" and then the incident with Pelet would repeat itself on a larger scale.

Nothing happened that day. That evening, we left before nightfall. We had been walking for a quarter of an hour when we had to pass over a viaduct. In the middle, I suddenly panicked. We were so high up the mountain stream below looked like a minuscule silver brook. I don't know why, but suddenly I had a premonition that my comrades were going to throw me over the rail, Baumé and Roger along with the others. I looked at them. No one was paying any attention to me. They seemed to be in agreement. I slowed down, lagging behind. But once we had crossed over the viaduct, I realized I had been mistaken, unforgivably so. No one had turned around even once.

A little further along, something else happened. We were crossing a field when a woman appeared not far in the distance. Labussière, who considered himself a very handsome fellow with his little moustache and almond-shaped eyes, said that he was going to ask for something to eat. I pointed out the imprudence of this. "Let me take care of it," he answered.

Then three or four others wanted to go with him. I realized they naïvely believed that a woman wouldn't refuse them anything because they were men. I saw them head off and negotiate.

Shortly thereafter they returned and asked us to wait. The woman had promised to bring them some bread. I told them that instead of bread she was going to bring her husband, her brothers, and some neighbors, and we would be wise to get going immediately. Labussière responded that I didn't know women, women had more heart than men, and so on. In the end we realized we had all been wrong, for the woman in question never came back.

The next day, my comrades were so discouraged I thought our escapade was over, that they wouldn't take another step; they were going to turn themselves in and force me to follow their example. They were claiming we'd never get there, that we had undertaken a super-human task.

Some of them had sore feet. Others, who had nothing wrong with them, neither wounds nor abrasions nor blisters, insisted they couldn't walk another step. Still others complained about their legs, their backs, their stomachs. The strangest thing was that I couldn't go any further because of my arms. They were paralyzed.

We took a break every hour. We no longer took any precautions. When we ran into people on the road, we sat down in a field without hiding and watched them pass. Whenever we saw a house or a farm, we went to ask for some food, and since up until now we had fared pretty well my comrades were becoming dangerously bold.

Baumé was more and more absurd. He was carrying a half empty chest he wouldn't get rid of. For the hundredth time, perhaps, I told him to pack up its contents and leave it behind.

Roberjack kept saying, "Cheer up, we're there. My sister-in-law is waiting for us. Grigau is right nearby."

As for Baillencourt, he had his hands free. Whenever he needed something he'd ask one of us. He had a lot of cash on him. He had the nonchalance and ease of those who figure they can always get along by paying someone off. And indeed, everyone was doing him favors. Yet some, even though they were broke, gave him the cold shoulder, reveling no doubt in the pleasure of showing that in certain circumstances money didn't matter. They were unpleasant about it too, as if to say that nothing was stopping us from acting as they did.

Chapter 19

We arrived in Grigau one evening. I had never said a word when Roberjack talked about it; I'd always thought that his desire to bring us to his sister's in-law's house would end up seeming like a mere obsession. But without saying a word, Roberjack led us there. And suddenly this distant danger, which I thought I had all the time in the world to avoid, was here. For the first time, we were going to put our fate in the hands of people we didn't know.

What worried me was that to boost our confidence, Roberjack told us how these rich farmers, to whom he was vaguely related, had already helped other escaped prisoners. They therefore must have been under surveillance. It also seemed odd to me that they would take such risks for strangers.

My comrades had a completely different take on the

matter. That others would help them seemed perfectly natural to them. They were aware, even though they were hiding out like me, of having done no wrong, of simply being Frenchmen seeking to return to their country. There was no crime in that. No matter how many times I told them we were being rash, it didn't sink in.

Among other arguments, I reminded them that we weren't the first Frenchmen these farmers were saving, and that in times like these such conduct could not have gone unnoticed.

I was wasting my time. Baillencourt, with the distinguished air he was able to assume despite his dirty, tattered uniform, when told of my objections, adopted the superior attitude of a man faced with small-minded stupidity. He didn't even bother responding.

Wasn't it surprising that people who were basically happy would risk prison and execution for the sake of some escaped prisoners, simply because one of their family members was French? Yet this reason was sufficient in my comrades' eyes. They had such an overblown view of their country that they found it quite natural for an entire family of Germans to risk prison and death for a Frenchman. I, more modestly, didn't think it was possible.

Thus I was quite worried. And then, there were so many of us. For Roberjack to go to his brother-in-law's house alone was understandable. But all of us!

The insistence of our comrade, I must admit, was a sign

of good character. Actions of this type are among the most noble. Roberjack wasn't thinking only of himself. You sensed he was more eager to be useful to us all than to save himself.

When I entered the home of this family of Krauts, I suddenly realized what disinterestedness and kindness really were. I had such admiration for these qualities that I would have liked to be the sole beneficiary. A confused feeling of envy came over me. I was suffering at seeing my comrades attended to by such exceptional people. I would have liked to sit alone with them at the family table and show them all what a true, intelligent Frenchman was. You can gauge by this detail how far I was morally, in this situation, from Roberjack.

I was especially jealous of Baillencourt, whom I considered deep down to be a hypocrite, for I remembered what he had said about these Germans. He had told me without knowing them that they weren't nice people, that he despised traitors of any country, that he wasn't going to think well of them just because they were useful to him. And now, he couldn't do enough to please them.

Yes, I would have liked to have been alone, but a few days later when I actually was alone, I realized that the presence of my comrades had always been a real support. I had thought being alone would make me daring again, would make me love those I came into contact with. In fact, I noticed that I became even more fearful. I regretted leaving my comrades. Setbacks and difficulties had more of an effect on me than before. When there were ten of us, our demands were taken much more seriously, a refusal bore heavier consequences. We seemed more military, almost as if we formed a regular detachment. Our numbers made the hardness of our hearts more visible. We could say anything, we could tell the truth, whereas as soon as I was alone I realized that whatever I did I seemed suspicious.

What these Germans were doing for my comrades and me, for I was part of the group, had a strange effect on me. I feigned great coldness, so that although I was the one who understood these Germans best, I seemed a typical nasty Frenchman, one of those Frenchmen who respond to kindness with haughtiness, who show great disdain for foreigners, and who, even in need, would never ask for anything from a German.

I realized that giving a wrong impression is the punishment for envy. Suddenly, I began joking around like everyone else, which was all I needed to regain lost ground.

They set us up in a barn. Bisson, who always looked at the dark side of things, said as he climbed the ladder that one could very easily break one's "spinal column." Shortly thereafter, the women brought us warm underclothes. I felt awkward around my comrades. I had made so many preparations for our escape, and all these preparations seemed so minor next to what Roberjack had done without saying a word! No one looked at me anymore. I had fallen in their esteem. Roberjack was the big man now.

When it was time to divide things up, everyone jumped on the clothing. A rather comical scene took place. I hadn't moved, not wanting to fight to help myself, and soon everything was gone and I still had nothing. Roberjack's brother-in-law learned of this and didn't want to see me shortchanged. He went to get some more clothes for me, so that without having to make any effort I received much more than my comrades.

There were so many of us in the barn and we made so much noise I was afraid of attracting the neighbors' attention. I tried to go over with everyone what we should do if someone complained. But staying with Germans had gone to their heads. No one paid any attention to my recommendations. I sat down sadly in a corner. Billau began singing a horribly sentimental song.

Then Baumé came over to me. He was the only one who acted like a brother. Whenever I was suffering, he noticed. Without my doing anything in return, without the least pressure on my part, he denied himself the pleasure of being with his comrades to stay with me.

I tried to use him as an intermediary. I persuaded him that they would listen to him. But he seemed so horrified by the role I wanted him to play that I didn't press him.

Suddenly a whistle blew in the alley. I was up in a flash. No one had moved. Baillencourt and Roger were off to the side. Four others were reclining on straw.

"Get up!" I cried. They looked at me amazed. I realized

they were wondering if murdering two guards hadn't caused me to become mentally deranged. I saw things from a false perspective because I was more compromised than they were. I was looking to expose my comrades to dangers they weren't running, under the pretext that I was running them myself.

Shortly thereafter, when the whistle didn't blow again, I realized there was some truth to this. I was a little ashamed of my sudden panic. I thought that, given my inability to discern real dangers from false ones, it would be better for me to be alone.

Chapter 20

One night during a rest break, we noticed that Durutte had disappeared. Even though I was angry at him I insisted we backtrack. He might have fallen from exhaustion. If we were in his place, we wouldn't want to be abandoned. My comrades grudgingly admitted I was right.

We retraced our steps. We had gone a few hundred meters when some started grumbling. We would never make it to the destination we had set for ourselves before dawn. Durutte, whom we thought had lagged behind, was perhaps ahead.

Labussière was yelling, "Durutte, Durutte . . ." I begged him to be quiet. If Durutte had fallen from exhaustion, he surely couldn't answer.

"He may simply have gotten lost," someone said.

"This is pointless," observed Billau. We're not even on

the right road." "We should really keep going," suggested another. I again insisted we continue our search. No one was listening to me anymore. My comrades had only one thing in mind: to keep walking forward.

I suggested we stop and wait for daylight to continue our search more effectively. Roger approached me. "That's enough, don't insist," he said in my ear. I didn't know what to say. "This is crazy!" I finally cried. "Where could he have gone?"

We set off again. From time to time, despite my protests, someone would yell at the top of his lungs, using his hands as a bullhorn. Suddenly I thought of a chilling possibility: Durutte had gone to the nearest village and told them everything. Tomorrow morning, when we would arrive at our destination, the Krauts would be waiting to surprise us.

I motioned to Roger and told him my fear. He told me it was exaggerated, but he didn't seem all that convinced. "I'm sure of it," I continued, "If we want to avoid falling into the trap we have to modify our itinerary."

He remained silent, so I called my comrades. They didn't seem to understand the danger I was warning them about. I told them that in my opinion we should change directions, even if it meant walking a few extra kilometers. "Again!" they cried. It was at this point that I made the serious decision to separate from them as soon as I could. I told them, to justify myself, that if we were recaptured I personally ran far greater risks than they did.

"We set out together, we're not going to separate," yelled Roberjack, as if leaving my comrades would put me out of danger.

I didn't change my mind, even though I was beginning to feel overwhelmed with terror. I remained silent. As I was walking, I thought about what I should do. Should I take advantage of the darkness to run away, or stay with my comrades, at the risk of being arrested? I noticed some of them giving me dirty looks from time to time.

I stopped suddenly and they stopped too. "I'm not going any farther," I said. "Why?" asked Momot. "I don't want to get caught." I heard some murmurs. "My case is far more serious than yours," I continued. "You'll get taken back to the camp, but I'll be shot. See the difference?"

Roger intervened, "Come on, come on, let's not argue. We're all in this together. In our situation, we don't have the luxury of arguing." Some of them agreed. "Well okay, I'll stay with you," I said. "But stop spying on me!" Everyone gasped. They had never been spying on me. What was I imagining? I had a persecution complex, and so on.

We started off again. Naturally, I was still determined to break ranks with my comrades. I felt like a prisoner. I had the distinct feeling that everyone knew where Durutte was, that a trap had been laid for me, that we were all going to be arrested at daybreak, but that my comrades had been assured no harm would come to them. They had betrayed me to save themselves. Which is why they didn't want to waste time in a pointless search, even though they were so sensitive when it came to matters of solidarity.

I shared my thoughts with Roger. He told me I was dreaming, that if he ever noticed something like that he would take my side; he would leave with me, if need be. He was right. None of my fears came to pass the next day.

In the afternoon, two other comrades separated from us. The first had gone to a small farm to ask for something to eat. We were waiting and watching for him from a hundred meters away. When he didn't come back, we began to worry.

We were discussing what to do when he reappeared, but without his knapsack and jacket. He announced that he had found some very nice people who had offered to put him up. He had come back only to say goodbye. He didn't want to leave without seeing us one last time.

How kind of him! Even before he turned back, we couldn't help commenting that this was some way to act! It's only natural for people to act in their best interests, but despite the feeling that we had no reason to reproach our comrade, we unanimously agreed that he was not very nice.

At this point a truly curious incident took place. We were about to leave him, we were saying, "Good for you, you're lucky, take advantage of it, and so on, when

Labussière pulled him aside. We realized he was asking whether these nice farmers wouldn't accept a second guest, in which case he would immediately apply. The response must have been negative, for Labussière rejoined us shortly afterward, without even bothering to hide his disappointment.

I told Roger I found this behavior even worse than that of the accepted boarder. Roger made a remark that pleased me no end: "What do you expect!" he said with a cynical wave of the hand, in which I sensed both profound disdain for and profound indifference to this petty behavior.

As for the second comrade, Lemoyne, he left us in an even stranger fashion. He was the simplest, the poorest, the most timid among us. He hadn't said a word since our escape. I think as a civilian he had been a dishwasher in a restaurant. Even though he had been mobilized over a year ago, he still had thick, black nails, and a face and neck furrowed with wrinkles. He barely knew how to read and write. At the camp, he always took on the most strenuous work himself, without even being asked.

We had been walking for several hours when we encountered two real vagabonds, ageless men carrying bundles. When we turned around, we realized our comrade had stayed with them. He signaled to us.

A few seconds later, he also came to say his goodbyes. He told us he was very happy. The vagabonds were going to get him what we all avidly desired: civilian clothing.

Then they were going to lead him to a safe place. A chance meeting was enough for our comrade to make friends and help him forget our common suffering.

After this new defection, we all felt very uneasy. The bonds uniting us—and some considered our attachment to be eternal—were based on very little. Deep down I now realized that however exceptional our adventures had been, we were strangers to one another.

Chapter 21

We were dead tired. We washed ourselves in rivers so we weren't dirty. I was the only one who continued shaving, which always ticked everyone off, ostensibly because I was delaying our departure, but really because they found the care I was taking of myself to be an uncalled for coquetry.

All these beards gave my comrades unexpected expressions, for each one grew in its own way: some outlined curves on their cheeks that seemed to be made by a razor, others covered just part of the face, usually the chin. Only Baumé had no beard at all, and his skin remained rosy, which meant that the humblest one among us had become the most splendid.

A bit farther on it was decided that one of us would go to a farm and try to get some provisions. We now made every decision by drawing lots! It had become a habit. As fate would have it I was selected.

I approached the farm very cautiously. From time to time I turned around. Even though I had told my comrades not to show themselves, I saw them signalling me. Nothing could be more detrimental to my mission, since if I could see these signs the farmers could certainly see them as well. My plan, which was to pretend I was an isolated hiker and eventually arrive at the desired result, would be compromised. Nothing would have been more unpleasant for me, just as I was telling my story, than to sense my comrades gesticulating behind me. And nothing could make a worse impression on the farmers.

I signalled my comrades to hide, but instead of obeying me they responded with other signs, which I interpreted to mean: "Take your time. We're counting on you. Go ahead. You have nothing to be afraid of, we're here." I kept signalling them to move away. As my efforts remained in vain, I stopped and hesitated. Finally I decided to retrace my steps.

My comrades came to greet me. They were wondering what could have happened. When I told them they were all annoyed. If I didn't want to go to the farm, they would go themselves. They all volunteered. No one even mentioned drawing lots; everyone wanted to go. I was in the position of the unyielding one being taught a lesson by others, who would gladly do what I'd refused.

Finally, Bisson decided he would go to the farm. I

continued to argue my point. I was so successful I arranged for us to wait for him in the hedge we saw to our left.

But as soon as Bisson had gone, I suggested we set ourselves up elsewhere, at a place where, without being seen, we could see him returning. Some were surprised. "Why?" they asked me. I explained that if Bisson aroused suspicion, if the farmers (we didn't know who these farmers were) detained him, made him talk, made him lead them to us, it was better, for our own security, to hide in a place where Bisson wouldn't find us and where we could watch for him. That way, whatever happened, we weren't running any risks. We had to foresee every possibility. Of course, I didn't think for a second that Bisson would betray us, but he might be forced to.

Everyone was shocked by my prudence. They found my attitude somehow selfish and unfriendly toward our comrade. I clarified that I had not for an instant thought he would betray us. They said that we were all friends and that I was over-complicating things.

It did seem to me that I was indeed being overly cautious. As necessary as it might be, you have to be able to accept risks for reasons which, deep down in your heart, weigh little next to your own life, such as friendship and other people's positive opinions of you. I was a little ashamed. I regretted what I had said, especially since my comrades were sincerely shocked. They didn't understand how one could be so lacking in solidarity. Far from thinking of hiding or running away, they would have gone to help Bisson if he hadn't come back for whatever reason; they would never have thought he had betrayed us but that he might be hurt.

Though it made me uneasy, this incident taught me a lesson which I hoped would be useful in the future. It's that by trusting people, in the end you can avoid traps, ambushes and betrayals. People are not mean. I remembered my surprise when they carried me the night I was unable to walk. And hadn't Roger rescued me from the bushes? Hadn't he shown that he would have been captured with me rather than abandon me?

These thoughts were going through my mind when Bisson reappeared, alone, his knapsack swollen at the side. Everything that had just happened was instantly forgotten. My fears vanished. Bisson told us he had received a splendid welcome, that it had been a comfort for him to talk to people with so much heart. He hid neither his joy nor his success. He even added that he might come back to this place after the war, because the farmer's daughter had looked at him in such a way that, without boasting, he could say he had made a strong impression on her. She was so pretty he was sorry we hadn't seen her.

These words struck me, as had those of my comrades. Decidedly, they were all better men than me. I brought my hand to my face. I don't know if it was fatigue, but I had the unfortunate tendency, just when my life was in danger, to become a hypochondriac. I mustn't exaggerate; my comrades weren't as perfect as I imagined after all. A small incident confirmed this barely an hour later. This same Bisson, for some unknown reason, suddenly wanted to fight with Momot. We had a terrible time holding him back. And later, when we thought all was forgotten, he announced that he would get revenge.

Chapter 22

Sometimes we took the wrong road, but our mistakes no longer mattered as much as they had in the beginning. One consequence of these eighteen days of walking was that I was constantly injuring one ankle with the heel of the other foot. No matter how much I concentrated I couldn't stop doing it. I would have had to think about it all the time.

The truth was we had lost sight of our goal. We were living day by day, and as our adventure grew longer and longer, we had gotten used to expecting the unexpected; as a result we no longer thought about our pathetic situation as a whole. The first days we had been determined to reach a certain point by a certain hour. Now we no longer worried about these details and we were all the better off.

One day, from a hilltop, we noticed a train in the valley. Since it was very far off it seemed to be going slowly, and its smoke seemed as if it were coming from a cottage chimney. It occurred to me that we were now in a position to approach the track and try to jump a freight train. A second later, it struck me how inconvenient it was to be so numerous. I kept this thought to myself, even fearing that someone else would think of it, for I had noticed how quickly a good idea is adopted by others. What is possible when you're alone, or even with one or two other people, becomes insane with a group of ten. One of us would certainly have missed the train, or even been run over, obliging those who had succeeded in getting on to run the added risk of jumping off the moving train to help him. When you're in a group, there's always someone who doesn't make it.

That same evening, we noticed a light smoke rising from a lumberjack's camp. They were sitting in a circle eating. My first instinct was to get away, but my comrades refused to budge; they said that if we asked these loggers for something, they would give it to us, seeing the state we were in.

Strange as it may seem, hunger has certain similarities to intoxication. One of these is that the world seems better than it is. No matter how many times I repeated that these loggers were Krauts, my comrades remained convinced they were going to help us; we might even get on well with them. All we had to do was speak to them nicely. They would understand us, we were all men, and so on.

I had a terrible time restraining them. I succeeded only

by promising I would go to the next farm we came to and ask for bread and potatoes.

Whereas before everyone had shied away from this task, going so far as to accuse the lotteries of being fixed, this time, just as I was preparing to leave, four of my comrades wanted to take on the mission, no doubt because with their gnawing hunger they felt they could count on themselves better than on others. I nevertheless succeeded in holding them back.

I entered the farm's courtyard.

After quickly examining the grounds, I figured the owner was too poor to help us, and returned to the meeting place. I was surprised to find no one there. I was looking around when I saw my comrades far in the distance. I realized that they'd wanted to play a trick on me, to show me that it was no fun to be abandoned in a strange country, to teach me a lesson after what had happened the other day with Bisson.

They had no idea how off-base they were, and how, while glancing around for them, I had hoped not to see them, how happy I had been at the thought of being rid of them. And these would have been the best possible circumstances for it: if they left me without my having to leave them, I would have had the pleasure of being the victim of an injustice, in addition to the joy of being free.

I told them I thought there was nothing to eat at this farm. They asked me the kinds of questions my family or a librarian would have asked, the kinds of questions that automatically make you seem like you're stupid or didn't do your work conscientiously. "You say there's nothing there. Did you at least take the trouble to see the owner?" Baillencourt asked me.

I said I would go back. Before I even left, some of them pointed out that my mistake had resulted from ignorance, that in the country what seems like poverty is sometimes prosperity, that you couldn't judge people the way you did in the city.

This farm was even poorer than it had at first appeared, even though from a distance the adjacent buildings gave the impression of wealth. Pots with holes in them, pieces of broken glass and hardened strips of fabric were strewn about. Children were playing. A pale tan dog was lying in front of the door, his lower jaw against the earth, unaware of course that he was living in misery, but appearing nevertheless, at least it seemed to me, to have an inkling that his situation was not particularly good.

I called out and no one answered. I went into the kitchen. A piece of the roof was missing.

I called again. Finally a man arrived. His indifference to his surroundings surprised me.

I told him my story, but I seemed to be speaking too quickly, too well, and the account of my misfortunes left him cold.

He was motionless. From time to time he moved a bowl.

I told him we wanted to ask his permission to rest in one of the buildings. He didn't answer. I had to ask again. He took a bucket that was sitting on the table and put it on the floor. Then, without looking at me, he left. He didn't even glance at his children. The dog didn't even wag its tail when he passed.

I saw him head toward the rear of the courtyard. I had the impression that I could do as I pleased. He entered a building without turning around. The children's little eyes rested on me. I had the feeling that these children, who had probably always lived here, who should have been completely backward, were not. On the contrary, they were perfectly normal, because they hid their faces to laugh, to make fun of my confusion over their father's behavior.

Then the man reappeared. He saw me on the doorstep but didn't come toward me. He headed for the other building, pushed the door open, and wedged it with a rock. I went over to the building he had just left. Since the farmer was still ignoring me, it suddenly struck me that we should simply settle in here without asking permission. I immediately regretted that there were so many of us. Alone, I could have stayed at this farm indefinitely. But surely this man would break out of his trance when he saw there were ten of us?

I returned to the kitchen. "There are several of us," I told him. He remained motionless, his eyes unfocused.

My comrades really should have come with me. Seeing all of us would certainly have woken him up.

Finally we settled into one of the buildings. Nothing is more ominous than a cowshed without animals, without hay, without heat. It felt like an abandoned factory. Taking advantage of the farmer's stupor and ignoring my protests, a few of my comrades had taken what they needed from the kitchen.

In the middle of the night I woke up. After sleeping at all hours, I was now waking up at all hours as well. My comrades were snoring, sometimes cheerily, sometimes sadly, as if in sleep they were moved by the same feelings as when they were awake.

Suddenly I got up. My decision was made. I looked for Roger. I wanted to say goodbye to at least one of my comrades. Now, on the verge of leaving them, I felt deeply moved. They weren't as bad as they seemed after all. No matter how different they thought they were from me, we had nonetheless shared the same suffering.

They all looked alike on the shed's grey earth. Where was Roger? I leaned over each face. I saw almost every one of my comrades this way, so distant from me with their eyes closed, barely seeming to hate me at all.

Finally I found Roger. It had been understood that we would travel together to his uncle's house in Brussels. I woke him. "I'm leaving," I told him.

He sat up after a moment and looked at me. He hadn't

understood. I repeated that I was leaving. This news, which should have shocked him, to my surprise left him cold. I was a little hurt. Then I realized that difficult and dangerous living makes you respectful of other people's personal decisions. I was the sole judge of my actions. If I wanted to leave, it was because I had to, and my best friend would not try to stop me.

"Good luck," he said, rubbing his eyes. "And Brussels?" I asked him. He told me he would soon do what I was doing and that if I wanted, we could meet slightly further along, in Maxotte, for example, at the local inn. He added without thinking, without calculating, haphazardly so it seemed, that he would be there in exactly eight days. "Good," I told him. "It's a deal," he said, his voice sleepy. We separated without making any other plans, without shaking hands, without mentioning our meeting. We were both free to go or not to go, and whatever we did, it was understood that we would remain friends.

Chapter 23

When it was completely dark, I approached the train station. Being alone gave me a profound sense of security. I thought of what would be going on at that very instant if instead of being alone, there had been ten, fifteen, or twenty of us. If at least my comrades had accepted one person's command . . . But no, each one gave his opinion, criticized what the other suggested, rejected something for no reason, just because he didn't like it, or because he had his own idea, without being able to say why his idea was better than another.

I imagined our group approaching this train station. One person would have said we should stop and wait, another that we shouldn't take this road, a third that we were making a big mistake, a fourth that he had heard a noise, that we should make a run for it immediately, a fifth that he'd had enough, that we should just walk up to it, a sixth that he was hungry, that before anything he wanted a bite to eat, and so on.

The snow had stopped. Never had I taken such intense pleasure in calm and silence. I made my way, hiding behind the train cars, then in the narrow corridor between two adjacent cars, then on the embankment.

The trouble was guessing which convoy was going to hook up to the locomotive I saw moving in the distance. The weather had suddenly turned milder. From time to time, I heard the sound of a steam engine, then train cars clanking together. Shouts rang out. But I was no longer afraid.

I had kept my soldier's overcoat, though I had taken care to empty the pockets, my intention being to get rid of it instantly if there was a chance it might give me away. The only thing that worried me were my French military shoes. It's true that they were so worn out you would have had to look closely to notice their make. As I hadn't eaten in three days, I heard my stomach making inexplicable noises from time to time, as if, on the contrary, I had eaten too much. Aside from certain unpleasant sensations, like a sudden flushed feeling and the impression, and only the impression, that my vision was blurring, I didn't feel physically weak. I could have lifted a heavy weight if I'd had to. Perhaps I'd get winded sooner if I had to run. But on the whole, I couldn't consider myself handicapped by my fast and that was the main thing.

Suddenly I heard someone walking. It had been a while since I had thought of my comrades; the sound of footsteps reminded me of them instantly. How lucky I was to be alone!

It was a railroad employee. I merely slid beneath a train car and waited for him to pass. A second later, I left my hiding place as if nothing had happened. I thought of the terror I would have felt had we all been there. I was sure my comrades would have been unable to remain silent. How many times had I been forced to quiet them down in similar situations, my light-hearted comrades, who, had they been alone like me, would have been ten times more cautious than I was being.

In the end, I figured out which freight train was leaving. I hiked myself up onto the platform of a car and slid under the canvas cover. Then I noticed that seven or eight people could have fit under this cover, which made me uneasy. It pained me to think how happy my comrades would have been here; to think that I was here, that there was so much room for them, and that it was being wasted, wasn't helping anyone.

Finally the train left the station. From time to time, I lifted the cover to see where I was. I felt something hard as I was turning over and groped in my pocket. It was a crust of bread. This little discovery made me so happy. I broke off a piece of the crust and let it soften in my mouth before chewing it, salivating as much as I could. To be warm, hidden, alone, and to have something to eat, to feel the earth moving beneath me, beneath the floorboards, as in a ship when one feels the sea, was truly, at that moment, all I needed to be happy.

At dawn I took advantage of a slow upward climb to jump from the train. I thought it was safer to travel only by night. After following the first road I came to for about one kilometer, I sat down on a rock to consult my map.

It was six in the morning. The thought of walking all day in the country, against the wind, made me sleepy. I would have given anything at that point, despite my hunger, to be able first to bathe, then to eat, smoke a cigarette, undress, and fall asleep in a bed. Dreaming of one's desires can go on indefinitely. Sitting on my rock, with this same pathetic map I had examined over and over, I thought of the joy of waking to nice linen, a good suit, good shoes, a good overcoat, and proper identity cards. I began walking again. I had covered four kilometers when, upon noticing a church steeple, a steeple hardly different from an ordinary roof, I told myself that I shouldn't stop being cautious simply because I now had greater freedom of movement.

I took a detour to avoid the village. I had barely walked a hundred yards when a new, taller steeple appeared before me. I looked at my map. I realized I hadn't paid close enough attention when I'd looked at it before and that I'd made a mistake. Instead of being in a remote area, as I had thought, I was on a road linking two villages barely 800 meters apart.

This was where carelessness had led me. I wanted to turn right, but a river blocked the way. The idea of backtracking was too unpleasant to consider turning around. I thought of cutting through fields, heading off to the left, but I could already make out human silhouettes here and there; I must have been a mere silhouette to them as well, but they were enough to petrify me.

Although there was really nothing to worry about, I was suddenly panic stricken, as if I had just discovered that I'd fallen into a trap. My situation, which a second ago was neither good nor bad, suddenly struck me as desperate. I was going to starve to death, freeze to death. I'd never get out of this populated area into which I had foolishly ventured. I would never have the strength to reach the little station in Bischoffhein where I was counting on taking the train again that evening.

I laid my belongings on a perfectly symmetrical pile of stones nearby and began jumping in place to warm up, and most of all to prevent myself from thinking. When I stopped I felt better. There was no real reason for me to panic. I had made a mistake. My mistake would delay me, but after all, it wasn't all that important that I complete the plan I established for myself in advance each day, without knowing the difficulties I would encounter. It was far more important that I remain cool and confident, even in the face of the most unexpected events.

I said earlier that I feared hunger only insofar as it would actually weaken me, and paid no heed to the fantasies it engendered. The next day, for the first time, I realized my physical strength was diminishing. I felt dizzy. My legs were weak. It became apparent that I couldn't go on without food. I had to find something to eat. It was an absolute necessity, and not, like before, a simple need to be satisfied. My comrades and I had thought that twenty-four hours without eating would sap all our strength. This was a whole different story.

I approached a village. I couldn't believe I had hesitated so long to do so. I hid behind a tree near a house with a garden, waiting for someone to come out. A woman appeared, a German woman whom I would have considered fat and ugly, but who that day seemed imbued with all the qualities of the mistress of a house, the mother of a family, a good wife who would surreptitiously give me a package and say, "Go on, quickly, now, and promise me you'll never tell anyone what I did for you!" But shortly thereafter I noticed a man looking out the window.

I stopped further on, near another house. A woman was hanging the wash. I called to her. She raised her head. I approached her, remaining hidden not from her but from other people who could have seen me. I told her that I was an escaped Frenchman. I begged her to have pity on me. I hadn't eaten in five days. She had nothing to fear. I would never tell anyone she had helped me.

She looked me over. She was a little afraid of me, but in her eyes I was still a man like any other, even though I was French. I told her I didn't want to go inside her house, that I would hide behind the bushes and wait there as long as I had to, that she should bring me a piece of bread and I would disappear. I would never forget what she had done for me, and one day, when peace had returned, I would come back to express my gratitude.

She was still hesitating, saying she couldn't, that she shouldn't, that if anyone found out she'd be punished, her husband would never forgive her. All I could do to make her change her mind was continue begging. We were all human beings. I was going to die of starvation.

Finally she went back to her house and from inside signaled me to follow her. She closed the door and offered me a chair by the fire. It was the first time I had seen a fire in a chimney since my escape. I heard the woman coming and going. The sound of footsteps in the kitchen seemed like the familiar sound of a loved one, of someone to whom I was emotionally attached and not the sound of a stranger.

She brought me a bowl of milk, some potatoes, a piece of lard, and as I was eating I heard her still coming and going. She was preparing a package for me to take away. I had left my comrades so recently that a strange idea crossed my mind. If there had been ten or fifteen of us, could she have prepared a similar package for each one?

"You must get out of here," she said to me. I was up in a flash so she wouldn't think, even for split second, that I didn't want to go. She handed me the package and I left immediately.

A few days later, when I was hungry again, I thought about trying the same tactic all over. But deep in my heart I felt repelled by the idea of reenacting the same scene. I felt it was somehow indelicate, as if the first woman who had welcomed me would have been hurt to learn that I had done with others what I'd done with her.

But necessity is the worst enemy of noble sentiments. I stopped in front of another house, I called to another woman. Everything happened as it did the first time, but my uneasiness prevented me from feeling the same sense of comfort. She too wanted to give me a package, but I refused. This package was much fatter than my first benefactor's, and it shocked me, as if she were being shown up.

In the end I accepted it anyway. But as soon as I was alone I swore I would never ask for anything from a woman again, that I would approach only men, openly, face to face, accepting all the inherent risks.

Chapter 24

Upon arriving in Belgium, I began to regret having left my comrades. Now that I was a free agent, now that I was less at risk (or so I imagined), having no one to talk to was weighing on me terribly. When, after a night of walking, I hid in whatever hovel I could find, a wave of depression would suddenly come over me. I told myself it was crazy, that the company of someone like Roberjack or Labussière wouldn't change my state of mind, and yet I would have given everything I owned—it's true it wasn't much—to have the least of my comrades near me. I would never have guessed that being forced into silence would be so difficult. I was so unnerved I resolved to ask the first person I saw for help. I couldn't take it anymore. It was the solitude more than the cold and hunger that did it to me. I figured that in the state I was in, it was riskier to do nothing than to take a chance and knock on a stranger's door.

I approached a house that was slightly isolated. That way it would be easier to get away if I happened upon Nazis. Also the house inspired confidence in me; it was small and clean. I walked by it three or four times, but at the last minute I lost my nerve and continued along.

I didn't know where I was anymore, or whether I was retracing my steps without realizing it. The sky was black. The lights were all dimmed, and whatever light shone through the cracks did so without the owners' knowledge, adding to my sense of isolation. I heard drunken soldiers shouting and sometimes a stir at the door of a house. Voices would ring out, a square of light would rest on the pavement, then everything would become dark and silent again.

I cannot imagine a more profound feeling of distress. In civilian life, there is nothing worse than being followed in the dark, on a winter night, down the streets of a foreign city. Where do you go? What can you do? When you leave a well-lit place you can't see for a moment. That night, this moment went on forever.

Finally I chose a door at random and knocked on it, then stepped back so the person opening it would be less frightened. No one answered. I knocked again and again. Still no answer. This annoyed me. Even though I didn't know the owners, I had the feeling that this was the only place where I could find the help I needed.

After knocking once more, I groped for the doorbell and rang it. This time I heard footsteps. The door opened. I hadn't thought of what I would say. It all depended on the kind of person I would be dealing with. It was a man of medium height. I had figured I would improvise, but suddenly, everything that might have given me insight into this man became foggy. Even though I was in the dark and he was standing in the light, he could see me but I couldn't see him.

"What do you want?" he asked me. Suddenly I realized I was no longer in control of my destiny. It was all over. Without knowing it, I had taken a step that put me at the mercy of my peers. Before a danger reaches us, there is a brief moment when logic and caution no longer count. I was experiencing that moment. In a second, I would either be a prisoner or I'd be saved. At this point I could only trust my stars.

"I am an escaped French prisoner. I'm hoping you'll put me up," I said, my voice sounding to me like I was speaking before a room full of people. A second passed during which I would have been unable to flee even if this man had called the police. Then, suddenly, before he answered me, I sensed I was saved.

"You're an escaped prisoner!" he said.

"Yes," I answered. "You must let me spend the night here. I can't go on any longer."

"But who are you?"

"I'm an escaped prisoner," I repeated.

Now that I could see the man in the light, I could see he was harmless as clearly as I could see he was bald. He closed the door behind me. Though he was unshaven, though his nightshirt with red embroidery was frayed and crumpled at the collar, he had the sort of family-style cleanliness of someone who doesn't worry about his personal hygiene but is taken care of by others. The warmth of the house, the little creature comforts gave him a relaxed manner. A smell of burned milk seemed delicious to me.

He sat me down by a furnace with shining copper parts and called his wife. They were good people. I sensed in them a kind of fear of not being nice enough, mixed with wariness, an ongoing examination of their conscience taking place in the very presence of the person in need. I knew they would never have the courage to send me away, and that at the same time all the possible consequences of their kindness were passing quickly before their eyes.

They gave me something to eat. While I was blowing endlessly on my spoon, for I was no longer in the habit of eating hot food, the wife went upstairs to prepare my room. For the first time in months I was sitting indoors, on a solid chair, and being served; I lowered my eyes with joy. The fire, all the objects intended for family use, reminded me of the life I had lost and to which I was now on the verge of returning. It was childish, but the design at the bottom of my bowl when I finished the soup, the little garland on top of the fork, the facets on the glass, the monogram on the napkins, gave me a feeling of incredible refinement.

Shortly thereafter, the man led me to a room on the second floor. A log was burning in a small black marble fireplace. He added another as I watched. A tapestry covered the window. Towels were laid out on a dressing table.

As soon as I was alone I sat down in an armchair. All I needed was something to smoke to be perfectly happy. For a second I thought of asking my host for a cigarette. He had done so much for me I was sure he would have found it quite natural, but I didn't want to be rude.

On waking the next day I reflected on my situation. Until now I had thought only of fleeing, that is, of getting further and further away from the camp. I had never stayed more than one night in the same place, as if the sooner I arrived in Paris, the sooner I'd be safe. Now it seemed to me I had all the time in the world. What I needed was not to reach a certain destination, but to find a safe place, wherever it was. And this house, with these nice people, was perhaps that place.

At eight o'clock there was a knock on my door. It was the first time I had ever heard someone knock on the door of a bedroom I was occupying. Everything was grey. The fire was out. The wife went to open the window. I was touched that a woman would enter a room where I was lying in bed so freely, as if I were a child. She announced that breakfast was about to be served.

I dressed quickly and went down to the kitchen. The husband was already there, a sheet of paper and an inkwell before him. He immediately informed me that he was sending me to his cousin's house, thirty kilometers away, so that I would be closer to Brussels. This news was disappointing. Yet nothing could have been more natural. He began to write, from time to time asking me a question. I sensed that from that moment on, something more serious had been established between us.

"You don't have any identity papers?" he asked me.

"I have nothing," I answered.

"It doesn't matter."

He was confused. My guess was that he didn't mind having troubles of his own, that he saw things from an enlightened enough perspective, but that he absolutely did not want to risk annoying his cousin, to whose house he was sending me.

When he had finished, he sat a long moment, pen in hand, as if he feared what could not be undone. When he gave me the letter I thanked him profusely, but I was a little disappointed. When you ask for someone's help and you're in a situation that concerns society as a whole, you have the impression that one individual is insufficient and does too little compared to what society would do if it knew where to find you.

I arrived at this relative's house the next day, January 4, at four o'clock. It was almost dark. Snow was beginning to fall again. I figured that as soon as he read his cousin's letter, the relative would welcome me almost like a member of the family. But as I knocked on the door I realized I was arriving unannounced, that the letter wouldn't be much use, and that the welcome I would receive would depend mainly on what I would say and the impression I gave.

An old woman opened the door warily.

"Your cousins sent me," I said.

"What cousins?

"The ones in Malines."

I was afraid this wasn't enough information. I froze. I don't know why but I was unable to provide further details. I remembered what they had told me before I left Malines but I felt it was not worth saying. I should have made a big scene like the day before. It was foolish of me to think I could keep counting on help from people who didn't even know me. I showed my letter. The old woman read it, but didn't seem to understand what it said.

"I'm an escaped prisoner."

This disclosure elicited no response.

And your cousin told me that you would put me up for the night.

"He told you that!" said an old man who walked with a cane.

"You're his cousin, aren't you?"

"Absolutely."

The old man shrugged his shoulders.

Chapter 25

I met Roger in Maxotte. Deep down, I would have preferred to go directly to Paris. I wasn't at all comfortable with the idea of going to live with Roger's uncle in Brussels; I was afraid the house might be watched. When I suggested to him that it might be best not to delay, he shrugged. Roger didn't worry in advance. He thought we would always get by. I thought so too, but the future worried me more than it worried him. You never know what can happen. Roger said that it had always been understood that we would spend a few days in Brussels, which was why he had come to meet me in Maxotte. His uncle would give us clothes and money. I remarked that this uncle might be put off to see two of us arrive and that I didn't want to impose. Roger said he had never seen anyone like me, that it was unbelievable I could have such scruples in a situation like ours.

We arrived at the outer limits of Brussels at about six in the morning. Tar had been thrown over the graffiti-covered walls. Rain was beginning to fall. I wanted to give Roger my raincoat. He was surprised: What about me, what was I going to wear? But I held firm; I insisted so long he had to accept. After a few minutes of seeing me get wet from the rain he wanted to give it back. When I refused he got angry. I was ridiculous to want to uncover myself for him! If I didn't take back my raincoat, he was going to give it to the first passerby.

The sun hadn't risen yet. We would have liked something hot to drink, but it wasn't possible. The hours shops could stay open were strictly controlled, so that shop keepers were no longer trying to earn extra money. No one was working. (Later on, I was surprised to see a small-time artisan taking the trouble to make crosses of Lorraine.) Stores were only open at the strangest times. To our surprise, we saw a lighted tramway pass, clean like before the war and full of laborers on their way to work.

We kept walking straight ahead. It was the first time since I'd been mobilized that I was free in a big city. We didn't want to go to Roger's uncle right away; arriving so early in the morning would make a bad impression. Our clothing was enough of a shock. We thought, however, that in our situation we could take the liberty of doing what a native couldn't—that is, knock on a door or window and ask for a cup of something warm to drink.

We followed a long boulevard. At an intersection, there was such a tangle of cables it was like being under a net. I was so nervous I was not only afraid of the police, but of accidents that would never have occurred to me before, like being electrocuted by a broken cable. I told Roger my fear.

"You're becoming an idiot," he responded.

Now there were stores all around us. They were closed, and those that weren't concealed by metal curtains displayed shelves of empty cans.

We took a side street and stopped in front of a small house where the lights were on. As soon as we had conveyed through the window that we wanted a bite to eat, they motioned us to move on, making no distinction between us and ordinary beggars. This was my first disappointment. I had thought they would guess what we were right away. I had thought that the unchanged facade of life was meant for the Germans, that behind it lay a spirit of solidarity, that all over this big city we'd be welcomed as heroes.

Day was beginning to break. We sat on a bench in the middle of a small deserted square which must have been the site of a market, because there were holes in the macadam, iron poles, tarpaulins and hinged boards. It was one of those moments when I wouldn't have resisted if someone had appeared out of the blue to arrest me. I had already found myself in this state on several occasions and nothing had happened. It would have been unbelievably bad luck for the police to find me at such a time.

Roger slapped me on the shoulder. When I didn't move, he slapped me harder. I told him he was hurting me and that I didn't feel like laughing. He pretended to get mad. It occurred to me that by giving in to depressing thoughts, I wasn't being a good companion. I got up and said, "I feel better," even though nothing had changed. I pretended I had overcome a moment of weakness, rediscovered my passion for life. I slapped Roger back. Then I starting joking:

"You get that way sometimes," I said, the way some of my comrades used to say, "Okay, let's change the subject . . .",which had always seemed ridiculous to me, as if true despair could pass so quickly. "I feel better," I repeated a few more times.

We headed slowly toward the neighborhood where Roger's uncle lived, a modern neighborhood with nice Parisian-style apartment houses, even though by certain details you could tell they were foreign, provincial imitations. After all I'd been through, seeing these calm, bourgeois streets with their false ritziness gave me a lift. I was really on my way back.

At the stroke of eight, Roger decided to knock on his uncle's door. All I could think of was washing and sleeping, but instead we had to talk. I thought I was going to be housed and nothing more. I quickly realized that the uncle didn't interpret the simple act of putting me up as I did.

This man, an industrialist (which tells you nothing about him), was the most mediocre, small-minded person I had ever met, unless the poor physical and mental state I was in made these qualities, which I must have come across before without noticing them, more apparent to me. I had grown increasingly accustomed to judging people not as they were, but on the basis of how the kind of suffering we had experienced would have made them.

Instead of welcoming us as cold and hungry escaped prisoners, the uncle greeted us as if our escape had been difficult, no doubt, but as if the real test had been in finding choice hiding places, catching Germans off guard, cunningly procuring information, and inspiring people's sympathy along the way. He considered us resourceful diplomats, but was oblivious to the real drama, to everything we had endured.

I soon noticed that he was also an imbecile who had a strange ambition, the interest or reason for which was hard to fathom: he wanted to seem as if the war, the defeat, and the occupation hadn't changed him, as if he had remained the same in the midst of this catastrophe—as though this were an indication of extraordinary nobility, proof of great strength of character.

He wanted to talk, he had many questions for us. Roger winked at me. I admired my friend for being able to forget our situation, for being able to make fun of his uncle when all I could think of was sleep.

The uncle led us into a dark office where tapestries, gold frames, and bronzes gave the feeling of a well-appointed salon. I noticed right away, as I was often to notice on subsequent occasions, that there was a sofa in the room that could easily be used as a bed.

He invited us to be seated. Roger winked at me again. He had changed a great deal in the past hour; he no longer seemed afraid of anything.

We sat down obediently. The uncle sat down too, without saying a word, and shifted the blotter with its thick paper so that he could put his elbows on the table, the way one moves a place setting after lunch. He began with a few words about the joy he felt in seeing young people unafraid to risk their lives. He spoke to his nephew and to me as if we were equal in his affection, as if we were so united by our common ordeal that family ties were irrelevant. It was painfully stupid.

I thought he was finally going to address the practical issues, but no. He spoke about family feuds, about his wife, about the twenty-seven years he had spent in Paris, about his reasons for moving to Brussels. I was so tired I fell asleep.

Chapter 26

Roger and his uncle were still talking when I awoke. I sprang to my feet, rubbing my eyes. The uncle led me to a bedroom. I told him I didn't want to sleep. In fact I could barely keep my eyes open, but before going to bed I would have liked to spend a moment alone with Roger, to find out what he was planning, and most of all what his uncle had said about me.

The uncle closed the door and remained with me in the room. It occured to me that deep down he was a good man after all. He might be an idiot, but he was taking me, a perfect stranger, into his home, and treating me like a son.

He showed me all the details of the room. Though I had no luggage, he pointed out the armoire. He advised me not to use the armoire key to try to open the dresser drawers. All of a sudden, he said that he understood my falling asleep, that I didn't have to apologize. Then, despite his jacket with its fancy trim, he knelt down, rolled up the bedside rug, and put it away.

I watched his fiddling about with profound indifference. All these concerns were so foreign to me! He told me it was a very expensive rug. He was about to leave when he returned to examine the bed. I don't know what he saw, but he immediately called the maid and asked her to change the blanket. She returned with a greyish white blanket stained with iron marks and laid it out in place of the thick, fluffy one. Then the uncle told me not to put my clothes in the armoire when I undressed. He added that all this might seem petty to me, but that it meant a lot to him. He asked me to sit in the armchair again. He stood tentatively before me, as before the door to a bathroom where a woman is undressing. He hated himself for being so meticulous, but this was the only room he had to offer me, and this was the room where his poor father had died.

I told him that if he preferred, I would be happy to sleep on the office couch. He seemed not to hear me.

When I was alone, I told myself I was dealing with a lunatic. Like so many people who complicate everything, he wasn't interested in the big picture, and despite himself was offering me the most cordial hospitality without realizing it. Roger had mentioned that I shouldn't take this man seriously. My only fear was that the police might suspect our presence here; respectability was no longer the protection it had been. People were judged according to different criteria.

I slept straight through to the next morning, twenty-two hours. I was awakened by short knocks on the door and realized there had been many of them. It was the uncle. He was dressed exactly like the day before, almost as if he hadn't gone to bed. I sensed that for a man like him, the events of one day had no impact on the next.

He asked me if I had slept well. He talked about the nice weather. But he attached great importance to my answer to his next question concerning the bed. It was very good. He made me say it several times. Then he explained how I should go about washing up; after a series of excuses, he asked me to use the kitchen. Wax had become rare and he was afraid that splashing water would stain the floor. He pretended to leave to allow me to get up, but as soon as my legs were out of the bed, he returned. He had forgotten to ask me about breakfast. What did I want? I told him that anything would be delicious to me. He remarked that I had no choice, that the so-called free population had no more to eat than the prisoners.

When Roger returned I told him what had happened. He gave me the following advice:

"Always say yes and do whatever you want."

Roger had told me that his uncle would give me some clothing. Mine were too conspicuous. They were the same ones I had worn during what is called "the '39-'40 campaign." I had worn them on the Maginot line, in the camps, on the work site. Then I had cut them up, modified them, trying to make them look less military-like. The most glaring element were the pants; I had taken down the hem and hadn't sewn it back properly, so that a little of my leg was visible above my shoes.

The uncle thought the clothes were still good; just a few minor alterations were required. He gave me a pair of pants. At this point I realized how difficult it is, not just in this but in any circumstance, to be given everything you need at once. I had to fight for each piece of clothing. Before I was half dressed it began to seem like I was asking for too much.

The uncle asked other people to participate in the effort he was making for me. I thought that his friends would think him stingy, but to my surprise they were not in the least put off by his behavior. Not only that, they were inspired by it, asking others to assist me as well.

I grew increasingly alarmed at this. All these individual gifts were starting to seem like a collection for the poor. Everyone had a friend ready to give me what was missing.

I tried to alert Roger to the risks we were running with all this good will. Too many people would know we were in Brussels. Eventually, someone would turn us in. He said there was nothing to fear, that I should simply accept everything that was being offered.

More surprises were in store. The uncle suddenly began to criticize the same people he had contacted on my behalf. To hear him, they were acting shamefully with a brave fellow like myself. He ordered me to refuse everything from now on. I thought I had been mistaken about him, that he was a man of character, that he was heartbroken to see his friends giving so reluctantly, that he was going to provide whatever was necessary himself. But to my surprise, he suggested a solution even worse than the first. Thanks to a card he would obtain for me, I could pass for indigent and thereby obtain good clothing through official channels.

Ultimately, I ended up dressed in an oddball fashion: I had an overcoat with two long rows of buttons and an imitation astrakhan-style collar; a pair of excellent quality pants that had belonged to Roger's uncle, but which were excessively straight at the bottom, and a pair of fine deerskin boots which were in good condition despite being crackled and somewhat long at the toes. As for the jacket, it dated from a period when they were made with little pieces of the lining turned up. I tried to change it, but the stitching, like everything else that had been given to me, was top quality, and it kept falling back in place.

Thus attired, I went out as little as possible. But Roger, who hadn't been treated any better, managed to wear all these old things with a certain elegance.

Chapter 27

I yearned more and more to be on my way, but Roger wasn't keen on the idea. He had gotten in touch with a woman from his past with whom he spent most of his time, and each day he asked me to wait until tomorrow. Naïvely, I kept telling myself that it would be a pity to separate for a difference of twenty-four hours.

I spent most of my days alone at the home of this uncle, a stranger who had no reason to put me up, since he did it neither out of patriotism, nor out of kindness, nor because I was a friend of his nephew, whom he didn't particularly care about. Once in a while I went outside, but because of my clothes, I imagined everyone was looking at me and I didn't feel safe.

I really didn't understand the uncle's character. The first thing a person who rescues someone in trouble should do, it seems to me, is give that person a proper appearance, make sure he can go anywhere, if only for the sake of the neighbors, the concierge, and the domestic help. The rest can wait. If I had told the uncle that no one but me would have wanted to wear the overcoat he'd given me, the fur as he called it, he would have thrown up his hands. "What! My father's fur?"

So I spent my days by the window. One day I saw two men who looked strange to me; since my escape I had become an expert at drawing conclusions from the way people were dressed.

These two men, like Roger and myself, seemed to have been dressed under somewhat special circumstances. They were wearing suits which, though of different shades, seemed to come from the same place and be the same age, suits that had been finely tailored, but on a model and not on their owners, with false pleats, and the look of clothing given to shipwreck survivors. They wore new hats and tan leather shoes, also new.

They stopped in front of the house and looked up toward the window where I was standing. My blood froze, my heart stopped. It occurred to me that these two men might be German soldiers dressed as civilians. They had the same awkward newness in their dress, the same taste for youthful-looking things.

I watched them from behind the curtain. Suddenly I saw them cross the street. This time I no longer doubted they were coming to get me.

I must say that I had imagined this possibility upon my arrival and had figured that instead of getting caught I would jump from the uncle's bedroom window, which opened onto the courtyard. It was two, rather than three floors up, because the courtyard had a small, one-story garage. It was still a long drop, but I'd always had the impression that if approached correctly, it was a height that an average man who was supple and young could jump without breaking a leg. The only things that worried me were the strength of the garage roof, the noise I would make upon landing and whether I would be able to get up immediately, because my success depended on disappearing before the noise of my fall attracted attention.

Suddenly the bell rang. I ran into the uncle's room. If anyone asked for me, the maid would look everywhere but here, where she would never suspect I was hiding, and would say that I was out. If the Germans searched the apartment I would hear them. By the time they broke down the door to this room, I'd have jumped.

I locked the door, removed the key, and listened with my ear glued to the keyhole. I heard the sound of voices; the Germans were going into the sitting room. They might wait there for me to come back. For a second I thought of running out the front door, but I didn't know whether the door to the sitting room was closed or not.

Suddenly I heard the bell ring again and the voice of

the uncle. I heaved a sigh of relief. He was talking to the two visitors. Then I didn't hear him anymore and the sound of footsteps approached. Someone was trying to open the door! I held my breath. Was it the uncle or the Germans? It was the uncle. He was asking who had locked the door. This was unbelievable. How could this door be locked? Who was in the room?

I didn't move. I felt as if the entire house knew I was locked in this room, and that it would be the uncle's fault when the visitors, if they were police, arrested me.

I lost all presence of mind. Instead of opening the door and signaling the uncle to be quiet, I remained silent. I went to the window. But just as I was about to jump, I realized how ridiculous it was to risk breaking a bone if there was no danger. The uncle was still yelling in the apartment. It occurred to me that he wasn't so dumb as to make this much noise if Germans were there, that he would have realized I was hiding. I opened the door. He was returning with the maid to try to force it open.

When he saw me in the room (nothing had been put away, some drawers were open), he was dumbstruck. "What are you doing in here?" he asked finally, as if he were surprising a burglar. I pointed toward the sitting room, suggesting that I didn't know who these people were.

"What are you doing in here?" he repeated. I pointed toward the window, "I was planning to escape through there." I sensed he thought I was mocking him. What, jump three stories!

I told him I was very fearful. I had hidden it from him as long as possible because I was ashamed. Now I wanted to clear myself. To my surprise, the excuse of being afraid didn't wash.

Concurrent with the talents the police bring to bear in arresting criminals goes a certain administrative gaucherie. It's hard to believe, for example, that while inspectors employ such sophisticated techniques and are able to tell by the sound of your voice whether you're lying or not, they are forced to execute orders that destroy their efforts, such as, for example, prematurely visiting the home of someone they're after.

This is what had just happened. As soon as he calmed down, the uncle mysteriously announced that he had to talk to me. He led me into another room, and, as if closing the door wasn't enough, he sent the maid on an errand. He liked to exaggerate other people's dangers, so the fuss he was making didn't surprise me.

Once we were alone, he took yet further precautions. Finally he revealed that the two visitors were Belgian police inspectors; they'd come to inquire whether he'd heard from Roger lately. They hadn't said anything else, no doubt so as not to arouse suspicion, but they must have known much more than they let on.

I suddenly felt a heaviness in my thighs; then this part

of my body alone began shaking. No one had said a word about me, yet I had the impression that I was a goner. My only thought was to find Roger and warn him. I don't know why, but I had the feeling he would fortify me, that he would take it all better than I did. He had told me that if anything unexpected happened, I should let him know.

Ten minutes had already passed and now I lost my head. I felt like I was surrounded by flames and that a slew of details had to be settled before running away. I was wearing slippers. I had no money. I went to the window. The two police officers were still stalking the house. From time to time they stopped and turned around.

I dressed hurriedly. The craziest thoughts crossed my mind. At the mere prospect of my cursed outfit causing the inspectors to confuse me with Roger I began trembling. I could show them my papers. But wasn't I wanted too? They might have neglected to mention me simply because they'd forgotten, for others may not place the same importance on something we personally can never forget.

When the maid returned I questioned her to find out exactly what they had asked. They had only mentioned Roger. I hesitated to leave. Then I realized that it would be criminal of me not to warn Roger.

I still couldn't decide what to do. A series of new dangers came to mind. I imagined an entire scenario. It wasn't Roger the police were looking for, but the one who had murdered two guards. They had come here by chance.

They had pretended not to know of my existence, but in fact they were only after me. It was unlikely their visit would have coincided so neatly with my arrival if they hadn't known I was here. And since I must be considered a dangerous outlaw, they didn't even mention my name.

All these reflections had me rushing aimlessly about the apartment. Then I thought about the worst-case scenario. All things being equal, it was better to be caught acting nobly, on my way to warn Roger. Anyway, wasn't my imagination getting the better of me? Wasn't it unlikely that the police would be so shrewd? Weren't they the stronger ones? Wasn't it ridiculous to imagine that they were fighting me as if I were an equal foe, when it would have been so simple to surround the house had they known I was here?

I grew dizzy as I descended the stairs. I was thinking of how people always get caught stupidly, as would be the case if I were caught now. I went back upstairs and returned to the window, hoping the police would be gone. They were still there. I felt as if every second I delayed could be fatal to Roger. What would I do if I saw him suddenly at the end of the street, heading innocently toward the house? Yell to him to run away, even if it meant getting arrested in his place?

Finally I decided to leave. I had returned to my senses. After all, my situation was no worse than before my arrival in Brussels. In case of danger, all I had to do was run for it. When you're fighting for your life and your freedom, you can't allow yourself to be paralyzed by new friendships, by ordinary events. I must never forget that I was alone, a man with nothing to his name and no commitments, who mustn't hesitate to abandon everything when in danger, as cowardly as it might seem.

Chapter 28

I went to the address Roger had given me and asked the concierge for Miss Perrotin. She lived on the fifth floor. I breathed easier. I couldn't miss Roger now, unless it was already too late. I climbed the stairs and rang the bell. No one was there. I went back to the concierge and asked if she'd seen Roger this morning. "He just left," she told me. "I'm surprised you didn't cross him on the stairs. He went to the restaurant."

I ran to the restaurant. They hadn't seen him. Someone told me he sometimes ate lunch on the rue Neuve. I went to the rue Neuve. He wasn't there. I thought perhaps he had gone back to Miss Perrotin's. I asked the concierge again. She told me she hadn't seen anyone since I'd left. "He might be at the barber," she added. She explained where the barber was. "In any case, he always returns after lunch."

I went to the barber. They hadn't seen him. I returned to the restaurant, in vain. I decided to go back up to Miss Perrotin's without asking the concierge. The young woman was there. She had heard me ring before, but hadn't opened the door because she was dressing. To think there were people who decided not to open their doors for such simple reasons!

I told her I absolutely had to see Roger, that I was his friend, that I had escaped with him, and so on. She asked me to stay for lunch. While waiting, I sat down near the window that looked out over the rooftops. How pleasant to be able to sit by a window without seeing people pass on the street, without wondering every instant whether someone was going to stop and enter the building, without fearing the doorbell!

Miss Perrotin smiled at me from time to time, like a woman who is oblivious to the perilous situation of her friends, for whom an escape is something that only happens to men. The calm with which she awaited Roger's return reassured me.

Looking around, I noticed that Roger had it pretty good. I understood now why he had been so keen to stop in Brussels. It wasn't to meet his uncle. I did think it a little selfish of him to have made me take such a detour only to stow me away at his uncle's house, where he himself never set foot.

She was a pretty young woman. The apartment had a

far-away, protected quality that I liked. I was being welcomed as the friend of a loved one, which didn't prevent the danger that was weighing on Roger and me from being present in my mind. Here in this hideaway I felt uneasy at the thought that my situation was far more dangerous than my comrade's, who was an ordinary escapee. He had the luxury of making less of a drama out of it.

When he didn't return, I began to fear that because he hadn't been warned, he'd gone to visit his uncle, that he'd been arrested and forced to give Miss Perrotin's address, that the police would come here, find me, and make two arrests at once. Following a lead from one person to the next until reaching the guilty party had always seemed to me one of the most common police tactics.

I wanted to leave. I told myself it was stupid to take risks for a friend who had less to worry about than I did and who would always pull through.

Finally Roger showed up. I heard him say through the door, since he didn't know I was there, "It's me, darling."

I told him what had happened right away. He didn't seem worried in the least. Seeing my distress, he told me I was a baby, that his uncle had made it all up, he knew him, there wasn't a word of truth to it.

I told him I hadn't been dreaming, that I had seen the inspectors. He began to laugh. "They have to do their jobs!" he remarked to my surprise.

I couldn't get over it. "Come on," he said, "let's not talk

about it anymore." I didn't cheer up as easily as Roger would have liked. Suddenly, I was overcome by a kind of horror of this uncle, of everything about him, of the entire neighborhood where he lived.

I told Roger I agreed with him, that there was nothing to worry about, but that now I couldn't go back to the uncle's. I'd had it with that guy. I added, jokingly, that I would just stay where I was. "Don't you think I'm right?" I asked Miss Perrotin.

Her response was quite charming. She said that since I was Roger's friend it would be easy to set ourselves up in this apartment. We'd squeeze together. She would make me a bed on the couch.

I accepted joyfully, but deep down I felt pathetic. I was a coward. Why didn't I go back to Paris alone, instead of imposing? I realized that I was waiting for Roger, not out of friendship, but because of my fear of going back. Yes, I was pathetic. What could be more indiscreet than forcing the hand of lovers, who, because they have to appear in the best light to one another, aren't free to refuse your requests?

That evening, I lay down on the sofa with my feet on a chair. The sofa was so small I couldn't sleep. I was thinking of my room at the uncle's, which I'd left without knowing I wouldn't return. I realized now that if I had known, I would have dressed differently, I would have brought my toilet articles, I wouldn't have left anything personal. For a second I thought of going back, just to tidy up, but then it struck me how pointless it would be.

Why should I care?

I lay awake. Suspecting they were listening to hear if I were asleep, I sighed and turned over, so they would know I wasn't. Roger and his friend weren't sleeping either. I heard them whispering from time to time, and this tacit understanding by which we didn't speak even though we knew we were all awake had a coldness about it that made me uncomfortable.

I spent several days like this at Miss Perrotin's. Roger might have been happy, but I was less than thrilled with the situation. I thought more and more about moving on. I had no reason to stay in Brussels. But every time I spoke to Roger about it, he repeated that we would leave together.

When I couldn't pull any further details out of him, I thought of leaving alone. Upon further reflection, I realized my reasons weren't serious enough if I were truly Roger's friend. No matter how mad I got about it, no matter how convinced I was that he was only thinking of himself and that I therefore should only think of myself, I sensed that he would consider me a bad friend if I didn't wait for him.

It was surprising when one thought of how different our two situations were, but that's how it was. What's more, I had become superstitious. It seemed to me that if I weren't more patient with Roger, if I weren't more understanding about his reasons for delaying our departure, it would bring me bad luck. After all, I couldn't leave him at a moment when love was in a sense making him less able to gauge danger than I, who was in full possession of my faculties.

I had to get a grip on myself. There's no great virtue in defending a friend who heeds your warnings. I had so much affection for Roger it was a pleasure looking out for him. Deep in his heart, he was aware of my devotion and was grateful for it, even if I seemed to matter little next to Miss Perrotin.

Soon I noticed a problem that ended up worrying me to no end. In my devotion, I was losing sight of my own safety! Occasionally I went on errands for Roger that I considered unwise for him to undertake, but which were even more so for me. He wouldn't take precautions. He had completely forgotten that two policemen had come looking for him at his uncle's apartment. I found such a heedless attitude admirable. I also found it admirable that he always seemed to consider himself the only one who was in serious danger. He was surprised I was so worried when he wasn't. In the end I felt like small potatoes next to him, almost innocent, even though in reality it was just the opposite. On his way out, he didn't even bother looking left and right. I wanted to remind him of our situation; he shouldn't think he was safe, as I personally had committed a very serious act. If we were stopped, they wouldn't bother checking to find out who was responsible.

In a word, I wanted to tell him that he was in as much danger as I was. But I didn't dare. I would have seemed shifty, as if I were trying to get him to share the responsibility for my crimes.

Chapter 29

Three days later, I informed Roger I was leaving that evening.

He must have realized I was resolute in my decision, for, contrary to his usual reaction, he made no effort to dissuade me. He changed the subject. But an hour later, he told me he was coming with me.

A long discussion arose between us. He wanted to take the train, of all things! When I asked him what we would do at the border, he said we would play it by ear when the time came. It was unbelievable. I listed the reasons that, as far as I could see, prevented us from taking the train. Nothing frightens me more than people who count on their presence of mind or their ability to act quickly, who tell you that just as they were asked for their papers a scuffle broke out and they escaped.

We had to leave on foot. I added that we shouldn't wait

for nightfall as the risk of encountering patrols increased. Finally, I insisted we exchange the clothes Roger's uncle had given us for less eccentric attire. Since the war, it was not uncommon to meet people strangely dressed who had nothing to hide, but we couldn't take the chance.

The first day was the hardest. We had walked about a dozen kilometers, when Roger, suddenly falling prey to a wave of depression, desperately wanted to return to Miss Perrotin's. I told him it was ridiculous to take unnecessary risks as we had to leave sooner or later, and since the deed was done, we might as well keep going.

But he became stubborn. I had already found myself in similar situations several times during the war, when a comrade had sacrificed a hard-won advantage for immediate satisfaction. For over an hour, I had to fight Roger tooth and nail to prevent him from acting on his idea. Finally, he agreed that I was right.

We walked for two days. We had been so traumatized by the war that, from a distance, we thought a cart with its legs in the air was a cannon.

We arrived in France. We were so tired that this event, for which we had skirted so much danger, didn't register. I nevertheless cried that we were saved. Roger was completely indifferent. I must say that things looked the same, except for the lettering on road signs, which was finally straight and neat. The countryside stretched on just as monotonously. We were no less fearful of approaching houses. Yet I exclaimed when I saw one in the distance, "To think that French people live there!" And when we saw a silhouette, "It's a Frenchman, it's a Frenchwoman!"

I thought people everywhere would be ready to help us, that they would instantly recognize us as one of their own and open their homes to us. But how should we make our approach? Roger stopped me each time. Now he was the one who thought I was careless. It was childish to imagine that people were better, simply because they were on the other side of the border.

On the fourth night we slept in a metal hangar that served as a storehouse for bails of compressed hay. When I asked the owner's permission, she granted it without any questions, as the usual vagabonds didn't even bother to ask. I had hoped after hearing the story of our adventures that she would welcome us into her home, but we had no such luck. She was mainly concerned that we not smoke.

We settled into a corner, at the top of a pile. The bails were hard as wood. I took my knife and sawed through the band of tinplate surrounding them. They wouldn't notice until after we'd left. It wasn't a nice way to repay their kindness, but we didn't feel accountable to anyone.

We fluffed up the straw, then examined our surroundings. By jumping out the back, we could escape through the garden. Far from feeling secure since our arrival in France, we realized the danger had only grown because of the occupation troops stationed everywhere.

Although I'd said we were escaped prisoners, I had the impression the proprietress hadn't understood and that if Germans had come looking for us, she would have led them to us without thinking twice. There was therefore no point in hiding. I told Roger this. He said that they wouldn't have told us to climb up here if they didn't intend to hide us.

We lay down. I wanted to go back and see the owner of the bail factory to repeat that we were truly at her mercy, and that she shouldn't tell anyone we were here. But Roger stopped me, claiming that she would ask us to leave. He added that people do much more for their fellow men when they don't know what it's about, that you should never give people details or you might scare them.

It was still light outside. Gawky pigeons, flapping their wings against their bodies, were gathered on the hangar's metal beams. They came and went with short steps. From time to time, one of them flew off and landed slightly further along; they took great pains to stay airborne for such a short distance.

The adjoining farm was silent. Darkness was slowly descending. Out on the immense plain, which we could glimpse unexpectedly between two bails of hay, the setting sun cast a red glow over the fog cover rising from the earth.

And what struck me was that, as is often the case in nature's grand light displays, it was all perfectly symmetrical. Where the sun and the mist met, from one end of the horizon to the other, was absolutely straight, without a bend or hitch.

Suddenly, we heard shouting. Someone was calling us. Instinctively I placed one hand over Roger's mouth to prevent him from responding. He pushed it away, asking what was wrong with me. It might be Germans. I started crawling to the spot from which we could see the courtyard. There were no Germans. I saw the proprietress and told her we were coming.

We went inside the kitchen. There was an adorable baby goat there, who seemed at home like a dog or a cat. He began licking my hands, then chewing my shoelaces and the hem of my pants. I pushed him away gently, but he kept coming back with an insistence all the more amusing as there was no reason he should take to me more than to Roger.

We were offered a cup of goat's milk, appropriately enough. Then the proprietress's husband appeared in the doorway. He eyed us suspiciously. I sensed he was wondering if we hadn't lied, if we were really escaped prisoners, and if we weren't going to denounce him later. Finally, when he had gotten over this senseless suspicion, he asked us if by chance we knew his brother, who was also a prisoner.

We chatted more and more cordially. Then he told us

that he was happy to help us; his only request was that if by chance Germans came, to say that we had snuck into his hangar without asking.

To emphasize the fact that he didn't know we were under his roof, he slowly shook our hands as we were leaving, as you do when you won't see each other in the morning, and said, "Good luck in your travels," even though we hadn't yet gone to bed.

I'd been sleeping a long time when I heard someone calling us again. I thought it was all over. I sat up, without knowing where I was or what to do.

"Come down, come down," yelled the proprietress. I woke Roger. "We're caught," I told him. "Come down, come down," she was still yelling. I could just barely see the light shining through the kitchen door frame fifty feet away. "Can we come down?" I asked, without knowing what I was saying. I then realized I had gotten excited over nothing. We obeyed. We were surprised to find our host a changed man. Now he insisted that we sleep in the house.

What had happened? I saw on a wall clock that it was midnight. I saw too that the fire was still burning. The young goat was asleep, his head straight, his fragile legs folded under, looking like an unruly child suddenly overcome with fatigue.

We went to get our things. Deep down, this invitation was no longer so appealing. When you've passed through the first stage of sleep, the attraction of a nice bedroom is no longer as great. Roger, on the other hand, was as happy as if we hadn't slept a wink.

The bed had been turned down for us and we lay in it. For a long while I wondered what could have happened in the proprietor's mind. Had he realized he hadn't done enough for a couple of escaped prisoners? Had he grown remorseful after a long inner debate? I told myself that in any case, he was a good man, but as often happens with people who think they are helping you, he hadn't thought for a second of sparing us emotional turmoil.

I trembled from time to time from the fright of having been woken in the night. But I was in France. Soon I would be in Paris, the city of my birth. I was saved, or so I thought.

No Place
(Case Dismissed)

Part One

Friends and Relatives

Chapter 1

 week had already passed since my arrival in Paris.

I was walking along the Boulevard de Courcelles, heading toward les Ternes. Everything was deserted. That afternoon it had struck me like never before how unimportant family, friendship, even being in one's home town, had become since the occupation. In the old days, when things got rough, there were thousands of ways for me to pull through, to make new friends, find a place to live, get help. But the way things were now, none of that mattered anymore, not letters of recommendation, references, not even kinship. Everyone was on guard. I had just realized this and felt a terrible void. I had been to see many of my friends. But all I had to do was visit again for them to become cooler toward me.

Where should I go? Accounts of the Revolution describe how fugitives gathered straw, made up beds in bandshells or slept in the park at Meudon, but today that kind of thing was no longer possible.

I looked at the Germans around me. Some were in the company of women so hard looking I had trouble imagining them making love. Since everyone ignored the Germans they had adopted a uniform attitude—they acted as if no one else were around.

Sometimes officers smiled at me benevolently, not as Germans, but as superiors on the social ladder. I was cowardly enough to respond, not wanting to antagonize them, which sometimes put me in a strange situation with respect to my fellow Frenchmen. I who had killed two of these Germans, who, risking my own life, had made it possible for fourteen prisoners to escape, I who was a wanted criminal, sensed that the time would come when they would openly hold me in contempt.

Of everything that had happened to me, one of the most extraordinary was the fact that I sometimes found myself seeming almost pro-Kraut with respect to Frenchmen who, had they been in my shoes, would still be in their prison camp working obediently for the Nazis.

It was eight o'clock at night. I absolutely had to find a room. I wanted to wait a while before looking for one, but the hotels were already starting to close. I encouraged myself with the thought that the junior police inspectors who visited hotels couldn't possibly carry around the complete wanted list. They must simply collect names and check them against the lists once back at the station. They couldn't get back before midnight. Even if they started checking immediately, they still had to return to the site. What is more, I had always heard that an old tradition forbade any police action between the setting and the rising of the sun. Obviously, there must have been cases when this was ignored. But if I left at dawn, it seemed to me that I wasn't taking much of a risk.

I headed toward Levallois, wandering the deserted streets for over an hour. I was looking for a hotel that wasn't more than one story, two maximum, so that if need be I could jump from the window. I also wanted it to be isolated, far from any major intersection, so that the inspector who covered this route would pass over it. Finally I found one, but at the last minute I didn't go in. When I looked through the windows, I noticed that the clients knew each other and that there was a familial atmosphere which I would no doubt have disturbed.

It's hard to be in such a situation. Every time I prepared to act I thought of something that stopped me.

Suddenly off to the side I noticed one of those all-night corridors. I went up to the second floor. A man was making a bed in an office-like room. In an instant the hotel, the corridor, and the stairway would be immersed in darkness, which certainly wouldn't be the case if they were expecting the police.

The office had no table. The man gave me a card to fill out anyway, but couldn't find an ink pot. I offered to complete this formality the next morning.

"Oh! no," he responded, sending a chill down my spine. "You never know when they're coming!"

For a second I thought of registering under a false name since the night watchman would be unable to verify it. Then I thought of writing my name so sloppily it couldn't be read, but I noticed this stern instruction in bold letters on the bottom of the card: *"Write legibly."*

The watchman asked me to pay in advance, a lack of faith I found comforting. The hotel didn't trust me. That meant they considered me a free man over whom they had no hold, a man who could leave when he pleased.

I went up to my room. A fringed bed cover hanging to the floor concealed a metallic mattress that sagged in the middle. I didn't even look around. I locked the door. The keyhole was crooked. I examined the twisted screw heads. There was a latch too, but it would break if someone were to ram into it with his shoulder.

I opened the window despite the cold. The fact that I was on the second floor was perfect, but unfortunately the window was directly above the entrance corridor, so that if I had to jump, I would fall right into the arms of the policeman below. I considered going back to the office but needed a pretext. I couldn't act difficult with no baggage. It was clear all I needed was a place to sleep.

I caught myself more and more often feeling proud of the courage I had shown after, and especially during, my escape, because it mustn't be forgotten that to ensure its success, to save my comrades, I had killed two Germans. But I also began to notice that my fears didn't diminish over time as I had thought they would. On the contrary, they grew.

On arriving in Paris I had naïvely imagined hiding in deserted places: fenced-in fields, open depots, fallow construction sites, and so on. But I would have run into other dangers. By entering such places, I was acknowledging that I was in hiding, I was breaking the law, and whoever might find me there was no longer under the usual obligation to respect certain rules of etiquette. In approaching these places, I would have had to make sure that no one saw me, and in the process risk arousing curiosity in people who otherwise wouldn't have paid any attention to me. When Baumé, Roger and I passed through villages at night, we hadn't hesitated to jump into a ditch when we heard footsteps. We were determined at every moment to defend ourselves.

Since my arrival in Paris, that special energy had disappeared. The trick was no longer to scale walls, crawl on all fours, or throw myself into corners, but simply to look like everybody else.

I also thought of going to Versailles, to my father's house. But I still couldn't remember whether his address or my mother's were among the papers I had been stupid enough to leave at the camp. Some of my comrades may have been caught. They may have talked, as had those, no doubt, who at the last minute had decided not to follow us. My mobilization instructions said 243 rue Saint-Jacques, but on the endless questionnaires the Germans had made me fill out, had I perhaps given a more recent address? I had planned to escape from the beginning and always acted accordingly, but wasn't it possible I had forgotten at one point or another? It's hard to be sure you didn't make mistakes once the details of your days are forgotten.

I'd be better off not going to Versailles yet, and above all not to expect too much cunning from the men who were on my trail. As much as they would have liked to capture me, I had to remember that my enemies weren't as driven to succeed as one would be, for instance, in searching for a loved one. I therefore forced myself not to exaggerate the danger I was in, and tried to consider everything through the eyes of a man with nothing to hide. It wasn't easy.

Finally I decided to go see Monsieur Georget, a professor and great friend of my father whom I had lived with a few years earlier during my first year of law school. With the big eye sockets that formed two large holes in his face and the air of sadness about him, he looked a little like an owl. He had a long, straggly white beard and blinked rapidly in the light. He had lived so many years surrounded by books that a man of flesh and bones who was not a professor or a student frightened him as much as a pretty woman. He was humble, honest, and kind, but I must say that in my current situation, I didn't place much importance on these qualities.

I imagined every possible scenario. Such a naïve and scrupulous man could be mixed up in some unpleasant business without even realizing it. He might have compromised himself by protecting others who were either unworthy or in the same situation as me, for as exceptional as it seemed, it certainly wasn't unique. Fortunately I soon realized that excessive caution and forethought were as dangerous as not being careful at all.

Monsieur Georget lived on the rue de Sèvres in an entirely unremarkable building. It was slightly fancier than its neighbors, since the number, instead of appearing on a blue enamel plaque, was engraved in a coat of arms just above the door. The narrow, tightly-spaced windows showed that the rooms were small.

I passed in front of the house the first time very slowly, as if strolling by, the second time with a quick step, as if I were expected somewhere but wasn't late, the third time very quickly, with a worried expression, as if I had forgotten something, the fourth with a self-assured step and a relieved expression. Each time I glanced rapidly into the lobby. It had been empty every time, yet I still couldn't make up my mind to go in.

If my father's friend could have guessed what was happening he would have been surprised. I was the dangerous one, and yet I was afraid of being stopped because of him, a quiet, respectable man. I was the one whose presence could mean serious trouble, and yet I was afraid of being arrested because of him.

Finally I decided to step inside. Knowing how affected I was by unexpected noises, I remained on guard. During a moment of distraction, a bicycle fell in the courtyard. I thought I was caught. I spun around as if the front door had closed behind me. I expected men to appear on all sides, as if I had fallen into a police trap. I went back outside and stood in the street for a few moments to catch my breath.

Finally, I knocked on the door to the concierge's lodge. He raised his head, questioning me through the window. Here was another dangerous hurdle, the moment when I would pronounce the name Georget, perhaps awakening a dormant affair.

— "Is Mister . . ." I pretended to be searching for the name, as if my relationship with the professor were so insignificant I had forgotten it. A name that begins with a G, an old man with a white beard.

— "You mean Monsieur Georget?"

— "Yes, that's it!" I exclaimed, attentively eyeing the concierge. "Does he still live here?"

— "Third floor on the left, Sir," the man answered. I

climbed the dark staircase. When I arrived at the first floor, I descended a few steps to look over the curtain masking the lodge's small window. At the end of the corridor, I could see the front door. It was still open. When I bent down I saw people passing without even turning their heads. The concierge was reading a newspaper, wearing a pince-nez. I knocked on the glass. "Are you sure it's on the third floor?" "Of course I'm sure," said the concierge, surprised.

As I climbed the staircase again, I told myself that I would get into trouble if I kept acting like this. I kept picturing the surprise on the concierge's face, and imagined him growing suspicious. Of course I was reassured as far as Monsieur Georget was concerned, but now I was worried about the concierge. I imagined him asking a million questions, thinking me strange, alerting someone. I almost went back down with the intention of secretly watching him to make sure he was reading and not thinking about me. The fear that he might see me was what stopped me. Imagine if the concierge looked up and saw me standing there staring at him.

Monsieur Georget welcomed me cordially. He immediately had a snack served, though it wasn't much: a darkish slice of bread with grape jam. I was afraid he might wonder why I didn't go to my father's house or to the home of closer friends; my reason for choosing him instead of someone else might not seem very clear. But he found it quite natural in the way that one accepts a compliment as natural. A look of flattered pride appeared on his face.

He immediately showed me my room. Naturally I would be safe there. If I never went out again, it would be impossible for anyone to find me.

The first day, I felt a tremendous sense of security. I was saved. The second day, this feeling stayed with me, although slightly diminished. The third day it disappeared. I realized that in reality, my situation was no better than before. Monsieur Georget was already surprised that I had chosen him. When you ask a favor, the person you ask has to be the only one able to provide it.

I tried several times to find out what Monsieur Georget was thinking, but when dealing with nice people this is easier said than done. Had he decided to let me stay in his home? From what he said, there seemed to be no limit to his generosity. But at the same time he remained vague. It was more his extreme kindness toward me than any specific acts that showed me I wasn't bothering him.

I didn't feel comfortable. He could easily change his mind. When he said, "You can count on me, my dear young man, you're at home here, my wife and I will never let you down," I was only partially satisfied. I would have preferred him to say, "Here's the key, whatever you do don't go outside. I'll give you a suit and try to find out how we can get you some papers."

I sensed that Madame Georget especially was beginning to find me inordinately prudent for a boy who claimed merely to have escaped from a prison camp. The first days it was understandable because of my fatigue. I claimed that I found it unpleasant to go out the way I was dressed, that I was very happy in my room, and so on. But my excuses had one major flaw: you couldn't say that things would be any different in the future.

After I'd stayed inside for twelve days without going out, they spoke to me about a cousin, also an escaped prisoner, who had returned to his job at the Industrial and Commercial Credit Bank. I got the hint. After lunch, I took a short walk for the first time.

I was dealing with very serene people in whose home my presence was entirely out of place. They were very proud to be offering me hospitality. They imagined it was an act of patriotism. I was bothered by this. They sometimes spoke to me with a hint of complicity in their voices.

Until I could find an equally safe haven elsewhere, I was forced to agree with them. But I acted a little cold. It bothered me increasingly that they didn't realize the tragedy of my situation and that they seemed to think that in a few days I was going to be able to resume a normal life.

I had imagined that once in Paris I would live in an atmosphere of struggle and exaltation, and now over the course of these interminable days at Monsieur Georget's, the feeling that I was wasting my time grew stronger and stronger. Was I? I couldn't be wasting time because until the war was over all I could do was hide. I was hidden, wasn't I? What more did I want? I understood that the greatest threat wasn't the police or people's selfishness, but the waiting I would have to endure.

I could have found some other lodging, but I was already feeling lethargic, the way you do when you're living in temporary circumstances. I told myself that there would always be some detail that wasn't quite right wherever I went, that it was better to be happy with what I had and not, as I had often been accused of being, perpetually discontented. My salvation didn't depend on what I would find elsewhere, but on my ability to make the best of what I had. Yet at the same time, I also thought that I should try to better my situation and not waste time in a place where it was obvious I couldn't stay. I found myself deeply puzzled. Now that my life was in danger, I realized that my shortcomings, to which I hadn't paid much attention until now, were enormous. Finally I decided to wait until I was forced to act. What else could I do?

I was safe, I wasn't taking much of a risk. I forced myself to be pleasant. I even felt that I hadn't been nice enough until now. I had been too self-absorbed. I had acted as if their helping me were only natural. I had been too aware of the worthy qualities I'd shown to even imagine that I could be held in anything less than high esteem.

Despite our differences, Mr. Georget and I were the same size. He had finally decided to give me one of his old outfits, a suit of shiny wool serge, which, though threadbare, was impeccably ironed.

The windows in the main rooms looked out on a courtyard covered in cement imprinted with false tiles. My room, like the kitchens with exterior pantries, looked out on another, smaller courtyard. The bed of varnished wood was very high and lopsided. A bearskin far more pleasant to the eye than to the touch served as a rug. They had brought in a folding table for me, and to make the room feel more lived-in Madame George had placed an inkwell, a pen, and a blotter on it. It was the second time since my escape that I had been pampered like this. In the beginning, I hadn't dared open the window because of the possibility of the domestics' passing glances and smiles. Now I opened it but was careful not to let anyone see me. This wasn't easy, since the room was small and cluttered with wardrobes and dressers. I heard people saying hello to each other every morning; they had a way of asking after each other's health that got on my nerves, it was so obvious they were fine.

The more time passed, the more I realized that it wasn't at the home of good people like this professor and his wife that I should live, but with men my age, brave men to whom I could reveal my true situation, who in case of danger would protect me and even proudly risk their lives for me instead of getting scared.

I finally realized that there had been a misunderstanding. Mr. Georget had agreed to house me but not to hide me. I had confused the two. He was afraid he had gone too far.

It was heartbreaking to see this good man constantly struggling with bad impulses, the fear of compromising himself, the feeling he wasn't doing enough, the secret wish that I would go away.

Another thing irritated me even more. I had thought that this professor would be crushed by all the difficulties that arose in these troubled times whenever one wanted to take the slightest action or satisfy the slightest desire. But not at all. He had never seemed more at ease. At the moment he was taking the steps necessary to obtain a change in category on his food card. It was all he talked about. It didn't bother him at all. He wasn't shy about sticking up for his old age and his infirmities. He wanted everything that was coming to him; when he read in the paper that he had the right to so many grams of butter, he immediately abandoned his books to go down to the dairy.

I decided to leave. I had no money. I didn't know where to go, but I felt a deep need to rely only on myself. If I stayed here, I was going to become prisoner to an excess of good intentions. I didn't want to hurt my father's friend, nor leave him with a bad impression. I never should have let him look after me so attentively.

As I was racking my brain for a pretext, I suddenly realized how crazy I was being. What! with my life in danger I was worrying about being polite? I clenched my fists. I had to be a man again, to keep reminding myself that it was me alone against my pursuers.

Chapter 2

As soon as I got outside I noticed that a freezing rain was falling and I didn't have a raincoat. "Serge may take longer to soak through than other materials, but once it's wet it also takes longer to dry," I thought. Everyone had a raincoat but me. My greatest fear, that of attracting attention by wearing the wrong clothes, was coming true. I almost went back upstairs to the Georget's but I didn't. I had agonized too much over my departure to question it now.

I headed toward the Luxembourg Gardens. In the end the rain provided a certain security, since it seemed unlikely that anyone would be looking for me in such weather. I went on foot as far as the rue Soufflot. As usual, I lacked experience. I realized this just as I was mixing with the crowd. There is nothing more dangerous than keeping to yourself, even for a short time. In my room on the rue de

Sèvres, I had exaggerated the dangers to such an extent that just visiting friends seemed terribly daring. I hadn't wanted to think about the future, to plan anything in advance. Writing or receiving letters, making plans, all that had seemed a mine field to me, whereas going to a friend's house as I was now doing without warning him, without his even knowing that I was in Paris, seemed to me on the contrary a way of guaranteeing my security.

There was an unpleasant side to all this nevertheless. How much nicer it would have been, in this rain, to know that someone was expecting me! Where would I hide if no one was there, if at the end of the day I still hadn't found a safe haven? Wasn't I needlessly risking being rounded up by a patrol?

Finally I arrived at the building where Guéguen lived with his mother on the rue Gay-Lussac. In the rain it looked dismal and forbidding. Some lights were on even though it was still daytime. I had the impression that the tenants were immersed in their own worries over food and heat.

I hid in a corner and took a long look at the building. Finally I ventured through the doorway, but I had barely taken a few steps when I stopped dead in my tracks. Two men were talking to the concierge. They scared me. They had the obvious manner of policemen looking for information.

I went back outside immediately. I had to restrain myself from running. I turned onto the rue des Ursulines. There, it got the better of me, I couldn't help but run. Finally I stopped. No one had followed me. I hid under an awning where a woman and child were already standing. Their presence made me feel better. We might look like we were married, as if I were inoffensive, a father and husband.

I returned to the rue Gay-Lussac an hour later. The lights were out. I stopped in front of the main entrance and scanned the hallway to make sure the two men had left. I still hadn't entirely recovered. I had to talk to the concierge.

I told her I had come before, that I had seen her talking with two gentlemen, that I hadn't wanted to bother her, that I had taken the opportunity to run an errand. When she still didn't reveal what I wanted to know, I repeated that I had seen her with two gentlemen, but smiling this time, pronouncing these last words in such a way as to imply that I could guess who they were.

The concierge smiled in turn. "Oh! no," she said, "it's not what you think."

This response made an excellent impression on me. It meant that the concierge was like everyone else, she didn't like the police. It was a good sign that she didn't hide it from a stranger.

René Guéguen was someone I liked a great deal. I had met him at Montparnasse back when I was taking painting classes at the Swedish Academy. Even then he was living in this dismal and ordinary looking building, in a very pleasant fourth floor apartment joined to an artist's studio on the floor above. He adored his mother and was convinced it was because of her that he hadn't married, which I myself doubted.

When I had told the story of my escape at length, leaving out its dramatic moment and already feeling slightly awkward in passing my adventures off as recent, Guéguen led me to the studio.

That night when I was alone, I felt for the first time since September '39, the date of my call to arms, like I was in a peace-time atmosphere. Sitting in a large garnet-red corduroy armchair, I gazed at the studio in the dim light of a bedside lamp. The familiar odor of turpentine, which seemed a rare perfume to me, floated in the air.

I was still happy in the studio. For a childish reason, I felt much safer than on the rue de Sèvres: if need be, I could escape over the rooftops. The only problem was that I was living much better than my hosts. Their apartment on the floor below, which was linked to the studio by an interior staircase, was very small. No matter what Guéguen said, a less privileged situation would have been more lasting. Thinking about this spoiled my pleasure. My only consolation was to remind myself that my situation deserved special consideration. I had fought brilliantly. On June 10 I had been nominated for the Military Cross, and if not for the defeat I would now be decorated. Then, I had escaped.

Guéguen was sensitive enough to official distinctions to realize this. If I personally placed no importance on these distinctions, he at least appreciated their value.

I locked the door every night but didn't want my host to notice. As a result I slept badly, waking with a start several times a night. I was afraid that it was morning, and I wanted to open the door before he arrived.

Aside from this, I was much better off than on the rue de Sèvres. I no longer felt like I was stuck in a dead end.

Unfortunately, my sense of security soon seemed inadequate. So many things could be done, so many details perfected. I carefully examined the roofs. I realized that the things that made me feel secure were in reality insufficient. Without a rope, it was impossible to pass from one of the studio windows to the roof of the four-story house five meters below. With the lack of precision that characterizes a first impression, I had pictured myself jumping onto this roof at the first sign of trouble, but what had seemed a cinch before now seemed enormously difficult.

I thought of getting a rope and attaching it to an outside bolt so it would be ready in place. But someone might notice it from one of the windows a little further down that also looked out over this roof. And what was worse, if he leaned out the window, Guéguen might wonder what the rope was doing there. As far as taking it off and putting it back all the time, it was the kind of precaution I might forget about after a while.

Once I had decided to hang it anyway, a new problem arose. Where would I get the rope? The shopkeepers laughed at me. They'd sold their last foot of rope ages ago. Then it occurred to me that the neighbors might have one. But everything was in such short supply, the strangest objects had taken on such value that no one wanted to part with anything. Whatever you asked for, the response was invariably no.

Some pieces of string were lying around the studio. But even twisted together, they would have been too thin and I would have cut my hands.

When you spend entire days feeling bored, you wind up doing things you told yourself you wouldn't do simply to keep busy. I braided my rope as well as I could and attached it to the shutter bolt, since the metalwork of the handrail threatened to break like glass.

For several days this simple rope gave me an extraordinary sense of security. I felt so confident knowing I could escape in a way that no one suspected, for who would have thought that I could get away through the fifth floor window?

But soon I was haunted by a new concern. Where could I go once I was on the roof? The idea of learning the layout, of basically rehearsing my escape, seemed increasingly necessary. I couldn't even think of asking people questions without taking infinite precautions. I tried to make friends with the concierge of the building next door. I failed, since there was absolutely no reason for us to exchange more than two or three words at a time.

I seriously considered lowering myself onto the roof one night with the cord. But I quickly gave up this idea. I was afraid of some sort of incident, and that while the cord might be solid enough for me to get down, it might not be sturdy enough to climb back up. It would have been ridiculous to get caught practicing for a possible future escape, an exercise that was of no immediate use.

The next day, though, it seemed like it would be a better idea to test this escape. I was always hesitating! As soon as a precaution no longer seemed urgent, I hesitated to take it. After, when it was too late, I would regret my cowardliness.

Since my arrival in Paris, I had unwittingly become rather similar to the man I was before the war. I had acquired certain habits. As much as it had seemed natural for me to run at the slightest danger when I was in Germany or Belgium, it now seemed unnatural on the rue Gay-Lussac, rue de l'Abbé-de-l'Épée, rue du Val-de-Grâce, rue Denfert-Rochereau. If I valued my life, I had to ignore my instincts, I had to be careful that my new family life didn't cause me to forget that I had to defend myself like a lowly thief.

One moonless night, I decided to explore the escape route I might have to take. If I had been hidden in a far-away village, I wouldn't have hesitated to do so. Why should it be any different in my home town?

At about eleven o'clock, I opened the window. The darkness scared me for a few seconds, the contrast between the comfortable studio and this windswept black hole.

Something in me was decidedly broken. I was no longer the man who had escaped from Germany and who had urged his companions on for twenty-three days. No matter how strong his character, a man cannot remain in a state of alert indefinitely. I was afraid of being taken for a burglar. I thought about it too much. What I was considering doing didn't seem all that useful. My plan seemed somewhat abstract. I sensed that if I gave in to this idea, there were a thousand other precautions that were just as important.

I forced myself to think about something else in order to get my judgement back. Did it make sense or not to climb down onto this roof at night? Was it useful?

"Yes," I suddenly cried to myself, and without thinking a second longer, relying solely on the strength of my fists, I climbed over the handrail and slid down to the roof. I lay on my stomach after my shoes made an unexpected noise on the zinc. I was my courageous old self again. I noted joyously that I was now ready to do anything to defend myself, to leave Guéguen's studio if need be at this very instant and in my present state.

The concierge, in her immaculate lodge, was one of those sad women who people say don't worry about anyone but themselves. Each time I ran into her she seemed not to see me, even though our first contact must have stuck in her mind. If someone had asked her about me she wouldn't have known what to say, which was even better than if I'd given her instructions.

Yet a new dilemma soon began to concern me. Things were too good. The more I perfected my hiding place, the more the difficulty of letting Guéguen in on it troubled me. In a sense I was creating a safety net for myself on top of the one he was providing me. I had to hide it to avoid angering him. But he noticed. I realized that I was acting increasingly in a way that I would have found unpleasant in someone else. I did not seem to appreciate what he was doing for me. He was too aware of the seriousness of my situation to hold it against me, but I could guess that he found the initiatives I was taking in his home strange anyway. I seemed to be suggesting that when life and liberty are at stake, friendship comes second. No matter what I did, I couldn't help coming across this way, which proves that just knowing where your flaws lie is not enough to hide them.

He probably wondered sometimes if he wasn't mistaken, when a new incident occurred that must have erased any doubts.

One thing, it seemed to me, would considerably increase my security and require no great effort on Guéguen's part. The studio was hooked up to the apartment below by a buzzer. I had to get Guéguen to agree to ring this buzzer as a warning if anyone suspicious came looking for me. I made several allusions to what a favor it would be if he would do this. When he didn't seem to understand what I was asking of him, I finally told him outright. He immediately agreed, but I noticed a strange look on his face.

Shortly thereafter, upon further reflection, it occurred to me that this agreement wasn't quite right. Though Guéguen readily accepted to do me this favor, he didn't seem to understand the importance I placed on it. In order to relax, I needed to feel that I could really count on him. But I didn't feel I could. I realized too that I hadn't been clear enough, that I hadn't told him everything because I hadn't wanted to upset him. For this buzzer system to work, Madame Guéguen had to be in on it too. Her son was often out and she might be the one to greet the suspicious visitors.

I brought it up again. Guéguen invariably said that he understood, but I could sense that he only thought about what I was asking while I was speaking to him about it.

As time went by, I don't know why, I attached more and more importance to this favor. A week ago I hadn't even thought about it and now it seemed indispensable, to the point that everything else seemed futile if I didn't have this security measure.

Finally, after insisting repeatedly, I had the feeling that I could count on Guéguen and his mother. I was then surprised to realize that in their minds, my hosts now considered the simple act of pressing a button the biggest favor they were doing for me, whereas it seemed to me it was nothing for them, especially since they might never have to do it.

This incident taught me three things that I wanted to keep in mind for the future. The first is that we always tend to take advantage of people's kindness, and it's when you ask for the most insignificant thing that they suddenly show they've had enough. The second is that one's self-interest, even when it doesn't interfere with anyone else's, causes ill will. The third, finally, is that it's hard to maintain your dignity when you're in danger.

Oddly enough, the same thoughts regarding my situation occurred to whoever happened to be around me. Mr. Georget, and this was one of the reasons I'd left, had offered to introduce me to the son of one of his friends, an escaped prisoner like myself. Now, Guéguen, exactly in the same tone, announced that one of his friends had escaped from Germany, and that it would be a good idea for us to get together.

I asked him apprehensively whether he had talked about me. "Of course," he told me. I didn't doubt that Guéguen had acted with the best intentions, but I didn't want anyone to know I was an escapee. I told him so. "But why? On the contrary." I didn't know what to say. Guéguen couldn't understand why I was so concerned with silence. If I continued to hide my merit, to not make use of a distinction which according to him would open doors for me and bring out so much kindness, he would begin to wonder what was wrong with me. I would seem like I wanted to rely only on him. Since his surprise seemed to grow, I finally pretended to agree. But after talking about other things, I refused his offer. As soon as I was alone, I was once again filled with remorse.

I finally resolved to visit this friend of his despite the dangers I saw in the visit. Deep down, even when your life is in danger, you get tired of taking precautions. You get used to the risks. You expose yourself more and more. It's like being under enemy fire. In the end you think you'll never get hit.

Just as I was about to pay the visit, I had a surge of independence. "This is stupid," I said to myself. Since the very idea of this visit was so unpleasant to me, why do it? So that I could tell Guéguen I did it? But wasn't I in a situation in which I had to forget about friendship, forget about all of life's little compromises?

That night, I told Guéguen that after thinking it over I preferred for the moment not to see anyone. Too bad if he got annoyed. It didn't matter, I was only worrying about myself.

I had the impression Guéguen was thinking, "No use insisting." He gave up on his project as easily as someone dispensing charity, not knowing if his advice will be followed.

I got a grip on myself. "You're right, I'll visit him," I cried. But it didn't matter anymore.

The idea of earning a living in one of the more humble professions had already come to mind. I figured that the lower I was on the social ladder, the more hidden I would be and the less attention I would attract. When I shared this thought with Guéguen, he looked surprised. I nevertheless began looking for an old friend from the Swedish Academy who bragged of having done all sorts of jobs.

I was so dazed by my sedentary life that when I found myself on the Maisons-Lafitte train I was unnerved to see the passengers getting on and off, talking to each other as if it were the most natural thing in the world. When would the day come when I would be like these people? When would I have the ability, as they did, to stop thinking about danger, to live and even laugh?

After an entire day of running from address to address I still couldn't find my friend. Finally I went home exhausted. But I didn't even think of complaining. As long as I was searching, I wasn't thinking about my situation. Whereas I was ordinarily so careful, I had taken no precautions, as if the honesty of my activities placed me above suspicion. Everyone had been generous in giving me directions and information. This had seemed a good sign. I had no doubt it would be like that every day once I was working.

That evening, when I told Guéguen about what a good state of mind this exhausting day had put me in, I was surprised to see him remain just as somber. My joy vanished. I realized that I was still moved by childish illusions, that my highs and lows had no basis in reality, that my situation was still just as tragic.

The next day, I wanted to continue my search. But the secure feeling I'd had the day before was gone. I didn't dare ask any questions. I felt as if everyone was suspicious of me. At noon I returned home having accomplished nothing and everything looked black.

A few days later, as if he had forgotten having already spoken to me about it, Guéguen announced that he was planning to entertain some friends whom he had told my story. Naturally, I had nothing to fear, these friends were all safe. I would also have the opportunity to meet the famous escaped prisoner who wanted to meet me.

The prospect of this little party was terribly unpleasant to me. It brought to light what separated us, Guéguen and me. He deemed that in such difficult times I should be glad to find sympathy and support. According to him, I was a member of the great family of Frenchmen poised against the invader, and had played a leading role. He knew my position was rather dangerous, but hardly more dangerous than that of the people I was to meet.

But I myself knew that I was quite alone. I had no desire to engage in conversations about heroism and the war. I had no desire to be introduced to ten people, one of whom might very well dislike me and work against me later. I felt that backing out would be very unfriendly toward Guéguen. In any case it would be physically impossible, the studio being the only room large enough for guests.

Since my escape, that is, since I was in danger of being shot from one day to the next, my character had changed. I had become totally indifferent to what others might think of me. If by acting in an uncouth manner, or ungratefully, I could increase my security, I didn't hesitate for a second. Considerations which in the past would have held me back no longer mattered. My self interest came first. In every circumstance, I considered myself a little like a man who jumps a sinking ship. Despite the efforts I made to be social I couldn't bring myself to respect the usual conventions when I realized that the other person wasn't devoted to me body and soul.

I managed to act as if I were looking forward to this party anyway. But as soon as I was alone, I thought at length about how I should deal with it.

I was especially wary of meeting this celebrated escapee. From what I understood, he was a brave man. He had demonstrated an extraordinary ability to keep his cool. He had risked his life several times. He had saved one of his companions. Once back in France, and this one pleased everyone, he refused a woman's hospitality for fear of compromising her on two counts, as a man and as an escaped prisoner. All these details should have made me like him. But I couldn't stand him. To me, there was something conventional about these feats. I sensed in the way he was hiding, the way he was living since his escape, a certain respect for the kind of order the Germans had established. I sensed that if he were caught, he wouldn't be treated the way I would be, but like a war hero. In escaping he had respected the rules. That's what everyone liked and why others weren't afraid to compromise themselves for him. I even had the impression that there were patriots who would turn themselves in in his place if necessary. It would all happen in an atmosphere of honor and legality which was completely lacking in my escape.

And Guéguen imagined that this man and I were brothers! I could see it already, the escapee sniffing out the differences, asking for details ostensibly as if I were an equal, but in reality out of mistrust, pretending to accept everything without verification. I would be forced to give the name of the camp, the names of the towns I had passed through, perhaps the names of my fellow soldiers and officers.

Guéguen was very kind through all this, aside from a moment of annoyance when he said that I was paranoid, that I had a persecution complex. While this had seemed true enough to me at the time, shortly thereafter I exclaimed, "And with good reason!"

The kind of friendship we are used to in normal times seems quite fragile when times are hard. I couldn't reproach Guéguen for anything. He was doing everything he could, but he had no heart. Until now I had never judged people according to their hearts. It was secondary. The important thing was that they acted like friends. And now suddenly I was discovering someone either had heart or didn't. And Guéguen, my friend Guéguen, did not . . .

All the efforts I had made to ensure my safety had been useless: the rope, the buzzer, the concierge, the neighbors. I would have to start over somewhere else. And not only with these efforts, but with all my plans, the benchmarks I had established for the future.

When you're in a situation like mine, you don't regret things for long. If necessary, you instantly abandon the most complicated plans, ones that took weeks to construct. You live like a soldier in a bunker, able to be displaced by a command at any time. I had developed habits. I remember the first night when, alone in the studio, forgetting where I had come from and what lay ahead of me, I imagined that I had always lived there. I had used objects that were unfamiliar to me as if they had always been mine. I hadn't even bothered to move the vases around, the knick-knacks. I didn't think about my own tastes. I had spontaneously adopted Guéguen's, I had put myself in his place and simply enjoyed things that in other times I would have immediately rearranged or even rejected.

I had admired everything around me as if I were never going to leave this studio. But whereas in normal times I would have suffered at changing my surroundings so quickly, today I would have left it all at any moment with no regrets.

Chapter 3

I hadn't asked anyone in my family for help for the simple reason that I didn't want to go where the police expected me to go. But I was beginning to realize that I was being too cautious. Without going to my father's house, I could stay with an aunt of mine who had married a colonial administrator named Xavier de Miratte, and who had been living alone for the past ten years or so on the rue Rambuteau. The police couldn't know my family so well that they knew this aunt existed. In the end, staying with her would be more normal than imposing on a good man like Georget or on Guéguen.

My first days on the rue Rambuteau did wonders for me. My aunt was a very good woman, capable of great devotion toward those who entered her life unexpectedly, which surprised her close friends who thought she was mean and stingy.

The trouble she took to hide her avarice was touching. She answered the most natural questions in incredible ways. One day, when she was drinking coffee without offering me any, I asked her if it was good. She said she didn't know. I looked at her surprised. She added, with a tremble that revealed her inner panic, that she had a cold, that she had lost her sense of taste. In the end maybe I was being unfair. You can't confuse the stinginess of a person who earns a living with that of someone scraping by on a small fixed sum.

I had asked her to write to my father and secretly convey that I wanted to see him. The response came without delay, which I found comforting—at least if I had to leave my aunt's house unexpectedly I wouldn't have to come back later to learn what my father's response had been. I don't know why but since my escape it was torture for me to have to return to places or homes I had left behind.

Through various allusions which I had directed my aunt to slip into her letter, I had told my father that he should be on guard and that most importantly he shouldn't tell anyone about my visit. On arriving in Versailles, I regretted this prudence. Basically, it is hard to know in advance if one should alert people to things or not. Alerting them provokes unexpected reactions which are sometimes very dangerous.

Indeed, when I arrived at the school where my father taught I was startled to find that the concierge was expecting me. Before I even said my name, he had guessed who I was. Instead of leading me directly into the main building, as he would have done with an ordinary visitor, he steered me into the small pavilion near the gate where his living quarters were. Then I heard him tell his wife to take a stroll around the courtyard and near the main buildings to see if anyone had noticed my arrival, if anything unusual was happening.

He locked the door. Shortly thereafter someone knocked. I jumped. There is nothing I hate more than being locked in, alone, in a place where I'm not supposed to be. What if the person knocking was the director, what if he wanted to know what I was doing here, why we had locked the door? What would I have said? Luckily, the knocking stopped. The concierge's behavior continued to surprise me. Instead of going to tell my father I was here, he claimed that he couldn't disturb him. I had the impression he was making this decision himself, and that he was being overzealous.

I could see the white high school with its peristyle through the window, a former Louis XVI mansion that had been modernized. I was struck by how different it was from my memory of it and to see that life, with all its daily concerns, went on here where for me only my youth had been.

I sat down in one of those magnificent armchairs you find in the waiting rooms of public establishments. Because of me the door was closed. Because of me, it seemed, visitors wouldn't know where to go or where to get information or where to leave packages or where to make phone calls. "What's going on?" they would wonder. They would summon the concierge, ask him to open the door. I purposely say summon. My presence would be revealed to everyone. I would have to explain myself and I wouldn't know what to say.

I asked the concierge to open the door. He thought that I didn't want to get him in trouble. Touched by my kindness, he told me not to worry, that he would know what to say if someone were persistent, that he wanted first and foremost to follow my father's instructions. No one should see me.

Finally, he sent his little boy to tell my father. A little while later we heard a knock on the door. I could see a shadow behind the opaque white curtains on the glass door. "It's me," said my father. "Open quick," I told the concierge.

My father closed the door behind him. After all that had happened, it was strange to see him hiding to speak to me, when I should have been the one to hide.

I had never liked going to see my father where he worked, where there were people higher up who could give him orders, and others below him he had to supervise. It bothered me. There is nothing worse than seeing someone you love preoccupied, fearful, forced to be obedient and to give orders so that the chain in which they form a link isn't broken.

The truth is I was over-sensitive, because all this made no difference to my father. On the contrary, he was proud to be seen doing his job.

As soon as he saw me, before anything else, as if we had just seen each other the day before, he told me that I had arrived a little too early, that he wasn't quite finished, and that he would be back in a moment.

It hurt me that a meeting as important as that between a father and son separated by war could be put off, even for an instant, because of work.

The concierge's wife said I had better move to the back room so no one would see me. They couldn't keep the door shut forever. Her husband, I realized just then, was one of those exemplary servants who put their family at the service of their masters, whom they allow to infringe on their rights as husband and father.

I waited an hour. The concierge and his wife went back to work. Finally my father arrived. I heard him ask where I was. I opened the door. My father apologized at length for having made me wait. He had told me not to come before eleven.

He was as moved as I was. He quickly explained what he had left to do, as if we had far more important things to discuss right after that. But he kept repeating the same things over again, in a staccato voice, even involving the concierge in the conversation.

I sensed that he was hiding beneath this agitated demeanor, that he was afraid to hear what I had to say. Yet he wanted to show me that I could trust him, my father.

He asked me to sit, but he remained standing. He told me he preferred to see me in the evening, that he couldn't concentrate when he was at work, and that he had to start back by ten after eleven anyway. He couldn't tell me how happy he was to have been able to talk to me, even for a second, right away. He would be thinking about me. He didn't want me to worry. Everything would work out in the end, but in this place (he glanced at the school building) the atmosphere was stifling.

They had tried to get rid of him for political reasons, but they couldn't, because in seventeen years he had proved his dedication. He advised me to remain calm and be patient. He had many contacts, but naturally it would take time to get in touch with them, and we shouldn't be pushy.

At ten after eleven, he became even more nervous. Suddenly he got up as if a train were leaving. We had a lot to talk about, but we didn't have time.

Then the concierge came in. My father began talking to him with the same feverishness, revealing his friendship with the man. This reminded me of his mania for making friends with people beneath him, with whom he was always cooking up schemes intended to help out someone in trouble.

My father and I decided to meet at four o'clock. I had told him that this might be a little late if I still had to find a place to sleep. He told me not to worry, that he would arrange things. But I knew my father. He meant well; unfortunately unexpected circumstances always prevented him from keeping his promises. After several fruitless attempts, you could see for yourself that there was nothing more he could do for you. He asked you to help him some more and if you couldn't he admitted to his powerlessness. He was sorry. You couldn't doubt his sincerity, but that's the way it was. He had tried everything humanly possible; you had to give up. He went home, resumed his quiet, simple life, but what happened to those who had counted on him, who for days had lived with the hope he had given them? And if you forced the issue, he seemed so unhappy being just a poor little teacher that you took pity on him.

I went for a walk in the city. I hadn't eaten anything yet. I didn't have any tickets. And everything you could buy was so expensive that after calculating the price of each bite I lost my appetite.

By observing how each restaurant functioned, I might have been able to find one where they asked for tickets afterward, but I was afraid of a scene.

I decided to go to a bakery and essentially beg for a

piece of bread. The baker had just given some bread to the young woman standing in front of me. I told him I was passing through. He refused. I got angry. I pointed out that he had just given some bread to a woman who didn't have a ticket either. He raised his voice in turn. He wasn't yelling about me anymore. He was already beginning to talk about bread the way one talks about one's country or one's patriotic duty.

I instantly calmed down. In retrospect it was just the kind of incident I hate the most and always try to avoid, the kind of thing that happens at military revues when your neighbor yells "hats off" to you as a simple flag is passing.

I left the bakery without pressing the matter, telling myself that some day I would get revenge, but in the meantime deeply depressed because my situation made it impossible for me to raise my voice.

Then I went to sit near the Neptune fountain. When you have to spend hours in a public place, it's better to sit than to walk in circles as if you're looking for something. There is always someone with nothing better to do looking for trouble, and you can wind up getting in a misunderstanding. If you don't respond to their advances, they may resent you, they may know some of the other people in the area, they may come back as a group to pick a fight.

I didn't move. To give myself a cover I pretended to read

a book on dowsing, which I picked up randomly from a bookseller's table on rue de la Paroisse.

I thought again about the infamous police searches one kept hearing about and which were constantly on my mind. I wanted to talk about it some more, but no one seemed enough of a friend to listen to me and comfort me at the same time.

Finally my father arrived. I have never met anyone so transformed by the satisfaction of accomplishing a day's work. His mind was much more agile than before. He thought he should be full of ideas. He spoke to me about his friend Mondanel, one of the people in charge of police headquarters. I absolutely had to go see him. I had to put my situation in order, I had to get a job, organize my life for the long term, and make sure I was forgotten.

As he was accompanying me to the train station (he never said another word about my staying in Versailles) I started talking about the police searches that were obsessing me.

In my mind, immediately after our escape, instead of alerting the various police units with which he was ordinarily in contact, the camp commander went to his superior, the director of all the camps. This was no ordinary escape. What had happened was so serious that more important people took over for our little commander. They had directly alerted the Kommandanturs of Belgium, Holland, and Paris. They in turn had alerted their detective units and police headquarters. I even imagined the scenario. The French bureaucrats who had been called in were greeted respectfully. They were called in so often for cases on which, deep down, they didn't agree with their German colleagues, that this time they were all too happy to be able to outdo themselves with a clear conscience. They would do their duty. You could count on them. They would prove their good will and their desire to collaborate. There were some things on which all civilized people saw eye to eye. The head of the French police, after having accepted what was being asked of him, withdrew respectfully, but without forgetting that he was French. That is to say he was polite, but didn't click his heels, didn't return the heil Hitler salute; his face bore an expression that suggested he was preserving his personality and that if he was obeying this time, it was because in such a circumstance an honest man had no choice. The affair would follow its course. All that remained was to find the assassin.

My father didn't like how I was portraying French bureaucrats. He told me I had no right to speak of my fellow Frenchmen that way. And besides, I was exaggerating. The French weren't like that! I was making unfounded assumptions.

Then, responding in the tone I had used, he added that the French and Kraut police had better things to do than run after us. What I had said had no basis in fact.

Everything was much simpler. The camp director was a nice fellow who was doing his military service because he had no choice. Naturally he had been obliged to fill out a report on our escape. This report circulated from office to office. Two guards had been wounded. (I didn't dare say they'd been killed.) This seemed very serious to us. But what did superior officers or chiefs of police care? They were looking for us, but with no particular malice. We shouldn't imagine that there was a price on our heads, that the entire European police force was after us, because by giving in to such hog-wash one really did start to look suspicious and fearful. In the end one wound up calling attention to oneself and getting arrested. It was even possible that no one was looking for us any longer. Other cases had come up after ours, and the old ones had been pushed aside to make way for the new.

Chapter 4

Several days later, I went to see Richard as well.
While I was a prisoner, my half-brother Richard had taken countless steps to try to help me. Richard was not the brother of my dreams, that is to say one who would have protected me and warned me about people whose dangerous side I didn't see. When he didn't hear from me at first, he thought I'd been killed. He had consulted every possible list. He had sent certified letters to everyone. It seems to me that in such a case one might prefer not to know the truth. Not him. He had exaggerated his interest in me. He had used it to gain everyone's sympathy. He supposedly couldn't stand the uncertainty. He was living through a true nightmare. Nothing was more cruel than doubt. When they told him they couldn't give him any information, he pretended to believe they were hiding the truth. He begged them, he didn't want to be spared. He

swore he had the strength to endure the most grievous news. Anything was better than not knowing.

Then, when he learned I was a prisoner, he began to take the most outrageous steps to try to have me released. He ran everywhere, obtained certificates covered with official signatures, all kinds of letters. He called on people who thought well of me to take action, like the director of claims at the National Insurance office, people who ultimately had no particular reason to bother helping me, and in the end he accused them of being lax. He slid messages into packages for me, wrote interminable letters in minuscule handwriting under the labels of jars of preserves; each time I received one I trembled, not knowing myself what new approach he would take.

I went to see him reluctantly because with all the noise he had made about me I wouldn't have been surprised if he had already received a visit from the police. But he must have heard I was in Paris and if I didn't give him a sign, he would start up again, always supposedly in my interest. He would claim I didn't know how to look out for myself, that as always I was lost when I had to deal with the difficulties of life. I should add that what made my half-brother dangerous was that he wasn't afraid to call on the authorities when it was a question of helping someone. I could just hear him, telling the police that he was very worried, that he knew I was having problems and that he was afraid that I'd been hurt. I had disappeared. He was so worried he couldn't sleep. "Look into it. Try to find out."

I told him I was doing very well and refused to give him my address despite his insistence. I told him that I was living with friends and had to leave the next day. He wanted to know which friends. I told him he didn't know them, that their names wouldn't mean anything to him, and I repeated that I was leaving the next day.

From then on, whenever I ran into people who had contact with him, I surprised them by asking them not to talk to him about me. But I explained to them that in his eagerness to help, Richard might do something foolish. I still couldn't relax. Later I learned that he was looking for me again. He was telling everyone that I was hiding something so I wouldn't worry him. He let it be known, so it seems, that he knew it was something very serious.

I was still wondering what to do when one morning my father came to take me to Mondanel. Every time I had done something wrong in my life, he accompanied me on a visit to the victim. Each time I had been in danger, he decided that the best way to help was by bringing me to see the very people who were threatening me.

We headed on foot along the boulevard Sébastopol toward police headquarters. There is nothing more unpleasant than going on an important mission in twos. It gives a distasteful impression of seriousness, compounded by the fact that you can't change your mind. To keep calm, I kept thinking that even if Mondanel didn't see my situation with the same optimism as my father, the fact that we were going to see him as friends forced him not to make any decision that might work against me. He could tell us not to come back, but he had to give us a cordial reception.

Soon we arrived in front of the headquarters. Policemen were standing guard. In reality they served little purpose, since the Germans were in charge. You could sense this by a certain slackness that suggested they weren't quite sure whether they had the right to question those entering and exiting.

We passed through one courtyard, then another. We headed up a narrow staircase that only employees were supposed to use. This unofficial aspect to our visit gave me confidence. I figured that since we were presenting ourselves like this, Mondanel could only consider us friends, that it would be easier for him to advise us without involving himself as director of his division.

I was impatient to see him in person so that I could judge for myself how kind he was. My father had told me he was nice. But sometimes we develop no affinity for people who are supposed to be nice, which is why I always ask several times before meeting a stranger, "Is he nice?" "Yes, very nice . . ." would come the response. And this reassured me. Deep down, I was expecting a lot of Mondanel. When you are told that a man will take care of everything, with a little imagination you can think up the most extraordinary things.

Mondanel had his own office, one of those minuscule administration offices which gives an impression of occult power. My father sat down. I remained standing since there was no other chair.

My father was right. Mr. Mondanel was indeed very nice. He was a small, bald-headed man with glasses. As soon as I arrived, he immediately understood that my father was going to ask a favor for me, and he looked at me with anticipated good will.

One sensed that in his amiability it didn't even occur to him that one might criticize him for keeping his job under German rule. The extent to which the Germans influenced his administration was too remote to be noticeable. He would have been stunned at the accusation. He simply lacked character. He spoke as if he were independent, as if nothing had happened. Despite the German presence, in his estimation nothing had changed. You couldn't alter the facts. All you could do now was inspire respect in our conquerors, show them that we were no fools, that we could adapt to reality.

He showed great friendship toward my father. As a measure of his confidence, he spoke to his subordinates in front of us, talked on the telephone, and made no attempt to hide his official secrets. Finally I grew afraid that if there were a subsequent leak I would be a suspect. But they weren't real secrets!

My father spoke about me at length, told him my story, or at least what he thought my story was, for I had been careful not to tell him everything. It hurt me a little to see him believe so much in this friendship; he seemed to imagine that you could expect everything from someone simply because he was a member of your family or because you'd known him a long time. I congratulated myself on not telling him I had killed two guards. I had suggested it, but so reticently that he gave up on knowing exactly what had happened. Mondanel didn't want to know either. He merely said that he was going to see what he could do, get information. He asked for an address where he could write to me. My father quickly gave it to him.

As soon as we were outside, I made no bones about my concern. What I was especially afraid of was the inquiry Mondanel was going to make for his own information. He might say that he was taking this action as a friend, and not as a police director, but I don't believe people ever forget their official duties.

I didn't tell my father, but I had the feeling that Mondanel was first and foremost a bureaucrat. Even knowing that he had nothing but good intentions now, there was no guarantee that when he had genuine official documents before his eyes proving that I was an assassin he wouldn't change his mind.

Another danger came to mind. Even allowing that Mondanel would remain true to his friendship no matter what he discovered in my records, he might let something slip, let someone know that he knew me. Others more interested in my arrest could in one way or another call on him to give me away, and he might cave in.

I was so apprehensive that even my father didn't seem as confident to me anymore. He was visibly disappointed. He hadn't seen his friend since before the war and he had imagined that Mondanel would complain, tell him how hard it was to be forced to work with the Krauts, etc. He imagined that Mondanel would share his misgivings, his inner struggles. Instead he had found a man who, though as friendly as before, was secretive and determined, who seemed to know what he was doing, and who wouldn't tolerate any personal questions of his actions. I was beginning to realize that my father regretted having brought me to see his friend, which added to my confusion. It was becoming clear that when you're in trouble, danger can come from all sides, even from those who wish you the best.

I told my father that it would be best for me to leave the rue Rambuteau immediately, since we had been foolish enough to give my address to Mondanel. But my father was a man who hated making fast decisions. He thought that even were Mondanel to betray us eventually, which seemed unlikely, he wouldn't do it right away, that he would first have a change in attitude, that he would only stoop that low after a slow evolution.

I said that I preferred to be cautious. I wanted to leave right away, go anywhere, not even pick up my things at Aunt de Miratte's. My father said he couldn't leave me on my own like that, that he was going to take me to Charles, his brother-in-law. I protested. Charles was a good man, but I couldn't see myself living with him.

In the end, I decided my father was right, the most important thing was to have a roof over my head. As for the fears that popped into my mind all the time, I had to realize that they were my personal fears, that others, no matter who they were, didn't share them. Charles would be like the others. It's like when you think about illnesses to come. In search of the perfect doctor you may find yourself without any medical care whatsoever. You can't kid yourself. You have to tell yourself in advance that the person who will heal you then, who will try to save you from death, will hardly be any different than the poor little doctor you wouldn't even ask for advice today.

Chapter 5

I returned to the rue Rambuteau and waited for my father to bring me to the home of his brother-in-law Charles. I waited a month. I had almost no money. I had become so fearful that I didn't even dare go into a bank to sell the ten thousand franc treasury note, payable to the bearer, which I had left with Madame Gaillard.

Being forced to stay with my aunt made me furious. Every day, I grew madder at my father for not being true to his word. Pride prevented me from reminding him of his promise. I became more and more obstinate. I'm astounded when I think back on my attitude. How could I have left myself open like that at a time when self-interest should have been my only guide?

Sometimes I went to visit Madame Gaillard, or rather Juliette. Since my return, I hadn't wanted to sleep at her house. But this situation I had stupidly placed myself in, of not giving in, of waiting as long as it would take for a sign from my father, caused me to act rashly. Thus I had gotten in the habit of spending the night from time to time on the rue de La Tour.

We didn't like each other all that much before the war, but ever since her husband had been taken prisoner she had developed a kind of passion for the one million five hundred thousand Frenchmen interned in Germany. I had been one of them.

Before going to bed I took the same precautions as at home, but deep down it was more protection against the unexpected arrival of her husband than out of fear of the police. I never wanted her to turn out the light. It was strange, but I felt less safe in the dark. I was afraid that if someone rang, Juliette would say, "Don't move," that she would have the silly idea of trying to act as if no one were home.

She snuggled against me. I had lost so much weight that while my face had become more refined, my body had become uglier. I sensed she was looking for protection, and I found it strange that she, who was overflowing with health and had absolutely nothing to fear, would cast me, who was also looking for protection and fearing for my life, in such a role. I couldn't fall asleep.

I felt a tremendous need to talk, to describe exactly what had happened when I escaped so that I'd be protected. I also wanted to dissolve whatever artificial quality there was to our relationship. But I was held in check by the memory of words she had spoken unwittingly, the way certain people do when they imagine that everyone shares their views, words in which I had sensed her hatred for what she called riff-raff. She hated the Germans, but she also hated certain Frenchmen. And, I don't know why, I had the impression that if I starting talking freely, despite our intimacy, I might suddenly become one of these Frenchmen in her eyes.

I told myself that the best way not to make a mistake was to keep quiet, but I knew it would also be a great relief to talk. What a pleasure to be tucked away in this haven with a woman who knew everything and who loved me all the more. She was all mine, and she alone would hear my words in bed. A secret thus revealed could never be repeated.

Each time I was about to speak, I reminded myself that the time before I'd been glad I hadn't. Nevertheless, one night I gave in. We spoke in hushed voices for two hours. I kept repeating the same things. When a subject touches you, you can talk about it forever without adding anything new.

I thought that Juliette would be surprised I had waited so long to tell her the truth about my escape. But what I was telling her was so serious she found my silence natural and didn't fault me for it.

"We have to get some sleep," she said finally. These words sent a chill down my spine. I told her I wasn't tired, that I wanted to talk some more. "We have to get some sleep," she repeated. "You've told me everything . . . Tomorrow, I'll see what is to be done." A great wave of joy came over me. Then I grew afraid of something happening before she could act on my behalf. I mentioned this. She started to laugh. "You shouldn't think about catastrophes all the time!" She kissed me. "Sleep," she said, "nothing's going to happen."

The next morning, I awoke long before she did. I still didn't know if I regretted having spoken. I waited for her to wake up. "What would you do if you never saw me again?" I asked her as soon as she opened her eyes.

"Don't say such silly things . . . ," she answered. I had no regrets. I felt uneasy just the same. I was thinking about her husband now. Something unexpected might happen, I might not be able to return to spend the night, I might not be here to keep telling her to be quiet. Would she keep my secret then? Wouldn't she use it as an excuse for her own behavior?

Anything is possible in life. Now I began trembling in fear lest others learn of our affair. Didn't I have enough worries already? The risk of our liaison being discovered, which had seemed unimportant to me until now, suddenly became as serious a danger as the others.

Until now, it would have been merely just another love

story. He took advantage of the husband's captivity. It's shameful. How could anyone be so immoral? I wouldn't have been alone in this. Juliette was also involved. But our crimes would have remained within the limits of amorous betrayal. Whereas now a word from Juliette would have been enough to take us beyond that, to place us on more dangerous ground. And in the course of an argument, Juliette might very well say that word.

Several days later, Juliette announced that she had talked about me to one of her friends, Mr. Bressy, who was in charge of the accounting office at the Ministry of Justice. She had made an appointment. She was going to bring me to see him. For a second I panicked, thinking that she had told him everything. She assured me she hadn't. She had only mentioned that I needed a job. Since that night, she spoke to me almost as if she were dealing with someone soft and negligent, someone who lets himself go, and who would end up falling into a terrible decline if he weren't saved. I shouldn't close myself off. On the contrary, I had to visit people, ask them questions, look for official protection. It was possible. We all hated the Krauts. To have killed two of them was something of an honor. Certain Frenchmen were capable of helping me a great deal. In all walks of life, there were men ready to help patriots because they themselves were patriots. And Mr. Bressy was one of them. No one knew about it, but he had single-handedly ousted a detachment of Germans from his property.

At the last minute, Juliette couldn't come with me. She had to sing at a friend's tea. I told her I didn't want to go to the Ministry of Justice alone.

She said I was being childish. Bressy was expecting me. He knew who I was. Besides, I wasn't asking him for anything. I was simply making contact. I agreed with her. I conceded that I had been wrong.

But as soon as she left, I began looking for a friend to accompany me. I was nervous. I didn't like this kind of scheme, approaching an important person through a woman, through an employee, or through a doctor. I had an hour before the appointment. I ran left and right looking for a friend who could come with me, not into Mr. Bressy's office but to the waiting room.

No one was free. I suddenly panicked. There is nothing worse, in my book, than having a request turned down like this by three or four people. I had the impression that I had come up against so much rejection because I was too demanding, and then my next thought was that I had stupidly attracted attention. In the end, I was lucky. I ran across an acquaintance from National Insurance who was on his day off.

After seating myself in the waiting room, I gave my name to the court officer. Then I stood up and began pacing the room. The officer returned a few seconds later and asked me to wait. I sat down next to my companion. I asked him a host of questions but was unable to listen to his answers. Each time I saw the officer stand, I thought he was coming to get me, and since for some reason I wanted my friend to be talking to me when that moment came, I asked him a new question.

Finally I was ushered into Mr. Bressy's office. Without looking at me, he motioned to a chair. I looked at him closely. I was afraid he might know more about me than Juliette had let on. He must have been interested in me since he had told Juliette to bring me in, but he gave no sign of noticing that I was in the room.

The phone rang. Then a strange thing happened. While listening to the person who was calling him, whom he naturally couldn't see, he looked at me. I thought that he wasn't interested in what that person was saying, and was taking advantage of this mental freedom to become acquainted with me. But I was soon surprised to realize that he didn't see me.

Just as I thought he was welcoming me visually, he suddenly said, "Oh! no, no . . . that's not possible. Put yourself in my shoes. What would you do? No. We'll talk about it later." He never took his eyes off me. He hung up without hesitating, without adding a word, and his face became immobile once again.

The fact that I witnessed these mood swings didn't bother him in the least. He began taking notes, then started looking for a file. Suddenly, I felt a great sense of relief. He had just said, *to himself,* "It's incredible, you can never find what you're looking for." I mumbled a few words to be polite, not knowing whether I should since he was talking to himself and not to me.

Finally he found the papers he was looking for and began writing again. When he'd finished, he looked at me, but this time he saw me. I thought he was going to say, "Pardon me. Now I'm all yours." His face bore a certain expression that I had already noticed on many people. He was trying to ascertain whether Juliette hadn't been mistaken, whether my troubles had really begun with the war and not before.

My situation, which was so exceptional in many ways, only weakened my sense of social distinctions, and I quickly realized that Mr. Bressy couldn't accept this. He found that I wasn't respectful enough of the rules from before the war, that I found it too natural that he should agree to see me. He made some remarks I found unpleasant. My situation was not as bad as I was saying. I couldn't complain, etc.

A secretary came in at that moment. As if distracted, Bressy began writing again. The secretary stood still. We both waited for Bressy to notice us. I said a few words to the newcomer in a low voice. He didn't answer me. I smiled at him. Then, so as not to be rude, I changed seats so that I wouldn't have my back to him. Finally the newcomer's face brightened. He motioned for me not to worry about him, which made me very happy, since in my situation I needed people to like me.

On my way out, I would have liked to say how uncordial Bressy had been. He really rubbed me the wrong way. He seemed to be wondering what my relationship to Juliette was. It was yet another consequence of my situation to never be able to say what was in my heart. A dismissed domestic can do it, but I couldn't.

My father still didn't show up and I went more and more frequently to Juliette's. I clung to her in my desperation. Sometimes I spent four or five days in her apartment. I preferred not to go out when she had forgotten to leave the key, since there was nothing scarier than waiting outside after ringing the bell. But soon the possibility of her husband returning from Germany, just as I had, began to haunt me. If he found me here, even though I was an escaped prisoner myself, it would still seem as if I'd taken advantage of his captivity. But I couldn't resolve to leave Juliette. Every day, I decided that tomorrow I would leave for good. Sometimes I got angry with her. I thought that instead of holding on to me, she should have forced me to go. She said she wasn't forcing me to stay. I told her she was putting on an act, that she was lying, that she didn't want me to leave. These discussions were extremely depressing. Nothing is worse than being attached to a woman during one of life's major moments. When she'd go out, I would experience a series of highs and lows. Suddenly I would decide to leave without even seeing her again. It seemed to me the only way. But the thought of making her suffer was intolerable. I didn't understand why we couldn't manage to get along like two partners. It would have been so easy if Juliette had wanted to. Even though we loved each other, we were seemingly unable to act in our common interest. Juliette should have arranged to hide me elsewhere. She could have come to see me. She could have brought me what I needed. She should have understood how tortured I was by the idea that her husband could come back at any minute. But no, she didn't even believe in the dangers that surrounded me. She thought I was just fine at her house, that all I had to do was wait. She was convinced that her husband was not a man who would attempt an escape. And she would laugh when I'd tell her that she didn't know men, that they can act differently away from home, and that I did know men and that we were all alike, all capable of great deeds. Every day I swore I would have a talk with her. But we had talked so much already without results that she refused to listen to me. I did all I could, using all sorts of threats to keep her attention. "Listen to me, Juliette, I have to have a serious talk with you. This time, I won't change my mind about what I'm going to say. I've made a decision. Listen to me." But she would only pretend to listen. I'd get mad again. I felt that I could only leave after a big fight. Yet I couldn't fight with her. It would have been mean. So I would stay. I would tell her that if the police caught me, it would be her fault. Her only response was a kiss. I gave in. I apologized. I kissed her back. But afterward I was so disgusted with myself I thought of suicide. It was just as impossible as everything else, but I thought about it. "Too bad," I would say to myself. "Whatever happens happens. Why worry about it? If I'm caught, it'll be on her head." "It'll be your head!" I would tell her. She would say she'd run any risk rather than be separated from me. I would get angry again. No, this was unacceptable. I had to fight. She would start to cry. In short, it was horrible. All these scenes interspersed with moments of tenderness were driving me crazy. Leave, leave, leave, that's what I had to do. But then, when I regained my calm, it appeared to me that men create their own unhappiness by their inability to be content with what they have. You wind up hating whatever's around you, you have it good and you plunge into the unknown. You wind up despising your present life. You can no longer bear your own happiness, and you expose yourself to real dangers. It's okay to act this way when there's not much risk, but when your life is in danger, it's insane. Suddenly I would realize that Juliette was right and tell her so. She wouldn't even gloat. She would simply think I was better, that all I had to do was get some sleep for my illness to disappear completely. She was certain that in time I would recover. I listened to her joyfully. I had the impression she was seeing things clearly, that I was the one who had a bad take on reality. Then, the next day, if it was raining or if I was in a bad mood, it would start all over again.

Chapter 6

My father finally came to bring me to his brother-in-law Charles' house. Charles was a lively little man who wore jewelry and was bald, with a few, very fine long hairs. On life's various occasions, he dressed in the fashion he thought appropriate to the circumstances. He lived in a small apartment on the rue Victor-Massé cluttered with knickknacks and objects which had once had a purpose but were now worthless: the workings of a clock, pieces of old cameras, generators, phonographs. Gambling, poetry, women, music, and mechanics had successively inspired great passion in him. He was basically a colorful character.

How could I have been mad at my father for taking so long to bring me to the home of this man? No doubt he was going to find a way to involve me in another sham. I had been through so many ordeals and was living such a dark time that a colorful character did not amuse me at all. Fortunately it was understood that I would only spend a few days on the rue Victor-Massé. In the meantime, my father would seek a haven for me to organize my life and do something useful.

Whenever the bell rang I panicked; since almost no one came to see Charles, the sound of the doorbell ringing during the day was ominous. I hated myself for being so afraid. But it was understandable. Locked up in this apartment, cut off from the people I knew, I realized that my fate now depended on two people in whom I had no confidence: my father and his brother-in-law.

Nothing is worse than misfortunes we hear about through a third party. When someone you love doesn't come home, for example, rather than staying inside and waiting for news from the concierge, a friend or a telephone call, it's better to go out and confront the danger, try to find out what happened before hearing about it through someone else.

This tranquility therefore did me no good. Whenever I was around Charles, I had the impression he was hiding something from me. He was calmly tending to his affairs, while I was going out of my mind. Thanks to me, he appreciated the nice little life he had organized for himself even more. Nothing was worse, in my anxious state, than feeling like I increased other people's happiness with my presence. I concluded that when you're unhappy you should only rely on people who really love you, who would truly suffer if something happened to you even though they personally have nothing to lose, or on people who are completely indifferent, like Georget and Guéguen, or else on people who have a personal stake in your security, who are in danger as well. But nothing is worse than these people who claim to be concerned about your fate. It's better to be alone.

But what could I do? If I followed my own advice, I wouldn't stay anywhere. I had to live somewhere. I knew that the unpleasantness of arriving at the home of someone new would pass with time. I couldn't afford to give credence to this feeling of disorientation.

Three days later, my father came to see me. He told me that he'd seen Mondanel again. He hadn't wanted to tell me. I felt uneasy. He certainly couldn't have hidden from him the fact that I was living at his brother-in-law's. The mention of Mondanel's name destroyed the secure feeling I was starting to have in my new routine. I would have to start all over again.

My father told me he hadn't given Mondanel my address. He swore to it, but I didn't trust him; not that he was a liar, but he had no scruples about hiding the truth when he thought he was being useful by doing so.

The worst thing was the feeling that people were trying to correct the situation without keeping me abreast of all the details. Instead of doing what would have been appropriate—hiding me, helping me in my struggle against the current authorities—I sensed that they were doing whatever they could to regularize my situation and trick me back into normal life.

There is nothing more worrisome than having your family and friends intervene on your behalf behind your back. One day they agree with you, and the next, after a conversation with so and so, they suddenly think just the opposite. It's a lonely feeling when you realize that just a few hours or a few days of separation were enough for them to develop ideas about your salvation diametrically opposed to your own. You can imagine them quickly agreeing that your situation is serious, far more serious than you had thought, that you can't judge it sanely, that it is urgent that something be done even without your agreement.

Whenever people discuss a third party in this way they quickly come to an understanding at the latter's expense. Unintentionally, my father had no doubt gone so far as to say things he wouldn't have said in front of me. I reconstructed the scenario. I heard my father saying that my situation was worse than he had thought at first, and Mondanel responding, "I suspected as much," each one considering with feigned objectivity what had to be done and agreeing that I had to be persuaded to turn myself in!

People had the impression that I was hiding something. I sensed that despite my efforts they suspected that my situation was difficult not only because I was an escaped prisoner, but also because I had no money. This was only natural. Certain indicators were identical to those that had formerly been signs of poverty. Even if I changed the date of my escape—saying, "Last month, when I arrived in Paris . . . ," no matter how much time had passed— the reasons for my destitution were increasingly difficult to attribute to my being an escapee. What was unclear to people was why I didn't stay with my family.

I realized then that I would be more secure if I could earn a little money. Even though, given the state of affairs, poverty was no longer what it was before, I sensed that it still looked suspicious to the Germans. They were so proud, so fond of flashy things, they so wanted to show off in front of these French snobs, that I had the distinct impression that if I were to get caught up in any kind of shady business, my fate would depend on how I was dressed. My threadbare suit, which had seemed a disguise, which in the past would have assured my total anonymity, seemed more and more like a give-away. I was told that there was far less surveillance when crossing the demarcation line in first class than in third, and the same was true in expensive restaurants. I had noticed that it was part of the German character to respect monetary distinctions.

Even though the obstacles were no longer the same, it was still difficult to earn money. Certainly my father must have had some. He spent absolutely nothing—his room and board were provided by the Sévigné school. But he was so stingy it didn't even cross his mind that others might notice.

I decided to talk to Roger. I had already gone to see him three or four times on the rue George-Sand, but he was never home. I went there not only to see him, but to see the neighborhood. In the past, I had loved this neighborhood, where my father's elegant sister lived. For me, who came from Les Ternes, from the working-class part of Les Ternes at the bottom of the avenue MacMahon parallel to the rue des Acacias, it had been like a vision of the life I would lead later on, when I would marry and have the means to rent a nice apartment. But now I found it disappointing. There were still little gardens, quiet streets. Nothing had changed, but the soul of the neighborhood was gone. The same was true of all the places I cherished in Paris. All the things that had made it so charming in my memory, the locals taking a morning stroll on a sunny day, the sense of earthly comfort, the care lavished on children, their carefree ways, had disappeared.

I was sure that Roger would help me find a few odd jobs. Nothing is worse than seeing your future, your health, your very life depend on money, on a certain lifestyle that others possess without needing it, without knowing its price, when for you it isn't a matter of vanity but of life and death.

When I finally met up with Roger, I was amazed that he had been able to erase any trace of what we had endured together. You would have thought he had never been a prisoner, or better yet, that there had never been a war. He introduced me to certain friends of his. In this kind of situation the first encounter is always excellent. Roger had only one thing in mind: to show me that he was happy, like a man reunited with a woman he'd left behind.

Roger must have told his friends good things about me, since they were always very friendly. They didn't take my situation any more seriously than Roger did. If the bell rang when they weren't expecting anyone, for example, they would motion me not to move. Then they would close the door to the room I was in, as if that were enough. And when the visitor was someone I didn't have to be afraid of, they ushered him in. I blushed each time I was discovered like this, without having the chance to show I wasn't hiding.

When Roger couldn't help me, I thought about trying to get my job back at the National Insurance claims office. It seemed to me that if the police were still looking for me I would know about it, there would have been signs of it other than the ones I'd had. Someone always warns you. I had often been warned. You have to be wary of the people who come to tell you that you're being watched. I had been tipped off several times, but I despise these kinds of messengers. I answered in monosyllables, I showed them that I didn't like how they were acting. I expressed no gratitude. I didn't even thank them, which made me some enemies.

"This takes the cake!" they would say. "We took the trouble to warn him, we didn't have to do it, we did it out of the goodness of our hearts, we had nothing to gain and everything to lose, and he didn't even thank us. He even looked angry."

Several days in a row I waited for Fridel at the exit to National office. Outside was a kind of peristyle with a large cast iron door. It was strange to see my poor little colleagues, minor employees, appear in this majestic palace entrance, oblivious to the contrast their presence evoked. It was strange to see them waiting for one another, talking to each other like before the war, and I couldn't help but imagine myself among them, rushing, uninterested in the world because I had only an hour and a half for lunch. Nothing had changed. Everything went on as if France were a free country. Fridel was never alone. I followed him several times, but as soon as he separated from his companion he'd start running, his conscience clear, to get to the train station sooner. Each time I was amazed at how he could draw attention to himself like that without worrying about it. To him it just seemed natural to run when he was in a hurry.

Finally, I was able to talk to him. I told him what had

happened to me, omitting the main event, leaving him to understand, nevertheless, that something serious had transpired. Twelve of us had escaped. There had been an incident at the last minute. I didn't know exactly what had happened. The fact remained that we were being sought by the police, etc. I had barely finished my story when I realized that I had already made the same mistake before. On several previous occasions, out of weakness, or fear of lying or of telling the truth, I had said more than one should when one has something to hide. One day, it would come back to haunt me.

We went to lunch together. I sensed that there was something wrong between us. No, it wasn't professional rivalry or jealousy. There was tension. I had the impression that everyone at National knew all about my story and that poor Fridel was in a situation in which I had already seen so many people, unable to choose between friendship and the fear of compromising himself. I told him right away that he had nothing to be afraid of. He said I was crazy, and with such profound sincerity that I thought I might be mistaken and that my marginal status was making me overly sensitive. But the tension didn't go away. Then I realized that the problem was not a fear of compromising himself; the problem lay in our differences, not of opinion, but in our reactions to the events at hand. And yet I hadn't said anything that I wouldn't have said before the war. The same for Fridel. Suddenly, I became afraid. All I could think was that I had to get out, to get away from Fridel before it was too late. I had the impression that there was nothing left of our friendship, that Fridel was my enemy, that he was going to stand up, call someone over, start yelling about how we didn't think the same way; I thought they would agree with him and arrest me. I couldn't even say, "Come on, Fridel, what's the matter with you?" He didn't know me anymore. He didn't know who I was. I couldn't keep eating.

It was after this incident that I became increasingly afraid of fanatics, of people who yell louder than others. I was afraid of misunderstandings, of group debates about politics. I felt as if people could read my thoughts on my face. I had the impression that anyone could point a finger at me and say anything he wanted; that I would be arrested without anyone daring to help me, without anyone having the courage to say that I had done no wrong. Which is why I would slip away whenever people raised their voices, but even then I feared that my departure would be interpreted as proof that I was guilty of something or other. "Hey you, over there, why are you leaving?" I would nod my head in a sign of agreement. It surprised me that such an insignificant gesture could inspire confidence. An approving nod and I was worthy of staying, of participating in the future . . . But the worst thing was that these dangers arose most unexpectedly. They could pop up at any time, when I was buying a newspaper, when I was saying hello to my concierge. He was a nice man, but one day by mistake I happened to be there just as he was voicing his opinions: everyone to the stake. Since then, each time I passed in front of his lodge I felt like he was doing me a big favor when he smiled, but that he might change his mind at any minute.

Chapter 7

It was about this time that I found a room in the home of an old woman who didn't know, strange as it might seem, that there were police restrictions. It was surprising to find someone who didn't even suspect that the police might be interested in her, who imagined that honest people never had anything to do with the police. She was living as I myself had lived before the war. She would have been surprised, and indignant, if they had asked her the slightest question. She imagined that no one in the world had the right to question her, to ask her to explain her actions, to enter her home. She imagined that she was free to do as she liked. If someone she knew had dealings with the police, it didn't even cross her mind that the same thing could happen to her. These people had to be guilty of something or other.

This naïveté made me uncomfortable. When I was staying

with people who could defend themselves, it didn't matter to me that I posed a danger for them. I had no qualms about putting them in a compromising position. But with this poor woman who was so trusting, I had such a terrible feeling that I was deceiving her that I almost moved out soon after moving in.

It didn't take me long to realize though that if I got so hung up about being honest, I would close myself off from all the places I'd feel safe. The choice became clear: either live with outlaws and add their risks to my own, or deceive innocent people and risk involving them in my troubles.

In any case, there I was living with this old woman. All I had to do was stay put. Maybe she wasn't as angelic as I thought; maybe I wasn't so evil. I wouldn't be arrested. Things would end here as they had everywhere else. I had to harden myself like a traveling salesman, who doesn't take it personally when he is asked to leave.

I therefore accepted the kindness of this old women despite the looming possibility that she might one day learn that I'd had no remorse about exposing her to terrible dangers. I went about my business as if this would never happen. And yet I was very fond of her.

I had been living there for a week when her son was liberated as part of the medical corps. I had never said that I'd been a prisoner. When there's been a defeat, no one is curious about your military past. No one asks what you did. "Maurice will be very pleased to meet you, Monsieur de Talhouet," the old woman told me.

Finally the son arrived. He spoke of his captivity like a prisoner who would rather see his jailers reeducated than punished. He was one of those people who seem to consider the events of their lives so important that the entire world should cling to their every word. He had a right to feel this way of course (his attitude was apparent by the way he allowed himself to be waited on), but ultimately his case was far less interesting than mine.

I found him pretentious, the kind of person who lectures about things their listeners know more about than they do. He arrived with suitcases like a civilian. He left them in the vestibule to be put away. When you return home and find a stranger, you rarely feel kindly toward him.

This boy was immediately very friendly toward me nonetheless. From time to time, however, he cast a wary eye. He said everything in a tone that was not to be disputed. Not everyone could have been taken prisoner. Yet one sensed that he had great disdain for anyone who hadn't been exposed to the life of the Oflag. He had the bearing of a man who comes directly from the very place where the fate of the world is being decided. He was telling us what was really happening: the prisoners would not be silent about all this. They would want an accounting from those responsible; at no time did one sense he thought the Germans might be the ones responsible, even in part. Then he spoke of the Jews, the freemasons, the English, and the Communists. He spoke of the bad Frenchmen, particularly those who had escaped without taking into account the reprisals the brave souls who remained behind would have to bear.

At this point I had no regrets about having kept silent regarding my adventures. He still hadn't changed his clothes. He kept wearing his faded uniform, with the ridiculous corduroy coat of arms of the pharmacist officers, breeches, and leggings; seeing the remains of our former military splendor, I realized how arrogant it had been. His pockets weren't cut like those of soldiers or civilians, vertically on the side, but horizontally in front; there was something vulgar about how he placed his hand inside, like when a man slips his hand between his belt and shirt.

I spent entire afternoons in remote neighborhoods where I had never set foot before because I sensed that my being in his mother's house got on his nerves. I imagined that if I felt lost, no one else could see me.

But as a result of being alone, of rehashing the same things all the time, I became more and more nervous. I couldn't live this way. The constant fear of being shot was playing tricks on my imagination. Sometimes I saw myself transported to the future, a Sunday stroller visiting my room the way one visits a museum. A crowd gathered. This was where I had been arrested. A guard was explaining what had happened. I had tried to jump out the window. They had caught me in time. A brawl ensued. I rolled to the ground. Finally they'd pinned me down. The visitors examined with interest the ceramic debris, the furniture and the broken windows, for the disorder had been treated with the same care as a great man's study. I must say that I had already fantasized about the place where my life ended becoming famous, ten years earlier, when I had been stricken with the pleurisy I've spoken of and thought I was going to die.

Sometimes I told myself that I should simply move out without saying anything. Why bother leaving a good impression? Yet I was aware of how imprudent such conduct would be. I might run into someone who knew these people one day. As big a city as Paris may be, you're never safe from random encounters. I had noticed something rather troubling: since the occupation, there were many more coincidences than before. For some reason Paris seemed to have shrunk. I used to come and go as if I had nothing to hide. But one day it dawned on me that by behaving so freely, I was exposing myself without realizing it, other people could see me walking around, that while I pictured myself as an individual lost in the big city, all sorts of preparations were being made for my arrest. A flash of heat rose to my head. I looked around, to the left, to the right. There were so many people everywhere that it was impossible to know if I was being followed or not. I wanted to get away from everyone. I took one small street, then another. Finally, I was alone. I stopped. A passerby occasionally ventured down this lane. I looked at him carefully and each time felt relieved by his indifference toward me. But occasionally a troubled looking man would approach, a man dressed like me, whose occupation was difficult to determine. Even these men didn't look at me. I must say here that later, when I had nothing more to fear from anyone, I would return this kindness by not paying any more attention to suspicious-looking types I'd meet than these people had to me, as if this might bring them the same pleasure.

It was during one of these interminable days that I made the acquaintance of Germaine Peuch. I was sitting on a bench in a little square.

Children were playing. But there was no room owing to that mad pre-war desire to include something for everyone, a covered area, two kiosks, a stage, extra benches, a cement sandbox. People had to squeeze together to make room for me and did so in such an accommodating way that it warmed my heart.

I was watching the children play. Sometimes they hurt themselves. Their movements were so chaotic I was surprised this didn't happen more often. They were so oblivious to the dangers around them, dangers that I could see from where I was sitting. There was one thing in particular that made me tremble, a large rake with iron teeth that one child had used to threaten his friends. His mother had shaken him and told him to put it down. The child had thrown it far away, and even then it had almost hit someone. And now this rake was on the ground, its teeth in the air. Children were running, pushing each other, and falling all around it. I kept thinking that a child was going to fall on it, and that if he fell face first it might poke out an eye. But the mothers, who made such a fuss over chocolate-stained fingers, weren't moving. I figured they knew better than I did what had to be done and that as usual I was seeing dangers where there were none. And, indeed, they were right; no one got hurt.

A woman was sitting next to me. She had no toys to suggest that she was the mother of one of these many children. She had straight black hair that hid part of her cheek, murky brown eyes, white teeth but with extraordinarily pointed canines. She was poorly and sloppily dressed. I don't know why, but this woman seemed very happy to me. She was sitting as if she didn't want to speak to anyone, as if she were interested in the sight of maternity and children. From time to time, she would smile at the mother of a mischievous child, but in such a strange manner, as if she weren't thinking of this particular mother or of this child, but of a past life she had lived or would have liked to live. She never waited for a response to her smile, she never seemed hurt by the mother's somewhat egotistical activity, full of slapping, shouting, and running after lost objects.

I struck up an acquaintance with this woman. She was a nanny. She was looking after one of these children. I told her my fear. She started to laugh. Shortly thereafter I learned her name was Peuch. I asked her if she was related to a politician of that name. It was vaguely familiar; I thought it might also be the name of a well-known artist. She said that there had indeed been a deputy by that name, from Rodez like herself, but that the name was very common there and they weren't from the same family.

Two days later, I went to stay with her in the maid's quarters she occupied on the top floor of her employers' building, without knowing whether I owed this favor to love or to a disinterested need for protection.

Chapter 8

The door didn't close right, and could have been pushed open with a shove. This bothered me. I could already picture the police bursting in. But on second thought it occurred to me that the door's fragility didn't matter. If the police got this far, whether the door was solid or not, I was caught.

I spent over an hour reinforcing it anyway. In the end I gave up. Apart from the door, I was very comfortable. It was a maid's room. There were a dozen of them off the hallway. It had a hinged skylight instead of a window. If I didn't go out anymore, I could consider myself saved.

I hadn't been downstairs in a week. I had the illusion of being in a situation similar to one I had experienced in the army, of being a man forgotten at his official post. He continues to receive food and a salary. His name is on the list. But no one knows where he is.

One morning, I woke up and decided to go outside. But the rain was beating on the skylight. You couldn't go out without a specific goal. I looked at my clothes, my familiar possessions, and for an instant I saw them as if they no longer belonged to anyone, as if their owner had disappeared or died.

As soon as Germaine had gone downstairs, I dressed, made the bed, straightened up. When suddenly I heard footsteps, I jumped. You would have thought my troubles had begun with a similar sound.

The hesitation I felt at this moment must be the downfall of many criminals. I waited with my eyes fixed on the skylight, but I didn't open it or move the stool that would get me on the roof.

Finally the noise faded. I considered going back to bed, but stopped myself; if the person returned I wouldn't have time to dress. I remained seated. I didn't walk around for fear of making noise, I didn't take off my shoes because of the puddles of water on the floor.

Germaine had said she would be back at about noon to bring me lunch. As soon as she'd left, however, I realized that we had forgotten to establish a special knock. Even though I knew she was coming back, the prospect of her knocking on the door made me nervous. I knew that at the first knock my blood would freeze. Even though I hadn't opened the skylight, the room had aired itself out. I listened to the sound of the rain. To kill time, I cleaned off the shelves and read the old newspapers from before the war that had been covering them. From time to time I glanced at the intercom. I was afraid it might ring while Germaine was out. Would someone come if no one answered? Shortly before noon, I got up. I had already smoked a twenty-four franc pack of Gauloises. The moment I dreaded was approaching. I was so tired from my seclusion I became despondent. What should I do? How could I get out of this mess? I saw myself stuck in this room, with no possibility of going anywhere else, of working, of being useful. I couldn't have been more unhappy. And yet this was just what I had wanted most, to live secluded from the world.

Suddenly it happened. There was a knock on the door. I was up in a flash. Instinctively, I took several steps back. I was about to ask who was there when I realized I would be giving myself away. Silently, I threw myself to the side so that I couldn't be seen through the keyhole. Germaine knocked again, calling my name. It was over, I was no longer afraid.

I opened the door. Germaine had brought me lunch and another pack of cigarettes. She was surprised that I hadn't opened sooner. I told her I hadn't heard her. She ignored my lie.

I closed the door behind her. "No one saw you?" I asked. She didn't understand the importance of her response. She put the tray on the bed, speaking loudly.

Now that we were both in this room at midday, I had another fear, that of no longer being able to run away if necessary, out of pride. I didn't know Germaine well enough to prick up my ears at the slightest sound, to keep her from talking in a raised voice, from standing in the middle of the room, from sitting on the stool I needed for my escape. I didn't want to seem a coward in her eyes.

I was so nervous she asked me what was wrong. "Nothing, nothing . . . ," I told her. I had only one thing in mind, I wanted her to leave me alone. Since she wasn't moving from the chair (which annoyed me beyond belief), I sat down on the bed and asked her to sit next to me. The sight of the empty chair relaxed me.

I ate my lunch in a semi-reclining position, propped up on my elbow. In my life there have been only a few occasions when I was in the position of seeming vain like that, a man being served by a woman, and it was so contrary to my nature it always surprised me.

I felt terrible each time she spoke to me tenderly, for in my mind I envisioned the scene in which suddenly, without giving her a second thought, without any explanation, even pushing her aside if necessary, I would be forced to flee like a madman.

Shortly thereafter, I kept her from going back to work, in a sense to punish myself. "Don't leave so soon," I told her. The chair was still empty and well-placed right below the skylight. No noise could be detected. I had the feeling that at this precise instant I wasn't running any risks, that I could allow myself to enjoy the moment. Everyone poses a certain threat, but when you've spent some time with someone, when you've gotten used to them, the threat fades away and they just seem kind.

Germaine was no longer an obstacle to my escape. On the contrary, I pictured her helping by stalling my pursuers, pointing them in the wrong direction, and when finally she opened the door saying with perfect ease, "What do you want? You can see there's no one here . . ."

I spent another week without going out. I felt more and more agitated. Suddenly I realized that there were dangers other than the ones I was protecting myself from, that I was exposed to far more serious risks that my cloistered existence kept me from seeing. I had the feeling that if I stayed in this room one more day I would be arrested. I absolutely had to leave to see what was happening outside.

The daylight, streaming in through the skylight, gave the room a certain solemnity. It could have been a dungeon, a crypt, or a cave. It was cold and the light was grey.

I kissed Germaine. I liked her at this moment, the way she never seemed to feel at home, the way she implied that her present life was temporary and that I could be a part of her life to come.

I had gotten so nervous that when I sat on the stool, each time I took a breath I thought the same immobile chimney in the distance was a person. And even though I should have been prepared, it still gave me a fright every time.

I hardly ate anymore. I had become impossible. I wouldn't talk to Germaine when she came home, except to criticize her or complain about what I needed. Every morning I would ask her to bring me something. If she didn't find what I wanted, I would close myself off in silence. Other times I criticized her for not coming to see me often enough during the day, for losing interest in me.

One day, my own behavior scared me. Germaine would end up getting sick of me. Then what would I do? I didn't have the luxury of being difficult in my situation. This was so obvious it transformed me overnight. I realized then how much stronger you are, how much better life treats you, when you are able to control yourself.

Indeed, a few days later, instead of having to leave without knowing where to go, which would have been inevitable if I had continued to act so insensitively, I had the pleasure of hearing Germaine tell me that I couldn't live like this anymore and that she was going to take me to her sister's.

I left without baggage so as not to attract attention. Germaine would bring my suitcase a few days later.

Here I must note a curious detail. There was no longer any romance between us. The seriousness of my situation had somehow prevented our amorous relations from blossoming and this without either of us blaming ourselves.

As soon as I was gone, I regretted this arrangement concerning my suitcase. If at the train station, for example, some mobile guards asked Germaine where she was going, if they rummaged through the suitcase, I knew at first she would repeat the story we had prepared perfectly. But eventually she might become confused. I didn't trust her stamina any more than I did anyone else's. I had warned Germaine that they would ask her where she lived, whose suitcase it was. She had told me that she would say she was living with her mother. "On what street?" I had asked her. "Near the train station." "And your brother, where does he live?" "He lives with my mother." "But what's the name of the street?" She didn't know what to say. "You see! You're going to get caught . . . ," I told her.

This rehearsal made me feel worse. The general population doesn't understand how far those slimy police can push an interrogation. They think there are limits, that you can't go beyond a certain point. They are incapable of preparing a series of answers. This is fine in everyday life. But in a situation like the one I feared, your average citizen loses his composure and you can tell he's afraid of giving someone away. He becomes indignant, he refuses to talk, or at least he thinks he'll refuse. But the police have methods of persuasion and it's best not to reach this point.

My stay at Germaine's brother-in-law's little farm was no fun. I was bored to death.

My heart beat faster whenever I ran into the police. I told myself I was being silly. When you see a policeman in Paris, it doesn't make an impression. But the police were treating me the way children treat a newcomer at school. This is the way people always act, no matter who they are, I reassured myself.

I always saluted them and when they didn't respond, or when I thought I sensed coldness in their salute, or when they didn't raise their finger to their cap, I would become terribly anxious. I figured they thought I was trying to get in good with them precisely because I had a guilty conscience.

Sometimes in the evening it occurred to me that I should leave that minute, that the next morning they would come get me.

Finally I would fall asleep and in the morning, when nothing had happened, I would think I'd been crazy to worry myself so. I found comfort in the idea that if they had been instructed to arrest me, they would have done so long ago. Basically, the role of the police was to arrest vagabonds and petty thieves; when I spotted them taking a poor farm worker who had stolen twenty francs to jail, as hard as it is to admit, I must say I felt relieved.

The nights I had insomnia were terrifying. I imagined that a crime—a serious one—had just occurred in the village and that my irregular situation brought me to the attention of the police. I even imagined that all I could do to acquit myself was tell the truth, and that I would escape the charges against me only to be tried by the Germans.

The first thing I did when I awoke was look at the weather. I also looked in the courtyard, at the leaves hanging from invisible threads that moved imperceptibly in the wind. When it was raining, I felt terribly sad. I had no clothes to protect me. I couldn't go out. I had to stay in this bare room with just a damp mattress and a chamber pot which I had no place to hide.

Because of the laborers in the vicinity I had gotten it into my head that I always had to be working, work being evidence of honor.

I must say that I was in such a muddle I couldn't sit still for a second. As soon as I got up I would fold my two covers, which were as stiff and heavy as frozen wet cloth. I would sweep everywhere. No matter how meticulous I was, however, the housecleaning never took me more than a quarter of an hour. Then I had to find something else to do. I would saw wood. I would take doors off their hinges and oil them, doors that no one had touched since the house had been built. I kept a rag in my pocket which I used not only for dust, but to dry off the dampness.

I became fanatical about order and cleanliness. I looked for things to perfect. I made latches, put up screens, repaired old tools. I spent three days trying to repair an old millstone that was missing several parts. I fed the hens. I even began cleaning the approaches to the farm. There was garbage everywhere, debris, stones accumulated over several years. I decided to collect everything in one place.

But one morning I suddenly became disgusted with this pathetic life. I didn't have the strength to go on. I told myself that this was too high a price to pay for my safety.

Barely two hours had passed before I found myself looking for the wheelbarrow. It was stronger than I was, I couldn't sit still.

Then I realized that if I could find something to keep me busy in the village, I could overcome the ridiculous habits I'd developed. But there is nothing harder than starting a love affair in a village. I have never been able to make a date with a woman in the country. It was as if love didn't exist, except perhaps on Sundays, but then all the men were there.

After a while I did manage to convey to a waitress in a café that I was flirting with her. After a while, we started to feel happy together. My life was transformed. But I couldn't lose sight of the fact that I wasn't in the same situation as everyone else. I couldn't indulge in love's impetuous acts. I found myself in that terrible situation for a lover of being unable to get jealous. One day, however, I couldn't help starting a quarrel. I immediately grew terrified, as if I had made an enemy, as if insults and shouts had the same repercussions in love as in normal life.

I went back immediately to ask forgiveness. Such a rapid about-face surprised her. I sensed that deep down she must have been thinking that I had to be terribly in love to come back so quickly.

Chapter 9

One evening, I suddenly decided to leave. The rain was beating on the window panes. It was warmer outside than in. I was feeling increasingly impulsive. My decision was made. Nothing had happened, and yet I was convinced that I couldn't wait another hour. The next day, my hosts would be surprised to find that the bird had flown the coop. I visualized the initial search, then the surprise once they realized I had left. I was going to make more enemies. This made me hesitate. Didn't I have enough enemies already? Finally it occurred to me that at this point, one enemy more or less didn't make a difference.

I opened the window despite the wind and rain to familiarize myself with that most terrifying feeling of being home in the country while a storm is raging. I figured that if I walked until dawn at the rate of six kilometers an hour I would arrive in Paris before daybreak. Once I was there, I would play it by ear. I would probably go back to Germaine Peuch's. The past two weeks had made me appreciate, and perhaps exaggerate, her devotion to me.

At nine o'clock I climbed out the window. Fat clouds, passing haphazardly in front of the moon, filled the sky and made my shadow appear small and familiar when it appeared alongside me for a few moments. I had brought my suitcase, but had left behind a pair of shoes and two battered volumes of Casanova's *Memoirs*.

I passed through a small wooded area. Soon I would be on the road. I had the feeling, now that I was alone in the country, that I was no longer in danger. I don't know why, but there was almost no traffic that evening. I hid when I heard a car approaching. When you're in a house or a room, you're at someone else's mercy; you're confined by walls and doors. Here I was free, as free as when I had escaped in Germany. In fact, I convinced myself that I was just arriving from Germany. This gave me more courage. I was wiping the slate clean of the last three months in Paris. I was more interesting that way than as someone who had been drifting for three months. Here, there was nothing to stop me from throwing myself to the ground when I considered it necessary. I could be as cautious as I wanted. The strangest thing was that I no longer saw any reason to be cautious. Instead of trembling when a car drove by in the middle of the night, I considered it almost a welcome event. I would hide, but casually, not crouching over but simply standing behind a tree. I would watch the car go by, then keep walking, joy and peace in my heart.

I spent most of the night this way. But suddenly, come morning, I became afraid. I had once again fallen prey to my own speculation. I hadn't learned from experience. I had calculated that I would cover six kilometers an hour. Yet just as dawn was beginning to break, I realized that I was still twelve kilometers from Paris. When would I learn to pace myself!

I quickened my step. Above all I had to avoid being seen coming in from the country. But I was so tired that I wasn't getting far. I left the main road. How could I enter Paris without attracting attention? I arrived at one of these small agglomerations that seem like villages, that have barns, farms, and courtyards. No one was awake yet. The gas pumps stood idle at the side of the road. I don't know if it was fatigue, the sadness of dawn, hunger, or the war, but I had a terrible feeling of distress. I hid on a path waiting for a café to open, but when it did no one would give me anything to drink. Three hours later, I took advantage of the increased activity to make my way into Paris. I sat in a café just opposite the slaughter houses of la Villette. I stayed over an hour. The room wasn't heated. Animal noises rang out incessantly. Train cars rammed into one another with a sound that could have been taken for explosions. Here too, there was nothing to drink or eat. The owner looked like a man whose business was bad. He stayed in the kitchen, even though he had nothing to do there, in order to leave the main room to his clients. I envied this man. Since my escape I envied anyone who lived calmly, despite the police and the Germans.

    I left the café and headed toward the center of town. From time to time I would see some exquisite German cars, mostly convertibles, and it struck me that the passengers were driving through this poor neighborhood as if they didn't know it was poor, as if foreigners, even when they were our enemies, couldn't fathom our biases, and took their pleasure wherever they could without taking into account our local distinctions.

    Several housewives were yelling in front of a grocery store. Two policemen were talking to one of them. Everyone was hostile toward the policemen, who seemed as if they had given a command that hadn't been obeyed, as if they weren't backing down but didn't dare use force yet. They weren't leaving. They weren't speaking. They were waiting to be obeyed, and the crowd, thinking it had detected signs of yielding, was growing more and more obstinate.

    I stopped thirty steps away. With a quick glance, I surveyed the gathering and noticed that it was composed mostly of women. The few men were old or looked like innocuous pensioners. It occurred to me immediately that I would look suspicious in this group.

Something told me I should move away. I didn't. Instead, I moved a few steps closer out of curiosity. I turned to see what was happening around me. Other people, scattered on all sides, were also watching the scene from a safe distance, like me, without getting involved. From time to time I said to myself, "This is nothing, I'd better go." But I stayed. The women were yelling louder and louder and the policemen weren't responding. They seemed to know that in the end they would have the last word.

I moved still closer, determined to leave as soon as the situation deteriorated. Suddenly, I saw six policemen arrive walking in twos. Even though they were few in number, I knew that this time I had to move away. Being overly cautious, I didn't want to leave immediately. As if the incident no longer interested me I turned around. At that point, I found myself eye to eye with three men I sensed immediately were plain-clothed inspectors.

"Where are you going?" one of them asked me. A policeman approached. When I was too overwrought to answer, one of the plainclothesmen took me by the arm, while the other two headed toward the gathering. Despite my terror, I noticed that they didn't seem to want to take sides with either the crowd or the policemen; they were scanning right and left, as if looking for someone. I was speechless.

The policeman turned me over to an inspector who might have been twenty-five years old. He looked like a new recruit, somewhat thin and delicate to be wearing a uniform, with a hint of the young boy who had wanted to be a policeman since childhood, something honest, well-behaved, a little overwhelmed by the responsibility he'd been given. Yet there was something unnerving about him nonetheless that made you glad to know he was part of a system, subject to a collective discipline, however little confidence the leaders themselves inspired. I told him I didn't have time, that I had to go, that someone was waiting for me. He didn't answer. He simply motioned for me to stay where I was. I lost my head. "You can see I didn't do anything." His lips remained shut. I took a few steps. "Stay right there! . . ." he said dryly. I lifted my arms in protest. Nothing is worse than being in the hands of people who merely obey orders. This policeman was one of them. And his youth, his honest expression, the good will I discerned in his gaze, were all at the service of his superiors.

I was led with nine women and one other man to the police station. Everyone was protesting except me. All these people had anger and indignation in their voices that I could not imitate. Better still, I guessed that they would have been disappointed to be released too quickly. They wanted to take advantage of the occasion to speak their minds, but I who had nothing to say was feeling more and more suspect. I adopted the air of an indignant gentleman, "They won't get away with this!" I said to each woman in turn. "What's this all about?" I asked. They answered evasively and I sensed a certain coldness, as if, even though we were in the same boat, as housewives who couldn't find vegetables they didn't care to see their respectable cause mixed up with mine.

At first the police made no distinction between us. I was glad to see that they didn't push me any harder or make nastier remarks to me than to the others. But suddenly I realized by the way they were looking at me that they were beginning to notice I wasn't like the others. Should I keep protesting like everyone else? If I made myself unpleasant, they might all turn to me when asked to designate the culprit. But if I stopped I was admitting I was afraid, I was admitting that they were right in judging me differently, and I would appear more suspicious still.

These housewives had just left home. They were warmly and cleanly dressed. It was evident, on the other hand, that I had just spent the night outdoors. I was covered in mud. My clothing, soaked several times by downpours, dried several times by the heat of my body, seemed to come out of a sweat room. If I had been old, it wouldn't have mattered. But I sensed how disturbing this vagabond look was in a young man with an alert face and in seemingly good health. As a precaution I began coughing. Suddenly

I noticed that no one would answer me anymore when I spoke.

They had taken us to the guard room until the police commissioner could get the affair straight. One of the policemen pulled up three chairs. None of the women wanted to sit. I was exhausted. Finally, unable to stand on my feet any longer, I sat down. A few seconds later an officer yelled that they hadn't put the chairs there for me. I turned toward the women as if to say, "Tell him that you don't feel like sitting!" No one moved. I stood up. But instead of mingling with the group I began pacing the room, which I found less tiring than standing still.

As time passed, everyone became acquainted with one another. I alone had no one to talk to. Then, like a rekindled fire, new protests arose. They were no longer as violent as they had been in the street or upon entering the station. None of the housewives was yelling, as they had before, "You have no right to do this to us," with the understanding that if they were arresting her they should arrest all the housewives in Paris. The problem now appeared to be that, as many as we were, we were to be questioned individually.

I began trembling. Until now, I hadn't worried too much. "Keep your cool," I had said to myself. I'd thought we were too numerous to be interrogated separately. But were we really? There were eleven of us. Nothing so extraordinary about that. I looked at the door. It was open, but blocked by two policemen. I looked at the window, a large office window with three hinged panels. There were bars behind it. Despite my situation, I noticed a curious thing. These bars, due to the architect's or the metalsmith's attention to detail, and in order to create extra space on the ledge, were not planted vertically like common prison bars, but formed an elbow at their extremities in order to rise up at a greater distance from the window.

Then I tried to speak to the only man besides myself who was mixed up in this affair. He was a little old man dressed in a suit far too big for him, for like everyone else he must have lost twenty kilos or so, and was decorated with military ribbons that in all good faith one couldn't imagine he had won himself. He listened to me, but didn't trust me any more than the women did. I kept staring at his ribbons, and told myself bitterly that even this man, this nobody, carrying a basket under his arm, probably had a thousand proofs of how honorable a fellow he was. He was a nice man nonetheless. I sensed that he would wake up only when he was personally attacked, and that then he might be more violent than anyone else.

We waited over an hour in this room. Finally someone came to get us as a group, contrary to what I had feared. Among the women, there was one who spoke for the group, who seemed more excited, who was threatening to cause a scandal, and so on. As long as she kept this up, I felt calmer. But soon she relaxed, which terrified me, as if, with no one else making a spectacle, I would be the one attracting attention. What should I say? That I had just escaped, that I was coming directly from Germany? Should I hide the fact that I had just spent three months in Paris? Should I tell the truth, say that I was coming from Verberie?

We entered the commissioner's office. Should I stand behind the women or in front? Instead of saying that I had only been a spectator, that I had nothing to do with what had happened, wouldn't it be smarter to also complain about the merchants? But I didn't feel natural playing this role. The problem with thinking too much is that in the end you never do anything and you always look suspicious.

I relaxed right away when I saw the commissioner. He was a thin man wearing glasses and dressed in dark clothes. There was nothing scary about him. Fortunately, he seemed to find those above him more important than those below. One sensed that his present relationship with his superiors required him to show proof of cleverness and flexibility, and that he was trying to satisfy their expectations rather than modestly acquire a good reputation by conscientiously performing his duties. I must say that all the police functionaries I'd met were like that. He spoke to us in a paternal voice without once referring to the occupying authorities. He nevertheless made it understood that his job had never been so delicate and that we should make it easy for him. He asked us to put ourselves in his position. Finally, he made us promise not to make trouble again.

At this moment a rather ridiculous scene took place. Everyone was agreeing to each of his requests when one of the women began yelling. It was obvious, she was saying, that he didn't know what it was like, that he wasn't the one who did the shopping, that he didn't have a family to feed. He must not be so bad off with the Krauts. The other women made her quiet down, telling her that you had to recognize when you were dealing with a good person.

A faint smile hovered on the commissioner's lips. He had the intelligent self-control of those who are attacked by inferiors. Finally, he gave us permission to leave. I took a deep breath. I was about to walk out, restraining myself from seeming hurried and not wishing to be the first to go, when suddenly I heard, "Excuse me sir."

I turned around. For the first time, the commissioner's eyes were on me. I looked at the other man, as if this word sir could have been referring to him.

"I'm speaking to you," the commissioner said, motioning for me to approach. I turned toward the others, hoping for some gesture of solidarity, but no one seemed at all concerned about my plight. I was completely alone. Even though they were all strangers, I felt abandoned. They left one by one, as if nothing were happening. Just when I thought I was out of danger, my greatest fear was coming true. I felt a trickle of cold sweat run down my sides. I smiled. "Certainly," I said.

The commissioner waited for everyone to leave. The last person hadn't closed the door; he motioned for me to shut it. I obeyed with exaggerated compliance, as if eager to please. A few seconds later, the commissioner stood up and left me alone in the room. Then he came back and left again. Finally he returned to his seat. His voice was instantly soothing. I wasn't as worried as I might have been. Increasingly I had the impression that this commissioner was an honest man and that if he were put in the position of having to turn in a Frenchman he would know how to get around it. The only thing that worried me was whether my being a Frenchman would be eclipsed by my appearance and whether the commissioner would see me only as a danger to society. No, I was going too far. Things weren't that serious. I was imagining things. This was an insignificant affair, the kind of raid that takes place a thousand times a day in the markets, nothing more.

But shortly thereafter he asked for my papers, even though he hadn't asked for anyone else's. I pulled out my wallet. I had a birth certificate supplied by the IVth arrondissement municipal hall, a soccer team membership card of no official value, and my infamous service record. On this record, they had written that I had been mobilized from Saint-Germain. But I had no paper proving that I had been a prisoner. Instinctively, like a criminal throwing his weapon away, I had gotten rid of anything that might indicate I had been in Germany. I didn't have a demobilization card either.

I showed him my papers, opening the military record myself. But the commissioner closed it, wanting to read it from the beginning. I comforted myself with the thought that functionaries, police, anyone whose job it is to examine papers, never discover the weak points.

The commissioner examined my record at length, but I could see that he was unable to reconstruct anything because there was so much written inside. In the end, he stopped at the sheet that had been added. It contained an error that had always disturbed me, an incorrect date. They had put 1940 instead of 1939. The commissioner didn't even notice, which made me feel relieved since, strange as it might seem, I worried as much about errors made by the bureaucrats themselves as about my little cover-ups.

The commissioner finally returned my papers to me, but forgot one on his desk. I didn't dare mention it right away. "You don't have anything else?" he asked me. I shook my head. I was relaxed now. My greatest fear hadn't materialized: I was afraid that the mere sight of my name would startle him. But since it didn't, since he was going into details, since I already sensed him backing down, I was no longer afraid.

When I left I ran into one of the women who had been taken into the commissioner's office with me. Our meeting should have created a certain bond between us. She should have smiled at me, she should have appeared to be glad that everything had turned out so well. I made a friendly sign and was amazed by her stupid, distant air.

Chapter 10

As a result of going from place to place, I was beginning to feel I was wearing people out, that everyone knew I had a habit of showing up unexpectedly; even when I went someplace I'd never been I had the impression I would be greeted as if I were returning for the tenth time.

And yet I wasn't a difficult guest. A room with a mattress, a table and a chair, someplace quiet, was all I asked. When I spoke of this, no one could believe I hadn't yet found what I sought. My needs were so modest, so simple.

I sat on a bench opposite a large café, like those passersby who want to listen to the music without eating anything. I knew that here no one would look my way. I watched people. Indeed, it was actually funny how, just as they passed in front of me, they would automatically turn their heads toward the terrace.

At noon I wanted to go to a restaurant but was afraid I might inadvertently get mixed up in a black market affair. I was hungry. I still didn't have a food card. At a certain point all these obstacles begin to get on your nerves.

It was incredible that I couldn't find a room, someone to say, "Come stay with me." How many times had I slept at friends' houses before the war, simply because the metro had stopped running. Today, it was impossible. Everything was impossible, eating, buying a raincoat, everything.

In the days when I was painting, I'd had no trouble finding a place to live or eat when my father had cut me off. I lived off my artist friends just as I had seen so many people live off soldiers during the war. I had slept in attics, or wherever I could.

I headed for Montparnasse. But everything had changed. This familiar neighborhood was as closed to me as the others! I told myself I had to start from scratch, make new friends, and so on. My mistake, I realized, was thinking that I would find things just as I had left them. The kind of people who would have helped me no longer existed. It's tragic to make these discoveries at nightfall. I was afraid of being outdoors. The shop owners had a way of dropping their metal curtains that sent chills down my spine. It sounded like a riot was about to break out.

When you're at a dead end, you re-examine all the possibilities that you've already rejected. You're surprised to find that you've been looking at things harshly. There was nothing really wrong with going back to the same people I thought I'd left forever.

Suddenly, the thought of simply returning to the rue Victor-Massé, to Charles' house, came to mind. But an unexpected feeling of pride held me back. I wondered whether one should take pride into account when one's life is in danger. After all, what difference did it make what people thought of me! Such concerns might be valid when you're sure you're going to live. But today! The main thing was to defend yourself.

So I went back to Charles's. I apologized for leaving. I said that I had been frightened. But to my surprise, as soon as I was back in the little apartment I felt exactly the same anxiety as before. My escapade had done me no good. I thought about leaving again. Another problem then came to mind. Should I follow my impulses or not? It was becoming increasingly clear that there was something wrong with me. If I kept changing my mind, I would be heading for trouble. I tried to be on good terms with everyone, but the importance I placed on my safety forced me to act outrageously. Should I stay with Charles against my will? I thought about it, but after several hours I realized that it was impossible for a man in danger to live according to a rational line of thought and that the only way to restore my soul's tranquility was to follow my instincts. Yet Charles had been a good host. I must say that those who wish to control us always react the same way in these situations.

They never get angry. They act as if they've always respected our independence.

I left the next day. I sensed that I was leaving behind a difficult situation, one that wasn't to my advantage. But when you're young, you fall prey to the illusion that the world is much larger than it is. You think that all you have to do is leave in order to never again see the people with whom you've acted badly, and that it'll all be forgotten.

I thought more and more about leaving France. Ever since I'd been living in a rooming house behind the Pantheon, rue du Cardinal-Lemoine to be exact, where my father had put in a word for me and where until now, no doubt for that reason, they hadn't asked to see any papers, I'd lingered before a large map hung in the hall.

All the lightly colored portions were those that remained for the Germans to conquer. I never tired of looking at them, even though they were always the same. It seemed to me that I was finally going to find a way to travel to the regions that were still free. I never did. I kept returning to the zone between Marseille and the Pyrénées. I saw myself crossing into Spain by night on a small boat, and from there heading to England. Another zone also attracted my attention: the Menton area. There might be a way to escape from there. "What if I did the opposite of what everyone else does?" I asked myself one day. I sensed that what made any escape difficult was that too many people were looking for the same thing. There were too many people everywhere in fact. I noticed this once food became scarce. In the beginning, I had been convinced I would always get by. I had pictured myself hunting out isolated grocers, making arrangements with them, winning their sympathy, and so on. But it didn't take me long to figure out that everyone was using these tactics which I had imagined I was the only one to have thought of, and that wherever I went someone else had been there before. It was impossible to be the first, to reach an understanding with someone first. It was impossible to obtain what I had so often and so easily obtained in peace time: small personal favors. I who thought I had a certain gift of persuasion, who thought I was easily liked, was surprised to find that everyone had this same gift and was as well liked as I was. When I heard that there were so many people in Marseille that you couldn't find a place to stay, I felt ill. I was blocked on all sides, not just by the police, but by my peers, by the masses, by all the French. The challenge was to find something on this map of the world that no one had thought of. One day, I found it. No one had dreamed of this. I was the only one to have this idea. I would be able to move freely. When asking for something, no one would have been there first. All I had to do was escape in the direction of the enemy, all I had to do was cross back through Germany and go to Russia. For several days, I was obsessed with this idea. I was so convinced it was brilliant that I was angry at myself for not thinking of it sooner; someone else might have thought of it by now. I found comfort in it. There were so many borders, mountains, rivers, and plains before my eyes that there seemed no reason why one day I shouldn't escape. But sometimes I felt I couldn't even leave Paris.

One morning, I decided to have lunch at a certain suburban restaurant near the aerodrome which I had been told was frequented by aviators who shuttled between France and England. I didn't know anyone, but I figured that my wanting to go to England was just like any such aspiration in normal times. You have to force yourself to approach the people who, because of their profession or their situation, can give you information, advise you, help you. People must be leaving France by plane.

I paced back and forth in front of the small restaurant. One thing I hate is pretending to look for something other than what people know very well you're after. From inside, watching me walk back and forth, they might have been saying, "Here's another one. He's a shy one. You think he'll come in? How much do you want to bet?" I, in the meantime, was pretending to be waiting for a bus. When it came, in order to show why I wasn't getting on, I would look at my watch as if I were expecting someone. After an hour, I told myself that I was being ridiculous, that it would have been better to go inside right away, that by hesitating so long I had drawn attention to myself. I thought of coming back the next day. But that was too soon. I would have had to wait at least a week; images don't disappear so quickly from people's minds. They would say, "Oh boy! here's the guy from yesterday. He took his time deciding."

Finally, I took advantage of an arriving group of diners and followed them into the restaurant. I sat next to two men who were finishing their lunch. What intimidated me a little was that I didn't fit in; not that I was dressed any worse than the others, but they all had an athletic, determined look. They spoke loudly, they all knew each other, they were like actors, journalists, or policemen when they gather at their regular café, they seemed to think the rest of the world didn't exist. I felt like an intruder. But the fact that no one was paying attention to me restored my confidence. The waiter came to serve me. I was glad to see that he was one of those waiters who makes no distinctions between customers, who has equal respect for anyone who sits down at a table. I didn't move. I was determined to wait for an opportunity, and especially not to seek one out. I was pretty proud of myself. I couldn't help thinking of some of my fellow prisoners. If they could see me here, I'm sure they would find me superbly daring, I who was always saying that I couldn't do things of this sort. Neither Baumé, Pelet, nor any of the others would ever have attempted such an exploit!

I soon succeeded in engaging my two neighbors in

conversation. They actually were aviators. I asked them a few questions, but soon noticed that they were starting to grow wary of me. I sometimes caught a look of caution in their eyes entirely foreign to the conversation at hand. I suddenly had the impression that they were wondering if I were from the police. It gave me a strange feeling to inspire this same fear in others that everyone inspired in me. The extraordinary thing was that I then grew afraid. I was the one they feared and I was the one who was afraid. I was afraid they would take me for an instigator, that they would want to teach me a lesson, that I would be obliged to call the police for help and that instead of defending me, appalled at my spying, the police would side with these men, who would seem sympathetic by comparison.

Chapter 11

I was not discouraged by this failure. I had been acting childish. If I was so eager to leave, I should simply visit my mother in Brittany. She lived in Quintin, on the Côtes-du-Nord. I hadn't seen her for a long time anyway and I would no doubt find a way to embark from there. But getting on a train scared me. During my escape, I had shown no lack of courage. But great danger, once passed, makes us fearful. Once we think we're safe, it's hard to put our lives on the line again. Today, just buying a train ticket seemed perilous to me. I had asked around, but still didn't know exactly how security worked on the trains, nor if Quintin was within a forbidden zone or not. The information I got varied according to the kind of person I asked. Some told me: "You've got to be kidding, they have more important things to do," others: "You can't get on a train without having them on your back."

Nevertheless, as soon as I was in the train station, I felt calmer. I had the impression, amid the general activity, and especially considering the complications that police measures would have brought to running the trains, that I had worried for nothing. None of the travelers seemed to be worried about the possibility of a security check, for instance. They were hastening here and there, complying with all sorts of regulations, even protesting when the regulations made them late. No one was thinking about the Germans. Had anything out of the ordinary occurred, everyone would have acted shocked. I had the comforting feeling of being one of the masses. I felt I was being treated with consideration, given special advantages, the kind of advantages given only to those one knows to be neither bitter nor angry. They weren't going to instigate a movement of widespread discontent for the two or three suspicious characters who might have slipped into this peaceful, benevolent crowd, a crowd that, while occasionally impatient, was well aware of its privileges.

I climbed into a car that was already full. All these people made me feel secure. How could they work their way through the corridor to examine papers? They would have had to ask everyone to get off the train. There were women, children, elderly citizens, all people who wouldn't have understood such a thing. And then, it was a pleasant feeling to know I was surrounded by innocent people. The Germans seemed only too pleased that everything was working so well, and all by itself, despite their presence. They only had to pretend to be watching over things. It occurred to me that they weren't going to risk interfering with this smooth operation, for fear that afterward it would be too difficult to put everything back in motion.

And besides, this crowd dispelled any somber thoughts, with its mix of vigor, independence, submissiveness, and especially with the feeling that emanated from it that there were some things you simply couldn't ask it to do.

Sometimes, however, a troubling thought came to mind. That suddenly, in one of those massive operations they don't flinch at undertaking, the Germans would try to find out what this crowd was made of, that, without concern for the cries and distress, they would slowly examine each of us.

Until now I had lived day to day, without thinking about the future. But now I had a goal. I wasn't taking this trip simply to hide in a calm isolated corner of the world. The thought of leaving France was anchored in me. I hadn't spoken to anyone about it. People are surprising in that they are not only afraid of being asked something, but of knowing something. Simply knowing something gives an impression of complicity that terrifies them.

I arrived in Quintin the next morning.

In a situation like mine, you can't imagine how comforting it is to have a goal, even an unattainable one. The goal before my eyes was a foreign land, that is to say, safety and freedom. And now that I had taken the first step, I was already growing afraid that I would be caught at the very moment when my efforts were about to be crowned with success.

I sat on a bench, next to a bandstand. It was childish, but ever since I had obtained a trench coat with a belt, not new but in good condition, a pair of brown shoes, not new either but not yet resoled, and a grey felt hat, I felt like a man and my capacities were doubled.

I was in no hurry to see my mother again. I wanted to think about this first step I was taking toward the unknown, toward freedom. Nearby, young people were pushing one another, running, hitting one another, laughing like fools. In other circumstances, I would have changed places like an old man. I have such a lofty idea of my youth, of what I was when I was twenty, that all young people today seem unbelievably crude, for time, in embellishing the past, embellishes the person one was as well. But that day I was so happy I didn't move. I thought I could smell the sea air. I was going to find a way to leave. And perhaps the sailors, on the boat on which I would set sail, would resemble these youths.

I noticed two German petty officers taking a stroll, stopping from time to time, admiring a facade or a statue like simple tourists. Suddenly I remembered my exact situation. I was no longer happy with what I had. I had arrived at the dangerous point at which one says it is better to risk death than to live in mediocrity. No matter how often I told myself that this new state of mind was risky, that I should just stay put, wait for the end of the war, it was stronger than I was, I wanted to take a chance, I wanted to undertake something grandiose. I recalled my idea of happiness at the time of my escape. It was so simple. I had pictured myself staying in a room without going out, without seeing anyone for as long as I had to, and this had seemed to me a marvelous life. And now, I was going to try to leave the country, risk being recaptured, and shot.

Finally after a few days, when I had grown accustomed to my new life, my courage grew. I began going out regularly, showing my face in town. The big difference between here and Paris was that here everyone knew me. If something were to happen to me, I would be forced to act a certain way: my response would have to be that of a man everyone knew. I couldn't run away anymore. I would have to explain myself, to protest against "unjust accusations," to defend myself, to use my mother's connections.

But nothing bad happened and every day I gained confidence.

Yet this situation was not without some terrible frights. I felt exposed as if I were on stage. My sole protection (and this is hard to live with when one has few illusions about men) was the kind of human respect that keeps people from interrogating you, from hampering your movements and actions, even when they find you suspicious. I had already experienced this in Paris when, though I knew I was being followed, I was surprised to find that no one questioned me, for fear no doubt of making a mistake.

This sort of respect is fragile. But here it was all I had. Out of sheer determination, I managed to play along with all these people who didn't dare bother with me yet. Sometimes I told myself that I was imagining things, that no one cared about me. But I still didn't dare make a move for fear of provoking my enemies. I strolled around smoking cigarettes—I had met a nice fellow who gave me his ration. I always wanted my mother to come with me. I told myself that all this was temporary, that after a month had passed I could begin seriously dealing with my departure.

You needed a serious reason to obtain authorization to go to the coast. For the first time since my escape, I had to deal with the German authorities. I had hesitated a long time. A Kraut who had spoken to me one day in a café told me he had a friend in Rennes, that I should talk to him.

I wondered whether I might have been better off going to Rennes. It is a strange feeling, in a case like this, when it appears that it would have been in one's best interests to go to a stranger, an enemy, rather than to one's own mother. I told myself I had been silly. I had followed my instincts instead of reasoning. What was done was done. But it was inexcusable that I hadn't tried to get other addresses. It could have been so simple. This Kraut officer had wanted only to help me. It's a mistake I always make. I imagine that just moving on excuses me from pursuing a line of inquiry, and that in another city I won't need anything or anyone.

I decided to go to the Kommandantur. It is impossible to express how difficult this was for me. It wasn't only fear. It was pride. How could I, a Frenchman, ask for something from a German? It disgusted me beyond belief.

Finally I was able to go to Saint-Brieuc. My mother had spoken highly of a notary named Mr. Buttin. She admired this type of man, impressive yet simple. Since I also appreciate this type of person, I was sure that we were going to get along beautifully.

First I went for a walk by the sea. I thought about the decorations my father had received in the other war, about his extraordinary courage which had all been for nothing and which surprised me now that I saw what war was.

I sat down in an isolated spot. I felt enormous pleasure looking at the sea. Nothing is more moving when you've been a prisoner. In Germany, I had gazed at the countryside through barbed wire, but the flat and motionless earth hadn't given me the feeling of freedom that emanates from continually moving waves.

I went to the notary's office. A color print of Marshall Pétain, his eyes so sadly blue, occupied the place of honor. I'm not sure in which historical painting I had seen a dead man whose foot, in an effort at realism, poked out of the sheet. There was a similar painting on another wall. Despite the solemnity of the office, a Cinzano thermometer splashed with color was hung near the window.

The notary was a man of about sixty, very agreeable, with no apparent bitterness. One sensed he had the narrowest views imaginable, and that as long as one didn't question them he would remain charming.

His colleagues gave the same impression. Everything in this study seemed to say that though more candid and honest than others, they were still just as fair and charitable. They would talk to anyone as long as you were polite and well bred. But if you fell short on your end, watch out! There would be no more help and recommendations on your behalf.

We went to see a plot of land that belonged to my mother over which there was some litigation. On the way the notary explained the procedure my mother had to follow to win her case.

We were in the process of measuring the plot when an incredible incident occurred. Two Germans approached us and asked us to follow them. They thought we were spies! On the way to see the Kommandantur, the notary kept repeating, "This is completely ridiculous!" I wasn't as worried as I would have expected. I had no doubt that the notary, with all his connections, would easily prove his innocence. Besides, the Germans didn't seem to consider us dangerous at all. After taking our names, they apologized. My only concern was when they noticed

I wasn't from Saint-Brieuc. I went home completely calm. The next day, when I went back to see the notary, he complained that they had come after him again that evening. He was nervous. He was afraid of being arrested. With Germans, he said, anything was possible. But I personally didn't feel threatened. I had the feeling that anything compromising in my past was overshadowed by this new incident, and the notary's fear ended up reassuring me. It proved that my particular case wasn't in question. But suddenly I began trembling. It seemed to me that I was suffering from a failing common to all men. The danger wasn't always the same. They might arrest me for an entirely new reason that had nothing to do with what I feared. And even though it was new, the consequences might be just as serious.

I told my mother the story. She asked me some questions and gave me all sorts of advice. Had I dared, I would have run away or hidden. But that was exactly what everyone was advising me not to do. By behaving that way, I would be admitting I was a spy. I couldn't run away. And the obligation to stay, to continue to live as if nothing had happened, threw me into an unspeakably nervous state. My only protection was the human respect I had sensed upon my arrival, which dictates that even when a person is suspicious, you don't dare question him, you let him come and go.

Finally, without telling anyone, I left for Paris.

Chapter 12

I didn't like being away from Paris. I always had the impression that I wouldn't be able to go back. When the train stopped in Versailles on the return from Brittany, I almost got off to see my father. I had been thinking about it during the entire trip. But I didn't feel like talking about myself all over again. I wanted to forget everything, to be alone, and most of all to get to Paris as quickly as possible. As soon as I left the train station, where police were posted every twenty meters, I felt a tremendous sense of relief. No matter how often I told myself that I lived behind the Pantheon (I always told myself that I lived behind something) the protection of this monument seemed quite illusory to me. But I was in Paris.

I returned to the rooming house on the rue du Cardinal-Lemoine. An old woman was reading in the lobby. The paneling and wall paper were discolored, but the dirt was only superficial. Naturally the housekeeping wasn't kept up as in a private apartment. But the basics were tended to every day. And I can't think of anything more pleasant than living in a place where all the details of daily life, while not going unsupervised by the mistress of the house, are considered unimportant. You could open the library and take a book without anyone saying a word. The men might have been considered overly polite, the way people are who live communally without knowing one another and who make a point of leaving a good impression. There was an aroma of bourgeois cuisine (the aroma was always better than the food itself) throughout the house. The mistress of the house was in the process of paying the washerwoman, a strange person who acted the part of a merchant unchanged by events, who kept the same prices and continued her service exactly as before. There was a safe in the closet-like room that served as an office. A decorated elderly gentleman was waiting to speak to the proprietress. A chambermaid was going from one person to the next, asking each guest if his towels had been changed. She asked me too. It's childish, but this question made me very happy. I realized my fears were stupid, that she wouldn't have asked me if something had happened in my absence. It was eight o'clock in the evening. I waved to Madame Meunier. She was one of those people whose honesty is never in doubt, and whom serious gentlemen—because they are alone, because they don't know how to take care of themselves, because they need advice—protect in a disinterested fashion. These gentlemen worried me some.

The next day, I received a letter from my father asking me to come to Versailles. A curious incident occurred as I was paying my bill. Madame Meunier asked me if I wanted a receipt. I told her that she shouldn't bother. A chambermaid, at this moment, spoke to her about something or other. When she returned to me, having no doubt forgotten her question and my answer, she took a pen and began writing up a bill. I repeated that she shouldn't bother. She responded, "Oh! it's no bother, I've already written it." Then, strangely, I said to her: "No, I don't want one. Don't write me a receipt. I'd rather you didn't . . ." It was incomprehensible. This little piece of paper was unimportant. My name wasn't even on it. But it made me feel so good to leave no trace of my passage that I couldn't resist. Madame Meunier looked at me in amazement. This is how, for an insignificant detail, I sometimes managed to arouse suspicion.

I went away mumbling confusedly, furious with myself. Once outside, I left my suitcase at a café. The owner gave me a lot of trouble about it too; in the end he told me, in a truly unfriendly tone, that he wasn't taking responsibility for anything.

Over the next few days, my father brought me on visits to four or five people he knew in Versailles. We always had little fights before going inside; he wanted me to tell my story myself and I wanted him to tell it. I said it would have more weight that way. He said that people would be much more interested in me than in him. I didn't insist, since I realized that merely accompanying me on these visits was already an immense sacrifice for my father, who took pride in never asking anything of anyone. Each time we entered someone's home, his nervousness pained me. He would try to hide it from me; he blamed himself as if it were a lack of affection on his part. I often noticed a similar attitude among relatives from whom one has been separated by circumstances and who, in the interim, have established friendships with people who in reality mean less to them than we do. First he took me to see those friends about whom he cared the least. Then when, precisely for this reason, these friends had no desire whatsoever to help me, he was obliged to bring me to those he cared about the most. Before going inside, he gave me numerous instructions. The one he repeated over and over was that I shouldn't harp on the dramatic side of the situation. I shouldn't seem worried, I should speak as if anecdotally about what had happened to me, I shouldn't provide any details that might scare anyone, I should give the impression of being just like everyone else.

 He was so afraid that I wouldn't obey him that as soon as we were in the company of these people who could so easily get a bad impression, and despite his desire to see me personally engage them in conversation, he couldn't stop himself from telling my story, but sugar coating it so much that it wouldn't have occurred to anyone that I needed help of any kind. When we left, they hadn't grasped what we wanted. I would look my father in the eyes to try to tell him that it wasn't enough. He would push me outside, as if to suggest that he would explain things, as if without my knowing it something had happened that changed everything. Once on the street he would explain that we had come at a bad time. He would tell me an incomprehensible story. Finally, he'd say that we would tell them next time.

When it finally became apparent that all these visits would never come to anything, my father rather mysteriously announced that there was still the high school. This made me very happy. I had never dared talk to him about the high school. Upon my return, however, it had seemed to me that there was no better place for me. I could work and be protected at the same time. I don't know why, but being involved with a group of people has always appealed to me. The only drawback was that I sensed this solution was difficult for my father. Just introducing me to the director was devastating for him.

We agreed to operate in a different manner. My father would talk about me first. I would only be introduced if he had the impression that I stood a chance. I told him that this time he had to clearly explain the situation. His answer was vague. He didn't want to talk about my escape. He wanted to simply say that I needed work, that he would be very pleased if they could give me a job of any sort. I pointed out that if he didn't even mention that I had escaped I was of no interest and there was no reason why anyone would help me. He claimed otherwise. He had been teaching at this same high school for seventeen years. In seventeen years he had never asked for anything. If today he asked a favor for his son, I could be certain that it wouldn't be refused.

Thus my father spoke about me to the director, but what I had expected to happen happened. They didn't need anyone. This failure had a big effect on my father. He was typical of people who never ask for anything: they imagine that when the day comes that they ask a favor, people will be so grateful for their discretion in the past they will go out of their way to comply. Which is why having his request refused, which revealed how little he mattered to others, threw him into a rage, the likes of which I would never have thought him capable. He was freed of all scruples. His thoughts turned bitter. If this was the way they were going to act, he was no longer bound to them at all. And just when I thought he'd gotten over it, he told me the next day that I had been right, that he would go back to see the director to tell him my exact situation. If at that point the director continued to refuse me, faced with such selfishness, with such cowardice, my father would resign.

Such a turnabout worried me. Since my escape, I had become terrified by people's unpredictable reactions, fits of anger, or bursts of enthusiasm. My father's announcement that he wouldn't accept being rejected the one time he made a request, that he would give the director a piece of his mind, that he would make a scene if he had to, all because of me, sent a chill down my spine. I told him that he mustn't do a thing, that he should pretend he hadn't noticed; if he responded, he might get into a conversation that could prove dangerous for me. My father didn't understand my caution. It wasn't just a matter of himself, or of his relationship with the directors, but of me, his son, the son of a teacher with seventeen years of service. I insisted that he remain calm, and whereas he had been so reluctant to help me, I suddenly found myself obliged to stop him from doing so.

In the midst of all this, my father learned that one of his friends, whose name he wouldn't tell me, had been hiding a young relative in her apartment on the rue Maurepas for several days. This young man had conducted himself admirably.

Before the war, he had written a novel. It was about the adventures of a woman of great beauty living among savages. In 1940, condemned to death by the Germans, he had succeeded in escaping. Recaptured while distributing leaflets, stupidly, by an old crank who had seen him putting one in his mailbox, he had managed to slip away before being identified. He then made his way to England. His wife was arrested. He returned to France to turn himself in. Once his wife was safe, he managed to escape again. In the face of such exploits, I felt like a young student next to a great scholar.

My father added that this young man had been compelled to procure a false identity card, without making the slightest allusion to the difficulties involved. This surprised me. Even I who found it quite natural to have false papers would never have thought to say that I had been compelled to get them. And the extraordinary thing was that I, who had worked hard to get them, without really thinking I was obliged to do so, had found only mediocre ones.

My father thought that a meeting could only be beneficial to both of us. He was convinced that I would be of interest to this hero and he thought that with all his experience, this hero could give me some useful advice. And, it has to be said, my poor father could never resist anything that might both please others and flatter his ego. I objected that it might not be a good time for me to meet a man who was wanted by the police, that in reality we had nothing in common, that I would feel extremely uncomfortable being presented to him as having also acted heroically. My only goal was to not get caught, to save my life. I didn't feel up to any new undertakings. I wanted to be as invisible as possible. But my father insisted. He said that all those who, like us, had given such shining proof of their patriotism, should know one another, should unite, combine efforts, that this admirable man didn't profess to be a hero any more than I did. I finally accepted so as not to put my father in an awkward position. He had done so much for me that I didn't want to back out just when he could be proud to be seen with his son.

We traveled to the rue Maurepas in great secrecy. There I was surprised to find that this friend was none other than Mademoiselle de Boiboissel, whom we had seen a few days earlier and who, at my father's request that she hide me in her apartment, had responded that she had no room. I felt a certain bitterness, but quickly chased it away. It would have been absurd for me to get angry at a stranger for not having done for me what she did for one of her relatives. Several people were conversing in hushed voices in the salon, a large old-fashioned room. They looked like people gathered to discuss a serious issue that hadn't yet been mentioned. I sat to the side. Jean de Boiboissel, the centerpiece of this gathering, hadn't yet arrived. I was excessively intimidated at the thought of the conversation I was going to have with him, of the questions he was going to pose, of the interest he would take in me. I felt so insignificant next to him, I felt that my adventures were so uninteresting. And what bothered me most of all was feeling my father at my side so proud of me. Being fond of my father, I was always afraid that my insignificance would be brought to his attention as a result of some sort of incident, something he couldn't help but notice, and that it would make him suffer. Finally, the hero arrived. He entered so discreetly you wouldn't have thought it was him. Even though everyone had been talking about what he had done, his character, his courage, no one moved. When he kissed his cousin, she didn't even stop talking. The conversation continued and these people who had struck me as if they were waiting for something continued on as before. I remained frozen. Though I was often in the position, out of necessity, of having to say that I had performed acts I hadn't exactly performed, I was afraid someone would notice and that instead of the usual indulgence shown to braggarts, I would suddenly be treated as suspicious, that things might escalate. This was always my fear whenever I didn't share the same opinions as the person I was talking to.

Then I realized that the heroism I had imagined everyone was going to discuss would remain absent from the conversation, and I was delighted. Nevertheless, the hero peered at me with particular intensity as we were saying our goodbyes, keeping my hand in his for a few instants longer than is usual, wishing to show me in this way that we were of the same family. I was overwhelmed. All the hostility I had felt faced with his apparent arrogance turned into profound and sincere admiration. My father, who hadn't noticed anything, criticized me on the way home for not striking up a conversation. Like a young girl whose parents would have liked her to be friendlier to a potential suitor, I kept what had happened to myself and merely responded that the occasion had not presented itself. After this meeting I was aware for the first time of the potential nobility of my situation, and it became clear to me how much my behavior, since my escape, was out of synch with what might be expected of me. I felt I could be useful to my country and thereby escape the horrible fear and solitude in which I was wallowing. But almost immediately the risks came to mind. I examined them one by one, but it struck me that though they were numerous, I would at least know what they were, that ultimately I would be safer than in my hiding place where the slightest noise made me jump. Danger, real danger, is comforting. I told my father that I wanted to meet the hero again, that I too wanted to make myself useful, and that if given the opportunity to serve my country, I would be the happiest man alive.

Chapter 13

The following afternoon, I returned to Mademoiselle de Boiboissel's. I felt like a different person ever since I had made this grand decision. The day before I had trembled at the thought of going to the rue Maurepas. As we were approaching, I had given my father a scare by telling him I saw people watching the house. My father, who wasn't yet accustomed to my constant fears, stopped abruptly. He took me by the arm, dragged me down a side street, then down another. When we had walked several hundred meters like this, a little bothered at seeing him take so seriously one of these remarks I had been making mechanically for the last few months, I told him that I had probably been mistaken. "Oh, certainly not," he answered. He forced me to hide in a little niche. Then he went back alone to the rue Maurepas. When he returned, he told me that indeed I had been mistaken. I knew this, but what surprised me was that he hadn't commented on how fearful I'd become. He was convinced that if there was someone who could never take too many precautions, it was surely me.

I visited with Jean de Boiboissel in the same salon as the day before. I immediately told him my decision. He asked me where I worked. I told him I wasn't working. He asked me other questions. I sensed, each time, that my answers were disappointing to him. In the end, he told me that he didn't see what I could do. I was surprised. I asked him why my good will couldn't be put to use. He said that good will wasn't important, that it wasn't a matter of good will, but of the possibilities that each of us might have in his sphere, that a simple railwayman was a hundred times more valuable than I was. It sounded as if he was looking for ways to make me feel bad, to hurt me. I was completely taken aback. Then, admittedly, I put my foot in my mouth. "But, what can I do?" I cried. He looked at me in astonishment. I sensed that if there was any doubt left in his mind as to my usefulness, it had vanished with these words. He told me with seeming kindness that he wasn't qualified to answer me, that I knew better than he what I should do. Wishing to redeem myself, I reminded him that I wanted to serve, to be useful, that I was ready to sacrifice my life, to accomplish the most dangerous mission. He smoothed his hair with his fingertips. Coldly, he told me that he didn't like for people to talk about sacrificing their lives. He wasn't questioning my desire to do good, but I mustn't forget that there was nothing extraordinary about this. It was natural. Everyone felt that way. Soon we were all going to be able to act. For the moment, he wished to repeat, only those who could harm the Germans—because of their positions or jobs—were useful to the country.

I left him shortly afterward. I must have fallen in his esteem; he didn't keep my hand in his as he had the day before. When it comes to friendship, love or money, warriors, ordinarily considered reckless, are the most cautious people in the world.

After I left, I went for a walk in the park, despite the many Germans there. I felt defeated. I had been unable to take advantage of all I had endured and all I had done. No one believed me. How happy I would be, right now, to possess the very proof of my heroism I had so carefully destroyed!

Perhaps this hero had already had frequent dealings with men like me and knew what to expect. I felt as if I had just been caught lying. That was why he had been so cold. I had wanted to sound interesting, to raise myself to his level. I chased away all these thoughts a few seconds later. My humble position disgusted me. "What a creep," I mumbled. Yes, he was the kind of man I despise. One often encounters such men in life. It is impossible to make human contact with them. "They take themselves too seriously," I thought. That night, I told my father what had happened. I told him what I thought of this hero. My father found that he had been perfectly reasonable. He didn't understand my anger at all. I told him this man thought too much of himself. My father said he had the right, that no one could hold it against him after what he had done.

I must not have made such a bad impression after all since as a result of this meeting I went to live with a friend of Mademoiselle de Boiboissel's, a Madame de Vauvillers. I was more and more confused. My room was exceptionally humid. Not one piece of furniture stood straight on the uneven floor. The bed linen, too, was in pitiful condition. The sky-blue silk of the bedspread was worn so thin a kind of grey stuffing showed through. Branches struck against the windowpanes when the wind blew. The first days, they made me jump each time. I hated myself for this childish fear, as if my other fears weren't enough. Eventually, however, I became accustomed to this little Louis XVI house, set below ground level on a deserted street. One thing I didn't like was how Madame de Vauvillers would repeat my name when she spoke to me. She was constantly trying to get to know me better. She would ask me questions about my family, my activities, and to show her friends that she hadn't made the same mistake she had the previous year she repeated everything

I said, omitting nothing, revealing everything, so that I couldn't be confused with my predecessor. The latter, a tax inspector, had been arrested one morning at the home of Madame de Vauvillers for having embezzled large sums. The old woman had sworn never to rent his room again. But after my father had pleaded with her for months on end, she decided to accept me. I must say that when I heard this story, I felt very ill at ease. I couldn't help but imagine the horrible trauma a second arrest in her home would be.

Luckily most of the visitors were just old ladies. Yet occasionally a gentleman would stop by. When I took part in conversations I was always on the alert, since Madame de Vauvilliers and her friends often talked about people I didn't know but whom I guessed, by certain comments, didn't live as retiringly as their friend. They spoke of people in high places who had just made major decisions and who were in the midst of making others; it never failed to worry me when their arrival was announced. Madame de Vauvillers was determined that I should make their acquaintance, which I tried each time to avoid since, other than that we never took to one another, I had the impression that once I left they would ask a string of questions about me. I was always afraid that these very proper gentlemen would want to spare Madame de Vauvilliers a second mishap, that they would generously offer to gather information about me, not because the old woman was particularly curious, but because of the way people in high places love to offer their services. I didn't dare share my fears with my father. He was determined to do all he could for me, but would have liked for nothing bad to ever happen. Every time I pointed out a new danger he lost his head. He acted as if he should go into hiding as well. Or at least that's what he wanted me to think, for I suspected that he hammed it up a bit, that he was doing this to get me to stay where I was and be content with what I had.

What characterized the people I saw during this time was that they were always talking about vengeance and what they were going to do to Germany. They were always talking about the Krauts, and it pained me to see how powerless they were. All they could do to show their disdain was make gestures which I was sure the Germans didn't even notice. They were constantly recounting little scenes they had witnessed: a woman who had turned her back on an officer who was offering her his seat, and so on. They valued gestures of this sort. It pained me that such worthless acts could monopolize their thoughts to such an extent. They braced themselves to avoid defeat and everything they did and said showed that they were already far more defeated than they thought. They were very nice to me because I was an escaped prisoner, yet I wasn't at all sure that if they knew exactly what I had done they would have continued to be so kind.

A short while later I decided to leave Versailles. I used

a very simple pretext to avoid causing a scandal. I didn't feel safe. That was all. I didn't go into any details. The strange thing was that each time I spoke about my fears I felt like a deadbeat, like a beggar asking for money from someone who has already lent him some.

When my father saw that I wanted to go back to Paris, he understood this time that he had no choice but to ask me questions, become interested in my fate, try to understand why. I told him that Madame de Vauvillers was very nice but that she was far too interested in me and that she had far too many friends.

My father listened to me attentively; on his face you could see the worries I was causing him contrast with the understanding impression he wanted to give. I sensed that he was suffering terribly, that every word I spoke caused him terrible pain. He was torn between his duty to help me and the fear of a scandal. "If you think you'll be safer in Paris," he said, "don't hesitate."

The next day he came to see me. He was sad, truly sad. I told him there was nothing tragic about my departure, that it was a simple precaution. But he didn't want to let me go. He wanted to write some letters of introduction for me. I went to ask Madame de Vauvillers for an inkwell. When she learned that my father was there, she got very agitated. She brought in a leather blotter and a Bohemian crystal inkwell. I watched my father make a great effort to be pleasant.

Chapter 14

I had been in Paris a short while when I ran into Guéguen. When I thought about this friend, whom after my escape I had found so approachable, so kind and so understanding, he now seemed odd, two-faced and extraordinarily petty. Nothing bad had happened between us. I told myself that I had to fight this tendency to interpret any silence or absence as hostile. On seeing him again, I still found him friendly, kind and understanding.

He asked me what I'd been doing. Deep down, I regretted having left his house. I told him that I was living in a small hotel room, that I was very uncomfortable, that they were growing suspicious because I kept finding excuses not to register. But I was careful not to tell him that I had bought false papers, that my name was no longer René de Talhouet, but Raoul Tinet. I tried to convey how happy I would be to return to his house. I inquired after his mother's health. Had he returned to work now that the studio was free? He seemed to have no inkling of what I wanted. This was only natural. And, in fact, did I really want to go back to his house? We often tend to desire things simply because they are there, and not because we really want them.

A few days later, he asked me to help him prepare for an exhibition. This show of friendship made me very happy.

Though I felt that he would never do anything for me, as soon as he made an overture I forgot my grievances. For I was afraid of everything, afraid of someone changing his opinion of me, afraid of losing friends, and I found kindness towards me infinitely touching.

When the exhibition was over, I returned to see Guéguen anyway. There is nothing more depressing than returning to see someone when you are no longer needed, when you have been thanked at length and there is nothing left to do.

Each time I saw Guéguen I asked him if he had anything for me. One day he asked me if I wanted to live in the suburbs with one of his mother's former seamstresses. According to him, it was just what I needed. The house, although isolated, was surrounded by other homes, which would make my presence less suspicious. It was not at all a provincial atmosphere. Since the woman was advanced in years, provisions were brought to her home.

I told Guéguen that I had no food card and couldn't possibly accept such a favor.

He didn't answer. He told me I would keep the woman company. I raised new objections. He began to get angry. He just wanted to warn me that if I acted with everyone like I was acting with him, I would make enemies. Soon no one would pay attention to me. To which I almost answered that I didn't, in fact, act the same with everyone.

I toned down. So as not to seem like he was forcing me to go to the woman's house, Guéguen gently spoke again about the advantages I would find there. I would want for nothing. I could take nice walks in the area. If I really wanted to live in peace, I couldn't do better. The question was whether I really wanted to hide, or whether I was looking to amuse myself, in which case, naturally, there was no point in insisting.

I sensed that Guéguen found it extraordinary that I was so difficult when it was the woman who should be wary.

I was so annoyed by this phony interest that I began asking Guéguen a series of questions. Was he sure no one would notice me? Did the woman own the house? Who visited her? Were there any disputes surrounding her inheritance? Wouldn't some people consider me a bad advisor? Why would she put me up when she didn't know me?

Guéguen responded patiently to each of my questions. But I kept finding something else. In the end he said, "You'll be better off in your hotel." I told him that wasn't the point. He annoyed me more and more, singing the praises of this old lady whom I could sense he didn't know very well. "Where will you go if you don't go there?" This question made me mad. I said I would always find something, that I had always found something until now. "In that case, let's drop it," he said.

Then I realized I was in no position to act smart. I was a little too quick to lose sight of reality. Though it cost me my pride, I backed up, apologized, and asked him to excuse me, I wasn't always in control of myself. But once I left him, I never went back.

Chapter 15

One morning, I woke with the feeling that all my efforts over the past year hadn't ensured my safety and that in the crummy hotel where I was living, I was in exactly the same situation as when I arrived in Paris. I reminded myself of all the changes I'd been through, all my comings and goings, all my hardships, all my anxieties.

The trouble I'd taken had gotten me nowhere, whereas someone else with far fewer worries might today be completely safe.

Instead of defending himself against imaginary dangers, looking for ever safer lodgings, he would simply have won everyone's trust in the first place he chose, made new friends, made himself loved.

I realized I was always making the same mistake, the mistake of wanting to have things pre-arranged. Basically, I hadn't adapted to circumstances. After a year, I still wouldn't dare open a window, distrusted the concierge, and checked that no one I had contact with was with the police. Since on the one hand I was wanted and on the other hand my goal was to be happy, I should have found a way to reconcile these two realities the way Roger had. With all my moving around, I may have had more opportunities than anyone to organize my life. And now that they were lost, it seemed to me that if I had been smart enough to take advantage of any one of them, I would be at peace. Then suddenly I remembered that dangers are unpredictable. We think we're not at risk and suddenly misfortune crashes upon us. It could have been easily predicted, yet we never gave it a thought. Consequently I spent my time wondering what would happen to me, without realizing that as a result of questioning myself like this, I wound up creating a certain confusion in my mind that prevented me from seeing this eventual danger.

Three weeks had passed since I'd left Versailles when I realized that since my escape I had forgotten to take one very important fact into account, which is that normally my father, no longer receiving any news from me in Germany, would have requested information. By not doing so, he was admitting to the Germans that he wasn't worried about me, that he therefore knew where I was. The next logical step would be to force him to denounce me. Obviously, my father would resist to the end. But like most people in poor health, he might also weaken. You can't predict how people will react on momentous occasions. The most cowardly are sometimes the bravest. I preferred not to find out.

I expressed my fears to my father. It was then that my obsession with danger almost created a real one. In my nervous state, I asked my father to tell the Germans he was worried about not hearing from me.

Fortunately, he did nothing of the kind. He got angry. He thought I was being completely ridiculous. "Fend for yourself," he finally told me.

My father was constantly feeling remorseful. A few days later, he came to see me. As always when he isn't sure of having done the right thing, he immediately announced that he had done some good work for me, that he had even had some luck, that the circumstances had been right. I thought he was talking about Boiboissel. But no. It was Mondanel. It hadn't been necessary to go see him. He had run into him by chance. As a result, he had been able to speak more freely about me. He had been able to ask him to help me out without it seeming premeditated. He had been able to tell him the story of the wounded guards. "Why didn't you tell me that sooner!" Mondanel had cried.

My face became covered with sweat. My father told me I was wrong to get excited, that I had nothing to fear, that he was as sure of Mondanel as of himself. He was waiting for me. He wanted to see me. He was interested in me. I reminded my father that I had asked him never to give the details of what had happened to anyone. He told me that in this particular case I had nothing to worry about, that Mondanel was his friend. My father couldn't stand seeing me live in this state of anxiety any longer.

The next day, we went to lunch at Mondanel's. He wasn't the least bit uncomfortable knowing about the things I hadn't told him. Right away, he took care to express this by being especially kind, no doubt to avoid any misunderstanding and to convince me that the information revealed in my absence hadn't made a bad impression on him. I could relax. He understood perfectly that I hadn't said anything myself, that my father had been obliged to do it for me. Sensing the distress my father's indiscretion had caused me, he added that I shouldn't dramatize things so much, that I could trust him, that he understood my caution and that, now that he knew everything (he no longer made any pretense of not knowing), I had only risen in his esteem. He added, as if it were what I was expecting from him without daring to ask, that he would quietly look into things at the various branches of police headquarters and even at the Criminal Investigation Department. I hadn't dared ask him, but he could guess that was what I wanted. He was going to question whoever was in a position to know something. Finally, I could consider that I had a friend on site and anything that could possibly be done would be done.

As soon as I was alone with my father, I could no longer hide my terror. For as long as the meal had lasted my nerves had been so on edge that without realizing it I had kept my head turned toward Mondanel; now I had a slight pain in my neck from a stiff muscle, as if I had slept in a bad position.

My father was shocked by my lack of faith. He repeated that Mondanel was there when I was born, that he had always been a friend, that he would do more for me even than he had said. He hated empty promises. That was why he had been so reserved. But I could count on him. I grew even more worried. I was afraid now that in the course of his inquiry on my behalf, Mondanel would fail to hide that he knew me, that instead of casually obtaining information, and to interest people more easily, he would say that I was the son of one of his friends. Everyone would sympathize with me. In time, my story would become less of a secret, until one fine day, despite everyone's good intentions and compassion, because of someone's indiscretion, blunder, betrayal, or jealousy, two inspectors would simply come to arrest me. At that point, I had no doubt, they would all have regrets, they would say that wasn't what they had wanted, they would recount what had happened in exhaustive detail, they would work to repair the damage they had involuntarily caused, they would do everything humanly possible to pull me out of the mess they had gotten me into, but in the meantime I would be in prison. It would then come out that none of them were responsible. An unfortunate combination of circumstances had caused this accident. They had taken every imaginable precaution. Nothing had been overlooked. And the best thing was that to a certain extent my unfortunate experience was going to serve a purpose. It would allow them to discover the person responsible for betraying me. They were going to be able to watch him more closely now. And at the first opportunity, they would nab him. Thanks to me, they had proof of a traitor in their midst, and knowing this they would soon expose him. Better still, my father wouldn't even hold a grudge against them. He wouldn't realize that I was in prison because of them; if I complained and reminded him that I had warned him, he would scold me for not knowing who my friends were, he would tell me that I had no right to bring such harsh judgements against people who, at the very moment I was speaking unkindly of them, were doing everything they could to get me out. What could I say to this from the depths of a prison cell?

The next day, I went back to see Mondanel. I had made all sorts of calculations to see if it had already been possible for him to take any action on my behalf. I figured that the day before, on arriving at his office after our lunch, he probably hadn't thought of dealing with my problem.

He had promised to deal with it, but he wasn't really a man who acts immediately, especially since he was planning a particularly delicate operation. He had to wait for the right moment. He couldn't speak to the Criminal Investigation Department about me out of the blue. It was even possible he hadn't given it any thought since we had parted. But you never knew. It's precisely when a favor can hurt us that it is done the fastest. After thinking about it, I figured that the wisest thing was to go see Mondanel again before he had a chance to take action. One afternoon had already passed. That was quite enough.

I arrived at Mondanel's shortly before nine o'clock. This was a terribly unpleasant business for me, especially since I was doing it behind my father's back. Mondanel wanted to be nice to my father, not to me. The truth was he didn't know me. I sensed that at the mere mention of my name when he wasn't expecting me, and so soon after yesterday's lunch, his first thought would be that I was taking advantage or that I was rude. The chambermaid, without recognizing me, asked me to wait. When she didn't come back, I was sure my visit was making a bad impression. Finally she reappeared and very amiably asked me to come in, explaining her long absence by telling me that her master was washing, that she had had to wait herself in order to speak to him, and so forth, giving me an abundance of details that she had obviously been told to pass along. Finally Mondanel appeared. He pretended to be happy to see me. He pointed to a chair. I sensed that he wanted to show me that as far as he was concerned, nothing had changed, that he was still in the same frame of mind as the day before. It was like calling on a person who has made you a promise before that person has contacted you. I told him that I had thought it over, that I was very touched by his offer to help me, but that I thought it was better that he do nothing. He showed no sign of surprise. "You really are being childish," he said. I told him my fears. He said I could have complete faith in him, that he had handled equally serious cases in his life (these words made me feel much better) and that I had absolutely nothing to fear, that I shouldn't forget he'd been my father's friend for thirty years. I told him I found his kindness very touching, but that I still thought that it would be better for me to keep a low profile right now. He was surprised at how afraid I was. I told him, in a confessional tone of voice, that that's the way I was, that I preferred to know nothing, that it wasn't exactly fear, but rather wariness. Still with the same kindness in his voice, Mondanel asked me if I really wanted him to do nothing. I nodded. He told me again, just as kindly, that if I should change my mind, he would gladly put himself at my disposal. I sensed that he didn't want to seem annoyed. I also had to ask him to keep everything my father and I had told him secret. He began to laugh. "My poor boy, do you take me for a child?" I apologized. I told him nevertheless that it was very important. Not daring to ask him to keep the secret again, I tried to do it indirectly. No one must know this secret. But no matter how much I emphasized how important keeping this secret was to me, Mondanel, despite his self-assuredness, had not yet spoken a word nor given me a look to convince me that I could count on his discretion.

As he walked me to the door, speaking, to my mind, quite loudly considering the people who could be in the apartment, I asked him, this time changing the tone of the conversation, almost imploring him, not to speak to anyone about what he knew. I was hoping he would look me in the eyes and squeeze my hand without even answering me; it wasn't an answer I was looking for, but something human to show me that he understood and would keep his word. But once again, he began to laugh. "I'm not going to answer you again," he said, slapping me on the shoulder with a paternal gesture. "If you weren't my best friend's son, I would say that your insistence annoyed me."

Once back on the street, I sensed that I had never been so clumsy. After this visit I had no doubt about it, Mondanel would not keep my secret. I had miscalculated. In trying to touch this man's heart, I had put him on the alert. It was too late now, but I realized that as I was leaving I should have simply said, "Naturally, not a word of this to anyone." "You can count on me," he would have answered in the same tone, shaking my hand. And, indeed, if things had happened that way, I could have counted on him.

Chapter 16

In his youth, my father had given lessons to a large, powerful family, the Riveyre de Seyssacs, one of whose members was a General. My father was in a rather strange position regarding them. For twenty years, despite his pride, he had maintained a relationship with the family, always telling my mother and me that you never knew what could happen in life and that people like them might one day be useful.

But he had never asked them for anything, not in 1914, not when he lost his job, not in any of the difficult circumstances in his life. Nothing had ever seemed serious enough to him to justify it. This is what often happens to proud people like my father.

More and more, I realized that I would never get anywhere and that I was going to wind up getting caught. I had almost no money left. I no longer dared live at anyone's house because each time, after a very short while, something would happen. And I couldn't find what I was looking for, a room that left me completely independent.

Nevertheless I wasn't all that worried. Fate was watching over me. Depending on if you are born under a lucky or an unlucky star, things work out well or badly for you. I was born under a lucky star. I had always been lucky. All these possibilities on my father's side, for instance. Every time I thought my situation was desperate, it worked itself out. There had been highs and lows in my life, but never an absolute low. I would climb back on top again, I could feel it, it was imminent. Yet just as I was telling myself this, I fell even lower. I didn't blame this accident on a change in my stars. I had made a mistake. I had thought that I was at the lowest point when I wasn't there yet. Nonetheless, I wondered if I hadn't been fooling myself about this divine protection.

Then, suddenly, I realized I had made a big mistake. I was no longer putting the same energy into defending myself as I had in the beginning. Too much time had already passed since my escape. I'd become lethargic. Seeing that nothing disastrous had happened, I allowed myself to be fooled into thinking that nothing disastrous would happen. I was being punished, but not too severely. It was a warning from above. If I wanted to live, I had to fight, to rid myself of this tendency to trust my luck. I was forgetting that I had already been free fourteen months. Now I was going to act. I put myself back in the mindset of the man I had been upon arriving in Paris. What could be dumber than getting caught just as the greatest difficulties seemed to have been surmounted?

This was why I decided to ask my father to contact the Riveyre de Seyssacs on my behalf. It was the least he could do for me. With the General's help, I could join the army or obtain some sort of official function where no one would think of looking for me, and in that position I could cross legally into the free zone.

And then, I had that odd feeling one gets when powerful people are on your side, when you succeed in letting them know you exist, that even if something terrible were to happen you could endure it far more easily. Deep down, what makes misfortune seem so great is the feeling that not everything was done that could have been done to avoid it.

My father, after a good deal of hesitation, decided to pay a call on Riveyre. I sensed that it troubled him to say that my name was now Tinet. Whenever he decided to do something against his wishes, it was important not to encourage him or rush him. Even when my younger sister died, which coincided with my father's troubles at the high school, even then he hadn't gone to see the Riveyres. And my situation was less serious. But fortunately years had passed, changing the relative importance of things.

I waited for an answer all day. Finally, my father arrived

at our meeting point. He hadn't changed into his everyday clothes. My father rarely dressed up, but when he did he never went home to change and spent the rest of the day in his Sunday best, acting excited, showing great willingness to accomplish other exceptional things.

He told me about his visit.

It was agreed. He hadn't dared say that I was going by a false name, but according to him it wasn't important. I was to pay a visit to Riveyre in a few days.

The General was seated in an overstuffed armchair, in the best spot in the room, beneath a kind of floor lamp. A portrait was placed on a small, highly polished easel, an idle reproduction of a work instrument. He was dressed in his uniform. He had put on his glasses. His wife was seated on the other side of the chimney. It was a veritable family portrait. His daughter Monique was reading, crouched over an Ottoman. In an armchair, his other daughter, Solange, was writing on her knees.

Riveyre de Seyssac was a large, muscular man. His wife was still pretty. They formed one of those bourgeois couples beneath whose respectability one imagines the satisfaction of possessing physiques as vigorous as that of peasants. Riveyre stood up. It showed great confidence for him to receive me like this, at home, among his family, instead of at the barracks. But since the war, the secrets of domestic life were no longer as important. He introduced me to his wife. She smiled warmly, with the air of a woman whose husband's high position brings her into contact with a wide range of people.

Riveyre was one of those men who seem sad, melancholy, as if they have seen their fair share of sorrow, but who nevertheless give the impression of not being easy to deal with. They are sad because life seems ugly to them, because men are not honest, because they are aware of how insignificant they are on this earth. But one has to struggle against sadness. And one sensed that in this struggle Riveyre was always the victor.

I told my story. I wanted to clear my name, live normally, no longer be obliged to hide. He listened to me attentively and asked me to return the next day. He informed me that he was going to give me a letter for Colonel D . . ., head of recruitment for Lyon. Shortly thereafter he asked for the papers I had promised to bring. I told him I hadn't had time to get them, but would bring them to him the next day. The truth was, I didn't want him to deal with me as the son of Professor de Talhouet, but as Tinet. And I didn't dare tell him my papers were false. I thought he would have guessed it. My response made a bad impression. But the General made such a pretense of impartiality that he didn't want to give in to a first impression. "Well, I'll give you the letter tomorrow," he told me. All evening I wondered if I should bring him my military papers or not. I was afraid he wouldn't give them back to me, that he would give them to other officers. I had naïvely thought he would help without asking for details. I still wanted to believe this and returned the next day, again without my papers, hoping he would give me the promised letter anyway. But I was wrong. He hadn't forgotten what he was expecting of me. The first thing he did was ask me for my papers, with the air of a man who didn't for a second doubt my good faith. He didn't flinch when I told him that I still hadn't brought them, but I sensed that it was over between us. He told me with a smile that sent a chill down my spine that he didn't like the way I was acting. Forgetting for a second time was to his mind unforgivable and there was no way to see eye to eye with me. I was definitively classified as unreliable. I was making a fool of him. I had lied when I'd said that I appreciated his kindness. He didn't show any anger. That was life. He had to act accordingly. He had no regrets about having taken an interest in me. He felt a certain sadness, one more disillusionment.

Then his wife entered the room. He asked her to leave us alone. I sensed it was a way of regaining his distance, that he no longer considered me worthy of being admitted into his intimacy, and the fact that such a trifling reason dictated his attitude was striking to me. It was increasingly clear that Riveyre no longer trusted me. I had thought I would be able to get help from him without his even noticing, he seemed so high up relative to me. But it's a mistake to think that people in high places don't know what is going on beneath them. They see it very clearly. I realized this now.

As I was walking along the rue de Grenelle, I had a dizzy spell. Over time, all this emotion was beginning to affect my health. It's all very well to live dangerously, but your health mustn't suffer. When you fall in the water, it's not only the immediate rescue that counts. You also have to avoid pulmonary congestion. I decided to do what I could to keep my emotions in check. Something strange had already been going on in me for some time. Occasionally, although I was in absolutely no danger, I felt a sudden shock as violent as if I were being arrested. I needed some sedatives, rest, and a healthy diet.

Part Two

Prison

Chapter 1

To make matters worse, it was at about this time that I fell in love. I hadn't foreseen that to my present fear another greater one would be added: that of losing a loved one. Until now, I'd had nothing to lose. I was fighting for my life, that was all, and suddenly I was stunned to find that I cared more about life than before. I had thought I'd found some relief, a kind of detachment; instead I found myself struggling with a concern I hadn't imagined: that of not allowing any little human frailties to show. I was always afraid of not being clean enough. I was constantly looking at myself in mirrors. Sometimes after hours of preparations (I lacked everything, lotion, toothpaste, clean underwear), I would change my clothes again just as I was about to go out. My hair, my nails, my teeth, everything was under constant scrutiny. The room where I was living, which had seemed so safe to me, suddenly became unlivable to my eyes. Every time I parted from Ghislaine, I trembled thinking that something would happen to me to prevent me from seeing her again. All sorts of fatalistic thoughts passed through my mind. If I had stayed one minute more, if I had taken this street instead of that one, this misfortune would not have occurred, and so on. One day, I had the idea of making a pact with her, which to my mind would have been a great relief: that we agree not to see each other until the end of the war, and take an oath of fidelity until then. But I didn't dare talk to her about it. Indeed, what I lacked the most was a friend in whom I could have confided, whom I could have trusted, who would have renewed my faith when I thought all was lost. I had noticed that in times of great danger, one often needs someone to take care of minor tasks.

Since my escape, wherever I'd been, I had unconsciously scrutinized the neighbors, the concierges, and merchants, and wondered if among them there wasn't one of those people to whom I could have whispered, just as the police were coming to get me, "Tell them you don't know where the key is; take the letter on my table, call my father later . . ." and who would have done it. But I realized that to perform such minuscule favors, people had to be great friends.

When I would return home after having spent an hour or more with Ghislaine, it seemed like an infinite amount of time had passed and that something serious had happened in my absence.

I would think about the thousands of nice things I had done, like reserving seats, running an errand, going to the post office, to city hall. How reckless it all seemed now!

I even found that that which brings the greatest pleasure—inspiring admiration, pleasing the other as much as she pleases you, exchanging things (as in the words, "I love you if you love me")—was extraordinarily frivolous in a situation as dangerous as mine.

The things that happened to Ghislaine were typical of what happens to people who don't know how to stick up for themselves: she would lend money to a friend who later claimed she hadn't lent her anything. She didn't tell me about these things because she'd noticed they upset me too much. Every time I saw her, I would stare into her eyes and try to guess whether anything had happened to her. She would tell me her little troubles. But since I couldn't do anything to help her, after a few weeks I asked her not to tell me anymore. I preferred not to know.

One day nevertheless I couldn't help getting involved. It was one of these problems over money. I went to see Ghislaine's friend. It hadn't even occurred to me that this might be risky. Yet this friend was not at all the shy young girl I had imagined. It seemed she knew she had nothing to fear from me. As soon as I began to defend Ghislaine she raised her voice. I got angry, still thinking I had nothing to fear. Then an extraordinary thing happened. Suddenly, this woman began pretending I had insulted her. Without clearly understanding what she meant, but sensing confusedly that it could be serious, I beat a hasty retreat. She yelled louder and louder. She said I wouldn't get away with it, that Ghislaine might have a boyfriend, but that she had one too, that there were some things you couldn't say to a respectable woman, and so on. Since my escape, nothing frightened me more than the assertion that I had said something that went beyond what I was thinking. It occurred to me that people might be called in to give their opinions. The mere possibility of arbitration made me tremble. I could already see these arbiters calling in other arbiters. Unable to resolve the conflict, they climbed higher and higher, until they reached the police. At that point, it was no longer a matter of the conflict itself, but of the participants involved. Before making a judgement, the police wanted to know whom they were dealing with.

    I grew increasingly afraid there would be another incident. I knew Ghislaine was devoted to me body and soul, but I was afraid something unpredictable would happen. Which is why I attached enormous importance to the timing of our meetings. The slightest lateness made me tremble. I myself left my room two hours in advance to be sure that nothing would prevent me from leaving at the last moment. I was also afraid that they would try to get to me through her. Every time we parted, we thought we might never see each other again. Which is why we had such a hard time separating and why, to buy a stamp, we entered the post office together. Nothing is more difficult than persuading a loved one to do everything for her own safety we would like. Once we said goodbye, I trembled thinking she might overlook a danger that I, had I been there, would have seen. I imagined that were she stopped, she wouldn't know how to defend herself, that she would get confused about what she was supposed to say, that she would contradict what I would say later. She would fall into every trap. I was ashamed of the precautions these problematic dangers forced me to take. They showed me that maybe I didn't love Ghislaine as much as I thought. I hadn't told her where I lived. Even though she knew that it wasn't out of distrust but out of fear of her weakness, and even though she didn't hold it against me, there was something rather base about these precautions. It was too obvious I didn't want to get mixed up in any of her problems. Of course, she had less to be frightened of than I did.

And if something did happen to her, how would she let me know? No method seemed safe enough. What if, in her panic, she used a method that I had forbidden! I was terrified of this happening. I couldn't keep lecturing her. I was continually torn between the desire to appear as if I trusted her and the urge to repeat the same instructions. But what was most difficult for me was seeing that she respected the matter of my safety as if it were even more important than our love. This caused me great pain, which in turn annoyed her. Of course, if I were caught, there would be no more love affair. It was therefore quite natural that my safety would be so important in her eyes. Which is why I sometimes forgot myself, I stopped taking precautions. "Let's love each other, by God," I would say.

One day she told me that she had met someone who could have told her precisely what I wanted to know about the state of the search for me, but that she had obeyed me and hadn't asked him anything. I told her she had been right to do so. I nevertheless felt a great sadness thinking that we had come to this and that with all my instructions I had caused the young woman I loved to feel so naïvely terrified for me. And the more time passed the more I worried.

Chapter 2

Since I had met Ghislaine, I visited Roger more frequently. I felt closer to him—the great seducer. We seemed to have more to talk about, and to take more pleasure in seeing each other.

Roger often slept at his family's house now. He saw no problem in that. I admired how comfortable he felt there, how calm. Then, upon further reflection, I realized that I too could have lived with relatives. I had no reason to envy him. I had only myself to blame. Deep down, I was suffering the consequences of my past conduct. This is what it is to enjoy being alone. There are people who hardly know anyone and who find help wherever they go.

Thus Roger divided his time between Lucienne and his family. He no longer considered himself in danger. There was no longer any reason why he shouldn't go home when he wanted. He had simply told the concierge not to talk to anyone about him. If someone were to ask for him, she should say that she didn't know where he was. He had given the same instructions to his parents, his friends, to the director of the little bank on the rue Drouot, to Lucienne, and to her young actress friends. All these people looked out for him, and warned him of any potentially suspicious event, no matter how slight. I found this admirable. With all these people knowing his story, he didn't seem the least bit worried, whereas I, in such a situation, would have perished with fear. Even though it unnerved me to know that so many people knew all this about him, I had a pleasant feeling of security in his presence. Despite it all, my status as a friend allowed me to benefit from his protection network.

I still preferred to visit him at his girlfriend Lucienne's house, where he said he felt comfortable and where there were always very few people. He hadn't gone back to his job on the rue Drouot. He had found something else instead and I had the impression that he was doing even better. He went out frequently, saw friends, made money. When I visited him, he seemed very satisfied. He would ask me what I was doing. He didn't understand why I wasn't getting along better, and was surprised that I was so afraid. He would tell me that our escape was long forgotten, that barring an accident we had nothing to fear.

What surprised me was the levity with which he imagined this accident. It was precisely the possibility of an accident hanging over our heads that made me so fearful, but he didn't worry about it. He said the Krauts were finished, that the police had better things to do than look for us (they were intentionally wreaking havoc everywhere, they were pretending to do their jobs but behind the scenes they were throwing wrenches into the works), that if they wanted to run after people like us, they'd have to join forces with the army, that we had absolutely nothing to fear. "How can you even imagine that they are thinking of you amid such chaos?" he would say. These words restored my faith. I came up with objections to prod him on. He never lost a beat. I shouldn't worry about it, I should just forget it. Unfortunately, he had reservations about special cases. I would tell him, as if he didn't know, that I was just that, a special case. I wasn't an ordinary escapee. No, he responded, I was like everyone else. "You know full well that I'm not!" I would tell him. He wouldn't answer me anymore. He would change the topic. It was then my turn to tell him that he was right, that indeed we had nothing to fear.

He never failed to tease me about Pelet. "Watch out for Pelet," he would say to me when the conversation lagged. Each time, I froze. Pelet was in Paris? I would ask him questions, I demanded information. He would say that he had seen Madame Pelet, that she had spoken to him about me. But why had he visited Madame Pelet when he was my friend? I asked him this. He looked at me and laughed and wouldn't answer.

Sometimes he took me to lunch at a fancy restaurant where everyone knew him. I have a great aversion to people who ignore those who are serving them, who forget that we are all human, who, in the theater, in restaurants, are so absorbed by their own pleasure that they never even glance at the little people watching them. I was forced to act like them and it was very unpleasant for me. Roger wanted to have fun. I told him he was crazy. He wouldn't listen to me and forced me to imitate him, which I did, as I could never resist him. Friends asked us what it was like in Germany. They only listened to him. No one seemed to suspect that I knew as much as he did.

In the beginning, I felt uncomfortable. I didn't have much confidence in the security of this restaurant, with its protection in high places. It seemed as if nothing bad could happen, yet I always had in mind the potential for panic and hysteria. I told myself that were there a police raid, all these select clients would be treated like the others. Havoc would break loose; nothing would remain of these fine appearances and the ones who would be caught would be people like me who had been taken in by the setting, who wouldn't have dared flee first. But Roger made me drink and these dark thoughts evaporated. Just one remained, however, despite my intoxication, a strange thought, that of misfortune befalling me just when everything seemed so pleasant, a thought that I always had, in fact, when I was happy. It would have been truly bad luck, and even though I didn't want my pleasure to end, I rejoiced in the passing of time, and with it the probability of an accident diminishing. I rejoiced in the idea of leaving, of the evening ending without incident.

Sometimes music was playing. With the help of a little wine, I suddenly had the impression that my current troubles were nothing next to the misery of my failed life. Years ago I had thought I would be rich, but I had failed at everything I'd tried. I had been a bad painter. Several times, my father had wished never to see me again. Then I began working at the claims office of the National Insurance Company—that was the best I had found to do with my life! Then the war. I had gone off like everyone else. I had been taken prisoner like almost everyone else. I managed to get out, but at what price! And now I found myself alone, hunted, in the company of a friend whom I admired but who would never be able to help me. I sensed it more and more, my abilities were limited. I was crying over this poor wasted life, over my destiny, but Roger couldn't have known this. He'd slap me on the shoulder, "Come on, old chum," he would say, "stop thinking about your buddy Pelet."

Roger introduced me to his friends. Thus one day I witnessed an incredible scene. Over an affair I knew nothing about, he had a disagreement with one of these imbeciles who takes sides without knowing what they're talking about. Their voices were getting louder and louder, so the owner of the restaurant asked them to leave. Then they turned on him. The owner went to get a policeman. A long discussion followed. A curious crowd formed, including some Germans. I was trembling with terror, especially when I sensed the anger mounting, for I was just as afraid of a false accusation as of a valid one.

The policeman separated them. Right away I realized that Roger automatically appealed to him more. By the questions he was asking, it was evident that he wanted to find him in the right. I grew afraid that the adversary would want to call in another, less biased policeman. When the dispute was settled, I was so shocked to see that Roger didn't even cast a grateful eye toward this policeman that I looked at him gratefully myself. But it wasn't the same and I sensed that the policeman wasn't the least bit moved by this compensation.

Finally, Roger took my arm and we left together. I couldn't help telling him he was reckless. He shrugged.

Lucienne had noticed that I was very impressed with her. As a result, when she was in good spirits, she would go out of her way for me. But when she wasn't, I noticed that my admiration was not enough to change her mood, and she hardly spoke to me. I was always afraid that she'd take my disappointment for bitterness. She would say I looked sad.

Roger must have told her everything, for she sometimes

alluded to the fact that I wasn't what I seemed. I didn't trust her all that much. I sensed that deep down, she didn't find me very genuine, and indeed, oddly enough, I no longer was very genuine when I was around her. I sensed too that for a friend of the man she loved, she didn't find me very charismatic. Obviously, I was an incredible guy if Roger said so, and he had certainly seen proof, but aside from that there was nothing out of the ordinary about me. I always had the impression that she considered me a curiosity, that she didn't understand what Roger saw in me, and therefore thought there must be something strange about me that I was hiding from her, which she resented. She scared me a little; not that she tried to harm me, but I was sure she would if Roger ever did her wrong. And she often fought with Roger. She resented him for preventing her from working, that is to say from dancing, for forcing her to live a cloistered life. She claimed that if she were free to do as she pleased, she would be making lots of money. If I arrived in the middle of such a scene, she didn't break off, and I sensed that on the contrary, she was pleased to have me there. Soon I noticed that Roger was becoming cool toward me, even blaming me for things. He would say that I was no friend. I looked at him surprised each time. He didn't push the issue and I sensed that deep down it was all the same to him whether I was or wasn't and since he didn't like having to keep his feelings in check, he preferred not to take this nonsense seriously.

One day when I arrived at their home, Roger came to me and said angrily, "You have some nerve coming here." I looked at him wide-eyed. "What did I do?" I asked. Still just as angry, he said that I had spoken badly of him. I protested. To my surprise, his anger dropped off just as quickly as a result of my vague denials. "Oh! well, that changes everything," he said.

Another day, I found the two of them a little drunk. They welcomed me warmly, but then began teasing me about my courage. I was a tough one, it seemed. I wasn't afraid of anyone. When I saw danger, I didn't hesitate. I was nobody's fool, and so on. From time to time, Roger pretended to be afraid of me. "Watch out, careful, don't get him mad," Lucienne would say. I couldn't help laughing, but something about these antics annoyed me deeply. I never claimed to be "tough," nor brave, nor anything else. But ultimately I felt that I had shown proof of courage despite everything and that, without me, we would all, Roger as well as the others, be carrying rails. Not to mention that it's profoundly unpleasant to sense people doubting your qualities, mocking what was done together in earnest, seeming as if they weren't sincere before. Roger must have sensed this too, for shortly afterward he said, "We're kidding . . . we're kidding . . ." and when Lucienne kept it up, he asked her to stop.

From mocking my bravery, they moved on to mocking my love affair with Ghislaine. I've often been kidded but,

I don't know why, coming from Roger, who I wanted to take me seriously, it affected me much more. At certain moments, I must say, he abandoned this tone and went back to being the man I loved, speaking to me like a friend. But even then, I sensed that I was no longer interesting to him. I don't even think Lucienne had anything to do with it, because deep down it had always been this way.

Sometimes I saw him alone. I did everything he asked of me. We would go out together, but the awful thing was that I quickly sensed his boredom with me.

I loved how Roger would get bored the minute he wasn't doing something. I was like that too, but whereas I didn't dare show it, he made no effort to hide it. I sensed that for him I was becoming just like one of those people who bore me as well, and that he saw me as one of them.

"Remember when we were in Belgium?" Roger would ask, when he was at a loss for words, seeming to think our troubles were over.

I loved tagging along with him more than anything, but even if he had nothing to do he would refuse my offer. I would ask him why. He wouldn't answer me. Sometimes he would suddenly stop in the middle of the street and say goodbye. I'd think he was going to walk away. When he didn't move, I would stand still. "Go on, go away," he would say to me. I'd walk away. When I'd turn around, I'd see him still standing in the same place, but not watching me, not even looking in my direction. Several times I thought of following him. It would have been easy. I would never have done such a thing before, but since he had changed so much one day I decided to do it. I saw him walking slowly. He turned around sometimes to look at a woman. (What I didn't like about him now was that he seemed to find Ghislaine ordinary. He would look at her like a rich man looking at a poor man's purchase.) He had a way of being excessively disdainful. He would just look at the legs. Each time, he would stop . . . Sometimes he would also stop in front of a store. But you could sense that nothing interested him. One day, he turned back, saw me, but looked away. I never saw him again.

Chapter 3

One morning, Lucienne came to see me on the rue Berthollet. She had never been there before, and had never shown the slightest curiosity about where I was living. I was flustered at being surprised by such a pretty women. I was hiding some shirts, putting things superficially in order when suddenly my embarrassment vanished. Two men had come for Roger. They had left together. Roger had said he would be back in an hour. Three days had passed and he hadn't reappeared.

I headed immediately to Versailles. I personally had no connections; only my father could do something. It seemed to me it was all over. I was so afraid that I didn't look at anyone, I no longer paid attention to anything. This incident was so serious that all my habitual precautions suddenly seemed pitiful, like being attached to a buoy when a ship is sinking. What would Roger do if he'd been arrested? Would he talk about me? When you've never been in prison, you can't know what happens in the mind of a prisoner. I had always trusted Roger. He was the only one of my companions from the escape who had affection for me. He had preferred me to all the others even though, in that miserable situation, we were all just about equal. What would he do now that he was caught? I was the one they were really looking for, not him. Would he denounce me to save himself? I kept asking myself this question in vain. It was as difficult as guessing the reaction of a man under fire. Will he allow himself to be shot down, throw himself to the right, to the left, forward, backward, will he run away? I remembered that Roger had always been perfectly honorable. But once he was caught, wouldn't he become a different man?

As soon as he saw me, my father realized that something was wrong. I immediately told him what had just happened. I begged him to help me, to enlist the help of his friends to find out what had become of Roger. He said it was difficult for him to do that. He was surprised at how excited I was getting. He naturally thought that I was overdoing things by worrying so much, but he respected my feelings. The same wasn't true of the other people I went to see immediately afterward. I gathered that they considered me utterly lacking in discretion. They had been willing to do what they could for me, but they considered it a form of insolence on my part that under the pretext that their interventions had been ineffective, I was again coming to solicit help for someone they didn't even know. They responded more kindly than my father had, but I sensed they would do even less. I had approached all these people with the confidence you have when something major happens. I was still in a state of shock. I imagined that until the war was won and peace restored, there existed a kind of solidarity among men that gave me leave to approach them, to be abrupt without warning, to be demanding, to ask for the most unexpected favors since it was for a good cause, since we were all, in truth, in the same atrocious situation. They hadn't liked this. I seemed to think I could do as I pleased, whereas the world was making extraordinary efforts to believe that things were normal, to brighten what little remained. Everyone was convinced that his own case wasn't as desperate as the whole picture suggested. And I, in my naïveté, approached all these egotists as if our misfortunes were just beginning, as if we had to band together, as if we were all equals.

"This guy never lets up," they said to themselves, "he sure knows how to take advantage of a situation." I practically came off as a war profiteer, having the gall to visit people whom I would never have had a reason to approach before the war.

I kept up my efforts nevertheless. I went to see Mondanel. I desperately needed to devote myself to something.

Lucienne's distress made me feel terrible. When one is in terrible need of others as I was, the day when the roles are reversed one loses all sense of perspective. Thus, when I think today of everything I did at that time, I can't help feeling both proud and embarrassed. I realize that my desire to do good uncovered certain faults which, in the course of normal life, did not have occasion to show. I had made it too obvious—oh, quite unconsciously—that I considered myself more qualified than anyone to help people in trouble. I had given too much advice and had tried too hard to comfort her. Basically, I lacked simplicity and true affection, just as I had, I now realize, in all the trying circumstances of my life. I acted too much as if this unfortunate event were an omen of what would happen to me, as if, after a long period of holding back, suddenly it was possible to act.

When I went back to see Lucienne a rather disturbing scene took place. After telling me she'd been looking for me all day, she suddenly started threatening me. She wanted me to find out by hook or by crook whether Roger was at the Cherche-Midi prison. I told her that I had already tried to find out, that my inquiries had been in vain, and just as I had been told so many times, just like all those people I hated, like my father himself, I added that I didn't see what else I could do. For the first time, I sensed a certain nastiness in Lucienne's voice. "I want to know what can be done," she said to me. "You're the one who knows. You can't tell me you don't know."

In spite of everything I continued to question people who could provide me with useful information. As time passed, the mystery surrounding Roger's case seemed more and more troubling. I felt something could happen to me from one minute to the next. I reassured myself by thinking that there was a whole side of Roger's life I didn't know about. He might have been arrested for fraud, for black market dealings. I questioned Lucienne on this subject to see if she had been aware of anything. Since Roger's disappearance, no one had come by, no visits had been paid either to his family or to Lucienne. It was nevertheless evident that something was brewing. If they had discovered Roger, there was no reason why they wouldn't discover me. I thought I should disappear, and not set foot at Lucienne's, at the home of Roger's family, or on the rue Drouot. But this would have been so cowardly I didn't dare. The next day, however, I shared my fears with Roger's parents and with Lucienne. I was undoubtedly being watched, and must have been denounced at the same time as Roger. It would soon be my turn. To my surprise, even though I was obviously in danger, no one even thought to give me the advice I was waiting for, which was to not come back. It seemed as if everyone had forgotten how serious my situation was. I felt as if they considered it normal that I should share Roger's fate, that my being a free man when Roger was gone was shocking. This selfishness showed me how indifferent all these people would have been if suddenly, for fear of being arrested in turn, I had never come back. I think it fair to say that no one would have done me the honor of thinking that I too had been taken away.

But the next day, I realized how wrong-headed and unfair I was. As soon as I arrived at Lucienne's, she took me affectionately by the arm and said, "Get out of here fast, and don't come back. Someone came looking for you yesterday. It must have been the police." I was so surprised by this kindness, it was in such contrast to my thoughts and made them seem so malicious that I was overcome with gratitude. Inspired by the blossoming of my nobler instincts, I said something that so visibly contradicted my behavior of the last two years, the behavior of a rather fearful man, that Lucienne couldn't help but laugh. "It'll take more than that to scare me . . . ," I cried. "You're crazy," Lucienne exclaimed. "Someone always takes advantage of a situation," I added in the same tone. "Go, go quickly,"Lucienne continued. "You mustn't get caught too . . ." I was so happy, so proud that someone was finally afraid for me that I couldn't help pretending to think it was undeserved. The roles were reversed. Now I thought I had to comfort Lucienne by posing as a self-assured man.

Chapter 4

Upon leaving my house the next morning, I noticed two men looking at a shop window. As I had already done many times, I immediately stopped. Pretending to think, as if I had just noticed I'd forgotten something, I stood immobile facing another direction, seeming to be unaware of their very presence. Then I turned back into the lobby of the building. I told myself it was outrageous to climb five flights because of two men who were certainly just ordinary passers-by. I waited several seconds at the foot of the stairs, then, realizing that I would call attention to myself, knocked on the door of the concierge's quarters. I said the first thing that passed through my head: I was expecting a friend. Then, walking through the lobby, I looked outside, peeking with only one eye as if I were hidden by a tree. The two men were no longer examining the window and were facing one another as if saying goodbye. I stepped back immediately. A few seconds later, I glanced outside again. They were still there. I went back to the concierge and told her, to explain my behavior, that there was nothing more annoying than waiting for someone when you're in a hurry. I began walking back and forth in the damp, dark lobby. I sensed that normally, since the weather was beautiful, I should have paced around outside. But I might have been afraid of missing this friend, after all. There are trivial reasons for our actions that fortunately people don't try to figure out. The two men still hadn't left. I was beginning to worry, even though they never looked toward the house. I even had the impression, seeing them talk, that if I were to go outside they wouldn't notice me leaving. I wondered what I should do. If I went back to my room, if I didn't go out and their mission was to arrest me, they would come get me. But were this the case wouldn't they already have done it? Perhaps there was a legal technicality that prevented them from arresting me at home. Once again, I looked outside. They hadn't budged. I finally decided to go back to my room, but when I reached my floor I felt disgusted at the thought of closing myself in. I walked to the end of the corridor, took the ladder, and opened the skylight. Then I waited, leaning on the railing. But the stairway was very narrow, and I couldn't see someone climbing up without putting my hand on the ramp and hugging the wall. After an hour, when nothing had happened, I returned the ladder to its place and went back downstairs. The two men were still there. This time, I was terrified. Should I escape over the rooftops? It was silly to be taken for a burglar if I wasn't in danger. I didn't know what to do. Finally I told myself I would wait until noon. At that point if they were still there despite the lunch hour, I would have to flee. I went back upstairs. I sat on a step. At noon, I went downstairs. To make everything that had happened seem normal, I told the concierge that this time I'd waited long enough. Then I looked at the street. The two men were gone.

I don't know if it was because of the events of that morning, but when I returned home in the evening I was so feverish I went to bed immediately.

I couldn't find any liquor. I wanted to make myself sweat. I was shivering. I got dressed again to go downstairs and asked the concierge to bring me some boiling water. I was bathed in perspiration but didn't have a shirt to change into. I wrapped myself in the mattress cover. Despite my fever, I wondered what I would do if the police were to break into my room. There's nothing like an illness to rid us of our worries, but I told myself right away one mustn't be fooled by one's constitution, which follows laws that are far too soft for the lives we lead. At ten o'clock, the concierge came upstairs. I had given her the key. I jumped up when I heard the door opening. She was bringing me another herbal tea. She saw that my shirt was soaked, and wanted to take it with her to dry in her kitchen. I tried to stop her but she took it anyway. It crossed my mind that if the police arrived just then, I couldn't get dressed. What would happen tomorrow if I weren't well? "May my health return," I said to myself. The concierge was very kind. She might inform the hospital without even telling me. When we're sick, people don't bother asking us what we want.

The next morning, I got up and dressed. I had that strange sensation of feeling better even though I still had a fever. I took three pills. I absolutely had to be in good health. The police are very clever, stationing themselves in places where one must inevitably go in time: hotels, hospitals, train stations, brothels. I had to be able to fend for myself if I wanted to avoid them.

I was preparing to leave when my father showed up. He wasn't his usual self. He told me some inspectors had come by the high school looking for me. I began shaking. My father was breathless. He told me he had taken countless precautions before coming, and that he was going to let Mondanel know about this immediately. What struck him most was that although the inspectors had spoken like Frenchmen, they seemed like foreigners. They had been excessively polite.

I regretted allowing my father to leave. I would have liked to have gone downstairs with him. Even though he couldn't have done anything in an emergency, I wouldn't have felt so alone.

I went down almost immediately after him. When I arrived at the foot of the stairs, I noticed a man in the concierge's quarters. He was fairly thin, with worn clothing softened by time. He had very black eyes, a receding hairline with long strands of hair stuck to the top of his head, one next to the other, leaving thick bands of baldness showing through. I don't know why, but at first I thought this man was a street hawker, a door-to-door salesman, a canvasser, that he was looking to sell something, basically that he wasn't very honest, that he was living on the fringes by way of some sort of scheme. As I passed in front of the lodge, I heard a knock on the glass pane. I kept walking, pretending not to hear. Barely a few steps later I heard someone calling my name. Since no one was leaving the lodge and it didn't seem very important, I stopped. "Are you calling me?" I asked the concierge. "Yes, you, come in." I approached the window the concierge had just opened. "This gentleman wants to talk to you." I was terrified for a moment. My fear was so extreme I immediately reassured myself by imagining that this man didn't dare sell his products directly, that he addressed the tenants by way of go-betweens to give a more serious impression. He was simply trying to make a sale to someone in the building or find out who needed life insurance. He began by winning the favor of the concierge. After that, all he had to do was prod her on. "Why don't you call this gentleman over," he might suggest. Basically, he was working with her. I entered the room perfectly at ease, but without daring to address the poor fellow directly. "What can I do for you?" I said, smiling at the concierge. "This gentleman wants to talk to you," she repeated. When the salesman remained silent, I suddenly got the idea that he was intimidated, as when you ask a third party to call on someone you're afraid to speak to directly. Conscious of being a little too courteous to someone I didn't know and who was using this kind of routine to approach me, I turned and asked him in a friendly way what it was about, being careful, out of a kind of inexplicable fear, not to appear as if I thought it might be about me. I must say at this moment I suddenly had a bad premonition. Superficially this man had given me the impression of having a one-track mind, of being a poor loner going from door to door trying to seem like a professional. But as I spoke, looking him in the face, I suddenly realized that he wasn't as pathetic as I had imagined. I had thought he would talk like a hawker, but not at all. He said what he had to say in a precise manner. I was further reassured by an ordinary sheet of paper with a few names on it sitting in front of him, on the concierge's round table. He told me he had already been by several times but that I hadn't been in. I asked the concierge why she hadn't told me. He didn't give her a chance to answer. There was no rush, and he had preferred to come back.

Finally he told me some business about a census. In this building alone, there were four of us he hadn't been able to lay his hands on yet. Since I was here, we were going to settle this question right away. He asked me if I would do him a favor and come with him to the office. My first instinct was to refuse, to find an excuse, to promise to come later. I asked him to leave me the address. He said it would be fine by him, but that it might be a problem for me. When I got to the office, I would be dealing with different employees. This census business should have been settled a long time ago. I might happen on someone who wasn't very accommodating and might give me some trouble. If I could spare a few minutes, a quarter of an hour at most, the office was nearby, he would settle this question immediately and we would both be done with it. "The offices are near here?" I asked. "Five minutes away. Just opposite the tax collector's office." I knew the tax collector's office. There was no police station in the vicinity. The prospect of these troubles the man warned me about, of an inquiry resulting from an insignificant misdemeanor, made me think it was best to deal with it right away, especially since this man was very reassuring. He was even pleasant. He didn't have the usual bureaucratic manner. One guessed he was a man fallen from higher social rank who had somehow managed to land a serious administrative position but did not let this bit of luck go to his head, who tried to hook up with people whom his new position enabled him to approach and wheedle small sums of money from them. On the way to the office, and considering how it all ended this is rather funny, he told me various stories that confirmed my suspicion. He didn't like working an administrative job. He confessed that before the war, he had managed to earn enough money at the track to live. Now, that was no longer possible. Since he had expenses (at this he made a gesture indicating that you could criticize him for many things, but not for leaving his dependents wanting), he had to earn a living and so had entered the police force, but only provisionally, because he didn't like this kind of work. I cringed. I asked him in a voice that I couldn't be sure was normal what the police had to do with this census business. He said that now everything went through the police, that since I hadn't answered, the census commission had transferred my file, and so on. Besides, I had nothing to fear since he was handling this case. I tried to be reasonable. I told myself not to be childish. "We're here," he said, pointing to a house just like all the others but slightly better built. "I don't understand what's going on," I said. "Show me some I.D. or something." He pulled several pieces of paper from his pocket. One of them had the name Tinet. It referred, indeed, to a census. "And what kind of building is this?" I asked. "It's the district office." "What district office?" "The neighborhood district office." "This is where you go for the census?" "Naturally, where else would you go?" At the time I didn't pay attention to this answer. I was so torn between worrying and feeling like everything was normal that this house impressed me as a kind of administrative annex. We passed under an arch. The words "District Office" were written on a white enamel plaque. We climbed one flight and entered an apartment without knocking, passing through several connecting rooms. In every room employees were sitting at tables. Finally, we came to a large room that must have originally been the living room. There were many tables here as well. In a corner, however, I noticed an Empire desk, behind which was a man who was visibly the boss. What worried me was that I couldn't tell whether all these rooms, including this large room, were public places, or if I'd had access only because someone had accompanied me. Then I saw my companion approach a table, whisper a few words to an employee, signal me to wait, and walk away alone. Was I caught? It seemed like it. "Aha! It's you!" the seated man said. I didn't answer. I didn't even have the strength to answer. Another man seated further away approached and, looking over the shoulder of the one who had just spoken to me, peered at the papers. "It's Talhouet! Boy, that was a tough one . . ." I began trembling, but luckily it was only my legs so no one noticed. I was caught. The blood rose to my head so fiercely I felt my vision blurring.

Chapter 5

After a few minutes, I was asked to take a seat and wait. A man, an inspector no doubt, sat down next to me. After half an hour, having regained my composure somewhat (I had to or I was lost), I said to him, "You know very well I'm not the one you're looking for." He said he knew that, which surprised me. People are much nicer in a one-on-one situation. Encouraged, I offered this policeman all the money I had on me if he would let me go. He shook his head no, but without the slightest indignation. I insisted, taking this to mean that he wanted to be coaxed. He continued to refuse limply. I told him that Frenchmen had to help one another, that no one would ever know a thing. Since he seemed to be on the verge of accepting, I pulled out my wallet and offered him the two thousand francs that were inside, but he pushed my hand away, not in a scandalized manner, but paternally, as if he didn't want to deprive me of money that I might need more than he would. I told him it was no problem, and that I could give him more if he wanted. He still refused, but like someone who doesn't want to make a bad impression. I told him not to think that he would fall in my esteem (it was a matter of putting him at ease with respect to his pride), that if I were in his shoes I too would accept, that perhaps he had "a wife and children," that he wasn't very well paid, and no one would ever know a thing. But he still refused. I begged him again. To no avail.

An hour later, I was taken before a man who seemed to be in charge of everyone I had encountered until then. I was briefly questioned about my identity. I maintained to the end that I was named Tinet, not Talhouet. Finally they handed me a police report to sign. Imagine my surprise when I read that I had attempted to bribe an officer. I was so furious that without thinking I cried that it was an abominable lie, I had never offered him anything. The commissioner called in the officer and told him that I claimed I hadn't offered him anything. "You didn't offer me anything?" said the inspector, in such an honest tone I got flustered. "No, I didn't offer you anything," I said, feeling like I was visibly lying. "You dare say that you didn't offer me anything?" continued the officer, with such profound sincerity that it was obvious he was telling the truth. I had never dealt with the law before. I imagined my word was as good as anyone's, that no one had the right to believe someone else over me. It therefore came as a shock when I saw the commissioner side with the officer following this confrontation. There was no doubt in his mind that I was lying. It suddenly became apparent that I was on shaky ground. "Okay, I'll tell you the truth." I told the commissioner that I had indeed offered some money (in my rage I was hoping to discredit the officer, to drag him down with me). That was the truth. I had denied it because I had been so infuriated by the officer's attitude. I added that I had only offered him money because I had been encouraged to do so, and that in his own mind, the officer knew that he had done nothing to stop me. The commissioner listened to me attentively. The care he took not to interrupt me led me to believe I had won him over, but when I finished he simply asked, as if not wishing to go into details, "Did he accept or not?" I had to say: no. "So, how can you blame him?"

I must say this business earned me the secret sympathy of an agent who witnessed the scene. He quietly approached and told me not to get discouraged.

A little while later I heard voices. I was sitting on a bench in the hall again. I saw one of the policemen look at me, no longer indifferently, the way they look at all criminals, but like a man who is no longer thinking of his duties. I have often seen that look on policemen's faces, almost as if their profession is so obnoxious that whenever they are simply curious or intrigued they no longer look like police. I pretended not to notice. There was only one thing on my mind: finding an opportunity to escape. And so they wouldn't suspect anything, I was still pretending to be angry. From time to time, I clenched my fists as if I wanted to fight with the inspector who had tricked me, or I pretended I was muttering to myself, or I swore out loud that I would never forget this.

Then I was led into a large room. I had the impression that if I wanted to escape, now was the time. I told myself that it would be harder later, when I was locked up, because then I would be exclusively in the hands of men whose sole job was to guard prisoners, while here people were still coming and going freely around me. I had to escape immediately. But I was waiting for a better opportunity, as in Germany. All I could think of was taking advantage of the right opportunity, which was enough to make me keep my cool. I was talking to my guards. I told them they should be embarrassed to be working for the Krauts. They didn't know what to say. I had the impression they agreed with me, that they were uncomfortable, that some of them were capable of the kind of generosity I've always found the most touching, the kind I'd experienced a few months earlier when an officer had taken me by the arm as he was sorting through a group that had been rounded-up, and, for no apparent reason, simply because he liked me no doubt, pushed me outside and said, "Quick, get out of here."

Suddenly, I was told to stand up. I caught sight of the officer who had arrested me. He was on his way out, a cigarette in his mouth. I stared at him, trying to give him a "you'll get yours" kind of look. But he was completely indifferent, with the air of a man whose duties often inspire hatred but whose conscience is clear.

Despite the commotion, I reviewed my situation. I realized that because of how I had acted at the moment of my arrest, I seemed guilty. Because of the shock and the surprise, I hadn't protested. I had seemed to find it natural that they were coming to get me, and even said certain things that made it clear I was guilty. I was wondering now whether all that mattered. One thing I didn't know was to what extent denying having said something aggravated the case of the accused. If my words were repeated to me and I acted surprised, would the law take that into account?

I needed advice. I shouldn't say another word until I had a lawyer. But wouldn't just making such a demand work against me? Of course, the lawyer would see me. At this point I wondered anxiously if it weren't better to follow my instincts. But wouldn't that be presumptuous in a world I knew nothing about? Maybe I didn't need a lawyer, and yet I felt I wouldn't have the courage to act without consulting one. I racked my brain over and over, but didn't know what to do. I was more disturbed by all these questions than by the policemen guarding me. I told myself that if I wanted to get out of this I had to keep my cool and not get upset about being trapped. Rather than trying to figure out what I should or shouldn't say, I had to force myself not to get excited by the fact that I was in the hands of the law. I reasoned that in a situation like mine, the loss of physical freedom shouldn't matter. You had to be ready to lose your freedom momentarily if it meant securing your future. There was no proof that I was the one they were looking for.

"My name is Tinet, my name is Tinet . . ." I kept repeating.

We were getting ready to leave the station when the inspector accompanying me, who for some reason was fanning himself with the papers he had in his hand, stopped to exchange a few words with one of his colleagues. There was an open door at the end of the corridor and beyond that, the stairwell. A few people were clustered around the passageway. I kept walking, my eyes fixed on the door, pretending not to notice that my guard had stopped. Suddenly I decided to take my chances and run for it, but I had barely taken a few steps when I was caught. The policeman fell into an indescribable rage. When I told him I had never intended to escape, he asked me if I took him for an idiot and threatened me for several minutes, raising his hand but without going so far as to hit me. He led me back to Mr. Hulot, the Police Commissioner. They had already made me sign one police report and the two of them were wondering whether it was worth it to start another one to include what they called my escape attempt. The incredible thing was that all these men were French. Aren't we all French? I wanted to scream. I held back. They would no longer have contented themselves with just threatening me if I had. In their minds, it was people like me who made the occupation so difficult. By trying to escape, by defending myself, I was being a bad Frenchman and putting poor innocent people at risk of being punished in my place. If I was so brave I should have fought earlier. Now, it was too late. All one could do today was try to get by, and they would take it on themselves to make me understand this. The discovery of this way of thinking perplexed me enormously. I had thought that I would be the hero, that they wouldn't know quite what to charge me with, that they wouldn't even dare look me in the eyes they would be so mortified at having arrested me, and suddenly I realized that my crime was a real crime to them. Instead of enduring the same fate as my compatriots, I had wanted to find a way out. What I had done had nothing to do with patriotism. Because of me, other prisoners might now be in jail. And I was trying to get away! That took the cake. At one point, I couldn't help but cry out that they should be ashamed to act this way to Frenchmen. I'll never forget the look on the policeman's face. It was as if he, a true Frenchman, would not take the blame for such a thing, and I sensed he would have killed me if he could have.

Back in the hall, the officer told me that Mr. Hulot had been a good sport, but that if I started my little tricks again, I would pay for it dearly.

I was surrounded by policemen. I have often seen wrongdoers in the street resist when their opponents were clearly stronger. I'd always thought they were crazy. How can you fight when you know you're going to lose? I was in such a panic, though, that that's what I did. Without comprehending the gravity of my action, I hurried toward the door. Two police officers grabbed me. Then, without the slightest hope of winning, I fought, I yelled, I called for help. For a second, I managed to break away, but I fell when someone tripped me. Several men threw themselves on top of me. I fought with all my might, I tried to bite (with no success in fact), and the more they hit me, the more I fought back. Soon I was immobilized. At this point I had a horrible, nightmarish sensation: not being able to breathe. I was going to suffocate to death. I tried to cry out again, but there were so many people on top of me it was impossible. I fainted.

When I came to, I was alone in a cell. The sleeve of my jacket had been torn off at the shoulder, but clung to my arm like a bracelet. My collar was gone. My shirt was ripped up and a shred was hanging down in front all the way to my knees. My face was covered with enormous, burning bruises. They didn't hurt. I tasted blood in my mouth. I got up and saw a small window with a grate over it, but so high I couldn't reach it. I looked for a chair. There was none. I approached the door, and grasping the bars, struggled to shake it. It barely moved at all, not enough to establish a back and forth which, in time, might have forced it open.

I circled the cell twenty times or so, rubbing the walls with my hands, knocking in the hope of hearing a hollow sound. Then I stopped under the window, looking up. I tried to jump. I told myself that if I could grab hold of the bars, one of them might not be as well-fastened as the others. But I was a meter short. Then I had an idea. I took off one of my shoes and my shirt. Twisting it, I made my shirt into a rope that I attached to the middle of the shoe. I threw the shoe up until it passed through the bars. Then I pulled it gently so it would get stuck. Once that was accomplished, I climbed up with my fists, but just as I was reaching the grate, the shirt ripped and my shoe fell to the other side. I started again with the other shoe. This time I managed to reach the bars, but they were as solid as the ones on the door. I then fell into a state of despondency that lasted many long hours.

Suddenly, I sat up. Luckily my dejection hadn't lasted. I saw things clearly now. I realized that I had acted foolishly, that I had done just the opposite of what I should have done if I wanted to get out. I should have remained a proper gentleman, asked for amenities as a favor, considered my loss of liberty not as a savage or an animal considers it, but as an abstraction that had to be endured but had no reality. I should have calmly followed them to the cell, stopped in the middle, surprised they could put me here, asked if I could have a blanket, when they would be coming to get me, and how long they would be leaving me here. Basically I shouldn't have acted upset. There was only one way to do battle, and that was legally. I had to keep something up my sleeve, not try everything all at once. If I had behaved in such a fashion, the police would have thought twice before acting against me, whereas in my current state, they wouldn't hesitate. "It's never to late to do the right thing," I told myself.

But an hour later, I realized I was really and truly in prison, whether symbolic or not. What surprised me was that when they came to take me to the criminal investigation unit, no one paid attention to how battered I was. They asked me if I wanted to sign some paper or other, as if I were a normal man. I thought of saying that I wanted to consult a lawyer first. If a lawyer had seen me so beaten, he would have wanted it on record. I hesitated. To attack the very people whose hands I was in seemed to me rather reckless.

Chapter 6

After my transfer to the criminal investigation department, I was led to a room which, although large, gave me a bad feeling. It was the kind of room you see in houses or apartments that are too big, furnished with a table and a few chairs. Individually, the four inspectors who were with me didn't give me an impression of physical strength, except that one of them was maybe a little brawny. They seemed more like bureaucrats, but in a group men always exude a certain power, even if none of them seem dangerous individually. They asked me to be seated. Then, as if I didn't exist, they spoke among themselves. They spoke of trivial things having to do with their business or leisure activities. I noticed that from time to time they alluded to me without naming me specifically, as if out of courtesy they didn't want me to notice. "Maybe we should get to work," they would say from time to time. Or else: "Let's wait a little. He'll like that just as well." I became more and more worried. This game went on for over an hour. I had the impression that they were trying to make me feel like it was my fault that they had to stay. As long as I had been moving from office to office accompanied by two guards, I'd had the comforting feeling, if you can call it that, that justice would take its course and even if things turned out badly for me, I would benefit until the end from the right of the accused to defend himself. But in this room, which was neither a cell nor a judge's chambers, in the company of four men whose duties were unclear, who were pretending to ignore the fact that I was here and yet didn't leave me alone, I was beginning to feel terribly afraid. I told myself that since I maintained my innocence, I had to find the strength to act calm and collected. I had to show that in my innocence I had no idea what they wanted from me. Finally I asked in a naïve voice, "Are we going to be here long?" One of the policemen answered me with perfect courtesy, as if we were the best of friends: "I don't think so." Then, to be agreeable, he questioned his colleagues: "Do we have much longer?" They interrupted their conversation for a moment but didn't answer. I tried to convince myself that they were expecting an order, that they found the wait as long as I did. From time to time, one of them glanced at me. No matter which one it was, they all looked at me with the same expression, as if they were looking at me without the others knowing it, as if the others didn't know I was there. Shortly before noon, another policeman knocked on the door and, seeing that we were occupying the room, left. This minor incident made me feel better. We weren't alone. Other people knew we were here. The policeman hadn't been surprised to see us. Anyone could come in. Strangely, my fear soon resurfaced, following an incident that was just as insignificant as the one I'd found comforting. One of the policemen took a chair and carried it to a corner of the room. "Go sit there," he said, turning to me. I obeyed, but from that moment on I couldn't help searching for the reason for this strange act. "Why are they making me sit in this corner?" Again there was a knock on the door. Another policeman appeared. Seeing me, he said, "Ah," like someone who has intruded and is about to leave. His colleagues detained him. They talked to him about a fishing trip they were planning for Sunday. At that moment, one of them voiced a reservation which I found chilling: "If we're free." "I'll leave you alone," said the newcomer, as if being respectful toward his colleagues' work.

The group resumed the conversation. They lit cigarettes. They seemed to have forgotten me completely when one of them said, "What about you, do you want a cigarette?" I accepted. He brought it to me, gave me a light. I thanked him loudly, in the hope that everyone would hear me. No one turned around. Someone came in again, this time without knocking. "We're tired of being disturbed every five minutes," one of the policemen yelled. A curious detail: while speaking these words he smiled at me, as if I was tired of it too. "Are you staying or going?" he went on to this same intruder. "Because now, I'm going to lock it." My cigarette revealed that my hand was shaking. I wanted to keep it in my mouth, but my mouth tasted so bitter that I threw the cigarette away. At this point I heard a voice say, "We should get something to eat. Do you want something to eat?" I didn't know who was talking to me. I looked at everyone and tried to appear delighted by the idea: "Yes, yes, I would appreciate that." Soon a policeman showed up with a plate covered by another plate, on top of which was a glass, a half-carafe of wine and a piece of bread. He was holding all this clumsily. "We're going to eat too," he said. Two of the policemen left. The others stayed close to me. At three in the afternoon, we were all together again. "So, how's it going?" someone asked me.

My cheeks were burning. No matter how often I licked my lips, a kind of sticky film covered them almost immediately. But I was determined not to let my terror show.

One of them came to me and said: "Well, buddy, how's it going?" I said that everything was fine, smiling as if to say: "As well as can be expected in such a situation." He took a chair and sat opposite me, while the other inspectors continued talking among themselves. He said I was indeed in a strange situation. Then, talking about the police as if he weren't one of them, said, "They weren't very sporting with you." I said that it wasn't their fault, that it was no doubt because of a woman. (I was thinking, I don't know why, of Lucienne.) "Oh!, women, that's how it always is." Then he called to his colleagues and spoke to them, but they pretended not to be interested. So he yelled even louder. "What is it?" they asked. "A woman turned him in." They all looked at me, pretending to be learning a piece of news, as if this fact changed everything. At this point, I don't know why, I found my courage. Seeing that everyone was looking at me and that no one seemed to have anything against me, I thought it was a good idea to address them all. I began talking very quickly, saying that I wasn't the one they were looking for. My name was Tinet and not Talhouet. In my eagerness I stood up as if dealing with a sympathetic audience. But I heard one of them say: "Sit down, sit down." Since I wasn't obeying, the man next to me took me by the arm and brutally forced me to sit. "She denounced you, is that what you mean?" I protested. He slapped one of his colleagues on the shoulder, who said, "What?" as if he'd been interrupted. "Come here, come here." As if against his will, he sat down next to me. It felt strange to be seated next to these two men with no table between us. "You'd be better off telling the truth. We know very well your name is Talhouet . . ."

A few seconds later, when they kept giving me the same advice in about the same terms, I became conscious of the terrible danger lurking over me. I'd had faith in myself. I had thought that I would always know how to respond to all these questions, and now I realized I was weakening, that a time would come when I would no longer be able to speak, when my explanations would no longer have any importance, when I would have to say yes or no, that's all. I nevertheless repeated for the tenth time that my name was Tinet. I'd had a glimmer of hope, when I heard: "You'd be better off telling the truth." I still had energy and exclaimed as before: "But I'm telling the truth," and I repeated the series of circumstances which, according to me, had caused me to be taken for someone else. Again, I heard: "You'd be better off telling the truth." I wanted to cry out again but I had talked so much that I couldn't. "You see," said a policeman, pretending to interpret my silence as an avowal, "you admit it yourself." I protested vehemently. A policeman approached: "Come on," he said slapping me paternally on the shoulder, "you'd be better off telling the truth." I cried out again that I was telling the truth. "No, you're not telling the truth." Then I heard two other policemen saying: "He doesn't want to tell the truth." I cried out again that I was telling the truth. The strange thing was, I sensed that the policemen didn't take me for a vulgar criminal and that with anyone else they probably wouldn't have insisted so much on the truth. They thought I was obsessed with the truth, and every time they wanted to strike a sensitive cord in me they said, "the truth." Since I wasn't a hardened criminal, they had thought that by being kind they would make me confess.

Chapter 7

When I arrived at the Santé prison, my first priority was to examine my cell. Three prisoners were already inside. Meticulous as I am, if I had been asked to draw up plans for a prison, I think I would have foreseen everything. I realized right away that other people were as capable as I was of doing so. It wasn't like Germany here. Even though it was hard to escape there, they hadn't thought of everything. They had improvised, done what was simplest: put us in barracks, surrounded the barracks with barbed wire, and placed armed guards everywhere. Here, aside from those who supervised the guards, no one was armed, at least not visibly. I understood this time that I was truly a prisoner. At first, realizing this plunged me into deep depression. I sat on the stool, which was attached by a chain, and began to cry. This made me feel better. I examined the lock, the window bars, but without touching anything. I realized right away that I shouldn't even think of escaping except through an administrative mix-up. My first idea was to substitute someone for myself. There were four of us. Maybe something would come up. But the very next day I realized that the guard knew us individually. I would have to wait. Before judging me, they would take me to court. I would certainly have an opportunity to get around. In the meantime, I was stuck here.

The next day, the guard opened the door and called me. I didn't move. I wanted to see what he would do. He looked at me and repeated my name. That the guard knew who I was had a very bad effect on me. I played dumb. The guard insisted, staring me down. I told him he was making a mistake, that my name was Tinet. All he had to do was check my papers. "I don't get into these details." I took on an aggressive tone. I'd had enough of being mistaken for someone else. I was naïve enough to think that feigning indignation with subordinates would be useful to me, that it would prove I was acting in good faith. For my denials to appear sincere in high places, I mustn't seem to insist on my identity only in the presence of officials, but in the most mundane situations.

The guard persisted, playing on my good sentiments. I ended up following him, but along the way I kept shouting that it was disgusting, and so on. It's a curious thing to say what you think of those whose hands you're in. How tolerant those in power can be shows you how powerless you are. The guard didn't even ask me to shut up. He let me do as I pleased, responding with utter indifference. I yelled louder and louder.

That evening, I pretended to believe that my final hour had come. I wanted to write a farewell letter to my father. But my father wasn't named Tinet. I therefore wrote to Mondanel, secretly hoping the letter would pass through many hands; it was a very simple letter, in which I said how incredible it was that one could be accused of a crime one hadn't committed, that I would certainly never see him again, that I forgave those who had done me in. It wasn't their fault. They had been tricked. I was the victim of a terrible twist of fate.

In retrospect, our actions are never what they should have been. Today when I think back on this letter I thought so correct in tone, I realize that it had a false ring and that nothing about my attitude at the time had been natural. Everything smelled of the crudest comedy and I don't think anyone believed me for a second. But you have to allow this much to the judicial system: its faults are also its virtues. Since the system is wary of everything, it is no more wary when there is reason to be than when there isn't. I was now beginning to realize that while this charade did me no good, it also did me no harm.

A few days later, it struck me that the only way out was to go on a hunger strike. I hesitated a long time, for even though I was making a lot of noise about my innocence, I was a little worried about attracting too much attention, about singling myself out.

Finally I made my decision. When the guard handed us our soup through the wicket, I refused mine, saying that I didn't want to eat. "Don't get cute, Monsieur de Talhouet," the guard told me. He handed my mess bowl to one of the other prisoners.

This happened two days in a row. No one wanted to admit I was on a hunger strike, and the guard might not know since my mess bowl always went back empty. I realized, at this point, that I had been foolish not to write to the prison director beforehand. I should have started the hunger strike on a fixed date, announced in advance. The way I was doing it was pointless; by the time someone noticed and the administration got into gear, I might be dead.

Should I interrupt the hunger strike and write the letter? My gesture would then lose its spontaneity and seem calculated, not like the act of an innocent man. "What kind of a hunger striker is this?" they might say. I realized that I would be in a stronger position if I continued even though I had gotten off to a bad start.

Despite this consideration, I began eating again. When I was feeling a little better, I decided to write my letter to the prison director. But should I write it in the voice of someone who doesn't know about the judicial system, say that I was innocent and that I was on a hunger strike, or rather compose an official statement written in legal terminology to the director, which would show that I wasn't a pushover, that I was aware of my rights?

I needed advice. I asked my fellow cellmates, who told me it didn't matter. Although they encouraged me, I sensed that they didn't like the air of innocence I assumed which made me seem as if I thought I was better than they were. Finally I wrote my letter. I handed it to the guard, telling him what it contained. Then, the next day, in the evening, I again refused my food. By the fifth day nothing had happened.

I told myself this silence must be due to the fact that as far as the administration was concerned I was still being fed, since my ration was being distributed. I not only had to refuse my ration, I had to prevent my cellmates from taking it. I told them this and they got angry.

Another problem came up. One morning one of my cellmates said, "This isn't such a bad idea after all." I sensed that he was beginning to think of imitating me. That would be a catastrophe. From that moment on, all I could think about was discouraging them. I exaggerated my suffering. I spoke of the punishment I might receive. I told them that if everyone went on a hunger strike, it would be ineffective. I had to stall for time. Afterward, my companions could do what they wanted. How hard it is to keep an idea to oneself! Your peers have no scruples about copying you when they realize that you're on the right track.

I grew weaker. The guards mistreated me and tried to intimidate me. They claimed I was trying to get them in trouble. I would pay for this. They would let me croak . . . Their main argument was that I shouldn't think everyone was watching me. No one cared. I could keep it up for as long as I wanted.

One thing I have never been able to explain is how an abuse or an injustice that could easily remain buried ends up coming to light. Indeed, despite the hostility surrounding me, a report was soon sent to the prison directors. I thought then that my enemies would become twice as nasty. Instead, to my surprise, they suddenly became very considerate.

Finally all four of us were taken to the infirmary—my companions had naturally taken advantage of the situation. I didn't like this infirmary right off. The idea of wanting to heal people while depriving them of their freedom created a strange atmosphere. You also sensed that they didn't want anyone saying it was more comfortable here than in prison. I was on my fourteenth day of fasting whereas my companions had just started. Thanks to me, without having suffered the same process of weakening, they were receiving the same benefits, which made me very angry with them. Yet shouldn't I have been glad if thanks to me they also succeeded in getting out? Nonetheless, when an administrator came to question us and put all four of us on the same footing, I couldn't refrain from telling him that my case was different than theirs. I was immediately sorry. At every moment, life endeavors to destroy our noble sentiments. They have to be firmly rooted to stay in place come what may. After thinking it over, I managed to obtain a sense of solidarity with my companions. They of course were doing me an injustice. I consoled myself with the thought that freedom was just as precious to them as it was to me.

Chapter 8

Once back in my cell, I had the impression that, as usual, I'd deluded myself about mankind. I would never get anywhere. I was feeling deeply depressed when suddenly it occurred to me that all I had to do was escape. I knew it was impossible, but the idea did me good. I went two days without feeling down. An impossible project managed to restore my confidence. I was determined to escape by whatever means possible and that was enough to cheer me up. I was careful not to think about how I would do it, since it was impossible.

Unfortunately, at the beginning of the third day, I suddenly had the revelation that despite the safeguards, the precautions, the slowness of the justice system, I was ineluctably approaching a tragic end. My life here was a model of human destiny, but on a smaller scale. All the hopes I'd clung to vanished one by one. The idea of simulating a suicide came to mind. I abandoned it almost immediately. The tactics that cause such a stir in normal life were considered here to be old tricks. At this point I became truly desperate. It was all over. I hadn't believed what I was saying when I'd written to Mondanel that I was going to die, yet without knowing it, I had told him the truth! Later, when I'd been handed over to the Germans, he would remark how insightful I'd been!

Then I had some other ideas. I could pretend to be deaf, or blind, but at the last minute I didn't have the courage. There is something blasphemous about feigning sickness that repels me, like the false blindness of a beggar. And besides, even if I won, even if I succeeded in having these imaginary infirmities confirmed, it wouldn't have been enough to set me free.

For several days I didn't know what to do, when suddenly I thought of madness. (Baumé used to simulate it perfectly. It's extraordinary that a person who appeared so simple could have such self-control, such skill when it came to passing himself off for what he wasn't.)

My madness consisted principally in adopting a haggard look, which was facilitated by the state I was in. I was repulsively dirty. I hadn't been able to shave for twenty-five days. To intensify this look, which basically could have been that of any prisoner, I laughed from time to time. I thought of bursting out laughing, like a real crazy, but that was too much. I limited myself to a little chuckle, which had the advantage of turning into a fitful cough if it wasn't being taken seriously.

My cellmates soon told me they'd had it with me. I could act crazy with the guards if it amused me, but not with them. I shouldn't take them for idiots. They knew the trick. I was wasting my time. I'd be better off saving my energy, because I was going need it.

It is difficult to persevere under such conditions, when no one is fooled and you lack confidence in yourself. Yet persevere I did. Then something remarkable happened which shows that perseverance can be very powerful: my companions began to wonder if I weren't crazy after all. And they complained to the guards.

When I was in the doctor's office, I pretended not to understand why I had been taken to see him. He was seated at a desk which, in contrast to the emptiness and coldness of the large room, was cluttered with photographs and familiar objects. The doctor wasn't even curious enough to raise his head. Finally he looked at me, the way someone might turn suddenly and say: "Ok! Now to us." I remained silent while moving my lips as if I wanted to speak. It was an idea that had just come to mind that instant. "What's wrong?" he asked, staring at me attentively. I began laughing louder than usual. He pretended not to notice. "You're nervous," he observed after a moment. I said a few disconnected words, but none of the ones I had prepared. The doctor stopped looking at me. He took a sheet of paper, wrote a few words, and called a nurse. I quieted down. Then I suddenly realized that there was something too reasonable about my madness. It only manifested itself at the desired moment. In between, I was too silent. I burst out laughing. "Calm down," said the doctor, with such sweetness that I felt disconcerted. I stopped laughing. I realized immediately that I had obeyed, that I had calmed down as I had been asked. I began yelling. "Quiet," said the doctor in a brutal voice. This command sent a healthy shock through my system. Deep down, I now understood, I needed to be mistreated to play my role. Cordiality and sweetness paralyzed me. Now I was free. There was nothing holding me back anymore. Instead of obeying this time, I began yelling at the top of my lungs. Still, I was afraid of falling into a trap. Was I really behaving like a crazy person? Does a crazy person yell all that much? I very clearly heard the doctor raising his voice, telling me that this had gone on long enough, that it was a ridiculous charade. I wondered what to do. I had the impression that the doctor had gotten angry to see what my reaction would be. Should I abruptly calm down or should I continue? I hesitated an instant. Above all I mustn't let it show that I was thinking. I began yelling even louder. At that point, the doctor raised his voice as well. He approached me with his hand raised to make me quiet down. I had the distinct feeling I was in the midst of an experiment, that if the threat made me quiet, I was admitting to being a fake.

An instant later he sat back down, looked at me with a smile, and said to the nurse standing nearby, note pad in hand: "This boy is fine. There's nothing wrong with him . . ."

Now I guessed what was coming. They would judge me as if nothing had happened and in the worked-up state I'd reached. "He'll stop playing the fool when he's convicted!" I would be treated like a criminal who doesn't even know how to defend himself. I could carry on in any way imaginable, no one would pay attention anymore!

Part Three

Toward Freedom

Chapter 1

When the judge dismissed the charge, I stammered a few words of gratitude. He gave me some advice, pretending to believe I hadn't killed any Germans. Nothing is more appealing than these men who don't mind being duped. I had been convinced that this judge hated me for lying to him and that he was looking to trip me up as if it were a personal affront. Now I realized I had been unfair. This man was truly a superior being. He had the coyness of someone who knows he is doing the right thing and yet pretends to be unaware of it. He did everything he could to hide his goodness, as if he had decided to dismiss the case taking only my file into account.

I announced the news to the guards. Nothing is more anguishing than the time that passes between a promise and its fulfillment. Two hours later, I fell back into my depression. No matter how much I told myself I was saved, horrible doubts kept creeping over me. A wild idea came to mind: Supposing I took advantage of the relaxed surveillance to escape! But wasn't that crazy? What can you make of a prisoner who escapes just as he is about to be released? I couldn't shake the idea. If the judge revoked his decision and they took me back to the prison, how I would hate myself for not taking advantage of this moment!

I was waiting in a hallway when once again I was escorted into the judge's chambers. It was only for a detail. The judge smiled at me. I then realized that this man, who as long as he was against me seemed to possess such extraordinary power, no longer had any at all now that he was on my side.

When I was released, a stupid bureaucrat told me that I shouldn't imagine they had done this out of sympathy. I shouldn't consider myself off the hook either, but should be very careful and stop acting so arrogant, or they wouldn't let me go at all. It occurred to me that this person had no right to threaten me. If I was being released, it was because the order had come from higher up and it wasn't in his power to change it. But just to be safe, I pretended to believe that he could.

After you're released from prison, there are still little reports that have to be filed to regularize the situation and clarify forgotten details, but which are accompanied by the same judicial apparatus as the serious things. Thus

I received a summons to report to the court clerk's office. And as everything that touches the law, whether before or after, is written in the same enigmatic fashion, I began shaking. I had a new fear: arousing suspicion by my sluggish response to a harmless summons. I regretted not having taken care of everything at first, when it would have been natural and easy, not having worked it out so I could avoid these final contacts. It's always the same story. When things are going well, you don't think about the future. It must be said in my defense that I never wanted to be taken for one of those people who keep worrying about their own interests even when they are given good news, and who act difficult instead of being glad. I had to fight this fear of indiscretion, because what could be stupider than worrying about tactfulness when your life and liberty are at stake.

I went to thank Mondanel. I thought that after what he'd done for me, he would help me settle the remaining details without even noticing, but I was surprised to find myself up against a wall. It was as if after having given me a gift of a million francs, he was absolutely refusing to give me the slightest piece of advice on how to invest the money safely. Coldly, he led me to understand that I had nothing to thank him for, that what he had done was perfectly natural and that anyone would have done the same. I suddenly understood that he did not want his part in all this to be exaggerated, he did not want to be the only one involved in the affair. He added that the prison director had been very kind and that at the Ministry of Justice they'd been nice as well. I didn't dare ask him the name of the high-ranking official at this Ministry who had intervened on my behalf. An official, so it seems, younger than his subordinates! I didn't want to appear to be scheming behind the respectable screen of gratitude. Whereas Mondanel had found it natural that I should come see him before my arrest, now that he had done me a tremendous service I sensed that I was disturbing him. To prevent me from coming back, he acted as if he thought I was plotting something, surmising that I would have never wanted him to think such a thing of me. I told myself nonetheless that it would be silly to allow a scruple like this to cause me to be impolite to the high official. Steeling myself, I asked his name. "Monsieur Messein," said Mondanel, without adding any details.

As I still hadn't received the paper in the name of Tinet attesting to my freedom, I continued running all over town. It was very unpleasant for me, but I still felt I was in danger and told myself I had to strike while the iron was hot. But the same protectors who had saved me from death were now unable to do me even a small favor. I wasn't yet aware that when people indifferent to our fate help us a kind of misunderstanding ensues, a regret even, which subsequently makes it impossible to have a good relationship.

What would happen to me if I were imprisoned again? What would Bressy, Messein, and Mondanel do? Once people perform a favor, they consider their mission accomplished. Having to intervene again gives them a bad feeling. And then, putting everything back in motion didn't seem like an easy task. Basically, the future looked bleak. They had saved me from a bad situation, it was true, but they hadn't exactly known what they were doing. My release was more of a lucky coincidence, as evidenced by Messein's surprise at seeing me free. Mondanel and he had worked at putting over a point of law. My self-assuredness vanished. I was paralyzed by the need to behave in such a way that these gentlemen would not have to regret their assistance.

After a month of useless comings and goings, a terrible fear began to creep over me. I kept telling myself that it was insane, but it grew stronger and stronger. I had the impression that the very people who had saved me were going to have me imprisoned again, finding me unworthy of what they had done for me. I felt surrounded by hostility, but was unable to explain the cause. It was such an unlikely scenario that I thought I was suffering from a kind of persecution complex. But after thinking it over, I realized that it wasn't impossible after all. It was quite feasible that those police who make every issue a question of personal pride, learning that I had been set free by my friends, would arrange to have me arrested without any formal order being given. It occurred to me that in the course of this last month I had been wildly imprudent.

When I saw my father, I didn't dare share my thoughts with him. He was triumphant. He told me that Messein wanted to see me. He also announced that he had learned that Jean de Boiboissel, whom I had judged so unfairly, had intervened on my behalf, which really surprised me. I mustn't waste a second, I had to thank him immediately. My father had already thanked him, but that wasn't enough. Since my liberation, though he used to pretend to leave me entirely on my own, my father had suddenly decided that he didn't have to consult me when it was a matter of my own interests. He was so awed by the importance he thought I had assumed that he'd become convinced I could no longer deal with the ensuing obligations alone.

We went to Messein's, and then I understood what had happened. Without daring to tell me, my father had solicited a post for me at the Ministry of Justice, and Messein, aided by Bressy, had used his influence to obtain one. My father was overflowing with civilities to compensate for my coolness. It pained me to watch him. He was at the point of losing all dignity. As if talking to a child, he even told me that I wasn't thanking Monsieur Messein enough, and this while we were still in Messein's office. The director's attitude was marvelous. He pretended he didn't want to be thanked and that my father was exaggerating. He hadn't done anything. The Minister himself, Monsieur Xavier de Languillonie, was the one to whom we should express our gratitude. He motioned as if to say that my coolness seemed far more natural than my father's gushing. He had certainly planned to get rid of us very quickly, as one always does to avoid cheapening a favor by too much familiarity, but when my father's overflowing gratitude showed no signs of tapering off, he allowed himself the pleasure of our continued company. He began explaining my future responsibilities to me several times without seeming to notice my father's joy, as if he weren't the one who had assisted us and was pleased on behalf of the Minister, our true benefactor, for our happiness.

After broadly sketching out what my responsibilities would be, Messein told us in an offhand way, as if it were a minor detail out of his domain, that I should introduce myself at the personnel office where my visit had been announced. I was struck that he wasn't taking his protection all the way, that he was largely leaving me to finish up alone, as if it were natural that I should contribute to an effort so successfully begun by others. I felt uncomfortable. We were on equal footing now, but not for long; while I was introducing myself to the personnel department, Messein would remain in this same director's office. Oh! I know, realizing that I was protected would ease the formalities. But I was so afraid of jealousy, the envy that this kind of protection provoked! I could just imagine the pleasure it would bring the petty bureaucrats if they could say to their superiors: "Do you know exactly who you sent us?" They might give Messein the sense that they found it impossible to hire me, ask him for a confirmation. I pictured the classic scene of the boss not being able to do what he wants, overstepping his bounds, being unable to require his subordinates to take a measure that would undermine his authority. "Why isn't it possible?" Messein would ask with astonishment. They would explain it to him. Experience has taught me that in circumstances like this, the underlings always end up winning. Their bosses, unable to enter into the details, leave it up to them. In the end, the fault would fall on my father and myself. "Why did I get involved in all this?" Messein would think, "I don't even know them," and so on. He would nevertheless try to work it out, without committing himself too much. He would talk about me, feign a continuing interest in my case, even though deep down he didn't want to hear about me anymore! For to do a favor that is directly in one's power and to ask others to do one are two different things. He would probably be asked more questions than he had asked us himself. And thus for a position that I didn't really want, they might end up discovering that my case's dismissal wasn't in order.

Chapter 2

The next day, I received an unexpected visit from Richard. Naturally my father had told him everything. He wanted to help me. The two of them understood one another perfectly where my interests were concerned. I have never heard friends talk about me behind my back, but I like to reconstruct this kind of conversation. Richard must have told my father how it pained him to see how inept I was at taking advantage of the kindness being shown me, adding that I didn't want this job, that I was pretending to be interested in it but that in the end I wouldn't accept it. Even better, he would give the real reasons for my behavior: I was pathetic, racked with fear. I saw danger everywhere. I distrusted my own family, my best friends. It was everyone's duty to act in my interest despite me! I was a child, I was emotional. I wasn't mean, but weak. You had to know how to reason with me, how to talk to me. And Madame Gaillard joined in the conversation. To add to what Richard was saying, she told of how I had left her. They didn't speak badly of me; they pitied me and simply wanted what was good for me. In reality, what would have genuinely contributed to this much-talked-about security didn't interest anyone. In this I recognized Richard's character. Even though he was able to see things clearly, he pretended not to see what threatened me. He claimed it was imaginary, though he knew very well that it was real. Deep down, he wanted to harm me, but in such a way that he would seem to be acting in my best interest, and he even managed to drag that idiot Juliette into the picture. My father was the only one who didn't buy it. He of course didn't see what Richard was trying to do, but he did sense that the situation wasn't exactly as he presented it.

A few days later, Juliette, whom I hadn't seen in a year, arrived at my home. She had a letter from Messein with her. She immediately told me that Richard had visited Mondanel, that he was acting on my behalf . . . He was doing all of this on his own, without talking to me about it of course. It seems he had even been to the National Insurance office to ask for some kind of certificate. In a word, Richard wanted me to disturb people who were well-disposed toward me, to make them do things for me that he knew I would later refuse. It occurred to me then that the best way to defend myself against this duplicity was to appear not to notice it. Messein requested in his letter that I come see him. I immediately took him up on his invitation. I was stupefied to learn that, knowing I would neglect to do it, he himself had completed the formalities he'd mentioned several days earlier. He had given my name and other information to Monsieur Brulot, the head of personnel. Messein considered me so unimportant that he would do for me what he wouldn't have done for anyone, as if he were helping an old lady cross the street.

When I found myself in the corridors of the Ministry with the note he had given me, I wondered what I should do. I was afraid of all these bureaucrats. I opted to go from office to office and play dumb, thereby rendering all this assistance useless, while still being able to claim that I had obeyed. I was just as afraid of several people in one room as I was of isolated managers. It always seemed to me that someone was going to give me a long look, take advantage of the fact that I was talking to someone else to get up and whisper something to a colleague. That colleague would stare at me in turn. Someone would remember seeing me elsewhere. "That's not who he is," they would say. Shortly thereafter, the entire Ministry would know my true identity. I would be arrested. Even those who knew about me would pretend I had tricked them. Obviously, they knew the truth higher up but didn't want to appear to have known and be taken for accomplices. They could defend me if the affair didn't go too far.

Otherwise, I mustn't kid myself. They would drop me without the slightest misgiving.

I ended up going to see this Monsieur Brulot after all. But I was so frightened at the idea of coming and going freely in these same offices where my file must have circulated not too long before that a strange thing happened. I suddenly had the impression that Brulot might think that the man introducing himself as me wasn't the same one to whom Messein had given the letter, that he might think that I was a usurper, that I had stolen it just now in a corridor, a waiting room, or a stairwell. I remembered how badly I had wanted Messein to ask the Personal Director to come up to his office. He had tried to call him but hadn't gotten through. It was when I'd said: "Maybe you can try again," that I sensed Messein found me a little nervy.

Finally I left. What joy to see clouds again, people walking, cars!

What was frustrating about my father and about Richard especially was that they didn't see things as I did at all. They thought I should take advantage of the interest in me to gain visibility and land a good position for *after the war*. I had the unimaginable luck to enter the civil service. What an incredible turn of events! Neither of them would have neglected to drop by my office, on the fourth or fifth floor, under the pretext that they were just passing by and wanted to say hello. Richard would have motioned me to point out which of my colleagues I liked best. Even better, he would have explained to them that I was shy in order to satisfy his own curiosity, asking everyone questions that I supposedly wouldn't dare ask. He would have been very respectful, as if I were going to be there forever and he wanted to make a good impression that would help me in the future. After he left, they would say I had a wonderful brother. Thanks to him, my colleagues would warm up to me sooner. It's a form of politeness among bureaucrats to talk to newcomers about a common future, as if they can no longer imagine being separated. Thanks to Richard, they would say, "Be patient, next month we'll get you a key to the coat closet," and so on.

More and more I was deemed an interesting case. People wanted to provide me with a means of existence. There was no longer any reason why I shouldn't have a good job. My father was working on it. He was always by my side. What confused me was that he seemed to think that I had everything coming to me. Justice was finally being served. When he encountered people who were not amenable, he threatened to get an influential official involved. He didn't even want to wait any more when we paid visits. He would walk around in waiting rooms as if there was no point in sitting down since he was going to be ushered in right away. I was afraid he would offend people. Nothing disturbs me so much as appearing to think that things are owed me. He seemed to be saying that if his wish were not granted immediately he would take action. I was afraid that people would get annoyed and throw us out. I mentioned this to my father. According to him, I no longer had anything to fear from anyone. On the contrary, they should be afraid of me. I didn't dare tell him so, but I was increasingly nervous about being arrested again. My father was talking too much about my being a hero. People looked at me strangely afterward. They didn't seem to doubt it, since it would have been indecent to do so in the face of such an assertion. But they weren't entirely convinced and didn't dare ask why I was a hero; instead they asked roundabout questions that I was always afraid my father would answer stupidly. But he didn't answer, as if such a thing were no one's business. And that worried me too, because there was something irksome about the idea that the beauty of my actions dispensed him from talking about them, that his mere assertion should suffice. In his pride, my father had lost all sense of social interaction; I therefore decided not to accompany him anymore. He would go alone, which worried me as well. He was so happy about my case's dismissal he acted as if I shouldn't bother coming along, implying I had every right to take it easy.

The most frustrating thing was how quickly he trusted people he was meeting for the first time. And he always seemed to suggest that after what had happened I didn't have to be afraid of anyone. He liked to say that one had to take advantage of success, which was rather strange when one considered the monotonous life he had led. In his eyes, success, as he put it, was a foot in the stirrup. It was finally an occasion to act. He had already been through this once, when after a great deal of effort he had received his job in Versailles. He had imagined that the proximity to Paris would allow him to make contact with editors, that he would write for newspapers, and he ran around so much that his clumsiness nearly destroyed his efforts.

Sometimes in a moment of weakness I became proud of what had happened to me and told the story of my case's dismissal to everyone I met. I pretended to be definitively saved. They congratulated me. They rejoiced a little too quickly at my success. They pretended to believe I was no longer in danger. They took the occasion of my present immunity to reveal things they had hidden from me. "We were so afraid for you! We didn't think things would work out so well, at one point we thought you were a goner," and so on. The knowledge of these past fears made me feel very uncomfortable, since deep down I didn't feel any more secure than before. No one was really thinking about my safety. No one was advising me to continue taking precautions. My belief that I was safe made things too easy. After all, no one wanted to risk being asked for help again if I myself was naïve enough not to see any need of such help. It was then I decided to act more modest. But this made a bad impression. No, I shouldn't underestimate my merit. I had been very clever. I had maneuvered perfectly. I resolved instead to explain exactly what had happened, to show that the danger wasn't over, that despite my return to freedom my situation was hardly better than before. Then something occurred that I hadn't anticipated. As long as I had being living on the edge, I had generally encountered a good deal of willingness to help me. People had found my requests entirely natural. But now that I was out of prison, a kind of distrust of a different sort came over people. When I seemed less than completely exultant, people thought I wasn't telling the whole truth, that there was something beneath the surface. I was surprised to see that my friends had done much more for me when I was sought by the police and there was some risk involved than now when it might seem that everything was in order. Stories of espionage and double agents passed through their heads. My fear of being arrested again after having been released scared everyone away. They didn't understand me anymore. My story was getting too complicated. So then I decided to keep quiet, which also aroused suspicion among those who knew what had happened to me and thought I wanted to hide it from them.

Chapter 3

It was at this time that my father was taken to the hospital. Even though I had been afraid that something would happen to him my entire life, I wasn't as affected as I would once have been. I had become hardened. Coming one after another, the worst calamities no longer had the same impact.

I went to the hospital. I headed for my father's room. I was struck by how courteous everyone was toward me. It was evident that whatever I might have done in life, I was considered in this particular circumstance to be a man worthy of respect and consideration, so much so that I stayed longer that I should have and they were obliged to tell me when it was time to leave. Suddenly I understood that my father was gravely ill, and that just because he wasn't in danger of imminent death didn't mean I could behave as if he were well. I pictured him immobile in his bed, moving only his hand from time to time when he spoke, and I started to cry. I was no longer thinking of myself or of anything. I left the hospital without even glancing at the people out front.

Two weeks later my father went to convalesce at one of the many residential hotels in Fontainebleau. He had always lived alone, which meant that at the critical moments of his life he had never been anyone's guest. Despite all his friends, he had never enjoyed personal hospitality.

I went to visit him sometimes. One evening on the train, or rather the omnibus, it suddenly dawned on me that all I had to do was leave for England. My case's dismissal, the authorities' recognition of my false identity, gave me a degree of confidence I had never known before.

Now that my decision was made, I realized that I had wasted a lot of time. How could I have waited nearly three years to decide to leave when I had always intended to do so? It may be, I told myself, that it is not enough to think of something in order to do it, nor even to desire it from the bottom of your heart, but that in addition the hour of one's destiny must strike. And this hour, I sensed, had struck. I saw everything differently. I became the man I had been before my captivity in Germany. I was surprised by all my fears, my indecision, and calculations.

I resolved to say my farewells to all those who had supported and helped me. Whereas until today I had felt alone, it seemed to me now that I had many friends, that everyone had done as much for me as he could and that I should be grateful to all. For deep down, the reason I had expected so much of my peers was because I had been diminished by fear and had an exaggerated notion of what was due me. In reality, I shouldn't just express my gratitude, but also make them forget how severely I had judged them.

I was living on the rue Rambuteau again. It felt odd that someone as insignificant as Madame de Miratte would be witness to such an important moment in my life, that she would see all my preparations, all my activity, that she would overhear my words of happiness, whereas so many people seemed dearer to me and would have shared so much more in my joy. But nothing's ever perfect.

A few days later, I began to say my farewells. First I went to see Juliette Gaillard, whom I hadn't seen in a month. We'd had an argument. She'd thought I wasn't appreciative of all she had done for me. I, for my part, found her way of helping me annoying; I had sensed more of a nosy need to get involved in other people's business than love. She had been to see my father and everyone I knew, and had spoken of me as if she thought I was a nice boy but she acted as if she had never been my mistress. Our love was gone. I sensed that deep down, doing good deeds and getting out and seeing people were more important to her than loving. But the great thing about success is that all your grievances vanish and instead you feel a great need to be kind. And this kindness is contagious.

It makes everyone around you kind as well. It's as if the positive turn of events were not affecting you alone. Your friends enjoy it too. I cannot express how happy Juliette was about all that was happening to me. She was no longer critical, and you would have thought that she too was going to leave this miserable life behind. She had not the slightest bitterness. There was no need to explain our actions to rekindle our friendship; my visit was enough to dissipate any misunderstanding. Now that I was leaving, everything that might have divided us in the future and been present in our minds no longer mattered. She had risen to my level. Deep down, I was a little disappointed. Never for a moment did she try to hold me back or even suggest that she would suffer at my leaving. She was sincerely as happy as I was, and seemed to think it would have been selfish on her part to hold me back. It was over between us, but she was happy that we would remain friends.

Next I went to see Guéguen. He was still living the same way, but was greatly changed. When I had lived with him, France had been occupied only a few months and he had thought it would all be quickly settled. But now it had been going on for two years and there was no end in sight. All the excitement with which he had greeted me, the desire to be useful, to help me because in his mind everything was going to come to an end quickly, had vanished. He was despondent and had developed filthy habits. He had arranged his life in mediocrity, and was surprised to find that this mediocrity had become permanent. Which is why, when I announced I was leaving, when I tactlessly thought I could speak to him as if he were still the man who had generously taken me in, I was surprised to find that he didn't seem to remember a thing and that I was unintentionally making him suffer. Indeed, nothing is more painful to people in such a situation than to sense that others have maintained their initial enthusiasm. He didn't envy me, but I sensed that I was causing him to confront his own life and see that his fate had been particularly doomed. He realized that other people were getting by, that they were undertaking new projects, and that he, without knowing how it had come to pass, was attached to the common lot. This made him bitter. He talked about his old mother. He loved her, that was why he hadn't been able to do anything. He explained to me at great length how he too had always wanted to go but couldn't because of her. It was one of the strangest experiences, hearing him complain to me, basically an indifferent observer, about the mother he so cherished. For over half an hour he talked about her in a way I would never have imagined, while I, a stranger, was obliged to persuade him that what he was doing was entirely natural and to his credit.

I left Guéguen's rather upset. I had thought I was making a gesture that would bring him pleasure, that would show

I held no grudge, and all these good intentions had vanished in the face of reality. I then decided to visit Mondanel, who was more stable. Everything he had done for me until now had seemed minor, but now that I was leaving I thought he had been awfully nice after all. He had done a great deal though he'd been under no obligation, which was commendable in a man so concerned with attaining a high position.

I found him in his little office. Just so he wouldn't think I was planning to ask for something again, I'd had the assistant tell him that I was coming to say goodbye. I knew that Mondanel didn't care for de Gaulle, but our relationship was such that he wouldn't take offense if I did. And then it must be said that according to certain of my fellow countrymen everyone had a right to like de Gaulle, there was nothing dishonorable about it, just as in peace time one can be a royalist. One could easily be a Gaullist without denunciation or harm from one's enemies.

When I announced my decision to Mondanel, he raised his arms to the sky, then, as he liked to give himself an air of importance, to make what he pretended were risky statements for him, he told me on the sly: "I would love to be able to do what you're doing," thereby leaving me to understand that deep down he wasn't at all what he appeared. I thanked him at length for all he had done for me when I was in prison. We shook hands warmly. Despite it all, I was touched that this man who trembled before the Germans and saw nothing wrong with collaborating, was visibly so incapable of doing me any harm, as opposed to people like Boiboissel and others, who didn't give me the same impression at all. Had they seen me talking to Mondanel, I know I wouldn't have felt safe. Finally I was going to leave all this behind: even more than not seeing the Krauts, the idea of no longer breathing this poisoned air filled me with joy. I asked him if he thought I should also say goodbye to Messein. He enthusiastically advised me to do so. I realized that all these men wanted was not to be judged any more severely than they judged themselves.

In the afternoon that same day, I went to see Messein. Now that I was leaving, I felt great sadness saying goodbye to all my friends. As long as I had been involved with them, fighting with them, I hadn't dreamt that they were basically in the same miserable boat as I was. But now that they were staying behind, it struck me that my judges, and even my guards, envied me, and that it would not have taken much for us become reconciled.

I went to see Lucienne. It was the first time I was visiting her with some credit to my name, no longer as a poor fellow but as myself. For the first time I would be in a superior position to hers. I was leaving and she was staying. I was happy and she was suffering. How the tables had turned! But it must be said that I wasn't doing this to satisfy any lowly rancor. I was doing it because I was happy and had a childish need to have only friends, to forget everything. I told her right away that I was leaving, that I was coming to say goodbye, and I kissed her. She was not surprised that I should come to her like this. Of all my friends, she was the one who was happiest for me. And it wasn't so that I would forgive all her spiteful little actions. It was strange but we were all so nervous since the war that what we did to one another no longer mattered as much as it used to. Friendship, even love, could come and go as if commanded by outside circumstances without anyone dreaming of being resentful. As long as the Krauts were among us, any feeling of resentment among Frenchmen seemed out of place and inopportune. You could hurt someone or help someone at the same time and no one would be surprised. Lucienne wanted to give me some money. I refused it after a scene in which the money changed hands several times. She put it in my pocket, I put it on the table. In a Russian-style gesture, she wanted to burn it if I didn't take it, so that at least no one would have it. I told her that was stupid. I mentioned Roger, and she began to cry. I consoled her by saying he would come back one day, and when he did she should tell him to join me. She promised me she would.

I went to see my father. After announcing my departure, I was surprised to see that what was for me such an important decision, what brought me inner light, made no impression on him. He simply said: "Oh! very good . . ." and I sensed that he didn't believe what I was telling him now any more than what I had told him before. I tried to make him understand that this was different, but he remained skeptical. I sensed he thought I was suffering from my usual bursts of enthusiasm, that tomorrow it would be all over. Then, suddenly, I realized what was really going on inside him. It hurt my father, who was sick, emaciated, and far from home, to hear me. He was suffering despite himself because I was happy, I was making plans, because so much was happening while he felt like he was at the end of his life. I hated myself for having paraded my future before him like this, for having overstated things so he would believe me. When suddenly we are happy, we think that everyone will join in our happiness, and it doesn't occur to us that this happiness can be hurtful. I abruptly changed my attitude and told him I would be facing great dangers. By his sad smile I guessed he didn't believe me. It is rare for a man who has always put on acts, and continues to do so, not to be irritating. He had always annoyed me with the way he liked playing the victim. But this time, it was real. He wasn't acting.

On the train home, I was sad my joy wasn't shared by everyone. What struck me most was how everything around me basically changed so little whether I was happy or not. I realized the dangers I had faced must not have been so great after all, since now I thought I was safe yet the world had stayed the same.

I went to see Ghislaine. Of all my visits, this was the

one I dreaded most. I even considered not visiting her. But I have always been horrified by the idea of treating the people I love worse than those who don't matter. Since I was seeing everyone else, it would have been strange to avoid the person I loved the best.

What struck me most of all was that I had made my decision without consulting her, and that I was treating this decision like an order. Ghislaine asked me why I had to leave. I told her I had to. She accepted this response as if I weren't in control. I was a little ashamed, for if I had to leave as I said, deep down it was only because I wanted to. And no matter how much I cried, no matter how torn up I was about leaving, it was nonetheless evident that nothing was forcing me to go. For an instant, I thought of bringing her with me. Basically, nothing I was planning to do couldn't also be done by a woman, nothing required any particular physical strength. We could just as well leave together. Ghislaine's presence would add no additional risk. I asked her if she wanted to come. I thought she was going to accept. But after a brief moment during which I didn't know what she was thinking, she told me it was impossible, that she would be in my way.

Finally I went to see Georget. He had been my first protector upon arriving in Paris. In truth, he had done nothing for me, and the irony was that he seemed to think that it was partially thanks to him that my affairs had turned out so well.

Chapter 4

Darkness had not yet fallen when I left the train station in Mâcon. Nothing is worse than arriving in a strange city in the evening. There was a crowd in front of the station since it was a Sunday and people were returning from the country. I asked where downtown was. I received a cold reply. In Paris I would no doubt have gotten the same sort of reply, but I wouldn't have paid any attention to it. So many people were waiting for the streetcar that I decided to head out on foot. I dined at a brasserie where music was playing. I have never felt such anguish. France seemed to be living like before the war. There were even groups of young people in the streets making a racket. The cafés were overflowing. I read all sorts of names which were familiar to the local residents, but meant nothing to me. I looked for a hotel. They were all full.

I had wanted to leave Paris with all my might, and now that I had left I felt a horrible void. It gave me a strange feeling to know that people could say to themselves: "He's not around any more" and that this observation wouldn't change anyone's routine. I saw my friends gathering without me. There were no great regrets about my absence. "He wanted to leave," they would say. I sensed that they were living in misery and couldn't disapprove of my having sought to escape, yet deep down they held it against me anyway. You could tell by their indifference to my fate. It hurt me to sense how quickly they lost interest in me, that I could only count on myself. Though I had left in the most correct fashion, though they had sincerely bid me well, all these people had suddenly forgotten me. They wished me no harm, they would even pretend to be sad if something happened to me, but in reality they considered themselves relieved of any obligation toward me. I had wanted to leave, hadn't I? This feeling increased my solitude.

Now I was gone. I had left behind everyone thinking I was leaving no one. When I left it had seemed to me that it was no big deal to rely only on oneself, persuaded as I was that I had always been alone. I had often been asked why I stayed in Paris. Now I understood. I had thought that it was only because it was easier to hide in a big city. But no, it was because I was Parisian, because I had family and friends there.

The next afternoon I took a train to a village close to the demarcation line.

When night began to fall, my distress grew greater still. From inside the train I could see the orange-colored sky, an immense sky that I had forgotten existed. Each kilometer was painful. I would have liked to be able to go back. I thought of the unfamiliar village where I would soon arrive. Nothing makes you feel more abandoned than arriving in a small town where you are the only stranger, where no one is waiting for you and where you have to pretend to know what you're doing so you don't attract attention. You enter the first café. Until then everything is fine. Even the locals stop in. But half an hour later, when the café proprietors set their table and begin to live for themselves, you begin to feel panicky because you are still there and don't know where to go. What should you say if someone asks you a question?

The café was emptying out. I was feeling better. I couldn't say where I was from, but I knew where I was going and could talk about it indefinitely. "Are you waiting for Gustave?" asked the owner, seeming to wonder whether he might be comprising himself by this simple statement. I said yes. "He's coming." I invited him to have a drink with me. I sensed then that the worst was over, that I was no longer alone, that a little life with its habits had just begun, and this made me feel relieved. The emptiness of travel had ended. I was reborn after a black hole of two full days. I sensed that little by little I inspired confidence without having said a word, simply because I looked lost. The proprietress came to sit down next to me, asked me if I wanted something to eat, as if she understood that I was hungry, that I came from cities where one couldn't ask for food, but that here it was different. A couple of policemen entered. They didn't even look at me. Their indifference was marvelous. They didn't want to know who I was. They were off duty and everything about them exuded the joy of leisure, the prospect of not having to worry about anyone. Finally, they could be themselves and reveal their thoughts. I invited them to have a drink as well. I told them that I came from Paris and that seemed perfectly normal to them. They asked me what was going on there. I'd had a bit to drink, and found my optimism increasingly natural. I felt I'd been saved. The worst was over.

In the company of Gustave, I crossed the demarcation line without a hitch.

As soon as I arrived in Lyon, I headed for a crummy hotel, cold and poorly kept, whose proprietor considered himself something of a protector of patriots. When I told him that Boiboissel had sent me, he didn't seem to remember him. He immediately handed me a form to fill out. I hesitated. My papers were in order but I preferred to remain anonymous.

He was a man who had done great things for many Frenchmen, but I sensed I was arriving too late, that it had gone on for too long. The initial enthusiasm had worn down. He was no longer interested in people who were crossing the border, who were living on the edge, who were sought by the police. And the most striking sign of this change was that he was beginning to see ingrates everywhere, people who, once safe, laughed about having compromised him. No matter how much I told him that I wasn't one of those people, he looked at me coldly. It now took him a while to do what previously he would have done of his own accord right from the start. And yet Boiboissel had done a great deal for him. I asked myself what he would have thought, hearing the man whom he had described so flatteringly say: "I can't do it, but so-and-so can . . ."

I went up to my room a little demoralized. It smelled like hard-boiled eggs from the falling ceiling plaster. That evening I went downstairs, and tried to put our relationship on more cordial ground. But the proprietor didn't seem to recognize me. He knew I needed him, but did nothing. I was a client like any other. I resolved to leave the hotel and try another one of the addresses someone had given me. It's incredible how useless these suggestions are, and I was beginning to understand that there never really is a special address. These tips are of no value because our friends forget that what was done once won't necessarily be done again.

I spent three days in this hotel where the proprietor

was an intimate friend of a friend and I was constantly a stranger. He didn't want to know me.

I couldn't make up my mind to leave Lyon. To go from Paris to Lyon was a natural, normal step, but to continue! I expected that the surveillance would increase as I approached the Spanish border.

I walked the streets all day. The weather was beautiful. In the sun, I'd forget my sorry nights, but as soon as evening arrived, I would remember and become depressed. I would have liked to avoid going to bed, but what could I do? In the morning, I heard streetcars. The sounds of continuing life were striking. I would have liked someone to join me. I asked the proprietor's son and another young man to come with me.

But the same thing happened every time. After seeming as if they wanted to leave, after telling me how happy they would be to go with me, when the time came these young people hesitated and changed their minds. It's not that they were afraid. But they felt as I had when I was a prisoner, that by waiting they would find a better option.

Chapter 5

Finally, I arrived in Sénac, at the foot of the Pyrénées. I looked at these mountains every morning from my window and the idea of climbing them made me ill. There is nothing more menacing than mountains in the distance. They were either foggy, rainy, or covered with a uniform grey pallor. Behind the first chain were others. After climbing to the top I'd have to descend and climb again. It would take an entire day to correct the slightest mistake in itinerary. I might encounter insurmountable obstacles. Faced with this wall of mountains, I found myself naïvely thinking how easy it was for a bird to fly over.

Then I thought of teaming up with a guide. The hotel where I was staying had been a summer resort. I told everyone I had come for a rest. It was discouraging to be in this border town—where you would have thought that everyone would be thinking about going abroad—and discover exactly the same life as inside the country. It was as if the nearby border didn't exist. No one paid attention to the signs, to the arrows pointing *To Spain*, and there were no extra police. The surveillance at the train station didn't seem particularly enhanced, and yet every day people like me must have been leaving. I had managed to find a pair of espadrilles, and went conspicuously without a hat. I bought a cane like the local people used. For those who might be watching me, I was posing as a tourist.

One morning, I suddenly realized that what I was planning wasn't so easy after all, that such inoffensive appearances must be hiding something. I felt a little suspect, having no other reasons to account for my presence than personal taste and chance. I don't know if he was doing it on purpose, but the hotel owner would indicate day trips I could take in the mountains. He would tell me where I could get a drink of milk, or find some local sausage, as if I had really come for that. There was cause for concern in all this; life couldn't possibly have gone on so simply if the police weren't sure of themselves. While in so many villages far from the border everyone looked at me with distrust, here every stranger welcomed me with a smile. And the feeling that there was an iron fist behind town hall made me hesitate to ask for information. I figured that that's where they were waiting for me, that so long as I was a tourist, no one would make a move, but at the first sign otherwise they would be merciless. I felt helpless in the face of this unforeseen problem.

I realized I'd been a fool. One of my biggest mistakes since my escape was that I never prepared anything in advance, that I never asked for advice. I had considered myself alone and had never counted on anyone. I realized now that if, under the same pretext of needing a rest, I had gone to Saint-Gaudens or to visit friends elsewhere instead of coming here, I could at least have talked to people and gotten information. Until now my independence hadn't worked against me too badly, however, since I was on the verge of seeing an end to my troubles. Unfortunately, this proximity was beginning to make me doubt myself for the first time. I pictured everything I had lived through over the past two years, three years really, since basically my ordeal had begun not when I was made a prisoner, but when I'd been mobilized, and the idea that it was all over, that I was at the Spanish border, that this very evening if I wanted I could be saved for good, made the danger of being caught at the last minute seem like an appalling catastrophe, like one of those horrible twists of fate, lightening striking a wedding party, a shipwreck survivor falling down the stairs. And this feeling stayed with me, to the point of paralysis. After all I'd done to come to this! I told myself it was my own fault. I had waited too long. When you're living the way I was living, you should never give yourself a chance to think, you have to keep moving.

Instead, I had lingered in Lyon, in Saint-Etienne, and in Toulouse. I shouldn't have stopped until it was all over. By my own doing I found myself confronted with what seemed an enormous obstacle, whereas if I had acted differently I would probably have overcome it like the rest, without noticing.

That evening I lingered in the hotel dining room. It was very crowded. I observed my neighbors, afraid that I would find someone who'd come here with the same intentions I had. But no one seemed to be in my situation. There was one man by himself, about fifty years old, but he wasn't paying any attention to me, which led me to believe he hadn't come for the border. He didn't notice my glancing at him. There was a woman with a child, an old couple, basically an assortment of harmless types. Sometimes I wondered if all these people weren't putting on the same act I was, and I grew terrified at the thought of failing, of something happening that would cause future conditions for crossing the boarder to be even worse.

I still didn't know what to do, so I did nothing. After breakfast I would drink a cup of coffee substitute at the city's largest café. It was barely any different from the ones in all the cities I had just passed through. Same regulars, same cashier, same atmosphere, same efforts to try to live like before, same regrets at not being able to satisfy the clientele. I thought each time that I would find someone to give me some advice, some direction. The heat was stifling. Afterward I would return to my hotel. I was beginning to know a good many people, but it was impossible to ask them anything at all. Nothing is more frustrating than not finding anyone to give you advice in a town that must be crawling with people who could. And the more time passed the more difficult it became. I had the impression that I would do better to retrace my steps and go elsewhere. Indeed, in this sort of affair, when you don't succeed right away, when you don't find what you're looking for from the start, a strange thing happens: after wandering about for several days you become numbed into a state of inertia, and subsequently, even if you find a way out, it becomes impossible to act without attracting attention. The more days passed, the more I was a slave to the front I had developed, which was precisely to seem as if I were seeking nothing, and I realized that even if an opportunity arose I wouldn't dare take advantage of it. There was no point in staying here any longer.

Chapter 6

I therefore took the train, but in the opposite direction. Though I knew that I would get off thirty kilometers away, in Perpignan, only to return to the foot of the Pyrénées a little further along, this voyage in the wrong direction made me ill at ease. Of course I did have the satisfaction of having passed for an honest man for over a week, and, by returning in the direction I had come, of confounding those who may have suspected me of ulterior motives, though some may have thought I was leaving because I hadn't found what I needed.

In Perpignan, I found a room in a hotel opposite the train station. I no longer had the same confidence as when I could tell myself, in all situations, that I was going to Sénac to rest. I went out to dinner. Basically, it was always the same story, I wanted to be on my own and once a day had gone by, I regretted not having a friend. Never would the presence of a friend have been as welcome as here. I realized now that I had been wrong to consider this need of another person to be a weapon against loneliness: it wasn't the fear of loneliness, or the need to talk, it was something else. The truth, very simply, is that in the company of another person you feel less suspicious. Everything you do can be explained, is confirmed. Why this hotel? Because he told me to come here. Why did you return to Perpignan, why are you gong to such and such a place instead of Saint-Gaudens? I could look surprised. I could answer not *I*, but *we*. We thought we'd be more comfortable, we were tired of it, and as if by magic, they would believe us.

 I resolved to get started immediately, as I didn't want to repeat my mistake in Sénac. As I was going up to my room I began a conversation with the bellhop. I told him I had come from Sénac, but that I had gotten bored there because there were no interesting excursions, that I wanted to go to Saint-Gaudens where I had been told it was livelier. What did he think, since he was from the area? He didn't understand my allusions. I didn't dare be more precise. It was beginning to surprise me that everyone ignored the fact that there was a border nearby, that life went on as if we were right in the center of France. I ventured to say: "There must be people who cross over to Spain, that wouldn't surprise me." The valet said that he had never heard of any.

The next evening I arrived in Saint-Gaudens.

After dinner, I went to kill time in a café. Suddenly my neighbor at the next table began yelling how horrible it was to allow ourselves to be governed by inept people, not to mention traitors. We were getting what we deserved if we couldn't oust such scoundrels.

Since my escape, this was the first time that a stranger was saying what he thought of Vichy in front of me. His outburst had been prompted by the undrinkable imitation bullion he'd been served. I had already noticed several times that people flew into rages and were ready to get arrested over insignificant details rather than hold in their anger—because they had arrived a minute after closing and were refused a drink, because they were asked to show their papers on a silly formality, because they were obliged to wait, or were asked to produce an additional ten grams worth of tickets. "What a bunch of bastards!" the stranger kept repeating.

We struck up a conversation. He had the most nondescript look imaginable, with his suit stretched out and full of wrinkles. He might have been forty-five years old. He wore a Basque beret. He had that air peculiar to men who seem to be unaware of the very concept of appearances. After chatting for a while, I alluded several times to the fact that one of my friends wanted to cross over to Spain. When I saw him again the next day, he told me he knew a guide who had already escorted many people. He charged five thousand francs but was a very careful fellow. He wanted to know whom he was dealing with. He took precautions. I said I wanted to meet him. That evening, when I saw the stranger from the café arrive at my hotel, I was a little worried. He was doing more than I had asked of him. He had undertaken to help me of his own accord, pretending to have understood what I wanted. I told myself that they were southerners who simply wanted to earn some money and were trying to act as if they were doing it out of political commitment. I pretended to believe this, even though their asking for so much money turned me off. There was another thing I found unpleasant—my visitor's attitude toward the people around me. He took no precautions, as if I trusted him enough to allow him this indiscretion. That evening I wondered what I should do. Should I get involved with them or move on? I was afraid that this man wasn't serious. His story was too complicated. But if I passed up this opportunity, I might never make it. I had to realize that I would never find my ideal, my dream guide. There are always risks on the road to success.

The next day, he came to the hotel with the allegedly great frontier runner. We sat in a corner of the large dining area with a bottle of wine I'd gone out of my way to order. I was surprised to see that the frontier runner didn't look at all like a mountain man. He looked more like a clerk. When I mentioned this, he said it was true, that he wasn't a mountain man, but that before the war he had spent one or two months every year with a brother who taught in a small village and as a result he knew the region well. His brother had since been sent elsewhere, but he had made use of his knowledge to bring over four people already. He even talked to me at length about the last one, the wife of a general. It was clear that these two men had as much to fear from the police as I did. I was almost certain they weren't laying a trap for me. They asked me if I really had the money. What worried me a little was that the first one, who at the beginning had seemed to know nothing, who had told me he would look into things, now had equal status to the expert in the expedition. But I figured it was because he wanted to collect half the money. We decided to leave that same night.

It seemed to me that it was all over now, that I was saved. I held back my joy nevertheless, since I hadn't actually crossed the border yet and optimism might make me soft. But shortly thereafter I began making plans for the future. Who would have thought, a few months ago, that today I would be in Spain, that my nightmare would be over? I spent the afternoon counting the hours. My impatience grew. I was angry with myself for not having set the meeting time earlier. I was more and more afraid something would happen at the last minute. I didn't dare go out for fear of encountering my guides and hearing them tell me that our expedition was postponed. I lay down on the bed. How dramatic a moment this was! It was all over now, I was going to be free. I even went so far as to ask myself if I was really doing the right thing. Wasn't it cowardly to leave France like this? It was lucky, it was special treatment, it was what masses of French people would have liked to do.

Finally I headed for the meeting point. Night was falling. We had decided to assemble on the outskirts of the city, on a bridge that crossed over a dried-up stream next to a cluster of signposts. No one was there. I sat down on the rail. I looked at the mountains which had become violet at the base. At the peaks, the setting sun cast pale rays from below. Soon it was completely dark. The moon had risen, and the presence of this calm luminous circle in the sky's mountainous horizon, made jagged as if nibbled by rats, was extraordinary. Still no one came. I began to grow afraid. The failure to keep one's word was certainly the most striking thing in France since the defeat. No one considered himself held to anything. People were always backing out. Nothing had any value. All that you offered, even if it was all you had, was never enough.

The moon was still rising. Suddenly, it occurred to me that I should just leave by myself. Hadn't I shown in Germany that I was capable of such a thing, that a night of walking didn't frighten me? All I had to do was follow the road and stay hidden. Near the border I would be on the lookout, I would take as long as I had to. After all, it wasn't any more difficult than in Germany. Then I told myself: "But I'm not in Germany. I'm in France. It's just incredible that I can't find a Frenchman to help me. It's incredible that I should have to worry about being rounded up by the police here in France." I got mad. No, I wouldn't leave under these conditions. I was the one who had botched things up. After all, maybe I was mistaken about the time or the place. Better to calmly return to the hotel. Tomorrow, I would try to find another guide. And if in the end I couldn't find one, well, then I'd go it alone!

The next day the two men paid me a visit. They began by telling me that at the last minute they couldn't make it because one of their friends had gotten married! Then, abandoning this wedding story, they told me they had thought it over and that there were many more risks involved and to do what I wanted, since there were three of them, for two people weren't enough, I had to pay more money. I told them I had eighteen thousand francs total, that if they wanted to take me across I would give them ten thousand. Again we arranged to meet that evening. This time, it was a promise, it was agreed. I headed for our meeting place. They were waiting. We left. Soon there were fewer and fewer little houses. The road was starting to climb, but so slightly that I was surprised on turning around to see the city down below, already indistinct, forming a brown mass with a few towers and a steeple rising in the center. My companions were walking next to me. Everything was completely deserted. The moon was shining in the sky, far more luminous than the day before since it was later. I was carrying my suitcase on my shoulder. I was in a curious state of mind. Even though we were still on the road and could have run into people, I had already stopped thinking about taking precautions. I had forgotten the danger, I had forgotten everything in the physical effort I was making. I was no longer thinking about my companions, whether they were planning to betray me or not. I didn't talk to them. Only one thing mattered, the time that was passing. Suddenly, as we were walking in front of a house where only the foundation remained, a man came into view. There was something so strange about this apparition that the idea of being caught didn't even occur to me. "Where are you going?" the man asked. I put my suitcase down and turned toward my companions. "It's none of your business," they answered. For a few minutes, a confused conversation ensued between them and the newcomer. Then, to my great surprise, my guides asked me for all my money. "What else can we do?" they said as an excuse. Shortly thereafter, I saw the three of them leave together, gesticulating as if they were still arguing, but in reality in perfect agreement. I had been dealing with bandits.

They were getting further and further away. For an instant I thought of running after them. Then I realized that it would do me no good. I sat down on the side of the road, and thought of how despicable they had been to do this to a person in my situation. How low! Could there be any greater crime that taking advantage of a man's distress to rob him? Then on further thought, it occurred to me that it had been a bit my own fault. Maybe if I had been less prudent, if I had been less secretive about my exact situation, they wouldn't have considered robbing me. But I had been wary, I hadn't revealed anything, and nothing frees the conscience better.

I asked myself what I should do, without money, with no home, without knowing the area. And once again I thought of the abominable act these men had performed. How could anyone be so lacking in conscience? They knew they were destroying me and they hadn't hesitated. Suddenly, I grew wildly angry. I wanted to get revenge, to find them, to turn them in, to let others know what had happened, even if it meant getting caught. I began descending hurriedly toward the city, but had barely walked a kilometer when I calmed down. No, I'd be better off trying to cross into Spain. The least cruel of the three, the one who had wanted to leave me three hundred francs, had pointed to the mountain and told me: "Keep going, when you get up there, there'll be a little farm below. You'll be in Spain. All you have to do is avoid the guard post on the left."

I told myself that I should just go to this little farm. I was so nervous that the distances to travel in one direction or another seemed interminable. I needed to do things immediately, to know, to talk, and whichever way I went I had the impression that I was making no progress amid this immense natural world. Had I been in the proximity of the border I would have crossed it running, at the risk of being killed. Die or be saved! But there was no border, no house, only this mountain which descended when you reached the summit. "What horrible people!" I kept thinking. What a fine example of the appalling mentality of bandits who think that when they rob you they have no responsibility to you. Why act this way? If they had asked me for everything I had I would have given it to them without their having to steal it, all I asked in exchange was that they put me on the right road, tell me what I had to do. But they probably had no idea. They were not only bandits but swindlers. And it occurred to me that nothing as appallingly stupid had happened to me since the war, whether in Germany or in Paris. This story topped off my pitiful adventures perfectly. Until now I had encountered plenty of selfishness, but nothing like this, nothing to this extent. Everything that had happened to me seemed normal next to this bad blow. And it was indeed a bad blow, the last thing I would have thought should happen to a man like me. I was dumbfounded. To strike me down like this! It seemed incredible, inadmissible.

Chapter 7

These thoughts were running through my head when suddenly it occurred to me that I would never cross the border. At the last minute, something was against me. Luck had never abandoned me before, but this time, my luck had turned. I had suffered too much. I had fought too much. At the last minute, I had no more strength. At this moment I felt more urgently than at Sénac the regret of having dawdled since crossing the demarcation line, of having done things in too comfortable a fashion. I should have been motivated by the same spirit as after my escape. I should have been thinking of one thing only, crossing the border. Instead, I had stupidly thought the hardest part was over, that what was left to accomplish was nothing compared to what was behind me. If it was what I had really wanted, I would have been in Spain long ago. I took my head in my hands.

Again it seemed to me that I should go back to the village. But I didn't have a cent. How could I eat, pay for a hotel, how could I live without attracting attention? Was there anyone I could ask for money?

I returned to the village completely hopeless. Lost in this unfamiliar part of the country, it seemed to me that I would be arrested in a matter of days. But things always work out. When everything seems absolutely lost suddenly there's a break in the clouds.

Passing before a small alley, I saw a shopkeeper sitting at the door to his shop. He was a sick old man, a diabetic probably since one of his legs had been amputated. He was enjoying one of those sad convalescences following operations that have not altered the deep-rooted pain. What was my misfortune compared to his? I spoke to this man. It made me feel good. He asked me to sit down. I felt far from the world in this alley, which was divided in two by the moonlight. He asked me questions in turn, and suddenly understanding who I was, what had happened to me, he asked me into his home. He called his wife. In my presence he told her what I had just told him. She listened to him seriously, without saying a word, looking at me with that very particular air of a woman who has no real power but whose opinion comes first. She had a slightly nasty, suspicious manner, mainly looking to see if someone had inspired a dangerous sympathy in the man she loved.

When her husband had finished, she said that I could

stay with them. I was so happy I began babbling. All I asked for were a few days to get on my feet.

They offered me supper, but I refused. When someone has done you a favor, the moments that follow are agonizing, for that is when your benefactors ask themselves whether they were wise to act as they did and you suffer sensing their turmoil.

I couldn't fall asleep. I was thinking about how many dangers I had run across, and that it was a lot for one man. Then I told myself that the most monotonous life might hold just as many dangers. The main thing was not to bear a grudge against anyone. No rancor, that's the secret to happiness, success, and achievement.

For several days now, I had been awake when the cocks began to crow. And instead of thinking, as before when I heard them, that it must be very early, I thought to myself: at last.

Two days later I decided to leave by myself the next night, no matter what. What would happen would happen. It was ridiculous to dawdle like this right at the border. And for the first time I thought about what my life would be like abroad. When we decide something with so much force, we wind up not seeing any other options. We believe our choice to be perfect. We put it to rest so as not to disturb our efforts, and when we attain our goal, we suddenly ask ourselves if it was really worth the trouble. For months, I had been dreaming of going abroad and now tomorrow, if everything went well, it would come true. I pictured the welcome I would receive, the politeness mixed with distrust, the sympathy for the man who had endured so many troubles. They would keep an eye on me nonetheless. You never knew. I might be a liar. There was no proof that I was telling the truth.

I was going to leave France where I had spent the most beautiful and fruitful years of my life. The others, those left for me to live, I was taking abroad. Would people there be grateful for them? Would they accept me during these years, which might be years of decline? I wondered. Would they accept a man who might fall ill upon arrival, who would need care?

When would it all end? Had the anxieties I'd just endured marked me forever? Until now I had generally smiled when I heard about the repercussions of misfortune. I thought that once a danger had passed, it was all over. I was wrong.

At nightfall, I took leave of the shopkeeper. He gave me a package of food. I thanked him, and was so moved that I kissed him. I told him that he might see me the next day escorted by two policemen. He seemed so sick that I didn't dare say I would see him again after the war.

The night was beautiful. Before beginning to climb, there were two or three kilometers of flat land. I was in low spirits. But as soon as I was alone in the country, I became a different man.

A shepherd approached me accompanied by his dog,

who was making large circles around him as if he were still circling the flock that I saw in the distance, continuing to graze exactly as before even though it was no longer being watched. I stopped. The shepherd looked at me a long time. He seemed so at one with the mountain that I wasn't afraid. I understood that he was telling me that I had to be careful on this side. I grew worried again. I asked him what I should do. He stood there an instant without answering, then ordered the dog to return to the animals. The dog obeyed like a person. Still without speaking, the shepherd motioned me to follow him. Sitting two hundred meters away, the dog watched us leave. We followed a trail. He walked in front, without hurrying. Each time there was an obstacle, he turned around slightly to see if I had cleared it.

We arrived in front of a small house surrounded by rocks. Other dogs began barking. It was striking to me that living creatures defended themselves here just like everywhere else.

An old man appeared on the doorstep, and his face lit up upon seeing me.

It was extraordinary that I should find such compassion only as I was leaving. Was the heart of France awakening just as I was saying goodbye? Then I realized that there were hearts like these everywhere, but that today they only showed themselves far away, in isolated places, that you had to look for them.

They offered me a glass of milk, then of wine. I sat down. I began talking as if I were among close friends and everything I said was listened to attentively. I told them what had just happened to me. Then I saw the old man glance at his son, and the latter make an almost imperceptible gesture. I saw the old woman get up. He wanted to give me money.

I began to cry. It was too kind. Most of all it was too late. I understood that my country wasn't dead, that it was like this everywhere. I kept the money in my hand for a long moment, so as not to insult them by returning it too quickly, then I laid it on the table. I said that I didn't need money, that what they were giving me was much more precious than all the money in the world.

That night, the father and son set off with me into the mountain. In the morning, they said goodbye. I was on top of the mountain. I turned toward France. The sun was rising. The plane was inundated with light and mist. I turned around. Two Spanish guards were approaching. I knew they were going to take me to jail, but it didn't matter: I was free.

About the Author

Born Emmanuel Bobovnikoff on April 20, 1898, in Paris, **Emmanuel Bove** was among the finest, most celebrated and most prolific French writers of the period between world wars—for both of which Bove was called up and in neither of which he actually participated. Born of a Russian Jewish father and a Belgian mother and raised poor, Bove greatly broadened twentieth-century French literature and staked out early on the territory of postmodernist writing. He brilliantly and devotedly described the horrors of the working poor and the poor without work. The literary world had no choice but to stand up and take notice. Discovered by Colette, admired by Gide and Rilke, Bove was awarded the prestigious Figuière Prize of 50,000 francs in 1928, beating competition that included André Malraux and Drieu la Rochelle.

Bove's creative output comprised thirty books, including nineteen novels, seven novellas, two story collections and two detective novels. In his heyday, during the late 1920s, he could write four novels a year and smoked one hundred cigarettes a day. Balzac, Dostoyevski, and Chekhov were major influences on him. But, as Peter Handke wrote recently after reading Bove, "Writing like this didn't exist before Bove, nor after." All his adult life Bove provided financial support to his mother and brother. He was a staunch antifascist. Reproached for the dark pessimism in his writing, Bove offered this definition by way of response. "A pessimist is someone who lives with optimists." Bove completed *Night Departure* and *No Place* just prior to his death in 1945.

titles traced

3 - 2/23/05